JAMES DELARGY

**SIMON &
SCHUSTER**

London · New York · Sydney · Toronto · New Delhi

A CBS COMPANY

First published in Great Britain by Simon & Schuster UK Ltd, 2019
This paperback edition published by Simon & Schuster UK Ltd, 2019
A CBS COMPANY

3 5 7 9 10 8 6 4

Simon & Schuster UK Ltd
1st Floor
222 Gray's Inn Road
London WC1X 8HB

Simon & Schuster Australia, Sydney
Simon & Schuster India, New Delhi

www.simonandschuster.co.uk
www.simonandschuster.com.au
www.simonandschuster.co.in

A CIP catalogue record for this book is available from the British Library

Paperback ISBN: 978-1-4711-7755-2
Ebook ISBN: 978-1-4711-7754-5
Audio ISBN: 978-1-4711-8317-1

Typeset by M Rules
Printed and bound by CPI Group (UK) Ltd, Croydon, CR0 4YY

MIX
Paper from
responsible sources
FSC® C020471
FSC
www.fsc.org

To those who never got the chance

1

His lungs burned as if he weren't breathing oxygen at all but the choking red dust that spat up with each footstep. Footsteps taking him nowhere. This *was* the middle of nowhere. That much he knew. The middle of nowhere and still the world was strangling him, the low branches stretching to take their ounce of flesh, to welcome him to the neighbourhood permanently.

It had so nearly succeeded. But he escaped. Now he was running for his life. A throwaway phrase that he never believed he would actually have to realize. He didn't feel alive. Far from it. The crushing fear of capture consumed everything, his focus constrained to each step, each rocky scramble and dive between trees. He felt like an animal, reduced to base instincts of survival, everything classed simply as dangerous or safe.

The long fingers of the relentless sun reached through the trees, baking the ground where it found land, dappling the bare earth in light but offering no glowing path to freedom. There were trees and rocks, trees and more fucking rocks. He had no idea whether he was heading towards civilization or further into the outback.

Around another rock scorched by the sun, his calves tightened, as if the manacles were still weighing him down. The cold, rusted metal he thought would chain him until that psycho decided to kill him. He couldn't stop. Despite the pain, fatigue and crippling lack of air in his lungs he couldn't stop. Stopping meant death.

He spotted a break in the trees up ahead. The edge of hell he hoped, where he would find a road, a farm, a dirt track – anything that indicated the real world. He forced more air into his lungs and pushed towards the light. Throwing his foot forward it met a rock that had probably been embedded for centuries, undisturbed until now. Knocked off balance, he flung an arm out. He found nothing but air. Then his shoulder jarred against a tree trunk which shook but stood firm. Somehow, so did he.

The treeline broke. Sunlight dazzled his eyes, his dreams of stumbling upon civilization dashed. He was faced with nothing but a small clearing with five or six distinct patches of loose soil; rectangular patches that looked like … graves. He knew that if he didn't get up now he would find himself in one.

He hauled himself up. His body hurt all over. Sweat soaked his clothes. Skirting around the gravesite without tearing his eyes from it he entered a landscape dominated by more trees and rocks. Almost as if he had circled back on himself.

Here the ground rose once again, his legs joining his

lungs in protest at the continued abuse. In the distance the faint blue shimmer of a cloudless skyline signalled the top of a hill; a vantage point to orientate himself.

He quelled the rebellion in his legs and lungs, but in subduing their protest, failed to see the tree root looping out of the soil. Over he went, no loosened earth to break his fall, just the hard, baked ground and a face full of dust. He stifled the bark of pain, terrified of giving his position away, but the echo of his grunt taunted him, the hard earth amplifying it, drowning out the chirps of birds, insects and the sound of his would-be killer.

The hilltop arrived and brought further dismay. There was no vantage point, only a sheer ten-foot drop. A panicked glance left and right confirmed there was no safe path down.

He didn't have time to source an alternative route. A shove in the back caused him to hit the dirt hard. He rolled around just in time for a set of knuckles to find his left cheek. A glancing blow, but enough to force his eyes closed for a split second. Balling his fist, he swung hard in retaliation. It found something hard – possibly a shoulder. In response, his attacker ground his sharp knee into thigh muscle. The pain forced his eyes open, his sight blurred. Without a plan, or indeed, much co-ordination, he threw a series of frenzied fists. Some found targets, others just air. But as many as he threw, double returned his way, accurate, finding his head and neck, dull fleshy strikes that set off a kaleidoscope of worthless diamonds across his vision. His hair was wrenched and his head slammed into earth that had no give, nor sympathy.

Blackness clawed at his brain threatening to switch it off for good. If he passed out he was a goner. Reaching up, he grabbed on to the dark outline above him. Pinning his attacker's arms, he rolled to the side battling for leverage.

Where there should have been ground, there wasn't, the roll continuing for what seemed like forever, weightlessness encompassing him as if the blows to the head had freed his brain from the effects of gravity. With it came a sense of bliss that was almost surreal. It was over. He had been killed and was passing on to whatever lay beyond this earth and there was nothing he could do about it.

The landing changed that.

The ground forced the breath from his body. As if his soul had fled. Opening his eyes, he took in the coarse grey-brown wall of the ridge rise high above, a little haze of waning blue above it. The browns, greys and blues darkened and he passed out.

2

The town of Wilbrook was Chandler Jenkins' home. Had been his whole life. All thirty-two long, dry years stuck on the Pilbara plateau in the inner reaches of Western Australia, a land mass conservatively estimated to be two and a half billion years old and once part of the ancient continent of Ur. Some days Chandler believed these pre-historic atoms had seeped into his bones and aged him prematurely. The copper-red dust, a fiery topping on a land scorched almost to death, did that to many people.

The town was a remote outcrop, a hundred kilometres from the nearest place of habitation, Portman, linked by a road that stretched into the distance like the twisting tail of a dragon. Wilbrook itself wasn't old, even by Australian terms, gazetted at the end of the 19th century and named after a famous prospector from Albany, who had left the lush green wine country down south to scrab-ble around in the dirt up here in search of wealth. And he'd found it. A fat deposit of gold; chunks that poked from the earth like marshmallows in a kid's breakfast cereal. Some even needed two hands to lift them. Word spread and soon shacks flew up, wooden structures that defied gravity and sensibility. After the shacks came the businesses: bars, saloons, brothels. At least two of each. The population exploded, thousands clambering for riches, newspaper articles proclaiming it as the place to realize dreams. But the dream died quickly, the hauls abruptly dwindling to little more than flecks caught in rusted pans. Yet more came, desperately panning rocks and dirt in the streams before drowning their sorrows with whisky and women they couldn't pay for. As the debts grew so did the tensions.

The result was a powder keg that exploded one summer night when ten men had a shootout on Main Street; the sole survivor, Tomato Tom Kelly, dying the next day from the punctured artery in his shoulder. As the violence increased, the prospects of wealth diminished. The doctors, lawyers and merchants were first to go, shipping out for the newest gold rush, leaving the once burgeoning town of five thousand cut down to barely a fifth of that, supported by a couple of bars and brothels that held firm. Nothing was better for business than desperation.

With the gold gone, families were forced to scrape an existence on land that was as harsh to them as it was to the animals they tried to raise. That was the way it remained for nearly forty years, the town barely breathing. Then the iron ore and blue asbestos was discovered beneath the scarred earth. A new rush started, the mining corporations buying large swathes of land, at prices too good to turn down. What followed was a rapid expansion and the erection of the town's first brick buildings. Then as before, yields suddenly collapsed, and the companies, without sentiment or remorse, shifted operations a few hours along the road to Portman like a moulting snake, leaving the thin shell of waste skin behind.

Chandler and his family lived in this empty shell and despite its flaws he was proud of the town. *His* town. He was the sergeant and in effect the sheriff of it; apt given that the town retained the look of one stuck at the turn of the 19th century. The wide main street boasted tarmac where packed dirt had once laid, gleaming almost white in the sun, and a concrete island down the centre offered unnecessary solace from the rare traffic. Colourful verandas arched over the footpaths providing shelter from the sun if not the unforgiving heat, the ornately crafted metal poles unmoved for the last century, the last bastions of a time long gone.

As he pulled up to the concrete sweatbox that constituted the station, Chandler glanced in the mirror. The steadily rounding face that stared back at him was of a handsome man tumbling towards his mid-thirties. A face battling late nights and life as a single parent, his blond hair losing volume if not territory as yet. The blondness plus the light tan he sported afforded him the look of an ageing surfer, though nothing could be further from the truth. Chandler stayed out of the sea as much as he could. At least on land he could see what was coming to kill him.

Bill Ashcroft, the old senior sergeant, had retired last June, leaving Chandler to assume temporary command. Not that there was much for the five of them to do: a few traffic violations and domestic disputes, or an occasional assault in one of the three pubs in town that didn't so much compete for business as welcome those temporarily barred from the others. Still, five was the quota assigned to the station and the Western Australian Police Force fought to keep the full complement in position, afraid that losing one would let the others fall, like dominoes.

As he entered, his newest recruit, Nick Kyriakos, was stationed at the front desk, his permanent lodging until Chandler was confident that the boy was capable of public duty. He had no need to risk putting an armed twenty-year-old out in the field, even if Nick had proved himself bright and respectful. A young man full of wonder, keen to please, keen to learn and keen to display his vast and unsettling knowledge of serial killers.

Tanya, his senior constable, and immediate number two, was already positioned at her desk. She was never late, as strictly bound as her ponytail. She did early shifts so she could collect her three kids from the primary school across town; kids popped out in quick succession during the five-year sabbatical she had only recently returned from. Chandler imagined it had been a clinical procedure for all three. It always was with Tanya, like a military operation. If he got promoted he would be recommending that she did too. She deserved it. Anyone who could balance kids and work deserved everything they got. He should know. He had two of his own. She at least had a partner to help.

Chandler slipped into his office. The air-con system had packed in again leaving the station feeling as sticky as glue. He took his seat and looked out of the window at Gardner's Hill in the distance, the rocky, wood-covered mound, named after the town's first mayor.

From this distance, the Hill looked appealing, trees enveloping the side visible from town tall, straight and rising into the sky, a lush green anomaly in an otherwise red land. Beyond the ridge lay thousands of acres of wilderness. The kind of wilderness that had always proved tempting for people to explore. But even experienced walkers used to extreme conditions found it difficult. It attracted those who wanted to find themselves. And sometimes, to lose themselves.

It was a typical day for Chandler, quiet and introspective. It was about to change dramatically.

A commotion drifted through the open door. A voice he didn't recognize but a desperation he did. He tried to pick the accent – south, far south, maybe Perth. If so, the person – a male – was far from home.

'Sarge, I think you should get out here,' called Tanya. Her usually equable voice sounded disturbed.

Swinging his feet off the table, Chandler let his gut settle. It had expanded in the months and years since Teri had left, as if his body thought that the way to deal with part of him being taken away was to create more to compensate.

He entered the main office. Sitting at Tanya's desk – the

first point of call after the high-banked reception – was a nervous man who looked to be in his mid-twenties, his T-shirt and jeans bearing the evidence of what appeared to have been a substantial beating.

Chandler felt for his neck and cursed. He had forgotten his clip-on tie. He wasn't a stickler for uniform in general but preferred to wear one when meeting a member of the public. It afforded an impression of authority.

'*Look like you own the place*,' Bill had told him, '*but act like you're managing it.*'

As he approached, Tanya stood close by, watching the man with caution. Even Nick had trundled his chair all the way from reception, as if by remaining in the seat he was fulfilling his assigned role of manning the front desk.

The visitor stood up. Tanya stepped back in response, ready to act. The man's terror was spreading. Chandler noted that they were of similar height if differing physique, the nervousness paramount in eyes that darted from Chandler to the walls, to the door, as if searching for somewhere better to be. His body seemed to recognize that his eyes sought the chance to escape and had narrowed into slits to prevent this. He looked like he was in pain.

'He wanted me to be number fifty-five,' the man spluttered, looking Chandler squarely in the eye for the first time. He shivered and squeezed his eyes shut.

Chandler made some mental notes. Definitely a Perth accent. Patchy stubble on his face suggesting it had been on the rough end of a blunt razor for a number of weeks.

An itinerant worker, he guessed; too lucid, a little too fresh to be a bum.

'What are you talking about?' asked Chandler, keeping calm, even if the sudden appearance of a bloodied stranger had knocked him off step.

'Fifty-five,' the man repeated.

Chandler looked to Tanya for help. She shook her head.

'Fifty-five ... what?' asked Chandler. The urge to reach his hand out and touch the man's shoulder as a show of support and comfort materialized but he was worried it might spook him.

'The g-g-guy. The killer.'

'What killer?'

'The one who kidnapped me. Took me ... there. The woods ... the trees.' The man pointed to the solid wall. Chandler realized he was pointing to Gardner's Hill beyond the brick.

'What kill—'

'A lunatic.'

The man's legs wobbled. Blood stained his jeans but didn't look fresh, as if it had dried in the sun. Chandler, however, didn't need him collapsing. He reached out to touch the man's arm and he winced in pain.

'It's okay, we're here to help.' Easing him back into the seat allowed Chandler to feel a little more in charge of the situation. 'What's your name?' he asked.

'Gabriel.'

'Very good, Gabriel. I'm Chandler. I'm the sergeant here. Do you know where you are?'

Gabriel shook his head.

'You're in Wilbrook.'

He noted a flash of something in Gabriel's eyes, something he read as hope. Hope that he had found safety. Chandler continued feeding information in an attempt to bolster this.

'Wilbrook, West Australia. This is Tanya, my senior constable and Nick, another constable. Where have you come from?'

Again a wavering finger pointed at the wall. 'From there.'

Chandler tried to offer a reassuring smile. 'I mean, where do you live?'

'Perth ... but I travel.'

He slumped back against the seat. For a moment it looked like he was going to slide right off it to the floor.

'Have you got any ID?'

'He stole it.'

Chandler nodded. 'Okay ... did you get his name, Gabriel?'

The man was quiet. The eyes that had darted around the room began to close. Chandler looked again at his clothes. The dried blood suggested no serious wound, though he couldn't discount an undetected brain haemorrhage.

'Did you—'

'Heeeeath,' said Gabriel, uttered in an extended sigh.

'Heath?' Chandler nodded to Tanya who was already scribbling it down.

Gabriel nodded. 'The maniac. He was called Heath. He stole my ID.'

The body that had seemed like jelly coagulating on the seat stiffened and tried to rise. 'I have to get out of here.'

Stepping forward, Chandler eased him back into the chair. The urge to flee was a reaction he was used to. Many people who found themselves in a police station wanted to leave sharpish, believing that if they hung around for long enough they would be charged with something.

'Stay there and we'll get you some medical attention.'

'No,' said Gabriel, his eyes wide. 'I want to tell you what happened and then get out of here. In case he comes back.'

'You're safe now,' Chandler assured him.

'Not until I'm long gone from here.'

Gabriel took a long, deep breath, fighting the nervous energy, wincing as he stretched what Chandler guessed were badly bruised ribs.

'We can get you a doctor,' said Tanya, creeping forward again.

'No, I want to tell you what happened.'

3

Nestled behind reception, the interview room was small and almost exclusively used as the lunchroom. Instead of the office's summery yellow, the walls were painted dark green. A colour that Chandler had read somewhere was conducive to making people talk.

The thin, plastic chair groaned under the weight of their visitor. Chandler took up residence on the other side of the desk, the grey PVC top stained with mustard. He needed to find out whose turn it was to clean up – probably his.

He addressed his visitor.

'It's 23rd November 2012. Please state your full name for the record.'

'Gabriel Johnson.'

'From?'

'Perth originally, but ... what do you call it? No fixed ...?'

'No fixed abode.'

'That's it. No fixed abode. Sorry my mind's a little ...' Gabriel's eyes darted around the room as if to take everything in. There wasn't much to see.

'Age?'

'Thirty.'

He spoke with a weariness that suggested he'd experienced hard times, thought Chandler. A deep tan had taken root in his skin, embellishing the acne scars that dotted his still-boyish cheeks.

'And what are you doing way up here?'

'Searching for work.'

'As?'

'As a labourer, a farmhand, anything. I thought I'd try some places out here.'

'Any in particular?'

'No. But I heard there were a few.'

Gabriel wasn't wrong. There were plenty of cattle stations and homesteads nestled in the vast plains, gigantic in size, akin to small countries. He had the lean, wiry physique required to work them, one used to living on a diet of meat and little else, used to doing anything from checking boreholes for water to mustering and branding cattle.

'And how did you meet this ... Heath?'

At the mention of his name, their visitor shuddered, taking a moment to compose himself.

'I was in Port Hedland. I'd come up from Exmouth the previous day with a trucker.'

'Got a name?'

Gabriel shrugged, as if it didn't matter. 'Lee something. Chinese guy in his fifties. Fat. Smoked pre-rolled roll-ups that were wedged in the visor. Nothing much more to him.'

'And he dropped you off in Port Hedland?' asked Chandler.

'Yeah, he was heading on to Darwin.'

'What did you do in Port Hedland?'

'I slept.'

'Where?'

'In the park.'

'Name?'

Gabriel shook his head. 'Dunno. I wasn't sightseeing. There was grass ... trees ... a bench. You know, park stuff.'

Chandler made a note to probe further. 'Carry on.'

The man's strained voice had calmed somewhat, but still jittered at the edges like the bark of a nervous dog. 'Next day I decided to head inland. Looking for work.'

'Why not stay near the coast?'

'A guy in Exmouth told me that inland was the best place to go. Said that most people stick to the coast for easy movement but competition for places means that the bosses pay fuck all. Also it seemed like an adventure.'

At this point Gabriel paused, as if he'd lost his train of thought. Chandler decided to let him vacillate, let the words and thoughts come naturally.

Gabriel blinked hard, returning. 'I was ... on the road out ... the main one.' He stopped and looked at Chandler. 'I don't have a name.'

Chandler did. Highway 1, the black vein that eventually turned off on to 95, which led to Wilbrook. A track he'd been up and down many times, especially when he was first seeing Teri, back when she was the bouncy party girl from the coast. He didn't know then that the coast would always have a hold on her.

'I was hiking along, the sun blinding me from what was coming. I heard an engine drone from behind and stuck my thumb out. Two had already passed that morning so I was expecting it to roll on ... but it pulled up.'

'Can you describe it?' asked Chandler. He looked at the two-way mirror and hoped Tanya was getting all this. It had been nearly a year since the last recorded interview in here. A domestic violence case. June Tiendali taking offence to her husband spending evenings with his pigeons rather than her and snapping his arm with a hockey stick.

'A boxy car. Don't remember the make. The badge had fallen off I think. Dark brown ... but that could have been the dust, which even covered the windows. One of the brake lights was out, I remember that much. I half-jogged towards it thinking that they might drive off at any moment.' Gabriel looked at Chandler ruefully. 'I wish he had.'

'Licence number?'

Gabriel shook his head. 'Covered in dust too. Maybe on purpose.'

'Okay, go on.'

'So I got in. Maybe I should've looked first but I needed to get work quick. Get housed, get fed.'

'So what did he ... this Heath ... look like?' Chandler readied his pen for a description. He hoped that it was more descriptive than that for the car: unknown make, unknown licence number, a dusty, boxy vehicle. Similar to most of the shit on the roads around here.

Gabriel closed his eyes and took a breath. Chandler let the silence play out. He glanced to the two-way mirror and his reflection. A weary cop stared back at him, the sharpness of his cool blue eyes highlighting the shadowy tiredness ringing them.

'Short ... a few inches shorter than me. Brown hair. Tanned, like he worked outdoors. Stocky too. Said he was thirty like me, but seemed kinda ... I dunno ... nervous.' Gabriel paused. 'I probably should have spotted it then that there was something *dark* about him.'

'What do you mean "dark"?'

'Something ... off,' said Gabriel. 'His beard disguised his features. As if he was slowly becoming a shadow.'

Gabriel stared at Chandler as if seeking confirmation that the words made some sense outside of his skull.

'And you don't have to remind me how stupid it is to hitch around here,' he added, suddenly on the defensive. 'He seemed okay, or my brain persuaded me that he looked okay. I knew ... or thought I knew ... if he tried anything I could defend myself. He said his name was Heath and he was travelling back from town with supplies. Even that made me feel better. I mean, no killer introduces themselves ... do they?'

Again he looked up for some form of confirmation. Chandler nodded, though he wasn't sure he agreed. If Heath's intention was to kill then why not spill details. But it did tell him one thing. The fact that Heath was confident enough to converse freely with his intended victim warned Chandler that he had done it before, that he was relaxed enough to take charge and assured enough to be open with his victim: number fifty-five. A feeling of excitement and dread swirled around his stomach, butterflies the size of eagles. This could be big. He needed to weasel out more details before his victim clammed up.

'Did he tell you anything about who he was?'

'Only that he lived around here.'

'In Wilbrook?' Chandler couldn't recall any Heaths in the area, though he supposed it could have been an alias. His attention turned to who around here could kill that many people. Wilbrook wasn't short on crazy people but none with enough gumption to pull it off. Probably.

'No ... I dunno ... just around *here*,' he said. His accent was from across east I'd say. Anyway, he seemed friendly enough. I was looking for a lift, not a soulmate.'

Chandler nodded for him to go on.

'I told him I was from Perth. When he said I was a long way from home, I told him that I had to go where the money was, that everything up here was barren but had a certain beauty.' Gabriel shrugged his shoulders and grimaced. 'That's a lie but I've found it's always best to flatter the ride in some way. Like a hooker would, I suppose.'

Chandler studied him. The grimace suggested that this wasn't a joke, but a philosophy he obeyed.

'An hour in we passed a couple of turnoffs for farms. I told him that this was good enough for me but he said that everyone dived into them. He said it was like stopping off at the first watering hole you come across, the big one, the one where the animals have already muddied the water. He said that they paid shit and that those further in were better. I asked him if he had worked them before, in case I could get a name or a slide-in, but he didn't answer. I thought that maybe he had but something had happened that he didn't want to talk about.'

Chandler made a note to check with some of the farms for a Heath; see if anyone remembered him working for them.

Gabriel continued, 'We went on for another half hour, the scenery turning to dust. I was starting to wonder how anything could survive out there never mind a herd of cattle. It got me feeling thirsty. Even with the windows cranked down the air was boiling. He must have read my expression. He told me there was water in the back if I wanted it. That's how he got me.'

'The water?'

Gabriel nodded. 'It tasted a little chalky, but by then I didn't much care. It was water and I was desperate.' He looked at Chandler wanly, as if disgusted with himself. 'I began to feel drowsy almost right away. At first I thought it was exhaustion or the heat, but it got worse and worse. I tried to lift my arms and couldn't. They didn't feel attached to my body. I remember turning to look at Heath. He was staring at me, as if there was nothing wrong. Just a process he'd watched many times before. He didn't even look at the road, or where we were going, just at me, for what seemed like hours. A shadow passed over his face until I could only see the outline of his skull.

Then I passed out, I think. He must have poisoned the water with something.'

Gabriel's eyes danced around again. Chandler recognized the look. The confused victim attempting to fill in the blanks and failing.

'I woke up in a wooden shed. Dunno how long I was out but there was still light poking through the slats so I guessed I'd only been out a couple of hours.' Suddenly worry drew over his face. 'Unless this is Friday—'

'No, Thursday,' Chandler assured him.

That seemed to bring Gabriel some relief. The fact that he hadn't lost a day of his life. The fact that he still had his life at all.

'He'd shackled my wrists to the roof beam.'

'Shackled?' asked Chandler.

'Yeah ... with these thick iron things. Two D-shaped loops linked by chain that was attached to the wall. The same just above my ankle. Those weren't attached but they were impossible to move in. Not that I was going to get away. He'd made sure of that.'

'Were you on a farm? In the forest? An outhouse?'

'Up there,' said Gabriel. 'That hill you said. I could see the trees through the slats. Shackled in a woodshed with saws and hatchets and stuff. Nothing that shouldn't have been there but 'cause I was chained up they all looked lethal.'

'Can you tell me anything more about it? Sounds? Smells?'

Gabriel shrugged. 'Dirt floor. Stock of wood in the corner for burning. I could hear movement next door so I guessed I was chained up next to a cabin. I called out for help. That's when Heath appeared. I asked him where I was – he said home. I pleaded with him to let me go and I wouldn't tell anyone about what he'd done. He told me to calm down. He sounded angry, as if I'd disturbed him from something important.'

Gabriel's legs began to chitter up and down under the table. His eyes searched the room as if trying to escape.

'Sorry, I . . . I'm just feeling a bit claustrophobic.'

'Do you want the door open?'

'Please.'

Rising from the chair, Chandler opened the door to reveal the office beyond and the series of small windows set high above a row of grey cabinets on the far side of the room. Gabriel stared at them.

'I got afraid he was going to do something there and then. He walked right up to my face. That's when he mentioned the number fifty-five. It was all he said before he backed off towards the door. I was afraid to ask him what he meant. But I guessed . . .'

Gabriel stopped.

'Guessed what?' asked Chandler, eager to hear his own assumptions voiced.

'That I was going to be his fifty-fifth victim.'

Even on a day hot enough to melt plastic Chandler felt the chill sear down his back. As he related the story Gabriel seemed to be reliving it, his wiry muscles dancing underneath the bloodied T-shirt, the sinews in his forearm permanently tensed. Sheer terror.

'He said not to worry about whether I was going

to be killed,' continued Gabriel. 'Because *of course* I would be killed. It had been written.'

'What do you mean, "it had been written"?' asked Chandler.

Gabriel shrugged. 'Your guess is as good as mine, Officer.'

'Okay, go on,' said Chandler, making a note of the phrase.

'I knew I had to get free, so when he left I tried to get out of the cuffs.' Gabriel presented his blistered palms and wrists, red raw circles around them, the skin scuffed, the fine hair torn from the root. 'I pulled on them, tried to rip them off the wall. Kept yelling out for help. Not once did he come in and tell me to shut up. He wasn't worried about anyone hearing me. That's when I knew I was in the middle of nowhere. I kept pulling and eventually managed to break one of the locks but one hand was still attached to the wall. I reached for the bench with my free hand to try and get one of the tools. I nearly put my shoulder out of joint, but managed to get my hands on the hatchet. I tried to chop at the remaining cuff without chopping through my own wrist. I was terrified that he'd come in and catch me. I just wanted a chance to get free. A chance to live. I went quiet, but worried that the fact that I had shut up would attract his attention, so I yelled out to cover the sound of the hatchet hitting the metal and ringing out like a fucking church bell.'

He looked up.

Chandler nodded for him to go on, intrigued by the

man's vivid recollection, how the words flowed from his mouth like water from a burst dam.

'Somehow I managed to bend the metal, like a super-human kind-of-thing and got my other hand free. The key for the leg irons was hanging from a nail so in a few seconds I was out. I felt more scared than I had when I was chained up. I remember trying the shed doors but they were padlocked. The only other exit led next door. The one he'd come from. So I opened it. There was a single room filled with supplies.'

Gabriel exhaled deeply. As if he had been holding his breath.

'And Heath?' asked Chandler.

'Sat at a desk covered in paper and maps. A big cross on the wall. I tiptoed to the front door but as I opened it, the hinges squeaked. He turned. We stared at each other as if frozen. Then the chase started. I made it outside but it was like I was in the middle of a hollow. Just trees and earth all around. I had no idea what direction to head in so I went right.'

'Why right?'

'I dunno . . . I'm right-handed I guess . . . I can't tell you why. Each way looked the same. My legs were stiff from being locked in the manacles but I knew I had to move fast, not knowing if he had a gun or not.'

Chandler could almost see Gabriel's heart pound under the T-shirt. The memories were flooding back, intense and uncontrolled. After a long breath that seemed to suck the last of the oxygen from the stifling room, he continued.

'I aimed for the ridge. I glanced back and he was about ten metres behind me. I kept running and running until I stumbled on some loose soil and fell into a small clearing. The ground was all dug up.' Gabriel stared at him. 'They were graves.'

The air in the room seemed to grow even more oppressive.

'Graves?' Chandler frowned. 'How do you know that?'

Gabriel shook his head. 'I don't ... not for sure. I only remember thinking at the time they *looked* like graves. Five, six, seven, maybe ... rectangular patches.' He paused and stared at Chandler as if only just realizing just how close he had come to death.

'I got up, kept running and came to a hill. I thought I'd be able to see from the top but there was nothing but a drop on the other side. I shouldn't have stopped.'

Another breath. Composing himself. The tendons in his jaw twitched.

'He jumped on me. I tried to throw some punches ... but none landed. None that stopped him anyway. We rolled over and over ... then I was falling. Like I was weightless. You ever experienced that?' Gabriel looked at Chandler.

'No, I haven't.'

'It was oddly exhilarating. Until the landing. As if I'd been hit by a train. As if I'd left my body entirely. I thought that was it and I'd entered heaven.' He looked to Chandler seeking understanding.

Though his parents had instilled the virtues of religion in him and his two kids, Chandler was never what he would call an active participant. Religion to him was like home-grown tomatoes. Easier to consume than nurture. It was also a reminder that Sarah, his oldest, had her First Confession tomorrow. Something he was supposed to help her with tonight, practise what to say, when to kneel, when to stand ...

'I woke up sometime later and for the second time that day I had to figure out where I was. I saw the ridge above me and realized I'd fallen off. The pain of the landing returned, then I remembered Heath. He was lying beside me. Flat on the ground, the dirt around us splashed with blood.'

'Was he dead?' A dead suspect would make Chandler's life easier.

'I dunno.'

'What do you mean, you don't know?'

'I dunno if he was alive or not. I didn't go near him in case he was only playing dead. I've seen movies, Officer. I had to get away. So I did.'

'And left him there?'

Gabriel nodded. It meant no confirmation of death. Chandler would have to assume Heath had survived. The lack of clarity was frustrating. He would need to organize a hunt for an injured man; a hunt through *that* forest. But if Gabriel had made it to town in a few hours it meant that Heath couldn't be that far in. There was a possibility of finding him, saving him, arresting him.

'How did you make it to town?' asked Chandler.

'Luck. I stumbled along for a couple of hours before

I came across a dirt road. I followed it looking for some help, but nobody passed. That's when I came across the old bicycle. It was rusted to shit but better than nothing. I made it to the end of the dirt road, saw the town in the distance and aimed for it, cringing in fear at every car that passed, expecting Heath to jump out of one, or to be side-swiped into the ditch and finished off.'

'What road?' asked Chandler. It would narrow the search down.

Gabriel shook his head. 'I dunno. It's all a blur, Officer. I don't think there was a name. Just a dirt road. He was after me. That bastard ... was after me. But I made it.'

With that Gabriel slumped in the seat, exhausted from relaying his story, the weight temporarily lifted from his shoulders. Chandler studied him. The eyes remained closed, the body language one of cautious relief curdled by ongoing trepidation.

'You're safe now.'

The eyes opened. The mouth followed, the smile weary and crooked, a set of perfectly aligned teeth flashed: good genes or excellent orthodontic work.

'I just want to go home,' said Gabriel.

'I thought you didn't have one?'

'I don't.'

'Then where will you go?'

'Anywhere. *Far* from here.'

'To another farm?'

'No, screw that.'

'I'd like it if you stuck around.'

Gabriel's smile turned into a frown. Not the news he wanted to hear.

'Why?'

His statement taken, Chandler had no authority to hold Gabriel. It was time to invent some reason to keep him around.

'In case we need to identify a body.'

The stare he received in return made Chandler wonder if Gabriel had seen straight through his ruse. The eyes that had previously desired escape grew still and focused. They seemed to implore Chandler to tell the truth, sitting in judgement on his lies.

'Where would I stay?'

Chandler immediately thought of the cells but they wouldn't entice a terrified Gabriel to hang around. But the offer of a night in luxury . . .

'We have an excellent hotel in town.'

That was a little disingenuous. Ollie Orlander's place was no palace, but for a farmworker used to sleeping in a twenty-bed dorm it might be luxurious enough.

'Okay,' said Gabriel, non-committal.

'I'll post someone outside.'

He would. Jim would enjoy sitting around all day with his half-completed crosswords.

'Do you have anyone we can call?' asked Chandler.

'No,' said Gabriel abruptly. The bonhomie that Chandler had tried to engender between the two of them fled. The subject of family seemed to have touched a nerve.

'No family?' asked Chandler, plunging in deeper.

The response was a slow shake of his head.

'Why?' Chandler was pushing his luck, but identifying pressure points so they could be manipulated under questioning was a skill he had nurtured and was a hard one to switch off. Sometimes it angered not only others, but himself.

Gabriel offered him the same cold stare. A stare that suggested Chandler should push no further, so he decided not to. The man had been through enough today without having to spell out why he had no family to call on. In the end, Gabriel saved him the trouble.

'They're dead, Sergeant.'

The statement was delivered without emotion, all twitching gone, the nervous energy spent. After the frantic escape, the running for his life, the abuse his body had suffered, it seemed Gabriel had finally shut down.

'Sergeant,' he said slowly, the smoothness of his voice coating everything in silk. 'The one thing we all have in common when born is the need for our parents and the comfort of religion. I was failed by both.'

'What do you mean?'

Gabriel sighed and closed his eyes. 'Nothing. A family thing. I'm tired, angry, scared. I just want to sleep.'

Chandler itched to fire more questions but the strings in the marionette opposite had been cut.

He led Gabriel back into the office, an unstable roll to his walk as if battling to remain upright. Tanya joined them, her subtle nod informing Chandler that the recording had been successful.

'What have we got clothing-wise?' he asked her.

'Not much,' she replied, fishing a shirt from the box

of clothes that even the charity shop couldn't sell. She picked the best of a bad bunch: a stained orange T-shirt with a small fiery logo above the breast.

'What's this for?' asked Gabriel when Chandler handed it to him.

'To wear.'

'I have one.' Gabriel looked at his bloodied top. 'I don't want to be an imposition.'

'You can't go around town like that. You'll scare our citizens,' said Chandler as he led them into the sandstone-walled yard adjacent to the station, towards the police cars.

Gabriel looked at him. Some of the defensiveness had disappeared.

'I don't have much, sir. I don't like to give away anything. Even this shirt.'

Chandler understood the sentiment. As a kid he was fiercely protective of his things. He had even got into a fight with his best friend – long-lost best friend – Mitchell over an old football that had been kicked so many times it was bent out of shape and rolled like Brian East down Prince's Street on a Saturday night.

'You don't have to. Just take the shirt and wear it. Call it a gift,' said Chandler.

Gabriel took it. 'I'll shower first,' he said as they reached the sparkling white police car.

4

Chandler pulled out of the station and into town. Immediately the afternoon sun set about cooking them from the outside in, the intense heat trying to glue them to the black plastic of the seat and stew them in their own bodily fluids.

As they drove past the family owned businesses and abandoned shops on the main drag, Chandler glanced across at his passenger. Gabriel was staring back at him, spread out on the seat, a calmness in his manner that matched his body language. Given that now he was under police protection Chandler hoped they wouldn't let him down.

'Are you sure you don't need a doctor?' he asked.

'They're only bruises I think. There's nothing he could give me. At least the pain reminds me to stay alert.'

Chandler offered a smile. 'Wait 'til you have an ex-wife.'

There was a stab of a smile from his passenger. 'When did that happen?'

Even Gabriel's voice had relaxed. The jittery squeak

31

had been replaced by the soft, enticing glow of a late-night radio DJ. A warm voice playing doleful tunes to send listeners to sleep. It was like he was in the car with a different person entirely.

Chandler paused, calculating it in his head. 'Seven ... seven and a half years.'

'Long time. You miss her?'

'Not since she threatened to take my kids.'

'Oh.' Gabriel stared at him. 'She got any grounds to take 'em?'

Chandler didn't really want to get into this with a stranger but the voice was like a shoulder to cry on; Chandler the midnight caller, unable to drift off, sounding off about his fears and woes.

'I don't think so.'

'How many kids do you have?'

'Two. Maybe the one good thing I've done in my life.' Chandler smiled and looked at his passenger. '*Two* good things.'

If discussing Teri taxed his nerves, he never wasted a chance to extol the virtues of his children, almost in compensation for not getting to see as much of them as he would have wanted. This job took its toll: long hours, odd hours, paperwork and procedure.

'How old?'

'Sarah's nearly eleven, Jasper's getting on towards nine.'

'Sarah and Jasper. Nice names,' said Gabriel.

Chandler noticed little feeling in the declaration. 'You have no one? Girlfriend? Brothers or sisters? Cousins? Uncles?'

A shake of the head. 'No. None.' The harsh, defensive tone from the station was back.

'Sorry,' said Chandler. He couldn't imagine being without his family.

Gabriel stared at him and said nothing for a few seconds. The stare was unnerving. Finally he spoke, the voice resigned.

'I'm used to it.'

'You said earlier that family and religion let you down ... '

Chandler let the statement float between them as they turned past the statue of Stuart MacAllen, the Scotsman who discovered the iron ore that had breathed life back into the town. For a few decades anyway. Now with the boreholes dry and abandoned, the youth were slowly being lost to more prosperous parts of the earth. He couldn't blame them. People had to go where the jobs were. And there were few here.

Though he gave Gabriel time, he got no response. Maybe there was none, just a slip of the tongue in a time of stress, or a family argument, not to be discussed with a stranger. Like an upcoming custody battle, he supposed.

They drove past the bright orange veranda of the Red Inn, an establishment that proudly stated that it had been in business since the end of the 19th century, despite having moved premises twice, before finally settling into its present location in 1950; the year his mum was born.

Gabriel interrupted his thoughts. 'So what's going to happen next?'

'Procedure.'

'Like what? It'll ease my mind to know that you know what you're doing.'

'You don't trust us?'

Gabriel's wavering smile offered no answer.

'We know what we're doing, Mr Johnson. I've been doing this for over ten years.'

'But how many serial killers have you dealt with?'

It was a fair point.

'After I put you up in the hotel, I'll put together a KLO4—'

'A what?' interrupted Gabriel.

'KLO4. Keep a look out for.'

'Oh.' Gabriel shrugged. 'Makes sense.'

'I'll send it out around the state, Northern Territory and the South as well just to be sure. Then we'll organize a search of the Hill, try and find the guy or his body then locate those graves. Though I have to admit that finding this guy, finding Heath, if he's adept at surviving out there, won't be easy given the size of the area.'

Chandler looked to Gabriel. He could see that his response had made his passenger a little uneasy.

'We'll send a chopper and plane up to look.'

'Like you're searching for a missing person?'

'Kinda. We'll start a ground search too.'

'Seems like needle-in-a-haystack stuff.'

Chandler shrugged his shoulders. 'It's all we have, strength in numbers – one man against hundreds.'

'Like Jesus versus the unbelievers.'

Chandler glanced across. 'So you're a religious man?'

Gabriel blew air out of his nose. 'I believe, if that's what you're asking. You?'

34

'I go along with it. Moral grounding for the kids, I suppose. They'll make their own decisions when they're older. It's not as if God forced anyone to follow him.'

'No ... if only his followers abided by the same edict.'

The conversation stopped abruptly. It didn't matter. They'd arrived at the Gardner's Palace, a squat, three-storey building that looked chipped out of a single block of sandstone, bright red, brighter even than the dust that scarred the landscape. It was perfunctory, the black tar on the roof painted white to reflect back some of the vicious heat, the wooden shutters guarding each window, protecting it further.

The pair of patched armchairs in the narrow reception area welcomed them. It wasn't the Ritz but good enough for the rare occasions they needed to keep some-one around.

The owner, Ollie Orlander, greeted them, his stomach bubbling over his trousers like an overheated pot of mis-shapen pasta. Ollie was more than happy to take their strays. The government always paid its bills and he could lease out his most expensive room, the misnomer known as the Presidential Suite, at full price.

Ollie eyed up his new guest to make sure that he under-stood who owned the place. An unnecessary attempt at intimidation and part of the reason Ollie got very few repeat visitors. In Chandler's experience, guests favoured a hearty welcome rather than obvious suspicion.

Ollie's beady eyes turned to Chandler. 'He's not going to cause any damage is he?'

'He's not a criminal,' said Chandler.

'Then what's he doing with you?'

'He provided us with some information. We need to put him up for the night.'

'The usual suite?'

Chandler nodded wearily. 'The usual suite will do.'

'Very good, sir.' A lopsided smile passed over the rotund face. He waddled off to ready a few things as Chandler led Gabriel upstairs.

'Don't expect too much,' warned Chandler.

'If it's got a warm bath and a soft bed that's good enough for me.'

Chandler studied his face. Some of the nervousness had returned, eyes that darted around as if expecting Heath to appear from behind every corner.

'I'll stick an officer outside.'

'I don't need one, Sergeant.'

They reached the door of the Presidential Suite.

'I insist,' said Chandler. He was not about to let Gabriel become a victim of his own bravery.

5

Constable Jim Fall arrived, book of crosswords in tow, extricating his lanky frame from the police car in stages; right leg, then left, then his arms gripped the roof before hauling his torso into the late afternoon. How he had survived down the cramped mineshafts Chandler still didn't know. Though they had joined only a couple of years apart, Jim had refused to rise above the rank of constable, happy with the minimal level of responsibility it brought. He was reliable to a tee.

'What's the job?' asked Jim, elongating the last vowel while scratching his unruly bush of greying hair.

'Watch the hotel. Make sure that our guest is okay.'

'He likely to run?'

'I'm not sure.'

Gabriel's wits seemed to have recovered enough to have the sense to get out of town – possibly why he had originally baulked at the offer of police protection.

'Just keep an eye out,' added Chandler as he left Jim sitting under the awning outside Annie's Cafe across the street.

Returning to the station, Tanya had already called in the final member of the team. Luka Grgić was wiping the sleep from his eyes. This was supposed to be his day off and he let Chandler know as much via his glare alone. He might have been young and occasionally reckless but he knew better than to question the orders of a superior, even if he was frustrated at being stuck behind Chandler and Tanya in the chain. The flashes of blind ambition reminded Chandler a little of Mitch. He chased the ghoulish presence of his former partner from his head. It was time to concentrate.

'So what's this about, boss?' asked Luka, yawning.

'We have a situation.'

Luka's jet-black eyebrows furrowed, shadowing a pair of smouldering eyes that much of the female population of the town had taken quite a liking to. If Wilbrook ran a most eligible bachelor competition then Chandler was dead in the water. Luka would win hands down.

Chandler continued, 'We have the statement of a man who claims to have been attacked and held captive out on Gardner's Hill by a man he's named as Heath. Heath, according to the description, is thirty, five foot six or seven, of stocky build, with brown hair and a beard. Tanned too. As in a working-outdoors tan. We're to consider him dangerous, possibly armed.'

'And he's wanted for? Assault? Kidnapping?' asked Luka.

'Attempted murder.' Chandler looked around his team. 'And we have reason to suspect he may have killed before.'

'Yes!'

Chandler turned to the source of the cry. Embarrassed by the outward show of delight, Nick drifted back to his desk and pretended to scribble on some paper. Chandler had known that this detail would spark him. His fascination with serial killers was such that Chandler believed there wasn't one he couldn't relay the entire history of.

Chandler looked at Tanya. She was the only one not listening to him, working on the KLO4.

'How long 'til we can send—'

'Ready,' she announced.

Chandler quickly scanned the details. 'Send it.'

With a click of a button the KLO4 winged its way to all stations in the Pilbara, Western Australia, Northern Territory and South Australia. The state police would get a copy too. Wilbrook would soon become the focus of much attention.

Seeking to get ahead of the game, Chandler brought up computer-generated maps to get an idea of the area they needed to cover. On the screen it looked viable for a small team, contour lines and markings scattered sparsely over the map, but the dog-eared paper copies spread across the meeting table confirmed the sheer size and expanse of the region. There might be nothing up there, but there was an awful lot of nothing.

'You're going to have to call HQ,' said Tanya.

Chandler knew that. He also knew what it would entail. HQ meant Port Hedland. And Port Hedland meant Mitch.

'I know.'

'We'll need at least ... twenty, don't you think?' said

Luka, immediately making it obvious that he had never set foot on the Hill.

'Triple that unless we strike lucky,' said Chandler. He looked to Tanya. 'See if we can get a chopper or a set of wings up today. Get them to eyeball for anything unusual, maybe narrow the area down.' He turned to Luka. 'Luka ... check up on the name Heath, any criminals with that forename. Or surname. Focus on anyone charged or convicted for murder or assault. Get me all the info you can.'

Orders given, the officers went. That left Chandler with a task he was dreading. Involving Mitch. A task that would reduce his role from leader to assistant. But if Gabriel was correct, then they had a serious criminal on the loose. He needed support to surround the area, erect roadblocks to contain the suspect, as well as organize a search of the Hill and nearby farms. It was too much for five officers on their own.

He reached for the phone but was interrupted by a cry from the main office. Nick's Melbourne drawl swooped through the air like a foreign language.

'Zero-zero-one, Sarge.'

An inside joke, code for a call from his mum. Chandler was her personal emergency service. Most likely Dad attempting something she didn't like. Given it was summer he was probably trying to haul the large rubber pool from the garage to the backyard. Another of Chandler's jobs. In exchange for free babysitting.

'What's it about, Nick?' asked Chandler. He could do without the distraction right now. The stifled chuckle might have been imagined but it was enough to irritate him.

'Something to do with Sarah.'

'Right, put her through.'

Chandler answered halfway through the first ring.

'Chandler?'

'Yes, it's me, Mum.' He sighed.

'What's with your new boy's accent, I thought I'd phoned the wrong place.'

'You phone twice a day, Mum.'

'No, I don't.'

Though her voice was soft, she stated everything with the confidence of a woman who knew her standing in the world and was content with it. Chandler decided to back down. He didn't need to get into a pointless argument.

'What's wrong with Sarah?'

'Oh yes, Sarah. I think you need to come chat to her. She's worried about First Confession tomorrow.'

'What's she worried about? She just needs to say the words, kneel down, stand up.'

'She's ten.'

'I know what age she is, Mum.'

'At that age you didn't like sleeping without the light on.'

Having heard this before Chandler cut in. 'Can't you deal with it? Can't Dad?'

'We could but I think it would be better coming from her father.'

'It's busy in here.'

'It can't be *that* busy.'

'Just deal with it for now, Mum. I'll be back later to talk to her. Or get one of her friends to talk to her.'

'So your advice is to have one ten-year-old counsel another ten-year-old?' She sounded incredulous at the idea. Chandler didn't blame her. It wasn't one of his best, but his mind was drifting to the situation at hand. To Gabriel.

'I've got to go, Mum,' he said and hung up.

In the momentary silence, Chandler thought of Gabriel. The terrified victim at the station and the calm, silky voice in the car on the way to the hotel. A notion arose that Gabriel had made it all up; crying wolf to get attention. Providing a spark to an otherwise mundane existence. Searching for fame. Or infamy. Like a serial killer might do. But Gabriel had genuinely looked scared. Plus, the blood and bruises were real. As was the chaffed skin around the wrists and the blistered hands. And if Chandler dismissed the idea of it being an act ... all that was left was the very real possibility that there *was* a killer out there.

He looked at the phone. There was a chance Mitch might send someone else. It was a faint hope. Like the one he had of never having to work with Mitch again.

6

2002

Even for late November it was a hot day. Chandler was hugging the treeline to steal any shade he could amongst the scattered branches, weaving a zigzag path from trunk to trunk. The others were doing the same, resembling a bunch of uniformed drunks lost in the outback, desperately seeking water and shelter. Salt stung the cut made by his zombie-like 6am shave. A twelve-hour shift trekking the outback wasn't really what he'd joined the police for, tracking through the middle of this hellhole in search of a lost hiker. But as rookies, he and Mitch were in no position to refuse the detail.

His partner at least had the advantage of long legs on the uneven ground. That and a chin which jutted out from his face like an antenna, guiding him over and around the protruding rocks. Though they were the same age Mitch looked older, gaunt, almost sickly in appearance, his arms and legs too long, as if stretched out and twisted back in an arbitrary fashion. When angry he had the tendency to flap them around like an inflatable sky-dancer outside a car dealership – minus the smile of course. Mitch rarely smiled.

Bundabaroo, the region that included the slopes of Gardner's Hill, was a wilderness that was particularly inhospitable. Impassable mountains, trees and rocks that either crumbled underfoot and sent you sprawling, or were sharp enough to slice bone. An experiment by God to set the most extreme conditions life could prosper in. A place where the only attendant civilization was Wilbrook, though, as the joke went, if Wilbrook was your last source of civilization you really were in trouble.

Despite it being the 21st century, the region had yet to be fully explored on foot. There were only two ways in: a dirt road that skirted the foot of Gardner's Hill; or a perilous descent in a helicopter through a thrashing mix of tall trees and wiry scrub on to the unstable surface below.

The reason they were all out here was a lost nineteen-year-old called Martin Taylor. It had been four days since Martin had disappeared and today a dog team had been bussed in from the coast to help, the canines afforded the luxury of a three-hour working day in the summer heat, while the humans toiled for twelve.

With the clack of the chopper overhead and eager barks of the hounds, Chandler concentrated on the noise closest to him: the crash of his boots through the undergrowth. Externally he was searching for Martin and internally for sympathy for the young man's plight. Another city slicker pursuing the great outdoors *despite being completely unprepared for what lay ahead. There was no defined trail out here, nothing for guidance other than eyes, compasses and maps. GPS was a pipedream. This was the earth as it was two and a half billion years ago, entirely undefined, rocks, trees and landscape blending into one, melting the land and sky together in a blur and offering no hint as to the way out.*

All the information they had on Martin's movements came from Eleanor Trebech, the owner of the Gardner's Palace, the hotel he'd stayed in the night before. Eleanor had conveyed all she knew in her disinterested style, her hair curled in never-ending spirals.

Her responses had been given in both smoke signals and words, her cigarillos never far from her lips. They had got a description and an idea of Martin's preparedness. Sturdy boots and sunglasses. A lightweight top that glowed a distracting radioactive green as he stood in the dimly lit lobby. A tiny backpack which couldn't have contained enough for an extended trek. An angry young man, she'd gauged, recently spilt up from his girlfriend. A nasty split she speculated.

Bill Ashcroft shot one further question, delivered in his inimitable gruff style. 'Did he inform you when he was coming back?'

Eleanor shook her head. Martin had not asked her to hold a room so what business was it of hers. She ended the conversation by returning to the glossy lifestyle magazine on the reception in front of her.

Information gleaned from his family and friends

marked Martin as a semi-experienced hiker with a number of weekend-long treks under his belt, but for this excursion Martin had disregarded a couple of the basic tenets: hiking alone and not informing a responsible person of his proposed route and expected time of return. No one would call Eleanor Trebech responsible, certainly not with her three and a half husbands and history of inebriated car crashes. But not providing her with any information on his future plans seemed a wilful act of abandonment.

The only clue as to where he had set off from was the rusty Holden found abandoned in the gash in the trees that constituted the dirt car park partway up Gardner's Hill. Tests showed that there was nothing but fumes in the Holden's tank, the suspension held together by prayers more than mechanics. How it survived the treacherous road to get that far was anyone's guess.

In the car they found a compass, tent pegs and a jacket, a necessity as the temperature could plummet overnight. A small first-aid kit was wedged under the passenger's seat, where it could be easily forgotten. Maybe on purpose.

At that stage no one had put forward the possibility – out loud at least – that Martin was dead. What was speculated was that he was very much alive and completely oblivious to the search operation now under way. That he had hitch-hiked somewhere else without informing anyone. Maybe even on to the old mining grounds. It wasn't uncommon. Three times in the past two years they had been called out to incidents where

*environmental activists had trespassed on to mining
land only to stumble into one of the many open pits.
Two had escaped with broken bones and a substantial
fine, but one had picked the wrong hole to fall down
and broken his neck. He'd gone undiscovered for six
months. It was the same up here on the Hill, natural pits
and hollows hidden in the undergrowth in abundance.
If Martin had fallen into one no one would have heard
him scream.*

7

It was the embittered screech that reached him first, followed by stout indignation. Chandler had been talking to Tanya about amending the KLO4 to include a warning about approaching the suspect, when a strange man limped into the station, his limp exacerbated by the shotgun barrel jammed into his lower back. The shotgun was wielded by Ken 'Kid' Maloney, fifty-six years old, born and as oft-said, ill-bred here, sporting a beard that was as wild as his eyes. He mumbled something about catching this bastard on his land, the rest was hard to make out in the garbled tongue few understood.

Sneaking a glance at his colleagues, Chandler offered a reassuring nod. A reminder not to react. Not yet. This was the second time Ken had marched someone in at the end of his shotgun this year. The first time it had been a young backpacking couple who he claimed had stolen things from his house. A claim that turned out to be nothing more than a thirsty couple in need of some water and – on Ken's part – wilful misunderstanding. This time he had a single victim. Chandler drew his eyes from the gun to the shaking hostage to try and calm him. His heart stopped.

The man at the end of the gun exactly fitted the description of Heath.

Around five foot six and, as Gabriel had described, with the stout, low centre of gravity of a farmhand, engineered to lug heavy equipment around. His nut-brown hair was tousled, as if it had evaded a comb for months, the week-old beard a shade darker than the hair. Sweat dripped from it. A small cross dangled underneath a green-checked shirt which was minus a ripped pocket. Accompanied by the three-quarter-length trousers he resembled a lumberjack, at home in the outdoors, at home with keeping someone locked up outdoors before murdering them. The blood staining his clothes lent credence to this hypothesis.

'Someone gonna come arrest him then?' said Ken, the gun firmly wedged into the small of the man's back.

With a flick of his hand, Chandler signalled his colleagues to back away. Ken's face was a picture of frustration. Dangerous frustration.

'We'll take him now, Ken. Just put down your gun.'

Chandler had hoped to convey authority in the command but wasn't sure he'd succeeded.

'Why the hell should I put down *ma*' gun?' demanded Ken. 'Someone's gotta keep him under control.'

'Just drop it, Ken,' said Chandler. He couldn't help but think that if Ken knew who this man probably was he wouldn't have dared approach him. Ken was crazy, not stupid.

'I'm not puttin' down ma' gun 'til someone comes arrest him,' said Ken, his voice trapped by the beard as if the hair had wired his lips shut.

Chandler inched forward to hear him better. A bad move. Ken readjusted his position menacingly.

There was an indecipherable mumble from his hostage now. Begging.

Chandler decided to try and placate Ken. 'Okay, Ken, what did he do?' he asked.

'More like what'a *caught* him doing.'

Chandler strained his head forward, not daring to move the rest of his body in case it set Ken off.

'He was trying to steal ma' car.'

'He was at *your* place?' asked Chandler. If this was Heath, he must have been looking for a car in order to flee. Or pursue his prey.

'No, I was out near Turtle's. Hunting some of those bastard rabbits. Was coming back to the car when I caught *this* bastard trying to start it. A fella's property is a fella's property,' said Ken, wide-eyed and acting as innocent as the rabbits he was supposedly hunting.

Chandler knew full well that the rabbit story was bullshit. If Ken had been around Turtle's then it was almost certain that he'd been stealing eggs from the chicken coops; but that was a follow-up for another day. Right now he needed Ken to back off and let him take his captive into custody so he could ask more questions and confirm his suspicions.

'Quite right, Ken, quite right,' agreed Chandler. 'Now if you let me have him, I can arrest him.'

'I wasn't trying—' started the man. The barrel shoved into his back stopped him.

'Ya bloody were, I caught ya,' said Ken, shouting into the ear of his hostage before diverting his attention back to Chandler. 'There'll be handprints ... fingerprints on the steering wheel. And before you think it, I ain't got nothing to do with the blood. Ya can't do me for that. He already had it on him.'

'I believe you, Ken. Now—'

'I didn't lay a finger on him. Tell him.' Ken prodded the gun into his hostage's back.

His hostage stuttered, 'It wasn't—'

Ken didn't let him finish. 'There, ya'see.'

'I see,' said Chandler. He directed the conversation to the hostage, who fitted Gabriel's description of the serial killer. 'Are you okay?'

There was hurt in the man's eyes. 'No, I'm not okay. Do I look okay?' he said, followed by a wince of pain. Not the barrel this time – something else was causing him discomfort.

Ken jabbed the barrel again, producing a grunt from his hostage. 'Tell them what you done, boy. Or what you were trying to do when'a stopped ya.'

'Ken, let us handle this,' said Chandler.

'If I get him to admit it you can't charge *me* with anything.'

'I'm not going to charge you with anything, Ken, but you need to put the gun down. Now!' Chandler realized that he needed to end this. The longer Ken stood there the more twitchy his trigger-finger could become.

Luka interrupted. 'We can't take any of this as evidence, Ken, as you have him at gunpoint.'

Chandler turned to glare at his constable. Luka was technically correct but it wasn't a helpful interjection. He already had a potential serial killer on his hands; he didn't need a separate murder investigation.

'Ken! The gun. Now!' Chandler held his hand out for the shotgun. Though he tried to will it, nothing he could do could stop it from shaking.

'It's my gun,' said Ken.

'And you'll get it back.'

'I've a right to have it.'

'But not a right to point it at people.'

'Even at bastards stealing ma' car?'

'You've brought him to us. That's enough.'

'He hasn't admitted it,' said Ken.

Again his hostage winced, his jaw clenched tight. A defeated aura encompassed him. The serial killer caught by chance, his carefully laid plans foiled by a slow-witted – but dangerous – local.

Seeing that Ken wasn't about to drop the gun, Chandler turned to the hostage. 'Did you try and steal the car?'

There was a nod. The confession at gunpoint. 'Yeah, I tried to steal his car. I had to. I had to get away, there's—'

His confession was halted by another jab of the gun. 'Bullshit, boy. There's no excuses, you city arseholes think you can get away with anything out here.'

'You've got your confession, Ken. You can let him go now,' said Chandler.

'But he isn't sorry.'

'Ken!'

Ken scowled, removing the gun from his hostage's back and aimed it at the ceiling. Chandler released the curdled air from his lungs and felt the collective tension ease, the mass of hitched shoulders dropped as one. Tanya and Luka darted forward to part Ken from his hostage. Chandler stepped towards him as Ken resisted Tanya's attempts to take the shotgun from his hands.

'The gun's mine.'

'Forty-eight hours, Ken,' said Chandler. 'To give you a chance to calm down. Next time you spot an intruder, call us.'

'I want it back. Two days, Sergeant. I need that gun.' Ken scowled, looking lost without his firearm, eyes wide in hurt as if his only child had been ripped from his grasp.

'Two days,' said Chandler, ignoring Tanya's look of frustration. He knew her opinion. She didn't condone anyone but the police having guns. It might have been her three kids talking but truth was she had never liked them. Not that she was afraid to aim one to hammer home a point. Chandler nodded at her to usher Ken out of the station. He was, for once, the least dangerous madman present.

With Ken gone, Chandler studied the suspect. His head was lowered to the ground with nothing in the sweaty, chubby cheeks that suggested he was capable of killing fifty-four people. The eyes that looked up as he approached, however, were narrowed and Chandler detected an undercurrent of malice in them. The man took a deep breath and grunted, teeth bared. Chandler's hands slid to his gun, grazing the metal, ready to draw.

'I had to steal the car. I had to,' he whispered.

Luka paused at the suspect's shoulder, awaiting further instruction. Chandler flicked his eyes to the side of the room. Message understood, his colleague backed away.

'Are you Heath?' asked Chandler, fingers curving around the butt of the gun. The seemingly wounded man slowly raised his head, jaw clamped firmly shut. The look of a man who'd been exposed.

The deep brown eyes stared at Chandler, before glancing at the others. Chandler prepared himself, his fingers tensing. If Heath were going to attempt escape it would be now.

Heath nodded once, confusion now rather than menace in his expression. 'How did you—?'

'Is your name Heath?' repeated Chandler.

'Yes, it's Heath. Heath Barwell,' he said, frowning. The pained expression had disappeared. It had all been an act. Though a very realistic one.

'You're from out East?'

'Yes. Adelaide.'

'And what brings you here?' Chandler was starting slowly, easy questions to lull him, like excavating at an archaeological dig, better to use a brush than a bulldozer.

'Work.'

'What kinda work?'

'Any. Farming, fruit-picking, labouring. You name it, I've done it.'

'So you know the place well?'

Heath slowly shook his head. 'No.'

Chandler noted the suspicion and tentativeness in Heath's voice as if searching for the safe path through the minefield.

'Mr Barwell, I'm going to have to arrest you—'

'I needed to steal the ... take the car,' spluttered Heath. 'I was running from—'

'We're not interested in the car,' interrupted Chandler, easing Heath's arms behind his back and slipping the cuffs over wrists that were chafed red, the palms of his hands blistered with heat or overwork. 'We want to talk to you about some murders.'

Immediately the cuffed hands ripped from his grasp. Heath turned to him, eyes ablaze. As he took a step away from Chandler, Tanya and Luka closed in.

'That's what I want to tell you about,' said Heath.

'You want to confess?' asked Chandler, fighting a curious mix of anticlimax and excitement. But if a confession meant he didn't have to bring in Mitch then—

'What do you mean, do *I* want to confess? I'm the one who was attacked,' said Heath, flicking his head as if signalling the direction. 'Up there. In the woods.'

Tanya and Luka corralled the suspect into a seat. Chandler stood in front of him wondering what Heath was trying to achieve. Misdirection? Lying to save himself? A game?

'What do you mean?' he asked, playing along.

'I *mean*,' started Heath, sounding affronted, 'someone

kidnapped and tried to kill me. I managed to make it out of there until I ran into the bastard with the mullet and the shotgun.'

'Who attacked you?' asked Chandler.

'Which one?'

'The one in the woods.'

'Called himself Gabriel,' said Heath, licking his cracked lips to wet them.

The name sent a million thoughts crashing through Chandler's brain but it was Tanya who spoke up, still coiled and ready to pounce. 'What did he look like, this Gabriel?'

'Tall ... taller than me. Maybe your height,' he nodded at Chandler, 'but slimmer. Talked ... I dunno ... like he was from around here.'

No, he didn't, thought Chandler. Gabriel was definitely from Perth, though he supposed that for someone from out East all Westies did all sound the same. He warned himself not to fall into the same trap. Casual stereotyping equalled lazy police work.

'Anything else?' asked Chandler. The description wasn't much to go on. Nothing to say for sure that it was Gabriel Johnson.

'What d'you want to know?' asked Heath. 'He was your height, tanned with stubble, but his face was kinda, I dunno, too young. As if they didn't match, like the beard was stuck on. He was softly spoken. Like silk.'

That nailed it. Heath had described Gabriel, almost exactly. In fact the recollection might have been a little too good, more of a prolonged study of the subject than a fleeting glance in panic. Especially for a supposedly startled brain.

Chandler looked to his fellow officers. Tanya seemed as stunned as he was. Luka stared at him, looking for direction as to what to do next. The final member, Nick, remained stuck behind the front desk, his eyes wide, enjoying the show.

Heath filled the silence.

'So that's why I tried to take the car. I was running for my life. You *have* to believe me.'

The plea was aimed at Chandler. Chandler didn't respond, his brain swimming in treacle.

'Sarge?' said Luka, pushing for an answer. The kid always liked it when someone was under pressure, even more so when it was his boss.

'Stick him in a cell,' answered Chandler. It was nothing more than a stalling tactic but it was the best he could come up with until his thoughts settled down.

As Luka nodded, Heath exploded, trying in vain to free himself from the two officers dragging him to his feet.

'You can't do this,' he screamed as he was led off towards the cells. 'I've got my rights. You can't lock me up.'

'I can if you're under custody,' replied Chandler to his protests.

'For what?'

'Stealing a car to start with.'

'He was trying to murder me!'

'You'll be safe in the cells then,' said Chandler, listening to the ongoing protest fade into the distance.

8

Chandler sat at Tanya's desk and tried to clear his head. He had two people, each claiming to have been attacked by the other. One he had locked up, and one he had let go. Who was telling the truth? Who did he *think* was telling the truth? The one who had entered voluntarily or the one presented at the business end of a shotgun? He would start by questioning the one he had.

'Will I call HQ?' Nick's enthusiastic voice interrupted his thoughts.

'Let me think.'

'We might have a serial killer, Sarge.' Nick's voice was riddled with excitement.

Luka stepped into the main office from the cells in back.

'He all locked up?' asked Chandler.

'He is,' replied Luka, grabbing a tin of Coke from the fridge. Chandler felt like the temperature in the station had cranked up a notch, impossible as it seemed in this scorching heat. 'You might want to stop young Nick's imagination getting carried away, though.'

Chandler agreed. It was his job to keep a lid on the

emotions, even if he was struggling to deal with his own. 'We don't know what we're dealing with. It might just be a dispute between friends that's got out of hand. We'll get some facts before we call HQ. We all need to stay calm.'

It was a mantra Chandler repeated to himself as he stood outside the interview room trying to calm his nerves. Inside was a man who had murdered fifty-four people. Or a kid who'd had an argument with a friend and posed no more of a threat than the flies buzzing around the ceiling light. Heath had been left to stew for twenty minutes before he had been transferred from the cell to the arena.

In the twenty-minute gap Chandler had checked in with Jim who informed him that there was nothing to report on Gabriel, their witness and victim, now implicated as a possible suspect. He'd ordered Jim to continue his watch and call if anything changed. After the interview he'd bring Gabriel back in.

Chandler entered the interview room. Heath was sitting at the table, bound in handcuffs, Tanya standing guard at the back of the room. Heath's eyes were firmly closed as Chandler sat down. He let him meditate for a moment, studying the man, both uneasy and excited over what he was about to uncover.

'Mr Barwell, are you with us?'

The eyes opened and focused on Chandler. Where he had been expecting cold and calculating there was only weariness and a look that suggested he had been awake for an extended period of time – or that his brain was struggling to contain a terrible secret.

''Course I'm with you,' spat Heath, raising the hand-cuffs. He might have been weary but he retained enough wit to bite back.

'I need to ask you a few questions,' said Chandler.

'I've told you everything I know. I've told you who held me captive and who tried to kill me. I've even given you a description – yet *I'm* the one locked up.'

'You stole a car, Mr Barwell.'

'And I explained why. I was fleeing from a murderer. That overrides any attempt to steal a car, surely?' There was a pause, before Heath backtracked, realizing that he'd just confessed to a crime. 'You can't use that, you haven't started the interview, or read me my rights.' Sweat dripped from the tangled brown hair, sweat that was quickly swallowed up by a beard, which seemed to have grown a shade darker in the last half hour.

'I already know about the car,' said Chandler. 'I want to know the rest. I want you to tell me *your* story. How you got here.'

There was a long pause as if Heath were deciding if Chandler could be trusted. It didn't matter; in his present situation he had no choice. Leaning back, Heath grabbed his hair, twisting it even more out of shape before dragging his hands down over a face that was as tanned and weather-beaten as Gabriel's. It was where their physical similarities ended.

Their stories, however, were almost a perfect match. Like Gabriel, Heath was out of work, broke and travelling inland to secure some farm work.

'Did you have a name? A location? A phone number?'

'What, ring ahead and book?' said Heath with a snarl.

'You must have had some lead to come all the way out here.'

Heath sighed in frustration. 'I was doing what I normally do – winging it. Some picker down the coast tipped me that way inland was the best place to go, that most stick to the coast to move around easily but there's too much competition.' Heath looked at him. 'But winging it's not a crime. Is it?'

It wasn't but it also made him less credible. Chandler needed more. 'Go on.'

'Well I was thumbing a lift out of Port Hedland when Gabriel pulled up.'

'What car was he driving?'

'I dunno. A piece of shit car. The colour of shit too.'

'Make?'

Heath shrugged his shoulders. 'It stopped. That's all I cared about. Battered piece of shit or not, it was better than slogging all day under the fucking sun.'

'Licence number?'

Heath sighed and closed his eyes. 'If I can't remember the make, what makes you think I'll remember that?'

Chandler didn't answer. Both Gabriel and Heath's descriptions of the car matched, both were equally vague.

'And you always hitch?' asked Chandler.

'Only if I don't have a choice.'

'You didn't get any bad vibes about him?'

'He was tall and skinny. Nothing I couldn't handle if

he tried anything. Introduced himself as Gabriel, travelling back from town with supplies.'

'Anything else?'

Heath's eyes wandered to the back wall. 'Only that he lived around here, on his own. Seemed true. I mean, he didn't say much and when he did it was so soft I could hardly hear it. Made me think he was possibly, you know, gay.' His focus returned to Chandler. 'Not that I've anything against them ... What people get up to s'their business. I mean, I don't hate 'em or anything,' said Heath, clearly struggling to express himself.

Chandler let him continue digging, hoping that he'd reveal something.

'What I'm saying is that I wasn't scared. I had it under control.' Heath closed his eyes in a moment of reflection. 'I *thought* I had it under control. I asked him what he did, being friendly and that, but there was nothing I wanted more than to sleep for a few hours. Because he was a stranger I didn't.'

'What did you talk about?'

'Nothing really. I told him I was from Adelaide and that the place up here seemed as barren as the haul from Coober Pedy to Alice Springs, but that it's where the money is. We headed out of town aiming inland. Passed a couple of turnoffs—'

'Did you get the impression that something was *off* about him?' interrupted Chandler.

'No, just that he was passing places that I might get work. He explained that everyone dives into them. He had a phrase ...' said Heath, rolling his eyes to the ceiling, 'like stopping off at the first watering hole you see.' Heath looked at him. 'You know it?'

Chandler shook his head, wanting Heath to continue.

'Something like you get there but all the animals have trampled the soil and made the water too dirty to drink. He said that the ones further along were better so on we kept going. It was nice to be moving, rather than cooking by the roadside. He told me there was water in the back if I wanted it.' Heath winced. 'I didn't see why not. I was thirsty.'

Chandler could see where this story was headed. Poisoned water. Like Gabriel had also described.

'It took a couple of minutes before I began to fade. Like I was shutting down. At first I thought it was just my body relaxing, the anxiety of being in a stranger's car passing and the hot air blasting in the window making me drowsy, but it gradually got worse and worse until I couldn't feel my arms or legs. Then I must have passed out. I guess the water had been spiked.'

Chandler let him continue, scribbling notes.

'I woke up in a tool shed.' Heath sniffed the air. 'It smelled like sweet sap, from the chopped wood in the corner. I was trapped in some old-style handcuff thing that hurt my wrists.' He showed Chandler the raw skin that branded his thick wrists, the skin rubbed off. 'Feet too. Chains like you see in old movies about Ned Kelly and the like. Thick iron attached by a chain to the wall. He didn't want me going anywhere.'

'Can you describe them *exactly*?'

Heath shook his head. 'Like D-shapes ... loops linked

by a chain. On my legs, too. My wrists were attached to the wall. My legs weren't but the chains were too heavy to move, like they'd been set in a concrete block. I yelled for help but there was nothing from outside but squawks and chirps . . . and someone moving next door. That's when I guessed I was chained up in a shed next to a cabin. That got me worried about what all the tools were for.' He stared at Chandler. 'Everything looks sinister when you're a prisoner. I kept calling out until my throat burned but Gabriel didn't care. He knew there was no one around to help. After a while he appeared at the door, not angry, not happy . . . just there. I pleaded with him to let me go and he told me to calm down, in that weird soft voice of his. I was afraid that he was going to do something there and then but he just mentioned something about fifty-five. I asked him what the hell he meant but he said he had work to do and left. I told him he didn't have to kill me. Then he said something that still creeps me out. "No need to worry about it," he said. "No need to worry at all. Of *course* you'll be killed."'

Heath stared at Chandler, as if the seriousness of the threat had to be reinforced.

Chandler played it straight. 'If Gabriel was that intent on killing you, how did you get away?'

His suspect put his handcuffed wrists on the table, the skin torn, blackened around the edges, dust ground into the wound.

'Luck. I kept pulling at the cuffs, hoping that they were so old they might break. They did. One of the locking mechanisms fell out. For a few seconds I froze, looking at it on the ground, not believing it had actually happened. Leaning over I grabbed a hatchet from the bench and swung for the other cuff, trying not to chop through my wrist. I kept hammering at it, listening for him coming back from next door.'

'And he didn't?'

Heath smiled, noticeable pride in it. 'I started shouting again, covering the noise of the chops, shouting louder the harder I hit. Managed to bend the metal enough to get my hand out.' Heath stared at the swollen palm of his hand. 'I was going to do the same to the leg irons but found the key hanging on a nail. I wanted to use the hatchet to bust through the shed doors but it was blunt so I went to the connecting door and peeked inside.'

Heath closed his eyes, recalling the scene. 'He was in there, facing away from me, papers and maps all around like he was planning something. Probably where to bury me.'

'So his back was turned to you?' asked Chandler.

'Yeah.'

'And you had the hatchet?'

'Yeah.'

'Why didn't you attack him?'

Heath paused, as if only now asking himself the same question. 'I just wanted to get out of there, Sergeant. Anyway, he turned and stared at me. Looked as startled as I did. I bolted for the door, got outside and started running. I fuckin' hate the outdoors.'

'But you work outdoors,' Chandler reminded him.

'Only for the money. Give me brick, tarmac and air

con any day but I haven't got the brains or qualifications to scratch my arse behind a desk.'

Chandler corralled him back to his story. 'So you ran but didn't lose him?'

'No. He's built like one of those middle-distance runners for fuck's sake. I managed to hold him off until I came to the graves.'

'Graves?' asked Chandler, feigning ignorance.

'Yeah – graves. Or at least I think they were graves.'

The instantaneous backtrack made Chandler suspicious – as if his suspect were pretending not to know too much.

'How many graves?'

'Six I think. It was like I'd stumbled into hell given the heat.' Heath flashed a weak smile, but it was quickly dropped when Chandler didn't return it. 'I aimed for the top of a hill thinking I'd find a way out but there was nothing but a ten-foot drop. Then he caught me and shoved me to the ground.' Heath cleared his throat. 'I don't remember much about the fight other than neither of us laid a decent hand on each other, rolling over and over to try and get an advantage before we must have gone over the edge. When we landed, I remember thinking that I was dead, no air in my lungs, unable to move my arms or legs. Then I guess I passed out and woke up sometime later staring up at the ridge. I had no idea where I was.'

'How long were you out?'

'I dunno. The sun was still rising so I guess a couple of hours.'

'Okay,' said Chandler. 'And where was Gabriel?'

'Beside me. Covered in cuts and bruises. Alive ... dead, I didn't care. I left him there.'

So neither suspect had tried to finish off the other. Chandler supposed that if either had truly been a serial killer they would have seized the opportunity. One thing was for sure – one of them wasn't telling the truth.

Heath continued his story. 'I stumbled along for a few hours before I came across a dirt road. Followed it and it came to a farm. Didn't look to be anybody in so I thought I'd try and borrow the car. That's when the gun-totin' arsehole found me. And here we are. Sitting here talking while that psycho is out there.'

Chandler decided to level with Heath to gauge his reaction. 'That psycho is telling exactly the same story about you – that you kidnapped and tried to kill him.'

Heath's face dropped, turning pale as his eyes blinked rapidly. 'You caught him?'

'Yeah,' said Chandler.

Heath paused. 'He's lying.'

'Okay. Why?' asked Chandler.

'What do you mean, *why*?'

'Why would Gabriel lie?'

Heath shuffled to the edge of the seat, the legs of the chair scraping on the floor. 'I told you. Because he's a psycho.'

'I mean, a specific reason? Is there anyone that would want to kidnap and kill you? Would hate you enough to set this up? Any enemies? Debts? Anything?'

'I don't have shit to owe shit,' spat Heath.

Maybe the first true thing you've said, thought Chandler. There was an intensity about Heath's posture that gave Chandler the impression that on the inside he was permanently on edge, as nervous as a startled cat, claws buried within the soft padding of his clothes.

'He's just a psycho, sir ... Sergeant ... whatever you're called.'

'Sergeant will do.'

The stocky man's nerves became more exaggerated, legs chattering up and down like pistons underneath the table. 'There's nothing more I can tell you, Sergeant.'

Chandler nodded. He'd wrung all he was able to from this stone for now. He needed time to plan his next move. All he had at the minute was one stranger's word against another and his opinion on who was telling the truth. If either were.

'Can I leave now?' asked Heath.

'Where to?' asked Chandler.

'Anywhere.'

'I think that it's best you stay here, isn't it? If a serial killer's after you.'

Heath opened his mouth as if about to argue but had nothing.

Chandler and Tanya left the interview room and re-entered the office. They were met by Luka pacing up and down between the desks, weaving in and out, as if tying himself in knots.

'Well?' asked Luka.

'We'll have to detain him,' said Chandler.

Luka's eyes lit up but it was Nick that spoke, his disembodied voice floating around the corner from the front desk. 'So he did it?'

'I don't know,' said Chandler. 'Their stories are identical.'

'They can't be *identical*,' said Luka.

Tanya interrupted. 'They are. Pretty much word for word.'

'So what do we charge him with?' asked Nick.

'I don't know yet,' admitted Chandler. He turned to Tanya. 'Stick him in a cell for the time being. And be careful.'

He meant it. He'd formed a close bond with them all. The last thing he wanted was to have to explain to Simon, Errol or Katie that something had happened to their mum. Likewise to Jim's invalided mother. Just last year they'd buried Jim's dad, the old man losing the battle with emphysema from his time down the mines. A man who had fought the war as bravely as he'd fought the disease. A man who had insisted that his funeral be a celebration of life. He'd got it. Three days' worth, an affair some mourners had barely survived themselves.

And though he knew less about the other two, he cared for both Luka and Nick; Luka despite his obvious faults and Nick because it was hard not to feel parental towards the boy given that he'd moved all the way across the country from Melbourne to work here. This fatherly concern added to his reluctance to put Nick in the field, though he accepted the cord would have to be cut soon.

'Stick him in the farthest cell. I'm bringing Gabriel

back in and I don't want them too close to each other.' He locked eyes with both Luka and Tanya. 'And don't do anything without getting backup from the other. As far as we're concerned *both* men are extremely dangerous.'

9

The town was quiet, even more than usual, as if the serial killer had swept through picking off the inhabitants while he was busy interviewing Heath. Chandler felt the heat crank up a little more, inching ever closer to boiling point.

The route to the hotel took him near his parents' place and he considered swinging past to deal with the Sarah issue. Maybe Nanna had tried to take her phone away. It was known to make her a little crazy. But he didn't stop; he had something more deadly to confront than a pre-teen girl's sulk.

At the hotel, Jim remained in position, as fixed as the minute hand on the town clock. It had clogged with dust a few years ago, a relic in this digital age. As Chandler parked, Jim unwound himself from the police car, dark and thin like a tree scorched by lightning.

'He's still in there,' said Jim, predicting his boss's question. 'What are we taking him in for anyway?'

'More questioning. Something doesn't add up,' said

Chandler as he started across the road. Reaching the hotel, he paused. 'In fact, Jim, it's probably the opposite. It's all too perfect. I need to find out why.'

They found Ollie at the front desk bent over a newspaper, the day's races highlighted in a mishmash of black circles and underlined names; Ollie's uncrackable code.

Ollie immediately furled his brow in surprise. 'What are you two doing back? You know I don't enjoy two visits in a day from you lot. One is sociable, two means trouble.'

'We need your guest.'

Ollie acted indignant. 'What do you mean *guest*? I've lots of *guests*.' He pushed the register towards Chandler as proof. Chandler waved it away.

'Just take me to his room, Ollie,' ordered Chandler.

Still muttering under his breath, Ollie led them to the Presidential Suite on the top floor.

Ushering him out of the way Chandler addressed Jim in a whisper. 'Plan is, we ask him to the station to answer a few more questions. If he resists, we cuff him and haul him in.'

Chandler knocked. He didn't state his name or business. No need to give Gabriel the chance to flee or arm himself. Assuming he was a crazed killer was the safest course of action.

Nothing. Chandler knocked again, louder this time in hope of rousing a possibly sleeping Gabriel to the door.

Again nothing.

Ollie approached, whispering at them, 'He ran the

bath earlier. Used up most a' my hot water. I'm having to hang the dirty sheets outside and let the sun bake any critters from 'em.'

'You got the master keys?' asked Chandler, impatient.

'Yeah, wait!' said Ollie in a loud whisper.

Chandler looked to him. 'Hurry up.'

Ollie fumbled the key into the lock, affording Gabriel plenty of advance notice to Chandler's annoyance. His size ten boot would have been more effective.

With the door unlocked Chandler eased Ollie to one side entering with his gun drawn. Jim followed.

The room was empty.

'Gabriel?' barked Chandler, striding through the bedroom into the bathroom. The wooden-panelled tub was full of water but there was no sign of Gabriel.

'Anything?' he shouted over his shoulder.

'Nothing,' replied Jim.

Gabriel had disappeared.

They searched. Rooms, cupboards, stairwells, the laundry and the lobby. Each drew a blank; no sign of their suspect or indeed any other guest. Their last stop, the kitchen, was empty apart from pots and pans and traces of rat droppings. Gabriel had disappeared into thin air.

As they ended the search a horrible thought entered Chandler's head. That in the short time between depositing Gabriel here and Heath's arrival at the station, Gabriel had somehow fallen victim to Heath. It was a tight timescale but could Heath have been waiting outside the station, before following them to the hotel and killing Gabriel? But then how did Ken manage to capture and hold Heath hostage? Could he have hiked all the way back out there in that time? Ken's place was a good fifteen kilometres out of town.

Reaching the reception desk Chandler questioned Ollie.

'You didn't hear anything strange?'

'Nothing apart from the bath.'

'And he couldn't have got past you?'

'I've been here the whole time. Not a chance he could have left without me seeing. What is it you want him for anyway?'

Ollie might have been unscrupulous but he wasn't stupid. The cops didn't put in this amount of effort without grounds for suspicion. Chandler downplayed it.

'He's a witness to an assault.'

'Really?' said Ollie, clearly sceptical.

He hadn't bought it but Chandler didn't care. He wanted to check Gabriel's room one more time.

The bed was untouched, nothing had been removed from the minibar, and the miniature bottles of shampoo and conditioner were unused. It gave Chandler the impression that Gabriel had left almost immediately. And if he hadn't gone out the front past Ollie and Jim, then ...

At the end of the corridor was the fire escape. Close inspection revealed that the safety tag was broken. It led to a set of metal stairs, the back alley, Anzac Street and freedom.

He sent Jim to stake out the town perimeter in case he

happened to come across their suspect fleeing town. It was a long shot, but long shots were all he had right now.

Back at the station, Chandler explained the situation to his assembled team.

'Do you think he's the killer?' asked Tanya without looking up from the mass of forms on her desk.

Chandler wanted to remain impartial but it was difficult. It didn't look good for Gabriel but Chandler recalled that he had wanted to get out of town and away from the threat to his life. It was the kind of fear that would make the idea of escape hard to resist.

'We'll have to bring him in and see,' said Chandler. 'Jim's out looking now. Me and Luka will go as well. Tanya and Nick, you'll stay here.'

''Cause I'm a woman?' scowled Tanya.

'No, because I trust you to look after the one suspect we have.'

'Don't you think it's time we called HQ?' she asked.

His team stared at him.

'The three of us can't cover the whole town,' added Luka.

Tanya nodded. 'He's right.'

Chandler knew they were right. He also knew what calling HQ would entail, and more specifically, who it would entail. Mitch.

They had once been best friends, growing up a rung above being dirt poor, joining the police force in the same class and under the same tragic circumstances. In 2001, near Newman, a plane crash had killed a number of police officers and opened up positions for new recruits. A tragic way to get an opportunity.

Chandler hadn't even considered applying at the start. Becoming a cop wasn't in his plan. He'd been drifting along in CJ's Grocery Store, stacking shelves and skiving out the back any chance he got. The only reason he applied at all was Mitch. And Mitch was only applying because of pressure from his family. His uncle had been amongst those who died. Chandler completed the application, partly in brotherhood with Mitch, and partly from curiosity over whether they would take him.

They were sworn in together in August 2001. He had stood shoulder to shoulder with Mitch, proud and astonished in equal measure, the shiny badges pinned to their uniformed chests.

After graduation they were placed in Wilbrook, together, firmly at the bottom of the ladder. Both of them would work their way up. Just not here. And not together.

Chandler sat in his office and stared at the phone, waiting for Nick to patch HQ through. He was dreading this; having to talk to Mitch again. He wondered whether his old friend had filled out from the pallid string bean with the unnaturally blue lips he'd known before. It was fully ten years since they had last seen each other, but through Mitch's cousin who lived in town Chandler knew that Mitch had moved up the ranks since leaving for Perth. Not that Chandler had cared. Not until the dispatch arrived announcing that a new inspector had taken over in Port Hedland, one Inspector Mitchell Andrews. That changed things. Mitch was now in effect his boss. So far, circumstance and the arid desert had kept them apart, but now their worlds would collide.

The phone rang.

'Inspector Mitchell Andrews, Port Hedland HQ, speaking.'

The voice was unruffled, comfortable in command. Behind it Chandler could almost hear the cogs in Mitch's brain whirring. The man he had known had an unerring ability to compartmentalize his thoughts, to foster rational judgement. Sometimes this led him to be too rational and remove any feeling. But maybe the edge had dulled in the ten years since. Maybe Chandler should wipe the slate clean, revert to simple boss and subordinate. His stomach twisted into a knot that couldn't be undone.

'Sergeant Jenkins, are you there?'

Chandler realized he hadn't spoken.

'Yes, Mitch, I'm here.'

There was a pause from the other end. The voice returned – backed with indignation and a touch of menace.

'It's Inspector Andrews, Sergeant. You will address me as such.'

That answered that. Rather than dulling Mitch's conceit, time had clearly exacerbated it.

'Is your whole team there?' asked Mitch.

'No, it's just us two ...' He couldn't bring himself to state Mitch's full title, his mind rejecting it, rebelling against such an egotistical request.

'Assemble them and put me on speakerphone. I want to address you all.'

Chandler waved his team inside, all except Nick who he kept on the front desk, unwilling to leave it unmanned. As a compromise he left the door open so that Nick could listen in. He tapped the button. 'You're on speakerphone.'

The commanding voice blasted over the speaker. 'This is Inspector Mitchell Andrews, Port Hedland HQ. I thought I would introduce myself as I know some of you have not met me before. As I'm sure your ... *sergeant* has informed you, we currently have one suspect in a possible multiple murder investigation being held in your cells and another on the run. So far the situation has not been handled as well as I would like but again that is no fault of yours.'

The implication went unstated but was all too obvious; Mitch was asserting that the situation going to shit was Chandler's fault.

Mitch continued, 'The situation calls for officers experienced in this type of matter, ones who are properly trained—'

'We need someone out here to help us organize the search, help to lead a sub-team,' interrupted Chandler, eager to put some emphasis on lack of support.

'That is all being taken care of, Sergeant Jenkins,' said Mitch calmly.

Chandler looked to Tanya, the only member of the team who had worked with Mitch before. Expecting an eye roll or a smirk, what he got was worse – a look of sympathy.

'I've identified someone with the suitable experience and who knows the area,' said Mitch.

'Who?' asked Chandler.

'Me.'

And that was that. Decision made. Chandler tried to take a deep breath but it stuck in his throat, lodged alongside the rotten memories of the last time he and Mitch had worked together.

10

2002

Martin's family joined the hunt. Chandler had been tasked with sticking close to Martin's father, Arthur, a man who looked constantly on the verge of a heart attack. He was in his late fifties and stocky, pressed to the ground as if sitting behind a desk all his working life had stunted his growth. His heavyset frame hung with the weight of expectation, drooping further every second spent out here, hope lost to the parched earth.

The campsite had seemed promising despite the blackened campfire stones being half-buried in dirt, any cinders long since blown away on the wind. Arthur insisted on searching it, despite Chandler's plea that they should move on and cover another kilometre before darkness fell. The old man fumbled around the site looking for clues to indicate his son had been here, trailing a stick through the dust, sweeping the ground in an attempt to uncover even the tiniest scrap of evidence. It was disheartening to watch him shuffling back and forth across the clearing, sweeping long-dead leaves and disturbed insects out of his path.

Chandler took solace in the shade as Mitch sidled up beside him. His friend's initial enthusiasm had waned and now, in a further notch to his increasingly grating personality, he had taken to ordering the volunteers around like personal slaves. No 'Thank you', just a warning to keep their eyes open. More scolding than encouraging.

Over the last few weeks Mitch's own appearance had altered, his cheeks were hollow with hunger, the pockmarks of his teenage acne had deepened.

Mitch whispered to him, 'I joined to do police work, not be a sniffer dog.'

'This is police work,' replied Chandler. 'We're trying to determine what might have happened to him. Do you not feel a sense of duty?'

Chandler had been as surprised by this sense of duty as most. It had been non-existent throughout his teenage years and he was still trying to come to terms with it. The Force and upcoming fatherhood had aged him. He was morphing into his dad, solid and dependable. Not a bad thing, but he was only twenty-two.

Mitch raised an eyebrow. He hadn't bought Chandler's attempt to motivate him. 'What I get Chandler is the sense that we're looking for someone who doesn't want to be found. If he wandered out this far he knew where he was going. And knew that he wasn't coming back.'

'What do you want, Mitch? Murders? Drugs? Prostitution? Try the big city.'

Mitch pulled a rotten branch from a tree, dry timber

exploding from the trunk. 'I'm thinking about it,' he said, crumbling the desiccated wood in his hand and letting the scraps fall to the ground.

'Are you serious?' asked Chandler, his attention removed from the old man scrabbling around in the dust.

Mitch nodded. 'I am.'

'You've only been in the force a year.'

'So?'

'So who's going to take you?'

Mitch licked his oddly blue lips. 'I've talked to a senior down in Perth. She's open to it.'

'Perth ...? Bloody Perth?'

'Yeah, bloody Perth. I'm not going to get anywhere doing this hide and seek shit.'

'Big plans,' said Chandler, not a little snarkily, 'big plans.'

'Just because you've got yourself stuck.'

'Nothing stuck about it.'

Mitch's grin was full of contempt and made Chandler want to punch him. 'You stuck it in Teri, now you're stuck here.'

Visions of his eight-months-pregnant girlfriend stirred Chandler's guts. He wanted more than anything to be with her rather than tramping through these woods. But he told Mitch what he had told her.

'Life goes on. It has to. There's no other choice.'

With that he left Mitch by the tree and returned to Arthur's side. The old man had uncovered some plastic wrapping and was trying to piece together what it had originally been.

What it was, was another false lead, the plastic too

old and degraded to have been recently discarded. They left the clearing, trekking on into the bush, guided by some indistinct rock cairns to a broad saddle between two rises, like a pass into the unknown.

As they reached the top the landscape opened out, the tops of the trees blanketing the ground, impenetrable but at least offering shelter from the unremitting sun. An overwhelming sense of isolation swept over Chandler, the view both wondrous and frightening. Not many people came this far, not even if they were crazy. He wondered why Martin would have come here. There were easier ways to kill yourself.

He reminded himself that it had only been a week. There was still a chance Martin was alive.

Taking his first steps down the other side of the Hill, Mitch's voice came into earshot, ordering the volunteers to spread out. Some of them didn't hide their irritation at the barked orders, but Chandler could see that Mitch didn't care a jot. He wondered again if Martin could survive out here for a week. He wondered if Arthur could. If Mitch could. If he could.

11

'Right, this is what you're going to do, Sergeant Jenkins.' The all-knowing, all-condescending voice came over the speaker again, impossible to ignore. 'First – make sure that the State Highway Police have a description of the man we want.'

'Gabriel,' interjected Chandler, feeling the need to add something of value. He wished that Mitch would dispense with the formalities. He was acting as if they had never met.

'Get them a good description, one that covers the fact that he might alter his appearance in some way.'

'Done,' said Chandler.

'Most importantly, lock down the roads. The main routes—'

'I don't have enough officers to do that,' said Chandler. The response was calm. 'Calls have been made to bring in the state police to help.'

'That'll take time, Mitch—' Chandler decided to play the game. 'Inspector Andrews ... and Gabriel may be long gone by now. Blocking the roads could be bolting the barn door—'

Mitch butted in, his stringent tone making it evident that he didn't appreciate his decisions being questioned. 'We have to try and put some sort of lid on things, Sergeant Jenkins. After your mess. Letting a prime suspect just walk out of the station ... no, worse than that, chauffeuring them *to* and putting them up *in* a hotel. At the taxpayers' expense. Extending an incredible compassion to criminals.'

Chandler imagined the smug pockmarked face on the other end of the phone and decided to remind Inspector Andrews of a salient fact. 'Gabriel might not be a criminal.'

'Let's catch him first and let the experts decide that, shall we?' There was a momentary pause. 'Plus, there's a third thing that you have to do – and that is keep this out of the papers. At least until we gather more evidence. We don't want the investigation hindered by the press.'

'Total blackout?'

'Total,' confirmed Mitch.

'What do I tell my townspeople?'

'Nothing, Sergeant Jenkins. Informing them only presents another opportunity for a leak. Five minutes and it'll be all over Twitter and Facebook. That's how things work these days. Instant access to instant news. You might not realize that down there. And reports that you let one of the main suspects go missing would not look good for you, Sergeant.'

This Chandler understood, but not warning his friends and family that a potential serial killer was wandering the streets wasn't particularly agreeable either.

'I think I should tell them.'

'I *insist* you don't, Sergeant Jenkins.'

'Chandler, Mitch – it's Chandler. You know that.'

There was a slight pause. 'If you put the word out, Sergeant Jenkins, it will only make matters worse. It may start a panic that could assist our suspect's escape. Plus, the consequences of disobeying a direct order are severe, as you know. Now I will be there very soon so—'

'You're more than four hundred and fifty kilometres away. You—'

'Three hours,' said Mitch in response. 'I'll be leaving promptly, so, Sergeant Jenkins, I would appreciate it if you made space at the station for myself and my team and have some form of refreshment ready.'

Inspector Andrews paused.

'And, Sergeant Jenkins ... try and not to make the situation any worse in the meantime.'

There was a click and then the dial tone rang out loudly, as if Mitch had dropped the mic after a final, unbeatable insult.

There was a momentary silence in the room – as if in remembrance of Chandler's dignity. Seeking to redress the balance somewhat, he spoke to his troops. The message wasn't positive but it was honest.

'Things are about to get nasty.'

There were nods from the group huddled around the table but it was Nick who was the first to speak up.

'I dunno what went on between the two of you, Sarge, but that bloke's an arsehole.'

Tanya chimed in. 'An arrogant arsehole.'

It was Chandler's turn to nod. 'I'd keep those opinions to yourself for now. Let's get to work.'

Despite the crushing feeling of being disrespected in front of his employees, Chandler set about following Mitch's instructions.

'Tanya, take 142 and the highway until State get in position. Luka, you're on Daly's, in case he heads south rather than north. I'll send Jim to Stockman's and we'll have to hope that's enough. And be careful out there. We don't know what he's capable of.'

Nick spoke up. 'Maybe he's using the same means to get out as he did in.'

'Unlikely,' said Chandler, but pleased that his young constable wasn't afraid to get involved. 'He came in by bicycle, according to his statement. But check for any reports of a car, bike, tractor, any vehicle, having been stolen today.'

Luka and Tanya exited just as Nick confirmed there were no reports of a vehicle having been stolen. Chandler had suspected as much. In a town this small anything as severe as grand theft auto, even grand theft bicycle, would have been pounced on immediately. It served as a reminder of just how serious things had become. From being relatively starved of action, they now had a potential killer in custody and another on the run. As life tended to do to Chandler, it never rained but poured, plague then flood, a wife, then none, no kids, then two to care for on his own.

But this flood threatened to overwhelm them all before they had a chance to draw breath.

*

Fifteen minutes later and he had confirmation that Luka, Tanya and Jim were in position and that all was quiet. He knew that it would be stupid of Gabriel to exit via the main roads – if he hadn't gone already – but it was the least they could do. The least expected of him by Mitch.

Nick was slumped behind the front desk, a picture of frustration.

'I'll get you out there soon,' said Chandler, hoping it was on something a little more routine than this.

'When? How often does *this* happen?'

Chandler sought to comfort him. 'Put it this way, Nick. I never expected this kind of thing to happen here and it did. So if it can happen here, it can happen anywhere and the best way you can help right now is by staying behind that desk at the centre of things. You might not think that you're seeing action but we can't leave the phone unmanned and the place unguarded, especially with one suspect in custody and another out there who might have tried to kill him. If he tried once there's nothing to say he won't try again. You might not be on the front line out there, but you are in here. Now get a description of Gabriel to the state police.'

Nick nodded, sitting up in his chair.

Chandler didn't like or approve of the next instruction but gave it anyway. 'And remind them to say nothing to the press. This is hush-hush, no Facebook, no Twitter, no Snapchat.' Chandler listed them off like he knew what he was talking about even if it was only what he had picked up from his daughter. He was stuck, with nothing to do but wait for news to filter through or backup to arrive.

His conscience squirmed at withholding this secret from everyone in town but he had to grudgingly admit that Mitch might have been right. They didn't need a general panic right now.

With no idea when he would get to see Sarah and Jasper again he called his parents. As ever, Jasper was first to the phone.

'Hello?' he chirped, full of enthusiasm. Chandler's youngest possessed an inquisitive nature or internal voice that insisted he poke his fingers into things he shouldn't or take things apart and leave them in a scattered mess for others to rebuild.

'It's me, Jasper.'

'Daddy!'

The boy practically screamed into the receiver.

'Yes, it's Daddy. What are you up to? Is everyone in the house?'

I'm just checking, he assured himself; he wasn't providing any forewarning, just confirming where they were.

'Umm, yes, Grandpa and Nanna are watching TV and Sarah's in her room.'

'Very good. Why don't you ask Grandpa to put a video on for you?'

That would keep them both inside and out of trouble.

'But you said that it's not good to be in the house all day.'

'I know but sometimes it is okay. Now go get Sarah for Daddy.'

The receiver clacked. His son had dropped it and left it to hang. He glanced at the front desk. Nick was talking to dispatch, putting out Gabriel's description.

'Yeah?' The voice was irritable, the complete antithesis to her brother. Sarah wanted nothing more than to get back to her iPhone. He had tried to wean her off the addiction but given the amount of time he spent at work it had proven impossible, engrossed as she was with everything from *Angry Birds* to *Candy Crush*, to well, any game where animals were shot in and around obstacles. He'd tried one of them once. He didn't get the appeal.

'It's nice to hear your voice too,' said Chandler.

'Yeah, Dad, I've got things to do.'

'How was rehearsal for First Confession today?'

It was the only thing other than her phone that she was excited about. The chance to show off in front of her friends.

'Yeah. There's a final rehearsal to go but we won't be wearing our dresses. They don't use the right words either but I've been talking to Nic and Amy and they—'

'Have you asked your brother to help?'

'Jasper? No! Why would I want him to help? He doesn't know ... he's a ... he'd just mess things up.' She sounded horrified at the thought.

'Ask him for me. I know he'd want to help.'

'But what help could he—?'

'Anything,' interrupted Chandler. 'Just so he doesn't feel left out.'

There was a pause, a huffed breath, the indignity seeping from the receiver. 'Okay, something,' she said, then added, 'Dad?'

'Yes, honey.'

'When are you coming home?'

'I'm not sure. Maybe not tonight.'

'Why not?'

'Something's come up.'

'Oh. Okay.'

And that was that. The disappointment at her father not coming home easily overcome. He was disgusted that she was so used to his absence she didn't even question it. No wonder Teri had brought a custody case against him. He wouldn't admit it to her but she was right, he did spend too much time at work. But what Teri failed to grasp was that he was in charge of a small force with a large area to cover. A valid excuse. Plus the fact that they were a man down after Bill's retirement last year. Another excuse that may not fly when it got to court. But that was a battle for another day. A quieter day.

'Daddy?' It was Jasper. How long had his mind drifted? Chandler scolded himself that he couldn't even manage to give them his full attention during a five-minute phone call.

'Yeah, I'm still here, Jasper.'

In his head he pictured his son at the other end of the receiver. Nine years old and only just brushing four and a half foot, his hair a briar untamed by brush or gel. Only a liberal dose of water anchored it down sufficiently enough to plaster it into shape.

'I seen the go-kart in the garage today. Can we take it out when you come back?'

The go-kart had been last summer's project. It already seemed like years ago. Since summer's end it had been sitting in the back of the garage waiting to grab the boy's attention again.

Chandler thought about getting him to ask Grandpa, but let it slide. *Keep them inside*, he reminded himself. He need not have worried. Jasper had already squelched that option.

'Grandpa's no good. He's too old. He can't push me around. He gets tired too easy.'

Chandler smiled at how angry Grandpa would be if he heard that. 'Yes, don't you go making him run around after you. I already warned you about that.'

'Yes, Daddy.'

Chandler glanced at the front desk. Nick remained on the phone. 'Now get Nanna or Grandpa for me, will you please?'

'Okay. Bye, Daddy.'

'Bye, Jasper.'

There was an immediate rustle of the receiver. His mum's voice seared across the wires, already on the warpath.

'So you're not coming back?'

'How much did you hear?'

'Enough.' The biting squeak of exasperation. 'What is it? What's happened?'

As ever, his mum was sharp as a tack. She understood that her son not coming home when he had promised meant something significant had happened and she wanted to know what. There was an insistence in the tone as if she felt she deserved to know and wouldn't stop until she had weaselled the information from him.

'Just something,' said Chandler. 'All I can tell you is to stay indoors.'

There was a slight pause. 'That sounds serious.'

'It might be.'

'You expecting a great storm?' she said, cryptically as if she thought the lines were bugged.

'Don't worry about me.'

'The day a mother doesn't worry is the day they put her in the ground.'

'Mum,' said Chandler, frustrated. 'Don't talk like that.'

'It's just a saying.' Her voice turned quiet. 'Just don't go putting yourself in danger.'

'That's what they pay me to do.'

'Not enough.'

On that Chandler could agree.

His mum continued, 'Okay, you go on. Your dad says hi.'

She hung up. It was her standard end to phone calls. Chandler knew that his dad hadn't said hi at all. In fact he probably wasn't even aware of the conversation, engrossed by something else entirely, the TV, the paper, or whatever it might be. When his dad got it into his head to do something, his attention was as hard to capture as his nine-year-old grandson.

Even though the phone had gone silent, Chandler could still hear his mum's words. *Don't go putting yourself in danger.* He might not have a choice. Currently there existed two options: that he had either a very scared and flighty witness on the loose somewhere around town – or a cunning and resourceful mass murderer.

12

Chandler itched to be out on the streets. But only once everything was in place could he consider adding his boots to the operation. So right now, he was in the same purgatory he had forced Nick into, having to accept his station behind a desk.

State confirmed they could have troopers in place within the hour. Nick's trawl through social media had confirmed that all was quiet in town aside from a couple of rumblings about the cops being more visible than normal. Nothing extraordinary. Things were being kept under control. *Swept under the rug*, his conscience reminded him. He had been able to indirectly warn his own family to stay inside but the rest of the town remained vulnerable.

As he awaited the inevitable slew of calls and requests he decided to test Nick.

'What do you think might have happened after Gabriel escaped the hotel?'

Nick tore the headset off, as if he had been itching for Chandler to ask.

'Right – so here's what we know, or can assume given that he left via the fire escape. From there he makes it down to the street, a stranger in a strange town, so to speak. If I was him, I'd head towards somewhere I know. Or something I know. That means whatever he used to get into town.'

'A bicycle,' recalled Chandler.

'Exactly. But cycling out of town is conspicuous. And we know no cars, or large vehicles, have been reported stolen. This leaves something smaller, a quad bike perhaps? Something like that might not be noticed by the owner for a while. Especially if it was stowed in a barn.'

'Okay, let's suppose that,' said Chandler, coat-tailing his young constable's assumptions. 'Then where? All the way out of town on a quad? And further? Pretty dangerous once it gets dark with the 'roos licking dew off the white lines.'

'Back roads?'

'Possibly. Hard for us to cover.'

'Or he stayed in town,' offered Nick.

'Possible,' said Chandler, 'but there aren't too many places for a stranger to hide here. *And* he said he was in fear of his life. Scared people don't stay still.'

'Assuming he's innocent, of course,' said Nick. 'If *I* was a killer on the run, I'd look for someone to get me out of town.'

Chandler nodded, as impressed with Nick's deduction as he was with the zeal with which it was delivered. He added to it. 'Maybe he acts like a lost tourist. He's picked up people blagging lifts or has blagged lifts himself so knows what to say, what to do. He uses his charm to get into the car and forces them to drive him out of town.'

'It's how I'd do it,' said Nick.

'That's good thinking, Nick,' said Chandler. 'Get on to Tanya, Luka and Jim and tell them to be on the lookout for locals heading out of town, in case it's under duress. Get them to check the vehicles but warn them to be subtle about it – don't escalate things.'

'I could be your resident expert on this,' said Nick, quickly undoing some of his good work. 'I have an insight into how a serial killer's mind works.'

Chandler was about to remind him that police work had little to do with TV but was interrupted. Heath was calling for attention.

Leaving Nick on the phone to Jim, Chandler entered the holding area.

'Who's that?' barked Heath from inside the cell.

'Sergeant Jenkins,' said Chandler and shook his head in disgust. The disease of using formal titles was catching.

'You can't keep me in here, Sergeant! I don't wanna be trapped while Gabriel's loose out there.'

'For all we know he's escaping from you,' Chandler reminded him.

'You know fuck all.' Heath paused. 'We can't *both* be suspects for the same thing.'

'At the minute anything's possible, Mr Barwell. And if he is out there and after you, then the safest place you can be is in here.'

Heath laughed, a shrill screech that Chandler noted

was a little unhinged. 'Safe? After you believed his bullshit story and let him go.'

'A story identical to yours.'

'They can't be exactly the same.'

Chandler yanked the metal flap in the cell door down to view his prisoner. Heath was pressed up close to the door, the cross around his neck strangling greasy, sweat-stained flesh.

'The guts of it, yes.'

'Like what?'

Chandler smiled. 'I can't disclose that.'

'So you're just gonna lock me in here and wait to see what happens? See whether he'll break in and finish what he started?'

'There's due process to go—'

'Due process, my arse. You just want to see if you can find him again. And if you can't find him, you'll pin this shit on me. I know how this goes down. What the fuck happened to innocent 'til proved guilty?'

'Some would say you muddied that line in attempting to steal a car. We have enough to charge you for with that.'

'Yeah? And why would I steal a car if I wasn't scared for my life? I'm no criminal.' Heath paused, his fingers playing with the cross around his neck, twirling it over and around. 'Okay, one little assault,' he continued, 'but I was drunk and they were drunk. They were mouthing off about a pal of mine.'

As Heath talked, Chandler studied his behaviour. He was finding Heath hard to read. He sweated like a guilty man but in that cake tin of a cell he would have to be inhuman not to sweat, as there was little or no breeze blowing through the tiny, square window. Heath was alone in there surrounded by walls steeped in the oily sins of those who'd come before. As his rant continued, Heath started to puff, his swollen cheeks filling with air. Given his aggressive manner and quick temper it was easy to mark him as a possible killer.

'So I hit him,' continued Heath. 'It was no big deal. He didn't want to press charges, I didn't want to press charges; but the manager called the cops anyway.' Heath stopped. He stared at Chandler, seeming to spot something he didn't like. Maybe a look that told him he was getting nowhere.

'You're making a *big* mistake,' said Heath, his tone suddenly threatening. 'Once I get out of here ...' Chandler waited for the explosion and rage-driven confession. If he could get it wrapped up before Mitch got here he'd avoid his own firing squad.

'I'll get my lawyer or any fucking lawyer on to you. Politicians too. They warned me the West was full of weirdoes, people who'd knife you for no other reason than for something to do, but to find myself in a town full of them ...'

Heath was now seething; flecks of spittle dabbled around his dry lips. The anger soon turned to desperation, slapping his palm off the greasy wall. 'Can I get something to drink in here? Or get the air con turned on? I've got rights.'

'Including the right to remain silent,' noted Chandler

as he left, experiencing a sense of disappointment. He'd hoped for something from the outburst, some indication that he had the right man behind bars. He'd got nothing but an unhinged rant.

Shutting himself in his office, Chandler went through the recording he'd made that morning, absorbing the voices oozing from the speakers.

Gabriel's voice was almost a distant memory by now, spawning a deep gnawing in Chandler's gut that he had let him walk, even though he couldn't have known then that it was the wrong decision. He listened to the entire interview, trying to visualize Gabriel's statement and mannerisms, identify where they differed to Heath's, places Gabriel seemed weak or unclear, something to swing the needle to or from him.

As he listened to Gabriel explain how he was following the casual tip to look for work inland, Chandler's instinct was to believe the silky voice oozing from the tape. Maybe it was the even-tempered tone, lulling him into agreement or merely because Gabriel's story had been told to him first, but subconsciously it made it seem truer, the cover song heard first and in his head becoming the original.

The recording continued. Gabriel's disappointment that Heath hadn't driven away. Genuine disappointment. The description of the car – identical to Heath's in colour and worthlessness. Then the phrase, 'No killer introduces themselves.'

Chandler stopped the recording.

No killer introduces themselves.

Delivered as if he understood what a killer would do, how a killer would act.

He pressed Play. Gabriel's voice continued, explaining that they had travelled inland, Heath convincing him he knew of better places to find work, fairer wages. Drinking the water, the funny taste and vivid description of how it paralysed him. The shed and being shackled to the wall. The cuffs and the workbench. A clear description of the room and the contents.

The threat of becoming number fifty-five. Trying to break free. The vivid red marks on his wrists and hands – on both their wrists and hands – from when he hacked his way free. Describing Heath at the cluttered desk, the plans and papers, the cross on the wall. A detailed account. The escape and the gravesite. Falling over the edge. Waking up to see Heath beside him. Fleeing without checking if his captor were still alive before arriving into town on a bicycle.

It was a strange choice. Not the immediate mode of transport that Chandler would choose if lying, but also one that was hard to track down. Plus, it was a decent ride from the Hill to town. Anyone who was being pursued by a killer surely could have found something better.

Like trying to steal a car.

Gabriel's statement ended there but Chandler dwelled on what Gabriel had said after, about having nowhere to go, a man alone in the world, a man without ties.

Leaning back in the chair he let the details sink in. What made sense and what didn't and what raised his suspicions. Top of that list was the comment: *no killer introduces themselves*. An extraordinary statement, a cold truth. There was also the depth of description regarding the shed and cabin, including the cross on the wall. Too well imagined. Perhaps more than would be seen in a panicked glance – perhaps a place seen more than once. But then again fear might have heightened Gabriel's senses, storing the details in his effort to get away.

With Gabriel's statement fresh in his memory, Chandler turned to Heath's interview. First thing that stood out was the lack of detail about where he was going, as if he hadn't had time to prepare the information in advance. Nothing else stood out between their stories until he got to being drugged. Heath's recollection was certainly hazier, the haziness continuing throughout his explanation of how he escaped, a little less descriptive, the details blocked by fear, a tremor in his voice as he recalled it, on edge even then, as if for that moment he was back in the shed, chained to the wall and trying to hack his way free. The haziness was apt if he had indeed been drugged but Chandler wondered if it were a ruse, masking details on purpose, trying too hard to appear innocent.

There was again a paucity of detail over Heath's escape, a brief mention of Gabriel at the desk before the graves, the encounter in the woods and fall. Waking next to Gabriel and running. What followed was a section that concerned Chandler, the rage displayed when accused of stealing the car, the rage and lack of remorse, insisting that it had to be done. The temper it exposed and the temper he still exhibited in the cell, the way he twisted the chain around his neck, reminding Chandler of what had been described as hanging in the cabin.

There were frayed edges with each story. Chandler needed to unpick them to find the truth.

13

2002

In a world capable of pinpointing everything from the tiniest atoms to sun-swallowing supernovae, Martin's whereabouts remained unknown. Thermal body scans had proved ineffective, as had the transmitters. The eyes in the sky had uncovered nothing but barren land, and the simple trace of his phone had yielded zilch, the battery long dead. All that was left were human eyes, ears and feet, and the gruelling terrain had taken a toll on all of these.

It was the first break of the morning and Chandler had reminded the group to sweep the rest area thoroughly; not for clues but to scatter any creature eager for a fresh meal. This morning Chandler found himself sitting with a couple of police officers from Mount Magnet, drafted in due to their experience of searching for missing hikers. He had noted already how they didn't chat as they walked, saving their energy, covering ground quickly and thoroughly, clearing an area in seconds before moving on.

Talk got around to how likely Martin's survival was after a week out here. Agreement was that it depended on how well equipped he was and how sound of mind.

'Fractious, from what we know,' offered Mitch, 'a mix of emotion, shock and anger.'

Jared, the Mount Magnet cop with a booming voice, interrupted. 'If he wanted to go away for good, he could, easily. Give a reasonably fit person a head start of forty-eight hours out here and the chances of you finding them are slim. It won't be the hunger or thirst that gets him, it'll be the panic. Realizing that you're in the shit but unable to do anything to solve it. He'll get desperate, make a mistake, and then bang he'll fall, break a leg and die at the bottom of some ditch.'

There was silence. Chandler was glad none of the family were there to overhear.

Mitch cut in. 'How often do you find 'em?'

'Maybe ten per cent of the time,' said Jared, causing the volunteers to mutter amongst themselves. 'Well ...' he corrected, 'actually probably four or five per cent.'

More groans erupted, the volunteers questioning why they were out here chasing a lost cause. Chandler fell foul of the defeatism too, his mind drifting back to Teri and their unborn child, and how unprepared they were for what was coming.

He had only met her this New Year at a party in town. And not as a guest. Being the ideal combination of young, a rookie and single, Chandler and Mitch had drawn the short straw for duty that night, allowing the rest of the force to get home to their families to celebrate.

Teri was in from the coast to visit her family, using the trip as an excuse to get into mischief.

Chandler and Mitch had been called out by a neighbour concerned about underage drinking at the party next door. It was a detail neither cared much for; they were going to get shit thrown at them either way, for interrupting the party in full swing, or for throwing people out.

They entered the house to the usual barks of disapproval, insults and people desperately fleeing the uniform. Not Teri though. She confronted both of them, already obviously worse for wear, blue dress slipping off her shoulders, exposing the straps of her red bikini. Easily towering over her, Chandler requested the owner of the house to make themselves known. Teri told them both to leave as they were fucking up the vibe, but it was only when she shoved him in the chest that Chandler really paid attention to her and her piercing brown eyes. They were wide and as dangerous as a bushfire. Seeing she was a little drunk he prepared to negotiate with her, but Mitch wasn't so lenient. It had only been two months, but already his partner wore the uniform like a second skin, basking in the authority and flashing his badge with a fervour that bordered on fanatic, keen to wield the power he never had as a reedy teenager.

With Mitch and Teri threatening to kick off the new year with some form of aggravated assault, Chandler was forced to wedge himself between them. Even as he ushered Mitch out the door, reminding him to stay professional – a request that only made Mitch angrier – he could feel Teri's tiny frame jostle him insistently in the back.

Leaving Mitch pacing around the cruiser like an angry bull, Chandler went back in to deal with the original complaint. Eventually, he persuaded the owner of the house and Teri that it was only going to be a talking-to and the sooner she agreed to it, the sooner she could get back to celebrating. He warned her about underage drinking and keeping herself protected – to which Teri replied that if anyone tried anything they would get a shot glass to the face. Shocked by her brutal honesty, he warned her against that response. She retorted by asking if she should mail them a letter asking them politely to piss off instead. Instantly he could see that there was no correct answer with her and possibly never would be. She was a force of nature and by the end of their talk she had somehow got him to agree to come back after his shift finished in an hour.

Chandler left it at that, warning the owner of the house to drag all the revellers in from the garden to keep the noise contained. And also to keep an eye on his younger visitors, warning him that he would be back to check.

In the end his shift ran a few hours late, Mitch still fuming about the girl at the party who showed such disrespect towards him and the badge. Chandler nodded and told his colleague to get a good night's sleep. Driving home, he detoured past the party house. The front garden was empty aside from the chirp of crickets … until the front door opened and a man stripped down to *his boxers tumbled out the door, the thud of the music seemingly forcing him out.*

Chandler went inside, still in uniform. Once again people parted for him.

'Where's your dog of a partner?'

Chandler turned. There she was. Teri. Still fully alert even after all the partying, her elfin frame somehow able to process all the alcohol.

'He's at home,' said Chandler.

Teri seemed impressed, maybe even relieved that Chandler had ditched him. 'He was a drag.'

'He's just serious.'

'A serious pain in the arse.'

Chandler didn't disagree. Already he knew better than to disagree with her.

'So, are you on duty?' she asked.

'No, strictly off now.'

'Good,' said Teri, shoving a beer into his hand. 'Take off the badge though.'

The rest of the night passed around them, drinking and chatting until four or five in the morning, Chandler quickly feeling the effects of the uncounted bottles.

After that night and for the first few months he drove up to Port Hedland to meet her when he wasn't on shift. By February she had turned eighteen. By April she was pregnant, and by June he didn't have to drive all the way up to the coast any longer. She had moved down to Wilbrook to live with him and his parents. June and July passed by in the excitement of a new place to live and a new life, but by September the leaves were falling off the roses, her arguments with his overbearing parents wilting what remained of the flowers.

Now at the start of December the frostiness encompassed everything. She was eight months pregnant, irritable and in the middle of a scorching summer out here in the arse-end-of-nowhere, as she had come to call it. He wanted to get back and support her. But he had a job to do. Out here in the wilderness. Looking for a boy who had got himself lost.

14

'State want to talk to you,' Nick shouted from the front desk.

The constable patched them through.

'Chandler?'

'Steve.'

No formalities here. Steve Yaxley was an old-school captain based out of Newman, hard-working but approachable, willing to help out where he could. His voice thundered across the electronics between them.

'I heard about the situation you have there. Our boys are in place, on the highway and on Ninety-five. No way in or out.'

Mitch had worked quickly, pulling strings to put everything in place without fuss and without Chandler's help. Flexing his muscles.

'Thanks, Steve.'

'Had Inspector Andrews on the phone too,' said Steve. 'Just to warn you, he's headed your way. Dunno what's worse. Him or a runaway murderer.'

'At least Mitch has to play by some rules.'

'I guess . . .' said Steve.

'Anything else you need from me?'

'Nothing more you can do. The main routes in and out of town are blocked. If you have any spare officers you might want to put them on the dirt roads we can't cover. You'll know those better than we do.'

'Thanks, Steve,' said Chandler, feeling somewhat bypassed, like he was part of the problem rather than the solution.

Hanging up, he checked in with his three. All had nothing suspicious to report, a few locals asking questions, but none carrying a passenger matching Gabriel's description. After that it was back to waiting, the rising heat only exacerbating the fear that something was going to happen, and the frustration that he couldn't do anything about it. It was all about time now. And they didn't know how much of it they had until Gabriel reappeared or another body showed up.

'Sarge?'

Chandler looked at Nick who seemed too restless to do paperwork.

'Yep?'

'You ever had a serial killer in the cells before?'

'Nick . . .' Chandler began, but there was no point trying to stop his officer's ardent imagination. For the next ten minutes Chandler listened to the fruits of Nick's informal studies, listing the infamous – Chandler had stopped him when he proclaimed them *the great* – Australian serial killers including Worrell and Miller, who strangled seven women around Adelaide in the seventies, Peter Dupas, who killed at least three in Victoria, before moving on to the top dog Ivan Milat. Even Chandler had heard of him, a man hard to forget, the psycho who had murdered seven backpackers around Belanglo State Forest in the late eighties and early nineties.

'You know, Sarge,' said Nick, breaking off from his gruesome biography, 'maybe this guy's a copycat, picking up young travellers, finishing them off, before dumping them on the Hill.'

This gave Chandler further concern. Maybe he did have the new Ivan Milat in the cells. Or wandering the town.

Nick carried on. 'There was also John Wayne Glover in the late eighties. He killed six elderly women 'cause he hated his mother-in-law. He eventually hung himself in prison—'

This statement induced a moment of dread. They had taken all the necessary precautions in removing belts and laces from their prisoner but the necklace cutting into Heath's skin ...

Chandler charged to the door leading to the cells, hoping to hear some movement, an echo, a snore, anything. He got more than that.

'I overheard you in there,' said Heath, his voice desperate, his breathing choked.

Opening the slit, Chandler peered in. Heath wasn't swinging from the window bars as he had feared, but was bright red, still playing with the cross, twisting it into his flesh as if trying to force God to help him.

His prisoner approached the gap, leaning down and twisting his head as if to try and squeeze through. 'I'm not a killer.'

Chandler took a step back, keeping his distance.

'I'm no monster either,' he said, pleading. 'Do I look like one?'

Nick's voice rebounded off the bare walls. 'Ted Bundy looked normal, he even volunteered on helplines; Robert Lee Yates too, and he killed thirteen prostitutes. Dean Corll was vice-president of a candy factory and murdered at least—'

Chandler interrupted his colleague. 'Nick, we get the point. You're upsetting our guest.'

In a flash of unexpected speed Heath slapped his hand off the solid steel door, letting out a howl of pain. 'Of course I'm upset,' he spluttered. 'I haven't done anything but I'm locked up like I'm Hannibal Lecter.'

'You have to be patient, Mr Barwell. If you're as innocent as you say, I'll find out.'

'I am,' whimpered Heath, looking at a hand that was now as red as his face.

'Plus, I'll need that necklace,' said Chandler.

'Why?'

'To prevent any accidents,' said Chandler.

Heath paused, cursed, then removed the thin, gold necklace and passed it through the slot before retreating to the bench and sitting down.

As he watched his suspect slump to the bench, something gnawed at Chandler. Though he had no proof, something warned him that he had the wrong guy locked up and that he was nothing more than a pawn in a game being played between Heath, Gabriel and now Mitch. The sense of helplessness didn't feel good at all.

15

In the end, Wilbrook didn't have to wait long for Inspector Mitchell Andrews' homecoming. Two hours, twenty-two minutes to be precise. With the roads all but clear, and with authority to speed at will, he had raced down the black tarmac that criss-crossed the barren landscape.

Chandler watched from outside his office as Mitch strode into the station followed closely by his entourage. Knowing Mitch, he had probably insisted on the rest holding back to allow him to enter first, king of kings. He was bedecked in a grey suit that wouldn't have looked out of place on a 1930's G-Man: wide, padded shoulders, tapered sleeves and peaked lapels, his trousers creased and tucked neatly at the leg as if he had stepped out of a freezer rather than the blazing heat. The rest of his crew were dressed in matching black suits and looked like a sinister funeral cortège, slyly glancing around as if they were yet to pick out the soon-to-be deceased. Chandler had a feeling it might be him.

Indeed there was a thin smile on Mitch's otherwise

placid face as he loped towards Chandler, completely ignoring Nick's welcome. *No need to fraternize with underlings,* thought Chandler.

A little to his surprise Mitch extended his hand. Chandler took it. The shake was cold and somewhat perfunctory, but more than he had expected. In his colleague's focused expression Chandler saw a connection, a fragile link to the past, good and bad strands wound tightly together. And tightly wound was how he felt. He wondered if Mitch felt the same.

Despite wearing a suit that aimed to broaden his physique, it looked like Mitch hadn't put on an ounce of weight in the intervening years. He still towered over Chandler, his chin jutting forth, his lips the same cardiac blue. One thing the advancing years and the zigzag of lines around his eyes had given him was a rather statesmanlike appearance. Possibly that was the aim of the suit, a furthering of the aura that he'd created around himself, lending authority to his position, but to Chandler he still looked and dressed like a politician moonlighting as a policeman; plastic, as if pulled from a mould and given moving body parts. The GI Joe of policemen. It was all a far cry from nicking sweets from Penny Hall's shop by the bandstand in town when they were kids.

'It's been a few years hasn't it, Sergeant Jenkins?' said Mitch, still soaking up the dreary view of a station that looked as if it had been carved from a single piece of concrete.

'It has,' responded Chandler, knocked off guard by the niceties.

'The town still seems stuck in time,' said Mitch. 'As are the people,' he continued, nodding towards his motionless entourage but aiming the jibe fair and square at Chandler. A preview of what was to come.

'We have business to do,' said Chandler, hoping to get straight back on the front foot.

'Yes, cleaning up your mess, Sergeant.'

'We don't know *what* it is as yet ... Inspector.'

'If you have to drag us all the way in from the coast to deal with it – it's a mess.' Mitch looked around again. 'And where's the coffee?'

'We didn't drag you; you came. I'll get someone right on the coffee,' said Chandler, with more than a hint of sarcasm.

'You do that, Sergeant, and while we're on it, we didn't have enough parking space.'

'I didn't know you were bringing the whole division,' said Chandler, pointing to the black suits slowly fanning out around the office like cancerous cells. 'Plus, if you're all parked out there, you might start some rumours – spark off some of the social media activity you're so terrified of.'

'Don't worry, Sergeant. The cars are all unmarked. And most are parked on the next street across,' said Mitch removing his hat and placing it firmly in the middle of the table, as if marking his territory. 'Besides, by now the first people going past the roadblock on the highway will probably have tweeted about it, so if our suspect has access to the Internet, he'll know what's out there. And who's hunting him.'

'That might not be a bad thing,' said Chandler. 'It might increase the chances of surrender.'

'Or force him into hiding,' countered Mitch. 'Assuming he hasn't escaped already.'

'Well, neither suspect possessed a mobile when they came in. Both claim that it was taken off them during the incident so there's a chance Gabriel might not know.'

'Might not is *not* good enough for me, Sergeant. *We* need answers. *We* need to locate and apprehend him.'

'What do you think we've been trying to do?' said Chandler, standing across the desk, not prepared to back down. 'Most of my officers are out there looking.'

'All three of them,' said Mitch with a smile.

'Yeah, three good officers.'

'Tanya, Jim and ...?' said Mitch, head cocked to the side, the smile persisting.

'Luka. Plus our new constable Nick over there,' said Chandler, looking to the front desk. Nick waved across.

Mitch didn't wave back, instead setting his crew into motion. 'Roper, Darren, Flo, you take that desk,' said Mitch, pointing to Luka's cluttered workspace. 'Yohan, Suze, Erin, you take that one,' he added, pointing at Jim's empty desk. 'The rest of you, find any place you can.'

Chandler watched as the Port Hedland team set up base, stuffing Luka's unfinished paperwork into a pile in the corner before whisking out shiny black laptops, jamming the ports full of electronic swabs and implements, the processors whirring as they started up, lights flashing like a control tower at an airport.

'Do you want to set yourself up in the interview

room?' asked Chandler. The more doors between him and Mitch the better.

'Oh no, that's not necessary, Sergeant. We might need it. I'm going to commandeer your office.'

'Right, I'll clear some space.'

'Clear *all* the space. We really don't need anything you have other than the testimonies.'

'You can't come in here and—'

'And what?' said Mitch moving closer, the volume lowered but the invective increased. 'I can do what I want ... *Chandler*,' he continued, dropping the formality but making sure none of the others heard.

Chandler felt like a dog being scolded by its master. He tried to retaliate. 'And where do you expect me to go ... *Mitch*?'

Mitch stepped back, undeterred. 'Let's not allow petty disputes to get in the way of this investigation, Sergeant. We're all here to work together.'

'Okay. What do you want me to do then?' asked Chandler, testing that theory. If the man had a plan – and knowing Mitch he had already developed one – then he should be able to rhyme off what Chandler and his team were designated to do.

'Let's get set up first,' said Mitch with a grin, before shouting across the room. 'Suze, get on to the sergeant's computer and rip me those two interviews.'

Suze, late-twenties in age but dressed like a forty-year-old banker, left her newly allocated desk and flew past them both into Chandler's – soon to be Mitch's – office. The black suit draped off her thin shoulders, the lapels of the white blouse flapping with each step. What was apparent was that in the years since they'd met, Mitch had grown adept at ordering his minions around. Whether he'd grown any better at listening to the advice of others was yet to be ascertained.

In a flash the small-town station became Mitch's headquarters, his staff darting around like spinning tops, setting up printers, taping numbers to phones, labelling equipment like an angry divorcee tagging items allocated in the settlement. There was a fury in how they worked and Chandler had to admit, a presence and authority in the way Mitch led them that he was impressed with, exhibiting an arrogance that Chandler wasn't capable of. Chandler supposed that to climb the ladder you had to be able to step on a few fingers.

'Meeting in my office,' announced Mitch. Chandler held his tongue and crowded into the office with everyone else, a dozen extra bodies raising the temperature in the small room a notch further.

Mitch addressed them, the ancient projector casting an overhead map of the town on to the wall.

'Okay, I assume we're all fully briefed regarding the situation, but to summarize, we have a suspect at large, possibly holed up in town, possibly on his way out of town. So far we've been trying to contain him, but now we need to be more proactive.'

Brandishing a laser pointer he aimed it at the screen. 'Roper and Flo, you take Watkins to Fenley; Darren and Neil, Pomarroo to the Creek. Erin, you and Mick take North down to Eagle's Brook; and MacKenzie and Sun, you have this area,' said Mitch, pointing to George Street and Dieskirt, where Chandler's house was situated.

'What about my team?' said Chandler.

Mitch didn't turn from the map. 'They can remain where they are and check the traffic as they have been doing.'

'And me?'

'You're in command, Sergeant,' said Mitch. 'With me.' With this he raised the laser pointer, guiding the dot back to the map. 'We have until dark to locate the suspect. If we cannot we will be forced to try something else. Everyone understand?'

His orders issued, he faced his audience to accept the obedient nods before his team swiftly exited one by one like unthinking robots. Chandler hoped that all emotion hadn't been whipped out of them like it had been in their boss.

Chandler remained behind. He was curious what Mitch had meant by being '*forced to try something else*'. It seemed to suggest that he had a plan for that eventuality. If Chandler was really in joint command then he should divulge what it was.

'So what if we don't track him by nightfall?' asked Chandler.

Mitch didn't bite. 'Then, as I said, we try something different.'

'I know you, Mitch,' said Chandler. 'You know exactly what you want to do.'

Mitch nodded. 'Correct, Sergeant. And if it comes to pass, I'll reveal it.'

If it wasn't bad enough being sidelined when Mitch

wasn't here, it felt ten times worse now that he was – it was an additional, personal, brush-off.

'So what do we do now?' asked Chandler. 'What else do you need to know?'

'What I need to know, Sergeant, are *all* possible ways in and out of town.'

'You can see that on the map. Why don't you use your laser pointer?'

'Yes, but I want to know from *you* which are the most viable. Draw them up and get them to me. Show me how a rat gets in and out of town with the least chance of being noticed.'

'Gabriel won't know them; he's from Perth or that direction. *You* know those runs better than him.'

Mitch stayed quiet for a second, taking a breath. 'Okay. I'll put it a different way. Let's assume he *does* know. Let's assume he *is* a rat. Find out how best he could get out, Sergeant. Come back to me when you do.'

And that was that. Mitch stopped talking and flicked his eyes towards the door.

Chandler took the hint, glad to get out of there. The office was empty, the ants having fled the nest to begin their hunt for prey. At the front desk Nick looked disturbed but eager.

'And that's Mitch,' said Chandler.

'He's very ... serious,' offered his young constable, pausing to find the right word.

'It's the badge talking,' said Chandler. He wanted to believe that the old, semi-reckless teenager resided within Mitch somewhere.

'At least he's getting things moving,' said Nick, before backtracking. 'Not that you weren't as well, Sarge, it's just that he's brought more people and ...'

It was obvious that his constable was impressed with the display of authority.

'It's okay, Nick. Just do what he says ... if he ever talks to you.'

With his own computer shoved into the corner of Mitch's new command centre, Chandler logged on to Tanya's and brought up a map of the town. He quickly discovered that there were no end of rabbit holes that might have shielded Gabriel's route out. The back of Fraser Street and down into the storm drain; Yoppy's Lane behind the football field; Rose Avenue; Lincoln Street; even the alley behind Cook if he were sneaky enough. He drew them all up, red lines sprouting from the hotel like lava flows and brought them to his superior.

Mitch was leaning back in Chandler's chair, the smile on his face confirming his delight at watching his former partner do his bidding.

'This is what we've got,' said Chandler. 'Plenty of ways in and out. Jim's here,' he continued, pointing at the image projected on the wall with his finger and trying not to be blinded by the glare of the bulb. 'Tanya here, Luka here. State are on 95 and 138. The hotel he absconded from is the Gardner's Palace, which is—'

'I know where it is.'

'Right. So if he took the fire escape, the quickest way out of town is Rooster's, tucking in around the side of the laundrette, before crossing the alley into the wasteland behind. No more than ten or fifteen minutes, if you want to make sure to stay hidden.'

'You know that laundrette's always busy,' countered Mitch. 'They're always out back hanging clothes on the lines.'

'Yes,' said Chandler, jumping on the opportunity to get one up on Mitch and persuade him that he needed his local – and recent – knowledge. 'But *that* laundrette closed down last year, so there'd be no one to disturb his exit. *If* he decided to go that way. Jim checked it out and saw nothing to indicate he did.'

Mitch seemed undeterred by being caught out. 'Plausible, Sergeant, plausible but as you said there was no sign of the suspect. You may know this shithole better than I do, but you haven't found him yet so some fresh thinking is needed.'

'You need my help,' said Chandler.

Mitch corrected him. 'I need your *input*, Sergeant. And I need the input of your team. But your *help*? If I need your help, I'll ask,' he said, the smile gone, face turning to granite; hard, pockmarked and impenetrable. 'And the input I need from you at present is to make sure that this place is running smoothly and that my team out there have everything they need. Paper, stationery, phones, a constant line to State and anyone else that they ask to be put in contact with. You are the cog that keeps this thing running, Sergeant.'

Chandler had heard enough. He turned to leave.

Mitch called after him. 'It's an important job, Sergeant.

The big boys get nothing done without their secretaries doing all the graft.'

Chandler turned. 'I'm not running around fetching cups of tea and feeding you biscuits.'

Mitch laughed. 'Of course not. My team don't need you to do *those* things, they are more than capable themselves. What you can do is take care of the local angle. There are bound to be questions regarding what's happening, police walking the streets and strangers in black suits moping around town. It's your job to allay their fears, Sergeant,' said Mitch, the constant use of formalities fraying Chandler's nerves. But his old colleague wasn't finished. 'You take care of the small picture and I'll do the big.'

Chandler took a deep breath. 'You haven't changed have you, Mitch?'

Mitch held back a grin. 'I could say the same. Shit never turns to gold no matter how long it spends in the ditch.'

'I thought this wasn't going to be a battle?' said Chandler.

A smile broke loose, a smile that seemed to hide something behind it. Chandler caught a glimpse of the old Mitch for a moment, the Mitch forever with a trick up his sleeve to shimmy his way out of trouble.

'The battle hasn't even started, old friend.'

16

As predicted, within fifteen minutes the phones started to sing. Nick quickly became swamped and started diverting calls through to Chandler. Most were from locals riding the biggest commotion the town had witnessed in years; anxious mothers and protective fathers, affronted retirees and giggling teenagers, all curious about the sinister black saloons slowly trawling the streets.

Some wanted to know if they were the Secret Service or a spy convention, their theories wild. As soon as he had calmed one resident down another would ring in, wondering if they should get dressed up and form some kind of vanguard for their obviously illustrious visitor. Some wanted to know who it was just to be the first to spread the gossip around. Others because they didn't want it to be the prime minister or one of those fucking crooks. To each Chandler offered the same advice, words that stuck in his throat and had to be forced out: that nothing was happening, that they should stay inside for the time being and that if something happened he would let them know personally.

He had fielded maybe ten calls before someone hit upon the question he feared the most, one about the roadblocks and why Jim, Tanya and Luka were actively searching cars. The query arrived from a furious source, Reverend Simon Upton, who couldn't believe that the police would stop a holy man and search his car, complaining a little too much for someone who was normally rather placid. As if he did have something to hide. Something to confirm the whispers around town that his past was less than holy.

'*Did* they search your car, Reverend?' asked Chandler.

'No, but they stopped me on my way to Georgina Patterson's house and she's very ill, you know.'

'I do, Reverend. Please send my sympathies.'

'*Why* are you searching, may I ask?' the reverend demanded, his voice now as imposing as it was on the pulpit every Sunday.

Before the notoriously gossipy holy man had a chance to spread even more – not entirely undue – panic, Chandler admitted that it was just a precaution.

'Come on now, Sergeant Jenkins, you wouldn't have roadblocks in place for a precaution. You cannot withhold this information from the town.'

Chandler paused. He would have to give the reverend something. 'You're right. We have a shoplifter that we suspect is trying to get out of town.'

There was a pause as if the reverend were waiting for divine inspiration on whether Chandler had spoken the truth. The answer arrived. The Lord was unconvinced. 'You don't set up stop and searches for just any shoplifter,

Sergeant, so I'll ask again: is this person you seek dangerous? Is he, or she, an escaped convict, perhaps?'

'No, Reverend,' said Chandler, calmly, 'just someone we want to question. But to help find them we need everyone to remain indoors so we can focus on the suspect without distractions.'

The reverend jumped on Chandler's slip-up.

'Suspect! Ah, so he *is* a convict. Or about to be!'

Chandler felt his brain click into crisis management mode, his voice rounding off the edges, seeking to calm the reverend down.

'Reverend, that's the term we use. A suspect. If I was to make a call, he's actually more a person of interest and we are merely checking that he hasn't taken a ride in someone's car, or taken one for himself.'

'I'm not a man who lays down for criminals, Sergeant. He wouldn't be in *my* car.'

Chandler was relieved. The subtle change in tone and direction had helped steer the reverend to where Chandler wanted him to go.

'I know, Reverend, but I've instructed my officers to check *every* car. At this stage we can't even be sure that he's still in town. He might be long gone from here making it the State's problem, but I would like to err on the safe side and search cars just to be sure. I'm sure you don't have a problem with that.'

The Lord's representative on earth had no way back from that. There was an almost incoherent mumble in reply, something that sounded like an offer to do everything he could to help. He would ask his congregation at morning Mass – all ten of them, thought Chandler – if they had noticed anything. After thanking him, Chandler hung up.

Still the calls kept coming, people stuck at the checkpoints, ringing in to ask why the hell they weren't being let into or out of town. By now even Nick had been seconded to help out Mitch's team, skating sheepishly past Chandler to get in on the action. Chandler was on his own, batting back the complaints of irritated locals while listening to Mitch and his team decide what to do and where to go next.

Suddenly the door to the station slammed open. Two of Mitch's crew entered and headed straight for Chandler's office where Mitch had set up camp.

Chandler zoned out the questioning voice on the phone and tried to eavesdrop on what was happening in his office. He picked up nothing but garbled words. Less than a minute later the two exited the station again.

Mitch came to the door as Chandler hung up the call.

'What's going on?' asked Chandler.

'Nothing that concerns you,' replied Mitch.

'Where are they off to?'

Chandler's phone started to ring again.

'Just concentrate on keeping the locals calm,' said Mitch, then asked, 'Has Mrs Juniper rung in yet?'

Mrs Juniper was the local busybody, Kid Maloney's ex-wife who married him in a fit of rebellion and divorced him when her senses returned. If it made a smell she had her nose in it. Or at least she used to.

'She's been dead four years,' said Chandler.

What should have been a moment of reflection or discomfort merely brought an unaffected shrug to Mitch's shoulders and his unhurried return to the office.

Nick passed Chandler, on his way back to the front desk.

'Where are they off to, Nick?'

The young constable shook his head and kept going. The speed of his escape made Chandler believe he was holding something back. Mitch was slowly unravelling the close-knit station he had built.

Chandler called after him. 'Nick?'

'I dunno, Sarge, honest. They whispered it to each other. I didn't hear.'

Mitch appeared at Chandler's shoulder. 'I want to interview Mr Barwell.'

'What's stopping you?'

'You have the keys, Sergeant.'

Chandler rose from his seat, shorter in height than Mitch but more intimidating physically; false padding wasn't needed for his broad shoulders. 'I'll come in with you.'

Mitch shook his head. 'No, I don't want any contamination from previous questioning. A fresh sheet of paper.'

'But I'll be able to tell if he's changed his story.'

'So will I,' said Mitch, pointing to his temple, 'I know it off by heart.'

'An extra pair of ears never hurt.'

Mitch paused, his lower jaw and chin jutting out, an involuntary and ungainly reflex he'd had since he was a boy. 'Okay, Sergeant, but I lead. You keep your mouth shut.'

'You lead,' said Chandler, biting his tongue. Anything was better than answering phones.

Chandler entered the cells, Mitch close behind. He opened the slat, the squeak echoing around the corridor. Heath's face thrust at the space like a dog seeking food, nothing but his mouth on view. His bark was full of questions.

'What's happening out there? Who are all these people?'

'Mr Barwell, please step back from the door,' ordered Mitch, calm but commanding, any trace of his boyhood accent gone. Chandler wouldn't have been surprised to find out he had gone to a voice coach to refine it, given the money and dedication he put into his clothing and manufactured style.

'Who's *he*?' Heath asked Chandler, indicating Mitch. 'My lawyer?'

'He's an inspector. He's come to interview you. Now please step back.'

As Chandler prepared to open the cell door Mitch eased his jacket back and rested his hand on his firearm. Chandler wondered if he had ever used it and quickly decided he probably had.

Chandler entered first and brought out his cuffs.

'There's no need for those,' said Heath, his hands up. 'I want a lawyer.'

'Why do you need a lawyer if you're innocent?' asked Mitch, frowning.

'Everyone gets a lawyer,' said Heath.

'Maybe so,' said Mitch, maintaining his cool, 'but only those who are guilty *insist* on one. All I want to do is go over your story. To catch up with my colleague here and understand what you've been through.'

Heath frowned, staring at Mitch, as if trying to gauge his real intentions.

After a moment's pause he turned to face the wall, allowing Chandler to slide the cuffs over his injured wrists. Chandler felt the man flinch in pain. Ushering him to the interview room, he placed Heath in a seat before carefully removing the cuffs.

'I'm only going to be repeating myself,' said Heath, gently rubbing his wrists while looking first at Mitch and then Chandler who had taken up position at his colleague's shoulder.

Mitch led the questioning, his silver cufflinks glinting in the light – large, angular and expensive, flashy but not showy, elegant with a sense of understatement. Silver had always been Mitch's favourite, possibly a reminder of the badge he held so dear, but maybe just because silver was a statement of grandeur. Mitch liked statements.

Heath started talking. He recounted a story which stuck pretty much to the original, maybe a little more polished as he recited it a second time, detailed when it came to the part about hitch-hiking, vague about the drugging and escape. Only one difference stood out to Chandler, a recollection of a name on one of the papers in the cabin: Seth. When Mitch pushed him on it, Heath said that it was something he only now recalled, a name written in big, red letters as if of utmost importance. Chandler made a note to check for Seths amongst the records of missing people.

'If you had managed to steal the car where would you have gone?' asked Mitch, eyes cast to his notes as if it were merely a question to pass the time.

'Anywhere,' said Heath, beads of sweat trickling from underneath his hairline.

'You claimed in your original statement that you were headed here. To town,' said Mitch, raising his eyes to stare at his suspect.

'I was ... but all I wanted to do was get away from him. I still do, but you've trapped me in here, while he—'

Heath's entire body shook, some stray beads of sweat escaping his flushed skin and landing on the desk.

'Trying to steal a car is hardly the act of an innocent man,' noted Mitch.

'Yeah, it's the act of a scared one,' said Heath.

'What about your past?' asked Mitch. Chandler knew Mitch was changing topics to try and throw the suspect off and get him to reveal something.

'What about it?'

'Family?'

'Don't have any.'

Mitch remained quiet, allowing Heath to elaborate. He did.

'My folks are dead.'

'I'm sorry to hear that,' said Mitch, indifferent.

Heath shook his head. 'They died years ago. When I was in my late teens.'

'How?' asked Mitch.

'Cancer. Mum, breast, Dad, bowel. Two years apart.'

Chandler felt that this was cause for a moment's sympathetic pause. But Mitch was on a roll.

'Do you still think about them?'

Mitch looked at the table for a moment. 'Yeah but I've accepted it. Also accepted that I may be more prone to cancer, too.'

There was a lassitude with how Heath let the words tumble out of his mouth that was almost morbid, as if he expected death were lying in wait just around the corner. Maybe his brush with Gabriel had confirmed this, or maybe this self-imposed death sentence merely made him feel that he should take as many people with him as he could.

'Have you been told you'll die?' asked Chandler.

Heath's focus switched to Chandler, Mitch clearly enraged at having his flow interrupted.

'Apart from Gabriel telling me, no. But everyone dies.' Again the words fell out with nothing to hang them on, just weary acceptance, as if he were already nothing but dust.

'It's just a matter of how, isn't it, Mr Barwell?' said Mitch.

The loaded question won back Heath's focus.

'What do you mean by that?'

Mitch waved his hand to suggest it was an offhand comment. 'Never mind. Carry on telling me about your family.'

'I have a brother and sister. Both older.'

'Names?' Mitch made a scene of preparing to jot their names down, a tacit promise that he would chase this information up, a warning for Heath not to lie.

'Ross and Pippa. Philippa. We don't talk to each other. A dispute over the will.'

'Your folks left it all to you? As the youngest?'

'No,' said Heath, tinged with disappointment. 'The opposite. I got a few bits and pieces; they got a share of the house. But that's long gone now. We don't speak.'

'Wouldn't they care that you're in custody?'

'They'll only care when word comes through that I'm dead,' he said, bitterly. 'Gabriel was close to granting their wish.'

Mitch nodded. 'But you don't have anything to confirm your identity?'

'He took all that stuff; wallet, driving licence, everything.'

'Okay,' said Mitch, non-committal.

'You have the wrong person, Sergeant.'

Mitch raised his eyebrows, a flash of anger at being inadvertently demoted.

'At the minute you're the *only* person we have, Mr Barwell,' he said, looking across at Chandler in apparent frustration before moving on. 'You mentioned the number fifty-five.'

'That's what he said I was.'

'Did he talk about the others?'

'No.'

'Nothing?'

'No. Nothing.'

Mitch took a deep breath, rubbing his thumb and forefinger together. Chandler recognized the habit. The lighting of a fuse, as if trying to create a spark between the two digits. Chandler was curious what form the explosion would take these days.

'What about this *Seth*, could he have been one of the victims?'

Heath shook his head. 'It was just a name I saw. It might mean nothing.'

'But you saw the graves.'

'I saw what *looked* like graves.'

'How many?'

'I dunno.'

'Take a guess.' Mitch's temper was building.

'It happened too quick. I don't know for sure.'

'A number, Mr Barwell, give me a number. Five? Ten? Twelve? More?'

Heath stuttered. 'Six, seven, eight ... I can't be sure. I was running for my life.'

With this Mitch stood up sharply, leaning over the table, face to face with the suspect. His voice was raised. 'We need something more than that, Mr Barwell. So far you've given us nothing but hearsay. What you claim to have seen and what you claim to have had done to you. So give us a straight-up fact we can work with, or you'll be in that cell for a *long* time.'

With Mitch close enough for Heath to grab him, Chandler stepped in, dragging Mitch away, his hands searching for purchase on the cool silk.

Mitch's ire switched target, glaring at Chandler. 'Get your hands off me, Chandler!'

'You're not going to get anything more out of him,' said Chandler under his breath.

'What the hell do you know? How many murder suspects have you interrogated?'

'None,' admitted Chandler, 'but look at him, he's a wreck – tired, injured, sweating. Anything we get out of him now could be the truth, a lie, or just something to shut us up. Let him cool down for a while.'

Mitch didn't drop his stare. But he didn't say anything either. The anger that burned in his deep brown eyes tempered. Chandler searched for some of his old friend in there but any compassion had been bled from them over the last ten years.

'Take him back, let him rest for an hour and try again later,' said Chandler.

Mitch batted Chandler's hands away from his slick suit, and swung towards Heath with a forced smile.

'I believe that's enough for now, Mr Barwell. The sergeant here will escort you back to your cell.'

Mitch strode for the door. Reaching it, he glanced back at Chandler. Angry though he was, Mitch wasn't about to be accused of deserting his duty and allowing a colleague to handle a dangerous suspect alone.

Chandler approached a now shivering Heath and clicked the cuffs into place. Looking up, Mitch had disappeared from the door, Tanya standing in his place.

17

Chandler steered Heath into the cell. He was like a drunk after a heavy night, manoeuvred without trouble or resistance. Not what Chandler would have considered the conduct of a dangerous killer. But what was the conduct of a dangerous killer?

As he entered his former office, Mitch was flicking the mouse furiously, eyes cast on the glowing screen.

'So ... do you believe his story? Or Gabriel's?'

Mitch tore his eyes away from the screen. His voice was flat; he clearly hadn't forgotten that Chandler had confronted him in the interview room. 'Mr Barwell's story seems plausible, even more so with the continued absence of our second suspect. We need to find him and find out who this *Seth* might be.' With that his eyes returned to the screen, the store closed, blinds drawn.

Chandler sat down at Tanya's desk and got to work. He felt like a dog that, despite the constant abuse, came running back to its master. He forced himself to focus on the job in front of him. In the database for Missing

Persons he trawled for people named Seth, hoping to find a match. The search engine brought up a result immediately. A complete blank. He recalibrated it to include the last decade. Murdering fifty-four people without drawing undue attention would take some time, even for the most brilliant mind – which Heath was certainly not. Or so it seemed. Again the search drew a blank. No Seths. He began to think that the name was the barely remembered thought of a frightened man.

Or an intentionally false lead to distract them.

Frustrated at being mocked and cast aside, *then* brought back into the fold only to immediately hit a dead end, he leaned back in the chair. Staring out the window at Gardner's Hill in the distance, Chandler's feet jack-hammered on the floor with growing impatience. The impatience forced an idea through. So far they had been unable to locate Gabriel but that didn't mean they couldn't locate the place both had described in detail: the woodshed. Gabriel might even have wound his way back to it seeking shelter, confident the police wouldn't be able to find it.

'I have to get out of here, Nick,' he whispered, even though Mitch was tucked away in the office and Yohan and Suze were wrapped up in their own tasks. 'I'm going to try the Hill. They both mentioned the same shack, so it must exist.'

'Yeah, but they both claimed not to know where it was,' Nick reminded him.

'It must be somewhere near Turtle's. Where Heath was caught trying to steal the car.'

'I might be new around here and all, Sarge, but that's a lot of ground.'

'I know but maybe I can track it down. At least I can give it a shot.'

'And what do I tell *him*?' asked Nick, arching his neck towards Mitch.

'That I'm following up a lead.'

'Okay ...' said Nick, sounding less than sure.

Chandler retrieved his keys and jacket and was within arm's reach of the station door when Mitch floated out of his office.

'Where are you off to, Sergeant?'

For an instant Chandler thought about making up some excuse.

'I'm going to check out the woods behind where Heath was picked up.'

Mitch's face turned to stone again, his eyes darting side to side, determining whether there might be traction in this idea, a bandwagon that he might want to jump on.

'I'm coming with you.'

Chandler formed a backup plan. 'Do you remember Turtle, Mi—, Inspector?' he asked.

'Turtle Siefert? Yes I do, Sergeant.'

'Good. But Turtle won't remember you. His memory's gone. He shot the last guy who tried to tell him John Howard wasn't prime minister. And that guy was his own brother!'

Chandler stopped short of mentioning that he'd only managed to wing his brother in the arm and no charges had been pressed.

'I'm coming with you, Sergeant,' said Mitch.

And that was that. Chandler had a partner once again.

The car ride was silent; a silence that Chandler dared not break in case he said something ill-judged in a confined space that neither could escape.

Thankfully it was a short silence. Twenty minutes later he pulled the car into Turtle's front yard. The first welcome sight was the banged-up Chevy tied to the concrete post like a horse in lieu of a working handbrake. Second was that Turtle himself wasn't in the yard, brandishing his shotgun at them. It was where his nickname had originated: always on the defensive, a shell on his back and another in his shotgun.

'Remember, he's not the biggest fan of the police,' said Chandler as they got out of the car.

'I know,' said Mitch, batting the concern away as he scanned the front yard.

'So let me do the talking.'

Mitch didn't reply as they cautiously weaved their way between the dilapidated barns and machinery, the subsided porch sloping away from the wooden building as if trying to flee. It was a farm in need of repair. A farm with plenty of places to hide.

They made it halfway to the farmhouse when they were greeted by a gnarled old man, who stepped out the screen door. His shotgun rested low, but high enough to make a point.

'What're you doin' here?' asked Turtle, in typical drawn-out fashion, his jaw grinding like one of the threshing drums in the harvesters now rotting in the yard.

Before Chandler had a chance to answer, Mitch spoke up.

'We're the police, Mr Siefert.'

'I ask'd what you're doin' here,' said Turtle, not advancing from his porch.

'Mind if we come closer rather than having to shout?'

'You mind tellin' me your name, boy?'

'Turtle,' said Chandler, interrupting. 'It's me, Chandler. Sergeant Jenkins.'

Turtle tilted his head, his good eye scanning the horizon, the other set straight but as blind as a bat's. Now within thirty feet of him, Chandler could also see that his eyebrows appeared to have been drawn on in thick black marker, halfway up his forehead in a look of permanent surprise. He'd done it again, lit the gas cooker on full, shooting a cloud of flame towards his already charred face.

'And what do you want, Chan'ler?'

Mitch inched closer. 'We want you to keep calm.'

'I was calm, boy. I *ammm* calm. What do you want?'

Chandler spoke up. 'We need to have a look around, Turtle.'

Turtle's head swung around so that his good eye faced Chandler. The unfortunate by-product of this was that the shotgun now pointed straight at them.

'I ain't done nothin' wrong. You can't prove I was poaching those fish.'

'We—' started Chandler. He flicked a glance at Mitch

whose hand had curled around the butt of his gun, wary of the shotgun and the increasingly perturbed old man. 'We're not here for that. We just need a look 'round.'

Mitch grunted at Chandler, his voice forced low. 'What are the chances he knows something about this?'

'Slim to none,' replied Chandler, equally forced, eyes trained on Turtle who kept the gun trained on them. 'He's not one for partners. Poaching's the most serious thing he's into.'

'I still want to search it,' said Mitch, his eyes on Turtle.

'The place we're looking for is further in.'

'I want to rule this place out.'

'I'm telling you—'

'You said yourself that his memory's gone. Our suspect could be here now, or maybe he had been here, pretending to be his son, the one who was fencing cars down in Sydney last I remember.'

Turtle might be losing his memory but there was nothing wrong with Mitch's. The youngest Siefert boy was still in prison outside of Sydney for running a chop shop out of an abandoned warehouse.

Chandler swung back towards Turtle. 'We'll be quick, Turtle. We aren't looking for anything *you've* done. We think someone might have been trespassing on your land.'

'Who?' asked Turtle, his face curling into a frown but his eyebrows remaining static.

'A guy from out of town.'

Turtle swung around as if the Devil would appear on command. With his failing brain and eyesight, it was a worrying possibility. 'Is he still on my land?'

'No,' assured Chandler. The last thing he wanted was Turtle storming off and getting in their way. 'We want to see if we can find any clue about where he went *after* he was here.'

The old man fell silent, considering the request.

'We won't touch anything we don't need to,' said Chandler, closing in on victory.

'Don't break any of my tractors,' warned Turtle.

Not a problem, thought Chandler. Most were already broken, relics of a farming past, back when the Sieferts had worked the land instead of chopping cars, poaching fish and threatening cops.

Mitch carefully backed off towards the car as Chandler made sure that Turtle was fully on-board with what was going to happen.

'You'll destroy my bloody farm.'

'If anyone damages anything, you can make a claim for it.'

'Really?'

Chandler pointed to Mitch. 'Direct them to Inspector Andrews. He's the man in charge, now.'

'That stick of koala dung dressed like a starched penguin?'

'He was born and bred here in Wilbrook. You can trust him.'

'Didn't sound like he was from here.'

Chandler nodded in response before rejoining Mitch by the car. He was studying a map of the surrounding area on a tablet.

'We'll check the outhouses first,' said Chandler, 'then the main house. I can go—'

'You won't be required, Sergeant.'

Chandler paused, struggling to process this new information. 'Why won't I be needed? You can't search this place on your own.'

'I know. I've called my team out.'

'But I know the area, I can—'

'We have this covered, Sergeant. My team will be here soon. They know how I work. I need you to explain to the old man—'

'You forget that I know how you work too.'

'How I *used* to work.'

'What exactly is your problem with having me around, Mitch?'

Mitch rested the tablet on the hood of the car and looked at Chandler. 'I need people I can trust.'

'And what have I done to lose your trust?'

'Nothing, Sergeant Jenkins. You never had it in the first place. You'll just have to accept that I give the orders and I choose my team.'

'You're letting the shit that went on between us in the past get in the way of this investigation.'

Mitch slowly shook his head. 'We have no past, as far as I am concerned, Sergeant. This is a decision based purely on what I think should be done. You know these hicks, that's true, but you're also a little too close to them and when you're this close it's easy to miss something. Or look the other way.'

'So you're accusing me of what? Unprofessionalism? Bias? Corruption?'

'I'm not accusing you of anything, Sergeant. This is

what an *inspector* . . .' he paused on the word, 'has to do. Make unpopular decisions.'

'And if I decide to stay?'

Mitch picked up the tablet again. 'I'd have no choice but to take you off the case and suspend you.'

Chandler didn't doubt the seriousness of this threat.

'Anyway, why are you complaining?' continued Mitch. 'While I lead the taskforce up here, you're in charge of base operations. With Suze and Yohan. In case any new leads emerge.'

Chandler understood that Mitch was fobbing him off but given the commotion with Turtle if Gabriel had been here he would have had ample chance to clear out. Plus, Turtle's farm wasn't where the kidnaps and killings had taken place. The crazy old man might have been blind but his ears were fine. Any cry for help within a few kilometres of his place and Turtle would have heard it. And been nosy enough to check it out.

18

2002

'Watch your step, Mitch!'

Chandler shouted even though there was zero chance that his colleague had heard him over the whine of the helicopter engine overhead. He retreated a safe distance from the murderous blades that whipped up a vicious whirlwind of dust that almost obscured the aircraft from view.

Five days into the search for Martin and still they continued to forge deeper into the outback, so much so that they now had to be airlifted in and out with enough supplies to survive for a few days in the dense woods and scrubland. Out here, the terrain was pretty in a feral way, wild and untouched, alluring and unknown, appealing to the adventurous side of Chandler's character, the teenage side, the lost side. He and Mitch had camped in the wild when they were younger but never this far in. It would have taken a full day and two tanks of fuel to get this far on scramblers, the terrain rough and undiscovered, lacking natural trails, which meant little speed and real danger.

As Mitch charged across the rutted ground, clear of the blades, the chopper began its slow ascent, whipping up dust in a wider and wider arc, causing the already disembarked Chandler to shield his face. Only as the helicopter cleared the top of the trees did the whirlwind die down, the craft angling forward and speeding back towards town.

They were amongst the second load ferried in today, bringing the group's number to fifteen, a figure that was shrinking by the day and in Chandler's opinion, a feeble effort given the area they needed to cover. Donning his backpack he set off to rendezvous with the others.

As their hearing recovered from the squeal of the engines, talk swung towards Bill's morning briefing. The area to search over the next three days had been marked out with a warning for them to find a clear spot by the end of the third so that the helicopters could extricate them. After that the rest of the meeting spiralled into attempts to rouse motivation but Chandler sensed that even Bill was frustrated at the air search having proved fruitless.

There was another reason for his frustration, too. Some bright spark in management had taken to inviting Martin's family to these briefings, amongst them Sylvia, the mother of the missing boy. Even in the air-conditioned room, her soft face glowed red in the heat. It lent the impression that she was on the verge of collapse, much as she had done on the second day of the search when they had to radio in the helicopter to transport her to hospital. After that, Arthur had barred her from going out again.

What the presence of the family had done was turn the briefings into formal affairs, everyone wary of what they said and how they said it in case it was deemed too negative. Words were adjusted to offer hope rather than state reality, each fruitless day in the wilderness sold as more area covered. The emotional attachment that they had brought had initially succeeded in driving the volunteers forward but now it was becoming a burden. Chandler was feeling more counsellor than policeman, concerned with the family's welfare as much as oversee-ing the search's progress.

Today, if anything, was worse. As if dealing with the tortured emotions of the parents wasn't hard enough, Arthur had dragged his remaining son along. Twelve years old and dropped into an alien landscape to battle with the rest of the group, his eyes were glassy and as wide as saucers, but Chandler could see that he was determined to make a difference, a stubbornness he no doubt inherited from his father – and brother.

As the group prepared to set off Arthur offered his morning prayer, red rings still evident around his eyes from the tearful interview on television last night that Chandler had watched after tucking an exhausted Teri into bed. The passion and hurt Arthur had displayed had turned the localized search for his eldest son into a national news story, resulting in Chandler being hounded by reporters at the station and the base camp this morning. They had been warned by HQ to stay silent about progress and to let those at the top act as the mouthpieces but Chandler didn't need to be told; he distrusted vultures who fed on human misery so he passed through the forest of cameras and microphones silently. If it hadn't been for the national attention and crippling fear of missing out on a scoop, none of them would have cared about the family's distress. And when the bones had been picked clean and they caught the whiff of blood on the wind, they would fly away again, hunting for their next victim.

Despite the inauspicious start, midday brought a clue, right before the two-hour break to wait out the hottest part of the day. One of the volunteers, a teenager all the way up from the Murray River area south of Perth, found a scrap of clothing caught on a briar, waving like a flag in the gentle breeze.

Chandler was soon on the scene, a crowd surrounding the strip of red almost afraid to approach in case it vanished in front of their eyes. First observations were that it had been torn from the original garment rather than cut, the edges frayed, fibres waving a thousand tiny fingers at him.

'What is it?' said Mitch, having caught up with them.

'A piece of clothing, possibly. Torn,' said Chandler, eyes fixed on it. The fact that it danced so easily in the wind told him it was a lightweight material. 'Pass me a bag.'

Mitch rummaged through his backpack for an

evidence bag. Teasing the material delicately from the barb, Chandler placed it into to the bag and zipped it up.

He held it up for a closer look. All eyes followed it, almost reverent of the find. Part of a logo was imprinted on to the material. An 'N' and what looked to be most of an 'O' in white capital letters.

'What do you think?' asked Chandler.

'No Fear... North Face... Mizu—no.?' offered Mitch. 'If it was torn off he must have been travelling quickly.'

'So where's the rest?'

'Let me see,' said Arthur who stumbled into the fray, his belly leading the way, his youngest son locked to his side.

Chandler passed the bag to the old man whose hand was swollen with the heat.

'North Face,' said Arthur. 'Martin bought a lot of that stuff. He has clothes in that colour too but Sylvia would be able to tell you better.'

'It's a popular brand,' said Mitch, gently.

'It's something,' said the old man, brusquely. 'Tells us that he made it this far.'

'Unless it blew—'

Chandler's raised eyebrow was enough. Mitch shut his mouth. Truth was that the discovery of the clothing generated as many questions as it answered. Had Martin made it here or had he not? Was it blown on the wind or ripped straight off? Was it even from Martin's clothing? The fact that it had been ripped could also mean that he had been attacked by something. Martin's disappearance remained as mysterious as the region they continued to scour. The best they could do now was search for further pieces of clothing.

Mitch was also concerned – but for different reasons. 'We're getting closer and closer to hell out here.'

'Where do you want to be, Mitch?'

'By the beach. Taking a morning dip before a shift. Maybe let the riptide sweep me silently away like Harold Holt. Like Martin.'

Chandler looked angrily at his partner. 'Don't let anyone catch you saying shit like that.'

Mitch glanced around. 'They can't hear me. And let's face it, there's no one else for miles. And that includes Martin.'

It was blunt but probably true.

Mitch wasn't finished. 'You think he did this on purpose?'

'What?'

'Disappear.'

'Like some form of elaborate suicide?' asked Chandler, humouring Mitch's wild theory.

'Faking it is my guess. Running away and becoming someone else. Mark my words, he'll turn up in twenty years, his fingerprints on some murder weapon. I mean, what reason is there to fake your death and assume another identity unless you have done or plan to do something illegal?'

As Chandler expected, a wild theory. An intensive search into Martin's past and present had brought up nothing, no ostensible reason for him to want to disappear and start a new life. Only the recent break-up with his girlfriend, bad though it might have been according to Sylvia, had caused any ripple on an otherwise flawless lake.

But Mitch's idea got Chandler thinking. If the teenager wanted to disappear – for good – then out here was the place to do it. Jumping country left a paper trail, at sea his body would float to the surface, but out here, after a while, they would have to surrender to nature and class him as missing, presumed dead – free to start his new life.

'He never intended on coming back,' continued Mitch. 'The car was fucked. No fuel, broken suspension, nothing but a trickle of water in the radiator.'

As tempting as it was to get caught up in them, Chandler decided to shut Mitch's theories down. It was time to do their job. 'Let the others do the thinking, Mitch, we're just paid to search.'

Mitch arched an eyebrow. 'Whoa, that's heartless.'

'If you haven't noticed this place is heartless.'

'You still didn't answer me.'

'I can't answer every one of your dumb questions.'

'You know I'm right.'

Chandler bit. 'Faking his death is a big leap.'

'But the correct one. That's why I'm going to go far in this game.'

Mitch offered a self-satisfied smile. Chandler was glad of the opportunity to burst his bubble.

'Not if you let the other kid get lost like his brother,' he said, pointing to Arthur's youngest veering off at a tangent from the others, his dad too busy *reading the earth to safeguard his remaining flesh and blood.*

Chandler set off to intercept the boy with Mitch in close pursuit.

19

On the drive back to the station, Chandler reflected on the fact that, once again, his lead had been taken away from him, his chance of stealing the thunder itself stolen. He was back to being an errand boy.

He was sufficiently distracted to not be paying much attention as he pulled into his parking spot. Stepping out of the car he glanced across the road towards the bakery. The Cheesy Chicken special was calling out his name but his eyes were drawn to the alleyway beside it and the hand that flashed into view for a split second. It was an alley the local kids often used to cut through to the football field behind.

His instinct told him to investigate, to send the kids home with a warning to stay indoors. He crept up to the corner and sprang out to surprise them. The shock was all his.

A few metres down the alley, clutching what looked like a long-handled kitchen knife, was Gabriel.

Reaching for his gun, Chandler missed, his draw hand wavering. Gabriel backed up a few steps. Chandler countered by moving forward a few, finally grabbing hold of his weapon and drawing it.

'Stay right there and put the knife down, Gabriel.'

Gabriel inched back, the knife unsteady in his hand, as if he wanted to let it go but couldn't get his muscles to comply. His face was twisted in pain or shock, almost as if he had blacked out and woken up to this tense scene.

'Gabriel, put the knife down!'

Chandler tried to speak loudly and clearly, allowing for nothing to be misinterpreted.

Gabriel looked at the knife and back at Chandler.

'Put it down, Gabriel!'

Gabriel's hand shook but the blade remained pointed at him. Chandler's finger rested on the trigger. *What the hell was Gabriel doing this close to the station?* It was almost as if he were begging to be caught. Or shot for threatening a police officer.

'Gabriel, I don't want to—'

As if suddenly unglued, the knife dropped from Gabriel's hand to the concrete and his hands shot up in surrender.

Chandler approached with caution.

'Up against the wall.'

Gabriel obeyed the command, his hands outstretched against the brick.

Chandler remained extra cautious as he whisked Gabriel's wiry arms behind his back, ignoring the stifled cry of pain.

'Please . . .' begged Gabriel.

'Why did you sneak out of the hotel?' asked Chandler,

not waiting to get back to the station to start the interrogation. 'Where did you go? And why are you back here?'

'I don't know,' cried Gabriel.

'And what were you doing with the knife?'

'I needed protection from *him*. I kept thinking he was going to burst out from around every corner. I didn't feel safe.'

Neither did Chandler, alone with his suspect in the alley.

'Get on the ground!' he ordered.

With the barked command some of Gabriel's pliant nature vanished. 'You don't have to do that, Officer,' he said. 'I'm giving myself up. I'm sorry for running but I got scared stuck in that room like I was trapped. Like in the shed again. I couldn't deal with it so I had to get out, get some space.'

'I said, get down, Gabriel.'

'I only wanted out—'

With his suspect refusing to obey, Chandler had no choice but to twist the man's wrist and force him to his knees. Gabriel yelped and tried to pull away but his knees gave up and he sunk to the concrete. Grabbing the cuffs, his heart pounding, his hands slathered in sweat, Chandler struggled to open the ratchet before finally slipping them securely around Gabriel's wrists. Only now did he allow himself to relax a little, pocketing his weapon and yanking his captive to his feet.

'You don't have to do this—' Gabriel hissed in pain.

'You've already escaped once.'

Gabriel fell silent.

'Where did you go after the hotel?' asked Chandler.

'Okay, okay,' said Gabriel. 'I tried to steal a car but they were locked. I didn't want to be on the street in case Heath made it into town too, so I just kinda sat in an alley. Dunno where … dunno how long. Then I overheard some people saying that they'd captured a guy called Heath. I was so relieved.'

'Why didn't you turn yourself in then?'

'I was building up the courage.'

With Gabriel cuffed securely, Chandler aimed him towards the station. Where he might have expected a fanfare there was nothing but an empty grey street.

'And you have the courage now?'

'I don't want him getting out to murder again. I couldn't forgive myself if he got free just because I panicked. I want to be a Good Samaritan. So you don't need the cuffs.'

'I do,' said Chandler, reaching the doors of the station. He decided to test the return of the self-proclaimed prodigal son. 'You were right that we have Heath. But he's telling exactly the same story you are.'

'What *story*?' said Gabriel, trying to pull away from Chandler.

'The exact same one you told.'

'Then that's good, isn't it?' said Gabriel, looking hopeful. 'It backs up what I said.'

'No, Mr Johnson, it's the exact same story. But implicating *you* as the killer.'

His charge resisted further. Chandler gripped Gabriel's wrists tighter.

'That's a lie. You don't believe him, do you? Is he still locked up? You haven't let him go, have you?' cried Gabriel, glancing towards the doors. 'I told you the truth. To lie is a sin, Sergeant. That's how I was brought up.'

'I can assure you he's locked up. You're safe.'

Gabriel stared at him, tears threatening to spill from his eyes.

As Chandler eased Gabriel inside the station, Nick's jaw dropped and he sprang up from his chair, which slammed into the already marked wall.

Chandler allowed himself a small smile. The win felt good, Mitch scouring Turtle's farm for clues to Gabriel's whereabouts while he had the real thing under arrest.

'Where did you find him?' said Nick, scrabbling for the paperwork to fill in but keeping his eyes on the second potential serial killer they had apprehended today.

'Fell into my lap.'

He looked around the station for Mitch's two minions, Bill and Ben, or whatever their names were. Nick anticipated his question.

'The inspector radioed in and told them to head up to Turtle's. Said you were on the way back to cover for them. I'm glad you're here. I was getting lonely.'

'Where's Heath?' asked Gabriel, nerves causing him to shake at the end of Chandler's arm.

'In the cells.'

'Don't put me in there too.'

'We have to. For the time being,' said Chandler. 'Cell number three, Nick.'

'And where is he?'

'Not cell number three,' said Nick.

'Oh,' said Gabriel. Chandler continued to feel the tremor reverberate through his captive as Gabriel looked at him. 'I'm sorry about earlier, Sergeant. Getting worked up and that. I was just so scared ...' Gabriel trailed off.

'You won't be in the cells long,' said Chandler.

'Good.' The worry in his suspect's face seemed to ease. 'You'll release me?'

'No. We need to question you again.'

The worry returned. 'Why? You already have my story. It hasn't changed.'

'We'll need it again. In more depth.'

'What do you mean?' said Gabriel, frowning.

'We'll clear that up later.'

'Okay. You're sure he's secure?'

'As secure as you'll be in a minute,' said Chandler.

His prisoner shivered with nerves. 'Can't we do the interview somewhere else, like back at that hotel?'

'Not after last time,' said Chandler, sternly. He wasn't going to fall for that again. If he did he may as well resign on the spot rather than wait for Mitch to kick him out of town.

'I won't run.'

'Doesn't matter. All our recording equipment is here. And so are you,' said Chandler, adding, 'Relax. You're under no threat now.'

Gabriel winced, the deep wrinkles ageing his face in an instant. 'When you've been drugged, captured, chased through the outback and told to your face that you're going to be murdered, there's threat everywhere, Sergeant. A killer in every shadow.'

Gritting his teeth, Gabriel closed his eyes. He inhaled deeply through his nose. 'But I'm ready to face him if I need to.'

'You won't need to face him,' said Chandler, leading him towards the door to the cells. 'Just answer a few questions.'

As he was about to enter the cells he shouted back over his shoulder. 'Nick, prep the interview room.'

'What about the roadblocks, Sarge? And should I inform the inspector that we have him?'

Chandler paused. He should call off the search immediately but there was no harm in it continuing for a little while. The danger was off the streets. Both Gabriel *and* Heath.

'Gimme half an hour,' said Chandler.

With a hesitant nod, Nick returned to the front desk. A feather of mistrust caught in Chandler's throat. Would his young constable obey him, or run off and tell Mitch and the others? At his age, Chandler would have followed every command given by his superior but Nick didn't seem to suffer from that kind of blind loyalty. Given Chandler's current conduct that might have been a good thing.

As they closed in on cell number three, Gabriel started trying to squirm from Chandler's grasp, directing his body anywhere but towards the waiting cell.

'Is he in here?' whispered Gabriel, his voice so soft

Chandler initially thought he'd imagined it. Chandler didn't answer but kept pulling him towards the cells.

'Don't,' said Gabriel, the colour in his tanned face almost washed out. His eyes darted over his shoulder at Chandler, his captor. His voice was soft like a summer breeze, barely perceptible but scorching all the same. A voice that contrasted with his scrawny beard and mien of fear.

'Who's that?'

Compared to the softness of Gabriel's voice, Heath's angry demand crashed around the cells, causing Gabriel to freeze, his eyes darting towards the sound, trying to pin the source down.

'It's me, Mr Barwell,' said Chandler, aiming Gabriel towards the cell. 'Now keep the noise down and get some rest,' he added, ushering Gabriel inside number three before undoing his cuffs. He swiftly backed to the door and closed it. He had them both. Locked up. Where they couldn't hurt anyone.

At the sound of the closed door, Heath became even more curious. 'Who are you putting in a cell, Sergeant? Is that him?' The sonorous voice stuttered, the power swiftly vanishing from it.

'Is that him?' repeated Heath.

Chandler didn't answer the question. He had two prisoners who seemed equally frightened of each other. But neither of them seemed to display the cold nature of a serial killer. At least according to the books and television he had seen.

*

That thought stayed with Chandler as he returned to the office. Nick was waiting for him, literally on the edge of his seat.

'Did he say anything?'

'No. One of the men in there is a very good actor.'

'Or both are,' noted Nick. 'The interview room's ready.'

'Good.'

'You know most serial killers are good liars. Ted Bundy was—'

Chandler was almost glad that another one of Nick's morbid biographies was interrupted by Heath yelling from the cells.

'What is it?' asked Chandler as he opened up the slat of Heath's cell.

Immediately Heath pressed up close to it.

'I'm hurt. I think one of my ribs is busted.'

'You didn't complain about it before.'

'I did to the other two. They didn't bother to check me over. I get that you can lock me up without any evidence – that kinda shit you've been doing for years – but I'm finding it hard to breathe in here.'

His plea was bracketed by a hand clasped to his side, against his bloodied clothes, pain riddling his voice. Chandler couldn't tell if it was an act or not.

'Leave it with me,' said Chandler.

'Are you gonna get someone?' barked Heath.

'I said leave it with me, Mr Barwell.'

Chandler turned to leave. He passed cell three. Despite Heath's outburst there hadn't been a peep from it. Curious to witness the reaction of his new guest and overtaken by an odd foreboding that somehow Gabriel had disappeared again, he opened the slat and peered in. To his relief his prisoner was curled up on the bed, staring at the wall in the direction of cell number one as if he expected Heath to burst through the reinforced brick. A pathetic creature, stricken with fear. He too looked injured but hadn't complained.

Chandler was torn. If he allowed them treatment he would lose valuable time for questioning but denying medical help might invite a lawsuit against the force and prejudice any eventual murder trial. There was only one choice.

'After you call Doctor Harlan, call off the roadblocks,' he told Nick, weighing up whether he could leave him to escort the doctor in to treat Heath while he questioned Gabriel. He quickly decided it was too much of a risk to leave an elderly doctor and a rookie officer alone with a potential serial killer.

Chandler left a message on Mitch's answerphone, informing him that they had Gabriel in the cells. It took less than five seconds for Mitch to call back.

'Don't do anything with the prisoner, Sergeant Jenkins. Hold him until I get back. Don't let him out of your sight.'

There was a fury in the voice that Chandler remembered well, a rage at being beaten to the punch, at being outmanoeuvred. Chandler thought of himself as a morally upright, do-unto-others kind of guy, but hearing Mitch suffer provided an intoxicating burst of energy.

Mitch was a good twenty minutes away. Doctor

Harlan Adams showed up in little over two. His house was barely two hundred metres from the station, but still the local physician was out of breath on entry, leaning on the reception desk, his gut heaving as if it were one huge lung.

'So what we got?' he asked between rasped breaths.

'Sure you don't need a few minutes?'

The doctor waved this off as nonsense so Chandler carried on.

'We have two men, mid-twenties or thereabouts, both exhibiting a series of cuts and bruises, one complaining of shortness of breath and self-diagnosing a cracked rib.'

'Self-diagnosis,' squinted Harlan, shoving the glasses back up his nose to sit in the well-worn crevice near the bridge. 'Self-diagnosis is for hypochondriacs and the weak of mind, my friend. I'll bet that there's nothing wrong with him.'

'You can go see for yourself.'

'That's why I'm here.'

'But I have to warn you not to approach too closely.'

Raising one bushy eyebrow, Harlan asked, 'And why might that be?'

Chandler knew that he should warn the doctor but he also knew that Harlan would react in one of three ways: with intrigue, horror, or by treating him like a celebrity. The jail-bound patients Harlan typically dealt with were drunks and down-at-heels sporting nothing but the most superficial of wounds. And though Gabriel and Heath's injuries seemed to be of the same inconsequential level, their crimes certainly were not.

Before they entered the cells Chandler ushered him aside.

'You have to promise to keep this quiet, Harlan. Once you leave here.'

The doctor's eyes loomed large in his strong-lensed glasses.

'I mean it, Harlan. I'm telling you this for your own security, but you must keep it secret.'

'My lips are sealed.'

Chandler could only hope against hope that Harlan was telling the truth. Things had a habit of leaking out with Harlan Adams, especially after he'd had a drink, his Hippocratic Oath conquered by the temptation of sharing gossip. But he was the only medic the town had. It was hard to get a young doctor to come and live in the middle of nowhere.

After a few seconds of forced silence, Harlan's brain couldn't cope with the intrigue and charged his mouth with saying something.

'Who's been fighting, then? Someone we know? Miners? Locals? A domestic? There's so little to do around here domestic violence counts as a hobby.'

With his hand on the door, Chandler stopped the rotund man, touching the damp, sleeveless shirt. 'No, none of those. And watch yourself in here.'

The lack of amusement in Chandler's voice succeeded in tempering the doctor's spirits. At least momentarily.

'Who have you got in here? They must be *dangerous*.'

'They are,' said Chandler. 'They might be.'

*

Since Heath was the one complaining, he was first up. As Harlan checked him over Chandler stood close, ready to intervene. As loud and irritating as he was Harlan was good at his job. He set to work cleaning up Heath's face with a myriad of gauze and swabs, explaining to both his patient and bodyguard that there was nothing major to worry about, a few abrasions and a cut lip, a clean-up job only, no stitches required.

Then Harlan commenced the small talk.

'So how d'you find yourself in here?' he asked, as he swabbed a graze on Heath's cheek that had turned black with dust.

'Harlan ...' warned Chandler.

'They think—' Heath began.

'Mr Barwell, you too,' said Chandler, interrupting. 'Any chatter and I take the doc away.'

'Just watch yourself son,' said Harlan with a mischievous grin. 'Don't go ending up like Skinny Bishop. Skinny didn't think he was guilty either. But after a while in here, it turned out that, despite all the evidence – or lack of – he was!'

'Harlan, I'll take you outside right now,' said Chandler, even though he was aware that, by ordering the doctor to shut up, he lent credence to the myth and that a similar stitch-up might befall Heath.

'Who's Skinny?' asked Heath, his ruddy face looking a little panicked.

Shaking his head and chuckling away to himself, the doctor's expert hands moved to Heath's ribs, prodding them gently. Heath jerked backwards, his hands coming up as if to ward off the doctor. Chandler stepped in to subdue him, but Heath lowered them again as the doctor removed his fingers.

Only when Harlan stepped back and rubbed his smooth chin did Chandler realize that his heart was pounding in his chest.

'Bruised. *Possibly* broken,' said Harlan.

'They feel broken,' said Heath, adjusting his position and wincing.

'You'll need to uncuff him,' said Harlan.

'Why?' asked Chandler, glancing at Heath, searching for any reason to deny the request.

'I need to check his range of movement. Make sure it isn't something more serious.'

'Is that necessary?' asked Chandler.

Harlan leaned in close. 'Unless you want him to twist some way and accidentally puncture a lung.'

Chandler looked at Heath.

'Okay, get up and face the wall, Mr Barwell.'

Heath didn't need to be asked twice and stood, staring at the wall, as Chandler removed the cuffs.

Chandler turned him around. Heath's face was beaded in sweat, pain and fear. 'Now no sudden movement, or you'll be back in these, broken ribs or not.'

Heath nodded so Chandler helped him back to a seated position. This time he stayed within arm's reach of his suspect, Harlan squeezing in between them to perform his diagnosis.

Grabbing Heath's forearms Harlan raised them.

'Hold there, son.'

Heath did as ordered, looking first at the doctor, then at Chandler. Chandler felt an unease rise within him, exposed as Harlan nudged him out of the way as he made Heath twist to the side.

'Well?' asked Chandler, wanting the cuffs back on his prisoner as soon as possible.

Heath opened his mouth. Chandler waited for him to emit a gasp of pain.

Instead he rose in a flash, shoving the rotund physician into Chandler.

'Don't move!' cried Chandler as he stepped back to try and avoid the collapsing doctor. He fumbled for his gun but an uncoordinated Harlan got his legs tangled, knocking them both off balance to the hard concrete floor like a pair of unwieldy dominoes.

Heath didn't wait and bound for the door just as Nick arrived to help.

'Nick, watch—'

Heath reacted first, lowering his shoulder and barging the young constable out of the way like a rugby player gunning for the line.

He didn't count on the second wave of defence though. Mitch had appeared and, using a strength that belied his skinny frame, grabbed hold of the off-balance Heath, buckling his legs and sending him into a sprawled heap against the far wall outside of the cell. Heath's cry of anguish seemed genuine this time but Mitch didn't stop, landing on top of the suspect in an instant, pinning him down, bending his arms behind his back and causing yet more angry declarations of pain.

'Why the *fuck* is Mr Barwell not cuffed?' roared Mitch, aiming his question at Chandler.

Chandler got to his feet, leaving the doctor to get up himself. He felt like there was a spotlight on him, the stabbing beam raising the temperature in the sweltering cell through the roof.

'Harlan had to check—'

'Are you determined to lose them both? Bring 'em in, tag 'em and release 'em like they're some bloody endangered species?'

'He was complaining of chest pains. We were check—'

'It hurts,' gasped Heath, pinned underneath Mitch's well-placed knee in the back.

Mitch ignored the plea. 'Get him cuffed and in the cell, Sergeant.'

'Please, sir ... chief,' spluttered Heath, 'they're working with Gabriel to frame me. Or kill me. I know what these hicks are like. You have to help me.'

'Why did you not inform me immediately that you had Gabriel?' asked Mitch before turning to Nick who visibly cowered from the question.

'It's got nothing to do with Nick. It was my call,' said Chandler.

'I know it was, Sergeant. I was just wondering if your stupidity was infectious.'

Though locked up once again, Heath continued spouting a mixture of complaints and wild conspiracy theories. 'Inspector, your sergeant and Gabriel are working together, trying to pin the blame on me.'

Mitch responded. 'Keep the noise down in there, Mr Barwell.'

'I'm not going to go down quietly,' shouted Heath.

Mitch ignored the statement and swung towards Harlan who was resting on the bare wooden bench opposite the cells, composing himself. 'Any chance you could sedate him?' asked Mitch.

As Harlan was about to reply Mitch cut him off, 'No, scrap that. I want to question him again. But first I want Gabriel.'

Flicking open the slat in the cell door, the inspector addressed Gabriel, his tone pleasant once again, the rage quenched for now. 'How are we in there?'

As Mitch fished for initial rapport with the suspect, Chandler could see that while Gabriel remained prone on the bed he had turned to face them. His expression was still one of shock but despite this his body was perfectly still, like a snake waiting to pounce. Chandler tried to shake the comparison from his head. It was nothing more than the previous encounter with Heath playing on his mind; how easily he had been tricked. Mitch had saved him from letting another suspect escape. It left him with an oppressive feeling of debt and a sour gratitude he despised having.

'Get him out of there, Sergeant,' ordered Mitch.

Chandler did, wary of any sudden movements, raised hands or attempts to disarm him. There was no need. Gabriel was compliant, merely shooting a nervous glance in the direction of Heath's cell as he was led out and into the interview room.

Sitting him in the chair and undoing the cuffs, Chandler asked Gabriel if he needed medical attention. Mitch butted in.

'No one's seeing the doctor until I've had the chance to interview them.'

There was no protest from Gabriel, but for a brief second his eyes flashed something else other than fear: coldness, either acceptance that he would be in pain for a while, or regret at voluntarily surrendering. This would be his third interview today. This time Chandler wouldn't be attending.

'You can leave, Sergeant,' said Mitch as Chandler tucked the silver cuffs into his belt.

'But I know his story. Same as with Heath.'

Mitch glared at him with little sympathy. 'I'll use my own men. It's time for fresh ears, Sergeant.'

Chandler turned to leave. He'd watch from the booth instead. Not ideal but better than darkness.

As he reached the door Mitch called to him. 'There are a few reporters hanging around outside. As you know, like zombies, when one shows up thinking that there might be something to feed on, they'll all show up. Let me make this clear, Sergeant,' he said, raising his voice, '*I'm* the only person to speak to them, okay? Tell your people that. I've already given a statement that we have no comment to make as inquiries are ongoing and I don't want you fucking it up by saying the wrong thing. Or saying anything, for that matter.'

Luka and Jim were back. Tanya too had returned and was in the recording room prepping the equipment to capture every word and action, twisting, nudging and adjusting buttons, headphones cast off one ear like a DJ in the world's smallest, dreariest club. The tune currently on deck was Mitch's abrasive whine, talking informally to his two sidekicks Sun and MacKenzie, ignoring Gabriel at the desk. His voice came through clear, the ebb and flow of his speech pattern captured, the microphones ready to record everything from the most insubstantial detail to the last moments of someone's life. The confessional was ready.

After a few minutes, Mitch faced Gabriel and started the interview. Gabriel's story remained unchanged, Mitch digging but finding nothing but rock at every juncture.

'What farms have you been working?' he asked, his voice fluttering through the speakers like an echo from the distant past.

'Some down around Murray River, then up to Carnarvon and Exmouth. Tomato picking, fruit picking, anything, everything. There isn't a patch of this country I haven't worked, or so it feels.'

'Can anyone verify you being at any of those places?'

Gabriel shrugged. 'You can try but it was cash in hand.' He paused. 'Before you say it, I know it's not legal but if taking a bit of swag is the difference between getting a job and not then I'm going for it.'

'The lack of an alibi seems rather convenient,' said Mitch as if he were offering counsel rather than leading an interrogation.

'It's the truth,' replied Gabriel. 'I don't care how convenient it is.'

Mitch went on to question him about his parents and family. From his overhead angle Chandler watched Gabriel's calmness alter somewhat. As if a nerve had been touched. The same way it had in the car on the way to the hotel.

Gabriel explained that both his parents were dead. His brother as well. An uncle and aunt too.

'Death seems to follow you around,' said Mitch. Though his back was to the camera, Chandler imagined a grin worming on to Mitch's face, a low blow, an attempt to shatter the ice from Gabriel's veins.

After letting it linger Mitch continued, 'How did *they* die?'

Gabriel said nothing. His body remained still, but his eyes were fixed. Even from afar the look unnerved Chandler.

'They died in a car crash,' said Gabriel.

Mitch's nod lacked any empathy, treating it as just another piece to the puzzle. 'And since then?'

'Since then I've been wandering, Inspector. Blowing around on the wind.'

'Very poetic,' said Mitch, not hiding his sarcasm.

'No. Just very true,' said Gabriel, now irritated.

Mitch had succeeded. He had hooked the suspect and was now reeling him in through the dark, muddy waters towards the shore.

But they still had no idea what they'd caught.

20

Gabriel sat back, his story relayed for the third time. Mitch immediately insisted on a repeat.

That was enough for Chandler. The same story four times in one day was something he could do without so he exited the booth to the belly of the station. Mitch's team was working without respite, displaying an impressive work ethic but a distinct lack of individualism, clones of their erstwhile leader.

Chandler found himself drawn to his own team: Jim, Luka and Nick milling around the front desk watching on, Tanya locked in the booth, likely to be there for another hour at least listening to the rerun.

'Is this police work?' asked Jim, looking at Mitch's team scurry around. As ever it was hard to tell if he were being serious or exercising his dry sense of humour.

'*Serious* police work,' replied Luka.

'Do we get involved?' asked Jim.

Chandler responded. 'If you want to. You might have to force your way in, though.'

'I've always liked a challenge,' said Luka.

Chandler thought that if anyone were going to worm his way in, it would be Luka. He was the most opportunistic amongst them.

Behind them Nick removed his headphones. 'Sarge?'

'Yeah, Nick, you can try too.'

'No, it's not that, Sarge. Ken's called in. Says there's something burning up in the woods behind Turtle's.'

'How far?'

'He says, and I quote: "Far enough that I'm not fucking checking it out."'

Chandler wondered if it was the place they were looking for.

'I'll go,' said Chandler.

'I'll come too,' volunteered Nick.

'No, you stay here.'

The young officer slumped back into his chair.

'Luka, Jim, who wants to go?' asked Chandler.

Jim raised one eyebrow and glanced at Luka, his expression suggesting that he had no desire to trek through Gardner's Hill in the height of summer.

'Looks like I'm up,' said Luka, grinning.

Disappearing from the station was easy with everyone occupied. With Luka driving, they sped out of town towards the Hill. Leaning forward to peer out the front window, Chandler couldn't spot any smoke on the hillside and hoped this wasn't Ken getting petty revenge for earlier. He wouldn't put it past the wiry old bastard.

As he continued his search for a trace of smoke, Luka spoke up.

'I know you don't think so, but I think he's done a good job.'

'Who?'

'The inspector. He's come in, taken charge, got shit done.'

'And pissed off a lot of people.'

'Mainly you, Sarge.'

Chandler ignored the comment.

'Sometimes you're a bit too soft,' continued Luka.

'You want me to treat you like robots?'

'Sometimes the law has to be tough. People respect that. They need that.'

Chandler glanced over at his young colleague. 'What self-help management shit did you steal that from?'

'It's true. Sometimes people have to see us use some force.'

Chandler was left disappointed that another of his crew had been impressed by Mitch but in Luka's case Chandler could see the appeal, the same naked ruthlessness in both to get ahead. There was no doubt Luka was a good officer, eager to learn, eager to do, but he also exhibited a recklessness that seeped into his private life. He had already gone through most of the eligible women in the town like a particularly virulent flu. Each of his crew fostered a clique they mined for information: Tanya, the eager tongues of the mothers' circle; Jim, the wet, blue-collar tongues down in the Black Stump and Luka with his female twenty-something brigade, which he was slowly alienating by dating then dumping. Chandler got the impression that Luka thought he could walk on water.

They were a kilometre south of Turtle's when Chandler spotted it, smoke rising into the sky deep in the scrub forest, the grey hand of a drowning victim waving for help above the surface of the trees. Anticipation rose in his chest. He tried to still it, reminding himself that it could be nothing and directed Luka a further ten kilometres down the road to the hidden entrance to Bluff's Bluff – a joke name from a former mayor who refused to let a dirt track be named after him.

They wound uphill, the car struggling on the rough, hairpin bends, increasing altitude, with the thin line of smoke passing in and out of view.

Chandler ordered Luka to park short of the car park. Getting out he prepared to hike into the scrubland his two suspects claimed to have scrambled through. He hauled on a backpack filled with water and other essentials. He didn't expect to be up here overnight but he wasn't going to get caught out.

Donning his own pack, Luka asked him, 'So which one do you believe?'

'We've been through this, Luka. First we get some evidence and then—'

'Your gut feeling, Sarge,' interrupted Luka. 'We all have a gut feeling. I'm picking Heath. He came in at gunpoint, was caught trying to steal the car, attacked you and the doc. It all points to a certain cunning, an ability to plan and the temper necessary to murder.'

Chandler drew the straps of his backpack tight. He was trying to ignore Luka but the young officer had some valid points. He had experienced first hand the menace

Heath offered but despite all of the arrows pointing to Heath, he couldn't rule out Gabriel. His varied demeanour from bag of nerves to icy calm nagged at him.

As he considered this Luka got the jump on him, bounding into the woods like a bloodhound on the trail, the impatient Sydney boy coming to the fore, the city he had grown up in before his artist parents moved out West for peace, quiet and inspiration. Luka had told him more than once that he was impatient to return to the city – or somewhere that boasted more than one nightclub anyway – and had been applying for jobs to get out. As he stepped to the side of the road, Chandler couldn't help but think that it was another reminder of Mitch, another reminder of the last time he was here.

They set off into the woods to look for whatever was on fire.

It proved difficult, the outback offering no reference points, leaving them to follow the wisps of rising smoke, barely visible at this angle above the trees.

On they went, fighting the waning daylight, struggling over rocks, boulders and fallen trees, discovering no recently dug graves nor ridges over which to tumble.

On the way, Luka advanced another theory he had been developing: that someone could still be in the shack, a partner or another victim. If the killer had locked up one then he could have another tied up for later, like hanging meat to cure; a store for the winter. Though only another of Luka's fanciful speculations it sped Chandler on, aiming for the smoke drifting above the trees. The land was eerily silent: no cicadas or crickets singing as if they had all gone quiet in anticipation of a gruesome discovery. It was unnerving, like the hush of a crowd before the jury delivered their verdict. So much so that Chandler welcomed the hiss of the radio interrupting the silence, right up until Mitch's voice erupted from the white noise. Their escape had been noticed, their destination and the possible importance of it raising alarms.

'Chandler, this is Mitchell.'

Gone were the formalities, a sliver of panic in Mitch's voice.

'Don't you do anything to that site. We're on our way.'

21

Chandler came upon little more than a smouldering pile of ash, the stunted remains of the walls poking up from the ground, charred black like matchsticks burned to the tip. He spied a small cast-metal water tank, about fifty metres from the ruined shack, perched on a self-built nest, weeds winding up and around the arms, using their support to reach for the sky. Despite the very deliberate order not to disturb anything, he couldn't just let it carry on burning and destroy any evidence that might be left.

'Luka, over here,' he said, running towards the tank. 'Can you climb it?'

His brash young constable wasn't one to resist a challenge. Casting off his backpack, he climbed swiftly up to the nest, the structure surprisingly solid despite its age and disrepair. With Luka in place, Chandler handed him one of the rusted buckets that sat at the foot of the tower and in return was passed down a full one, water slopping over the sides and soaking his clothes.

Chucking the contents of the bucket into the smouldering mix, ash and smoke exploded out and around him like dry ice at a concert. Coughing up some rancid ash, he returned to the tank for a refill.

Back and forth he went with bucket after bucket, dampening sections of the buildings in turn, trying to avoid being scorched by the heat and random flicker of flames that popped out of nowhere.

Blinded by the searing heat and intense light he struggled to the tank.

'Is there much left?' he asked, spitting out ash that had dried out his tongue.

'Half. Plenty,' shouted Luka as Chandler returned to the embers, turning his head to the side and casting the water on to another smouldering patch, the ash whipping up and away, revealing what looked to be charred metal remains flashing in the waning sunlight. The discovery drove Chandler on, his eyes stinging, and after about half an hour he had the fire under control. The pair of impromptu firefighters exchanged congratulatory pats on the back, Chandler's blackened paws smearing his colleague's sweaty shirt in dark handprints. What lay in front of them didn't look like much, but they had saved whatever was left.

Chandler stepped to the edge. Peering into the warm sludge he could see twisted metal. It would need to cool a little more before he could handle it.

'Arson?' asked Luka.

'Hard to know for sure but looks like it.'

The fire had been savage, destroying whatever dwelling this had been, but though the surrounding trees had been scorched by the flames the fire had remained localized, the parched wooden slats acting as kindling.

Chandler knew that they were lucky that it hadn't started a major bushfire.

Grabbing an already charred branch he began to circle the ruins, combing through the debris, discovering chunks of metal that had resisted the heat of the flames: right-angled joints of a table or workbench, a saw that had welded with the heat to a hatchet to create an unwieldy instrument. Fishing into the mess with his stick, he looped it through a set of manacles, the chain-links solidified, and dragged them out on to the ground to cool.

Stepping around the cabin, carbonized wood and paper floated on the thermal draught, suspended in the air, too heavy to float away but too light to fall back to earth. Chandler reached out for a few pieces but they crumbled into dust.

He swept the stick through the debris again, whipping up a whirlwind of soot. Something yellowed and singed at the edges made a break for freedom. Paper. He grabbed it at the second attempt, delicately, trying not to damage it further. Another careful sweep of a corner, where the wall had not quite burned to the ground, brought a second piece, fuller than the first. Pretty soon he had recovered a number of documents – including something very important, Heath's missing driving licence, the plastic surviving the inferno better than the paper. The name had burned away, but Heath's face stared back at him in black and white, unsmiling, almost sullen. Like a mug shot.

*

Mitch and his team arrived suddenly, appearing from the woods like Marines on a covert mission, armed with evidence bags and latex gloves. It had taken them barely forty-five minutes.

Rather than grateful, Mitch was angry. Chandler expected nothing less.

'What did you do?' he said, accusing Chandler.

'Put the fire out. We had to make sure there wasn't another victim in there.'

'And is there?' spat Mitch.

'No, but there's some paper—'

Mitch grabbed Chandler's shoulder and pulled him aside, the contact unexpected and unwelcome, crossing an unspoken line for a brief second before letting go.

'You should have informed me of the call, Sergeant. Like it or not, I am your superior officer and in charge of this investigation. Any fuck-ups will fall back on me and I'm not prepared to let that happen. It's not how I work.'

'I dealt with it how I saw fit,' said Chandler, standing his ground.

'You deal with it how *I* see fit, Sergeant. Understand? And if that means coming to me to get the go-ahead to have a piss, then that's what you do. Everything runs through *me*. You made your decision to stay here, Chandler. That was up to you. Don't let jealousy cloud your decisions.'

'No, Mitch, you *think* I'm jealous. I chose to have a family, you chose to have a career.'

This received only a grin from his opponent. 'Maybe I have both,' said Mitch.

'What do you mean?'

Mitch didn't reply. Was he intimating that he had a family? His cousins had said nothing about marriage or a family when he'd last seen them. He certainly wasn't sporting a ring on his finger but of course that proved nothing. Chandler wondered why he cared. Mitch was – had been – ten years and hundreds of kilometres removed from his life. It was only this unfortunate series of events that had brought them into contact again.

'Let's get back to work,' said Mitch, markedly pointing at Chandler and then to the trees. 'Go put a cordon around—'

A loud *pop* interrupted them, causing Mitch to stumble backwards and reach for his holster. Something black soared into the air and landed beside Mitch's crew who were busy logging the evidence Chandler had dragged from the wreckage. The charred object smoked at their feet, an exploded aerosol can which had successfully escaped the cabin.

'You might want to question it,' said Chandler, making for the trees.

He wound the yellow and blue tape around the clutch of nearby eucalyptus trees and watched Mitch's team fish more scraps from the blanket of ash, Luka welcomed into the fold as one of them. As the minions combed through the debris, the master prowled the outskirts, an iPhone pressed to his lips recording his thoughts and observations, while Roper, a muscular guy whose mouth hooked

downwards in a permanent scowl, recorded every movement with a video camera.

After all immediately visible evidence was marked
with cones or tags, Mitch organized his team to start
at one side and carefully sift through the ash, spreading
slowly but thoroughly over the ground. A few more
shreds of paper were discovered, including a fragment
of a map, the lack of contour lines suggesting an area
of flat ground rather than the hill they were on. With
the preliminary search completed Mitch extended the
remit from evidence only to indications of how the fire
started; for containers of flammable liquid, or unusual
distribution of fuel, like piles of newspapers or furniture
pushed together. They hunted for incendiary devices –
aerosol can aside – lighters, matches or even some form
of timing device. They fished more metal from the ashy
mulch, including the rest of the chain-links, one roughly
shorn through, the clean cut indicating that it had been
hacked through rather than cracking in the heat.

Next they moved on to the job that would prolong
their stay deep into the night – finding traces of people
who had been there, voluntarily or otherwise: hairs,
fibres, fingerprints, blood, bodily fluids. The fire would
have destroyed much of it but Chandler knew that Mitch
wouldn't give up easily. He ordered Chandler to return to
the cars and retrieve more evidence kits. It was a menial
task, for someone of a lesser rank, but Mitch took great
pains in picking Chandler out.

As Chandler left to trek back to the cars, Mitch was
geeing up his troops, the calm, assured inspector that had

sauntered into Wilbrook station beginning to melt under the pressure, his side parting plastered to his scalp, the wet look undiminished even in the heat. It was as if he was oozing sweat solely from the top of his head, his face still unnaturally dry, as if the pores had been plugged up with bitterness.

22

2002

Mitch swept his lank hair back into place, each strand like a sailor clinging to the deck of their sinking ship. 'Come on! Come on! No time for rest,' he announced. 'Another kilometre and we'll stop for the day.'

The volunteers were crowded around a huge red sandstone rock that looked out of place amongst the trees, a beacon in the desert, vegetation using the abundant shade to grow at its feet. The volunteers were also taking advantage of the protection from a sun that was lowering in the sky, gaining pace every minute as if being reeled in by the horizon.

'Five minutes,' pleaded one.

'You can rest all evening,' said Mitch. 'Martin might still be out here.'

It was Mitch's fallback motivational tool: the lure of Martin. But Chandler knew that there was only one reason his colleague now wanted to find Martin. The one that Mitch had confessed to in the last few days and which had caused the drastic change in his attitude: Mitch wanted to be known as the officer who found the teenager – alive or dead – and to get his name in the paper.

From that side he didn't have much competition. Only Chandler, in fact. The search for Martin had been scaled back, resources diverted to the gruesome murder of a trucker in Port Hedland a couple of days ago. Chandler's and Mitch's roles had subtly – and unofficially – changed too. Given that the chance of finding Martin was minuscule, their main job was now to keep the volunteers and family from meeting a similar fate.

But with this command came the authority. The option to call off the search. That morning – day thirteen in total and the second day of this leg – Chandler had broached the topic with Mitch who had immediately stated that they had to keep going.

The phony enthusiasm was grating. Mitch was hunting glory in others' despair and Chandler had told him as much. Chandler believed he was at least being honest with his intentions; the quicker they found Martin – or his remains – the quicker he could get back to Teri. There had been another argument with his folks the night before last, and another long night of her tears and cursing that he had to go away for another three days on this bloody search. Teri was sorry that the guy was dead but she wanted Chandler with her.

To rouse the troops Arthur launched into one of his well-intentioned but overemotional prayers, the old jack-in-the-box cranked up one more time, the springs now worn. He cajoled the remaining volunteers to keep pushing and only succeeded in getting their hackles up.

As they set off Chandler took Arthur aside and reminded him that he and Mitch were the professionals.

'I'm sorry. I know,' said Arthur, wiping what Chandler couldn't tell was sweat or tears from his eyes. 'I know you're the professionals but your calm logic also needs some heart.'

'We have heart,' said Chandler. 'No one would be out here if they didn't.'

The old man nodded for his youngest son to go on ahead. Only after a second, firmer insistence did he go, the roles switched, the boy acting as his father's guardian rather than the other way around.

Free now, Arthur walked alongside Chandler in silence for a few seconds before he sniffed a choked laugh. 'We're all a lot like Martin, you know.'

'How so?' said Chandler, peering into the scrub beside him, expecting nothing and finding exactly that.

'Out here ... slowly getting lost. We're all no more than one, maybe two hours from walking into the wilderness and disappearing.'

Chandler's concern for Arthur's mental well-being grew. 'What makes you say that?'

'It's the truth.'

'If you're not feeling okay ... ?'

The old man shook his head. 'There's nothing wrong with me apart from the blisters and the sunburn. It's just the weariness talking, the finding nothing, stepping on the dead every step we take: dead plants, dead animals, dead earth.'

He turned to face Chandler. 'I know you don't want me offering prayers and blabbering on, but they have nothing to do with motivating the others. They're about motivating me.'

Chandler watched Arthur pace off to join his son. Then he took up station at the rear with Mitch.

'It's time to call this off, Mitch.'

His partner was incredulous. 'What? It's only been two weeks.'

'Yeah and the dad's about to collapse, the boy's practically a zombie, more volunteers are quitting every day. I'm more a grief counsellor than policeman.'

'We'll go on as long as the family want to try.'

'That's not realistic and you know it.'

'Are you going to tell him?' asked Mitch and leaned in closer. 'If we find him, then his death will result in something positive, it will mean something.'

Chandler shook his head. 'To you. It already means something to that family.'

'Yeah,' replied Mitch, 'but if we give up now it was all a bit pointless, wasn't it? Walking into the unknown. And don't give me that newspaper shit about a soon-to-be adult going on Walkabout. A Walkabout has meaning to it, not just a depressed kid seeking annihilation.'

'You say that, but you didn't know him, maybe this was his Walkabout, his transformation into an adult.'

'Is that what Teri's going to do to you? Turn you into an adult?'

'Let it go, Mitch.'
Mitch shook his head. 'Giving up on life.'
'No, the opposite.'
'You can't be sure of that, Chandler. Not 'til you've gone through it.'

23

The light was fast disappearing, but Mitch had come prepared, his team erecting a series of searchlights around the site. Chandler watched from the sidelines as more scraps of metal and paper were sifted from the ash, fingers black with soot, searching for the tiniest shard of evidence that could definitively point to what had happened here.

Mitch stalked past, focused on nothing but the scene, recording details on his iPhone.

'Are you going to run shifts?' asked Chandler.

'Run what?' scowled Mitch, frustrated at being interrupted.

'Run us in shifts, to keep going through the night.'

Mitch paused. 'No. My team can take it. You can head home.'

'You really that pig-headed?'

'Go home, Sergeant. Get some rest. You've had a long day.'

With that Mitch walked away. Chandler had been given the brush-off. He considered staying on anyway to help retrieve what they could from the ruin but an evening with his kids and a warm bed was better than a cold night up here trawling through the debris. Let these arseholes do it. Even if they managed to find something to charge one of the suspects, all Mitch was going to be able to charge them with was kidnapping, maybe attempted murder at a stretch. Nothing more. Not until they located the graves. And that was work for a new day and fresh daylight.

As he passed the yellow glare of the lamps, Chandler watched Flo fish something from the wreckage. A piece of metal, charred but still in one piece, unmistakably the figure of Christ, free from the wooden cross that once held him, arms spread out, a reminder to Chandler that both suspects had mentioned a cross in their statements and that waiting at home, was a young girl nervous about her First Confession. Suddenly, he couldn't wait to get back home to see her.

First though he dropped by the now eerily empty station. Only Tanya and Nick were on duty, Tanya completing paperwork and Nick drumming a solo on the front desk. Both reported the all-quiet from the cells, their prisoners coming to terms with the fact that there was no point complaining now, they were stuck there for the night.

The brief check-in completed, Chandler drove home and was disappointed to find that the kids were already in bed. It was a disappointment shared by his mum – at him for not coming home earlier.

She met him at the door, her blonde hair striated with grey, falling long and straight back over her shoulders, perfectly set despite the late hour. She was a Wilbrook girl through and through, her humour as dry as the land she'd grown up on.

'I'll go in and see them,' said Chandler.

She stood in the way, arms out like the metal Jesus rescued from the fire. 'No, don't wake them,' she said, her voice squeaked but assertive.

'I won't.'

'They were angry with you. For not coming home.'

This only made Chandler want to see them more. 'I was held up. There was nothing I could do about it.'

'Caroline, stop it.' His dad's voice floated in from the living room, the voice of calm. 'The boy not being here isn't the reason they were angry.'

From this angle it appeared the old beige armchair was talking, ink marks from thumbing the newspaper staining the side. Most wives might have been angry at the mess but Chandler knew his mum was glad to see them, for if Peter was planted in the seat he could get up to no mischief. In the past she had tried to scrub the ink marks off but as soon as she did another set would magically appear, more pronounced, the artist creating a new picture over the shadow of the last.

Using the arms as support his dad stood up. Now in his late sixties, whatever hair he had was disappearing, his face lined like a relief map, a pointed nose dominating his features. It offered the impression that he was a harsh man but nothing could have been further from the truth.

He was a puppy, as excited and curious about life as he had been sixty years ago.

'They were angry because of the First Confession thing—' began his dad.

'Mass,' corrected his mum.

'Mass has been cancelled. The other kids are blaming you cause you're in charge.'

'Not with Mitch around,' muttered Chandler.

'And how is young Mitchell Andrews?' asked his mum.

The last thing Chandler wanted to talk about was Mitch, so he shrugged and pretended he didn't know.

'If he's come to town something major's taking place,' she added.

'I'll sleep here, if that's okay,' said Chandler, changing the subject. Though both suspects were locked up tight and it would have taken just two minutes to return home, he wanted to sleep under the same roof as his kids tonight.

His mum's inquisitive expression broke into a beaming smile. 'Do you want some food?'

'No, it's okay.'

'I'll make you something,' she said, pushing him towards the kitchen.

Chandler made for the marshmallowy sofa that swallowed him up into its brushed-white goodness. Unable to sleep he reviewed the evidence behind his eyelids. He had two suspects who were pretty much mirror opposites: a scared Gabriel Johnson, the tremor in his voice implying nerves but also possessing an unnerving silky quality, a voice that could no doubt persuade an eager hitch-hiker into a car. But if he *were* the kidnapper and killer, why had he escaped only to come back and let himself get captured? More likely he wanted to be the Good Samaritan and stop Heath from killing again. A Heath who was loud and vehement and violent, denying everything apart from stealing a car and protesting even being under the same roof as Gabriel. If his was an act it was very convincing, again the kind of acting that might persuade a nervous hiker to get into a car with them. Though Gabriel had in effect surrendered twice, Heath hadn't voluntarily done anything.

They were physical opposites as well, Gabriel tall and reedy, Heath short and stocky. Both sported the unmistakable tan associated with working outdoors. Both were parentless with negligible contact to any remaining siblings; through choice in Heath's case, through death in Gabriel's. Chandler didn't have enough to favour either as a main suspect so both had to be. And if both were, then there was the possibility that they had been working as a partnership until another, as yet undefined, event caused them to break ranks. Was that why they were so scared of each other? Because each knew what the other was capable of?

The shack also bothered him. The evidence found so far pointed to it being the place where the murders took place, or at least where the victims were kept chained, but how had it caught fire? An accident? The sun's rays magnified on to a stack of paper? Maybe when they were in pursuit of each other a gas heater had been knocked over and turned the shack into an inferno. But why would there be a need for a gas heater to be on in this heat? That left the theory that the killer had purposely set the fire. Possibly an incendiary device set by timer to go off if he/they didn't return by a certain time? And if so, when? Heath – in the time between Gabriel entering the station and being led in at the end of Ken's shotgun? Or Gabriel – after sneaking out of the hotel and trekking back up the Hill to destroy the evidence? But how could Gabriel make it there? And why return and give himself up at the station? Why not set it ablaze and then run?

The gaps in time and motive were frying Chandler's already addled brain but it wasn't about to let him stop. A final thought nudged its way in. What if they *weren't* working with each other but had a third partner helping them with their crimes?

That opened up a whole new avenue. Chandler needed something to narrow the possibilities down. He'd always preferred working within set parameters. That was why he'd stayed in Wilbrook. The town and his kids were like his sun, their gravitational pull meaning that he couldn't, and didn't want to, stray too far from them.

Though it was 3am, one of his suns wandered into the kitchen. Sarah, in her nightgown, poked her head in the fridge without spotting him. She was growing fast, almost the same height as her mother already, with the same high cheekbones and narrow face. Those she could have as long as she didn't inherit her mother's disposition.

She didn't even try to be quiet as she pulled the milk out, the fridge door slamming and the glass rattling on the counter. She was hindered as ever by her insistence on using her phone at the same time as she was trying to do something else.

'You can't be texting someone at this hour?' he said.

She gasped, the milk that was until now finding the glass making a break for freedom.

'Shi—' started Sarah then stopped.

'You'll have to confess that,' said Chandler.

His daughter resumed pouring.

'Will I? Is it going ahead?' She looked back down and the tapping on the phone recommenced.

'We'll see.'

She didn't respond.

'Who are you texting at this time?' he asked, curious and a little concerned.

'No one. I'm pre-texting.'

'Pre—?'

'For tomorrow,' said Sarah. 'Wait . . .'

She held the phone at arm's length and took a selfie. Of her holding a glass of milk. Chandler didn't understand why. Maybe he wasn't meant to. Maybe this was what passed for entertainment these days. And that was okay, he supposed. His notion of entertainment was probably just as foreign to her. A bottle of beer and some sport on the TV after the kids had gone to bed: cricket, golf, AFL, he didn't care. Sometimes he could watch a whole game and not know the score at the end, his mind cleared and his gut that little bit larger.

Sarah finished taking the selfie and was studying the results.

'Are you angry with me?' asked Chandler.

The pause suggested that she was.

'Naw,' she said, her jet black hair washing around her face.

'Sarah?'

Escaping the sofa's clutches he met her in the kitchen where she had sped her way through half the glass.

'I know you're disappointed.'

She tossed her head from side to side as if her brain were a Magic 8-Ball and she was calling on it for an answer. 'They think that it's your fault. That you stopped Confession from happening.'

'We had to stop it.'

'Why?' she said. He could hear a trace of bitterness in her voice.

'There was a chance I wouldn't be there.'

'Why?' she asked. 'And *only* you wouldn't be there? You always told us not to be selfish.'

Chandler smiled. Put that way it did sound selfish, postponing the entire event because he had other plans.

'It is selfish, but I'm not going to miss something as big as your First Confession because I've got an investigation.'

'What did they do?'

'We're not sure. He hasn't confessed his sins. We haven't *made* him confess his sins. But we will,' he added, determined, as if trying to convince his daughter that he was capable. 'And even if the Mass doesn't happen on Sunday, it'll happen another time.'

'Part of God's plan then?'

'Only God can tell you that.'

A smile returned to her face so, with the glass of milk empty, he gently nudged her in the direction of her bedroom. Within seconds she was back on her phone, thumbs tracing crazy patterns on the touchscreen, updating her status in as few words as possible. It was easy to see her being seduced by the wonders of the big, bad world outside this hole in the hedge. It worried him. Worried him that the chance to go and live in Port Hedland with her mother would appeal to her. If that was the case he was unsure if he could – or even wanted to – stop her.

24

Morning arrived with the typical regret over lack of sleep. Crawling off the sofa Chandler was gone before the house stirred.

Entering the station, Jim was wedged behind the front desk, looking awkward as he always did out front, one finger bashing loudly on the keyboard. As Chandler nodded his welcome Jim pointed towards the back office. Bathed in fluorescent light, was Mitch, his head down and paying little attention to his arrival.

Chandler approached the office. He doubted that Mitch would brief him on what he had missed, but he had a duty to ask. As he stepped closer, what had looked to be deep study of the files in front of him was in fact Mitch talking quietly into the iPhone. Chandler sidled up to the door hoping to eavesdrop on the case.

'It's going,' said Mitch, before pausing. Chandler realized that rather than dictating, he was having a conversation. 'No, I haven't seen them yet, why would I? I'm here to work.'

Chandler's conscience told him to step away from the

door but whoever was on the other end was giving Mitch shit and this was too good to pass up.

'No ... Yes, I'm fine with the kids being ready made.'

An odd statement. Mitch must have thought so too, glancing up after he said it and finding Chandler lurking outside his door. For the first time since he had returned, Mitch looked nervous, his limbs jerking, reverting back to the nervy, gangly teenager Chandler remembered. The one with some empathy and compassion.

There was an audible and insistent hiss from the other end of the phone, the caller still on the line. He waited for Mitch to acknowledge his presence and then return to his call but he did neither, frozen, the dull electronic squawk from the other end growing louder.

Finally Mitch spoke.

'I'll talk to you later,' he mumbled into the phone and hung up. Now off the phone the authoritativeness quickly returned. 'Yes?'

'Morning,' said Chandler.

'Is it?' said Mitch with a scowl, rubbing his face in his palms, emphasizing the fact that he had been up throughout the night.

'Find anything last night at the site?'

His wry smile suggested success. But a subtle response wasn't going to be enough for Mitch. Undertaking a quick scan of the cluttered desk, he presented an evidence bag.

'Take a look.'

It was a scrap of paper like the couple Chandler had found floating amongst the ash, but this section seemed to be particularly well preserved, containing what he made out as a list of hand-scribbled words marked 'named at the Beginning' at the top.

'From the crime scene,' said Mitch, stating the obvious. 'We're trying to find out if it's a list of the people he's killed.'

'Are they all listed as missing persons?'

Mitch's smile dipped momentarily. 'Some. We're checking.'

'How many?'

'It's early days.'

'So it *could* be a list of anything.' Chandler was getting used to throwing water on fires.

'We just haven't found the connection yet, Sergeant. The potentials are from different parts of the country.'

'You should have called me in,' said Chandler.

The response was sharp. 'Now you know how that feels.'

'I thought we weren't being petty.'

'We aren't, but you need to spend time with that family of yours.'

'How is that your business?' asked Chandler.

Mitch closed his eyes. 'It just seems like you spend the bulk of your time in here babysitting this lot.'

'They're a good bunch.'

Mitch screwed his face up. 'There may be hope for Luka, but Tanya's too old, Jim's too dim, and Nick ... well he doesn't stop rabbiting on like he's got to get everything in his head out.'

'He'll make a good officer.'

'Maybe, if he'd shut up and let his brain do the thinking.'

With that Mitch tucked his mobile into his pocket and turned to his laptop.

'So what's happening today?' asked Chandler.

'I'm going to put the discovery of the list to our two suspects. See what we can stir up. Someone set that blaze on purpose. We found a bottle of camping gas with a wire leading to a now destroyed battery. Deliberate and premeditated, not particularly smart but certainly effective.'

Chandler watched from the recording booth as Mitch read out the list to each suspect in turn. Names, ages, places of birth of the three they had linked to the missing person's database. It drew a blank reaction from both. Next, he tried descriptions but again received nothing. With each non-reaction Mitch probed deeper, divulging names of parents and siblings, loved ones, dangling the hook to make them comprehend what they'd done. He crowded their space, leaning in so close that Chandler was wary that they might attack but every time he got up to leave the booth, Mitch would back off, almost as if he were toying with Chandler rather than the suspect.

Despite the pressure tactics Mitch came up empty, both suspects sticking to their story, professing their innocence. Neither had heard of these people and just wanted to be freed.

After spending an hour with each man, Mitch stormed out, frustration etched on his face.

'Nothing new?' asked Chandler as Tanya began to

shut down the equipment. All that was left was to review the evidence again, trek up to the shack, or track down a witness who might be able to place Heath or Gabriel at the scene of a disappearance.

'Do you think he's robbing them?' asked Tanya, as they left the booth.

Chandler turned to her. 'What do you mean?'

'Kidnapping them, torturing them to reveal their details and then stripping their accounts?'

'Nothing we've seen points to a financial motive. It's obvious that neither have access to great means, given how they were dressed.'

'So if it's not money, what is it? Revenge? Bloodlust?'

'Maybe just plain lust,' said Chandler. 'A sex game gone wrong?'

Stalking around the office as if spoiling for a fight, Mitch shot Chandler down immediately. 'There's no evidence from either suspect of anything like that taking place. We didn't find any implements or devices of that nature in the wreckage either.'

'Nothing except the stick up your arse,' replied Chandler.

A hush fell over the office.

Mitch finally broke the silence, turning to the office. 'What we have here is a partnership,' he announced, 'or a former partnership. Each is now trying to frame the other.'

'I've already considered that,' interrupted Chandler. 'There's nothing to connect them—'

'Other than the crime scene and their matching stories?' said Mitch. 'No, there *was* a partnership and there *was* a falling-out. It caused a disagreement and each blamed the other. It explains why their stories are so similar.'

'I don't see them working together. They're scared of—' started Chandler but Mitch had already moved on and was lecturing one of his team, MacKenzie, a young man who looked barely old enough to shave. Or maybe he had been cowed enough by his boss to regress back to being childlike. Mitch was instructing him to organize a press conference with the vultures outside.

What Chandler had been about to say had been playing on his mind for a while but the discussion with Tanya had brought it to the fore. If Gabriel and Heath were in fact working together as some sort of dual killing machine and then had a falling-out, each would have a different story of how they got to the woods, stories conjured up independently of each other. Mitch might have thought himself smart but Mitch was wrong. He was being driven by the story rather than the evidence. One of them, and *only* one of them was the true victim and the killer was piggy-backing their story. There was no other explanation.

25

The press conference began, Mitch on the steps of the police station, flanked by his cronies, his suit freshly brushed, staring the reporters down.

It was surreal to watch Mitch parade in front of what Chandler had come to think of as his station, even though he was nothing more than a cog in the machine. A bigger cog had taken his place.

As he spoke, cameras flashed and reporters jostled for prime microphone position, each trying to grab the perfect sound bite from the circus that had rolled into town, fuelled by social media rumours and the road-blocks put up.

Mitch answered the questions fired at him, focusing on each interrogator, a born politician. He was all smiles and nods, his hands moving decisively to try and instil a sense of assuredness into the proceedings. He was good at talking without saying anything.

'As I'm sure you can appreciate, I cannot give too many details at this stage – '

Because you don't know too many, thought Chandler.

'– because it is too early to discuss certain aspects of an ongoing investigation. All I can tell you is that we are currently detaining a pair of individuals who are assisting us with our inquiries.'

Cameras and microphones jostled back and forth in front of Mitch like seaweed on a heavy tide.

'Inquiries into what?' shot a question from the mass.

The question elicited another winning smile. 'When the time comes you can be sure I will inform you of the details.'

One difficult question batted away. The next one was bowled.

'Is it true that one of the suspects escaped, and was that why you set up the roadblocks? Did you in fact have a suspect on the loose, Inspector, and did you fail to inform the local population of that fact?'

Mitch snorted. 'Nothing as sinister as that. The person we were seeking at that stage had no means of contacting us, and so it was decided that a series of roadblocks was the only suitable option to secure contact with him. So, nothing sinister. I don't need the press spreading fear and rumours around town.'

As much as he despised Mitch, Chandler had to admit there was real skill in the way he handled the crowd.

Thanking them all for coming, Mitch reminded the reporters to respect the job that the police now had to do. He signed off by wishing them all luck in finding places to stay for the night, joking with one blonde, Port Hedland-based reporter in particular, that she might have to sleep in her news van. *He's making friends*, thought Chandler, *friends in all the right places*.

But Mitch wasn't entirely finished.

'As a final note can I just point out that all future enquiries should be directed to Sergeant Chandler Jenkins over there,' said Mitch, pointing to Chandler, 'who, of course we all know is the head of this local branch.'

With that Mitch walked off, leaving Chandler as the designated – and reluctant – post box.

26

2002

Sixteen days in and the police involvement had been scaled back once again. From six, now Chandler and Mitch were left with a base support of two, Sylvia and Arthur tearing strips off them and the force in general for giving up on their son, that they paid their taxes for this miserable effort.

By now the distance covered every day had decreased and it wasn't just the fault of the rough terrain. The disease of false leads had struck, hope spotted in every disturbed rock or patch of soil, any fragment of civilization treated as evidence that Martin passed by recently.

Though he understood the desire to find their son, Chandler didn't really comprehend the desperation, how it clawed at the family and gouged out any remaining logic from Arthur, an intelligent man who had spent his life perched behind a desk but was now thrown into the outback in the middle of summer, on what was turning into a fruitless hunt for his child. Though Chandler had grown close to the old man, he tried to distance him-self emotionally, which was easier said than done with the kid hanging around, needing constant supervision, wandering off without care and only returning to the fold when barked at. This remained an adventure for him, better than school could ever be. His enthusiasm should have been infectious but those days were long gone. Logic dictated that the boy be left behind in town where it was safe, but logic was in short supply.

'He's doing nothing other than get in the way,' Chandler admitted to Mitch.

'What do you suggest then? Tie him to a tree and pick him up later?'

Chandler shrugged his shoulders. 'Maybe. Shit, I am turning into you!'

'I'm proud you've seen sense,' said Mitch.

'But not quite you.'

'Not quite. I'd have shot the little bastard in the leg so we'd have left him behind already.'

Mitch followed this with a piercing laugh, just unbal-anced enough to make it difficult to tell if he were joking or not. Chandler decided he didn't want to know.

They came across a creek that wound through the dusty rocks, raising its silvery tail occasionally to make a brief appearance on earth before slithering back to cooler depths.

The small group crowded around it, staring at it in wonder. It was the first hint of running water they had seen in three days. They'd lost another three volunteers *when they had returned to town last time, people who had lives and work to return to. Life carried on, Chandler reflected, with or without Martin.*

'Should we fill up the bottles?' asked Arthur.

'I'd be wary of drinking it,' said Chandler.

'Why?' asked the boy, waving the toe of his dusty trainer over the surface of the water.

'Never know what's leached into it. Might have picked up some mercury from the rocks and that's very bad for you.'

The boy stared blankly at him.

'It could have kept Martin going . . .' said Arthur. 'If he got this far' went unsaid.

After a swift glance around, Arthur turned on his heels to continue onwards, as if afraid that if he stood still for any length of time someone might persuade him to stop.

As he went, the others followed, a sad group of wanderers following Moses across a vicious wasteland, Arthur's heavy steps crushing the scorched earth beneath him as if he were punishing it for taking his son, trying to torture the rock into giving up its secrets. He won all the minor battles, the dry, crusted dirt disintegrating beneath the tread of his boots, but the war was gradually being lost.

A cry went up. A scream really. Chandler felt hope and fear. Hope that it was over, that they had found Martin even if it were only his desiccated corpse. He could call in the choppers and transport them all out of here inside a couple of hours.

Scrabbling through some shrubs he found the source

of the cries, the Murray River teenager, with his fresh face and lack of fear, the kid who wanted to be a bushman in the future. When Chandler had warned him that work as a bushman was rare, and for those of vast experience, the young man had waved it off with the revelation that he had learned to track people in school, following a different person every day, learning to follow from a distance. He had never been caught. Chandler didn't have the heart to explain to him that what he was describing were the skills of a stalker rather than a bushman.

As Chandler arrived on the scene the teenager was dancing around wildly, hands ripping at the white stuff glued to his body. It was immediately obvious to Chandler what had happened. He had blindly walked into a massive undisturbed spider's web and was trying to rip it away before whoever spun it exacted revenge.

'Get it off me,' he screamed, countering the efforts to help by dancing away from the hands that tried to pull the sticky silk from him.

'Stand still,' said Chandler, pulling a wad of tacky web from him.

'Is it on me?'

'You're supposed to be a bushman,' said Chandler. 'Calm down.'

Chandler informed the teenager that he was in no danger. It was a huntsman's web, a big, hairy but harmless spider that would flee at the first sign of trouble. With this declared, more people stepped in to help, including Arthur's kid. Chandler watched the boy laugh *as he shook his hands furiously to remove the sticky web and scolded himself for getting caught up in the yearning to find Martin's dead body to further his own selfish desire to get back home.*

27

Chandler quickly discovered that the press was desperate for information. They wanted to know who the people of interest were, what they were suspected of, background and beliefs, anything and everything about them, seeking the tiniest crack to edge into and take root.

As he finished his latest briefing, Erin and Roper had returned and were updating Mitch, Luka floating around the outside, a new planet orbiting the sun. A few minutes later Mitch addressed the station, failing to hide his disappointment. Mostly at them.

'So far we've had no luck in identifying a gravesite near the shack, so I'm making this our number one priority. Without graves, without bodies, we do not have a murder, we do not have a serial killer, just two men who are accusing each other of such. If – *when* – we locate the graves, then we can pressure one of them into giving up the other. They'll fold like a house of cards.'

'Assuming they are working together,' said Chandler. Mitch shot him an angry glare but Chandler continued. 'And if they were and had a falling-out then they'd have created differing stories of how they got to the woods. There would be no reason for them to match.'

'That could be their plan. To put us off the scent. And it's succeeding,' said Mitch.

'No,' said Chandler. 'If they have the same story that means the killer is using it to piggy-back. That means only one—'

Mitch fought back. '*Both* admit to having seen the graves.'

In full flow now, Chandler wasn't going to be stopped. 'Explain to me why they would admit seeing the graves if they were trying to get away with it, *or* trying to pin the blame on the other. That would make no sense. It only gets them into deeper trouble.'

'They may not be too smart, Sergeant.'

'Smart enough to have us running in circles.'

'Ever-decreasing circles,' said Mitch. 'We'll get them soon. What I want now is a positive attitude.' He turned to the group, but continued staring at Chandler. 'I need teams on the Hill searching for the graves. I'll be co-ordinating.' Pointing at pairs he continued, 'Erin and Roper you're up again. Yohan and Suze. MacKenzie and Sun.' His eyes scanned the room, straight past Chandler. 'Luka, you can pair with Flo. Jim and Tanya, you too.'

Tanya interrupted.

'You should take Chandler,' she said. 'Give him a team.'

Mitch tried to ignore her. 'Everyone ready in ten minutes.'

Tanya continued regardless. 'He knows the region. You both do. You want to find those graves, don't you? Then you have to bring him.'

It was an impassioned speech from a loyal colleague. Pride shot through Chandler.

Mitch paused, licking lips the colour of the evening sky. 'You are right, Senior Constable. Any personal differences Chandler and I may have will be put aside.' Mitch looked at them all. 'Let's solve this case.'

Chandler was back in the inner circle.

'If we do go searching for the graves,' Chandler said, 'we can't go by what they stated in the interviews.'

'And why's that, Sergeant?' asked Mitch.

'Because their info is vague. Maybe even mis-remembered.'

'It's the only information we have,' Mitch reminded him.

'I know. That's why I think our only option is to drag one – or both of them – up there to guide us. We need their eyes.'

'That's—' started Mitch.

'– a risky strategy,' interrupted Chandler. 'I know. But it's the only one we have.'

He expected immediate disagreement but Mitch seemed to have been thrown off-track. There was no dissent from the others either, all waiting to take their cue from Mitch. It seemed like an age before anyone spoke.

'Which one do we take?' asked Luka in an unusually reserved tone, staring at Mitch rather than Chandler.

The question allowed Mitch to find his voice. 'We take Mr Johnson,' he stated. 'Mr Barwell cannot be trusted. He's already tried to escape custody.'

'So has Mr Johnson,' reminded Chandler.

'But Mr Johnson is calm.'

'Too calm.'

'Tired, I reckon,' said Mitch.

'Or displaying the unruffled temperament of a killer.'

Mitch straightened his lapels. 'Or, Sergeant, he's a guy who has accepted that he has been caught. If you are so worried about letting him escape again, we could do it over video link. Use the new body cameras.'

Chandler had received the memo that Port Hedland were pioneering the cameras, the images downloadable and available as evidence. And Mitch's plan was sound apart from one – major – flaw, which he explained.

'You won't get any signal for a link-up there.'

Mitch stuck his chin forward. 'Then in that case we have no choice. We take Mr Johnson. I'm not having both out at once. And we move now. Five minutes.'

But in those five minutes another hitch occurred. A pair of court-appointed lawyers landed into the station, flown in from Newman on a chopper. Both were respectable practitioners who were delighted to be involved in such a tasty case. As such, both entered the station in much the manner Mitch had: demanding to see their clients, demanding to know what they were being charged with and finally demanding that they be released. They received nothing other than time in the interview room to brief their clients and, Chandler assumed, record their clients' numerous grievances.

Chandler considered his options – Mitch's options, really. They needed the men to take them to the graves, but there was no way the lawyers would permit that. And without charging them with anything, they couldn't keep them in the station much longer. Mitch was going to have to come up with something, anything, in order to keep them nearby. Probably the lesser charges of stealing a car and threatening a police officer. Mitch wasn't going to like that. Chandler certainly didn't.

'My client would like to help you find those graves.'

The voice took him by surprise. Chandler looked up. The blonde lawyer who had been appointed as Gabriel's counsel was standing at his desk.

'He would?'

'Against my advice, yes,' she sighed.

As if he been waiting to pounce, Mitch came charging out of his office. 'Excellent! Let's get to work!' he said, grinning from ear to ear.

With no similar proposal from Heath or his lawyer, Chandler offered to fetch Gabriel from the cells. As the door opened the slender figure didn't move from the bed. Chandler couldn't help but recall an article he'd read about criminals having the best night's sleep after being caught, the anxiety of being constantly on the lookout finally gone.

Gabriel roused himself as Chandler was putting on the handcuffs.

'Do we need those? I've agreed to help.' His voice was weary.

'Standard operating procedure.'

'But I'm cooperating.'

'For which we are grateful.'

Gabriel leaned in close to Chandler, as if he didn't

want anyone, especially Heath, to overhear. His voice turned to silk, regaining that elusive, mesmerizing quality Chandler had first noticed about him. 'Have you – have *they* – not realized yet that he's lying?'

Chandler studied the man who stooped forward slightly, his back bent as if he'd aged greatly after his night in the cells. He looked for all intents and purposes, beaten.

'Not yet.'

'You still think that I . . . ?' he trailed off.

'Neither of you can be ruled out, even now.'

Gabriel looked a little shocked by the answer. Chandler led him from the cells. Mitch addressed the suspect as his lawyer watched.

'I hope the sergeant has explained what we are requesting you do.' Gabriel nodded. 'Just so you are fully aware, you are under no obligation to help. But we hope that you will.'

'I've got nothing to hide,' said Gabriel, making for the door with Chandler guiding him.

'*Where are you taking him?*'

Gabriel stopped immediately. So did Chandler. Heath's disembodied voice rattled from the cell. Gabriel turned towards the voice. And the face. The narrow slat in the door had been left down to help air flow in and out. The suspects stared at each other. Chandler kept his hand on the cuffs but didn't pull Gabriel away, curious to see how the scenario played out.

The two suspects held the stare, both silent. Gabriel didn't move, a vein popping from his sweaty temple.

Inside the cell, Heath's face twitched, his eyes blinking irregularly. He looked scared.

Heath broke first.

'He's a lying bastard,' he screamed, striking his fists hopelessly against the steel door. 'Admit it, you bastard! Admit that you picked me up, took me to that place and tried to kill me. This lot might be too dumb to realize it but *I* know.'

Gabriel turned his head away at this, eyes closed as if trying to compose himself. Drawing a long breath he looked first at Chandler and then Mitch. 'I'm not ... He's ...' There was another deep inhalation. 'Can we please go? Now? I'll help you find those graves, those people.'

It was another hot day in hard country. Chandler sat in the back, guarding Gabriel, and Mitch rode up front with Roper. After putting up a fight, Gabriel's lawyer had remained in town. Behind them trailed four police cars with a convoy of news vans closely behind them. The terrain was especially challenging for the vans but each made it up the forest track, their vehicles obviously as dogged as the reporters inside.

Chandler watched as the tiny car park, cut into the trees and rock, appeared in front of them. Like everything up here, it hadn't changed in years. He peered into the front seat to gauge Mitch's reaction. There was no flicker of recognition.

Pulling up, Chandler kept Gabriel hidden from view as the reporters were corralled into the far half of the car park. A hurried press conference was arranged, Mitch shouting over the murmur, explaining to the crowd of microphones that they were taking one of the people of interest back to the scene to gain a better understanding of the timeline and events.

'What events?' asked a sharp reporter.

'To say anything at this time would be premature,' said Mitch, bringing disgruntled mumbles from the crowd.

'You haven't said anything yet,' noted an anonymous voice.

Another spoke up. 'Are you in a position to charge anyone? And if so, for what crime?'

They were valid questions, thought Chandler, and questions they'd have to deal with soon now the lawyers were involved. They would have to charge one man – or both if Mitch had his way – soon. It was either that or let both go. He studied Gabriel's reaction to the clamour that he had caused and was being shielded from. There was nothing, passive, as if he were purely background, a minor player rather than lead actor. Like Mitch, he seemed to be able to mask his feelings. Or had erected a shield to what he had experienced. And survived.

'I'm afraid this is as far as you lot go,' said Mitch to an audible groan of disappointment from the reporters. 'I know, I know, we're all disappointed but we have a possible crime scene that I don't want disturbed.' Pointing, he continued, 'Roper here, and Big Jim, will stay behind to prevent any of you good folk from attempting to follow us. I don't want you getting lost out here. I know what can happen.'

Mitch's mask fell, briefly. Chandler couldn't see it but the tremor in his former friend's voice said it all. Mitch *remembered*.

Handcuffed and under watch, Gabriel led the trek to the burned-out cabin, Erin and Yohan charged with sticking close by him in case he attempted to escape.

Chandler picked up the rear alongside Flo and Luka. The pair had struck up an immediate friendship, both young and disgustingly pretty. They whispered to each other, discussing the case, believing that they couldn't be overheard.

'It's all a ruse,' said Luka, dodging a low branch. 'A wild goose chase with nothing at the end. A prank they can't back out of.'

Flo half-shrugged her slim shoulders, her black hair crinkled in the heat, her dark skin glowing in the sun. She had a different angle. 'If that's the case what are Mr Johnson and Mr Barwell getting out of it? Are they fantasists?'

Luka's shrug matched hers. 'Maybe they wanted to create the perfect crime; maybe they even believe they have committed the perfect crime, without having committed one at all.'

'For what though?'

'For something to do? To write a book about it?'

Her hand snaked out to touch his arm. 'It's one way to get a book deal, I guess. "My time locked up as a serial killer."'

Luka doubled down by putting his free hand on hers,

risking his balance on the rocky ground, risking it being slapped away.

'Anything's possible.'

Despite feeling a mix of envy and nausea as he watched the young love blossom before him, another idea popped into Chandler's skull. Even more outlandish than theirs had been, but just as conceivable. What if their pair of suspects were wangling for a false imprisonment lawsuit? They'd already been held in custody longer than was legal without access to a lawyer or any form of representation. Maybe this was what they were counting on. Stall and stall, give half-truths or no-truths, let it fizzle into nothing and sue the department later. Make off with a generous settlement and/or book deal as Luka suggested. Once they got off this hill, Chandler decided that he would need to get on to the magistrate quickly to smooth things over, something Mitch didn't seem to care about, a bloodhound on the trail, blinkered to anything around him.

On reaching the cabin Gabriel was offered the chance to get his bearings. The site was quiet, the police tape oscillating in the gentle breeze. The fire was well and truly out, the remains sifted thoroughly and any surviving evidence collected. All that remained of the dwelling were a few charred planks of wood and guesses about what it had once been: a hunter's cabin, possibly even a meth lab, though they didn't often get that type of thing around here and never this remote. Chandler hoped to discover what exactly had gone on in there, find the truth. It seemed Gabriel wanted to know too.

'What happened here?' asked Gabriel, staring at the ruins. A tremor seemed to course through his body. 'Why is it burned down?'

'You tell us,' said Chandler.

Gabriel shrugged, the tremor persisting. 'I don't know. Did *everything* burn up?'

Chandler tried to read the lightly bearded face, judge whether Gabriel was pleased that everything had been destroyed. His study was interrupted by Mitch who placed himself where the front door of the cabin used to be. 'So, tell us where you went from here.'

As Gabriel closed his eyes and set about reliving the story of his escape, Chandler glanced towards the crest of the Hill. About a hundred metres up the slope and framed by the low angle of the sun he noticed faint shadows in the dirt. Stepping closer he made out two sets of footprints leading towards the ridge in the distance. Were they from some of the many officers who had trampled through here logging evidence? Or the suspects? Were they a remnant of the chase between Heath and Gabriel?

Reaching the first set, Chandler bent down to take a look. The tread was clear in the dust and didn't match those from standard-issue police boots. A pair of trainers, he guessed, and hopefully of the kind Gabriel and Heath wore.

Jabbing a pen in the soil to mark the spot, he set off for the ridge carefully following the prints, leaving everyone else behind. Two different sets of footwear had come in this direction, the prints following almost the exact same path, stride-distance apart, a litter of broken branches and torn leaves marking the route, including what looked to be a few fibres of clothing torn off by the rough bark of a tree trunk. He reached the crest of the ridge. It sloped gently away on the other side. It was difficult to see much beyond the first layer of trees. He'd need help to search further. Turning around, he went to see what was going on back at the cabin.

Gabriel strode past him.

Chandler almost fell backwards in surprise. Gabriel glanced at him, offering a hint of a smile.

But his suspect wasn't free. Closely behind him trailed his uniformed entourage, gradually making their way into the bush.

An hour passed, Gabriel moving in anything but a linear fashion, zigzagging, twisting and turning, practically chaotic in nature. It seemed obvious to Chandler that their hound dog couldn't recall the route he'd taken earlier. Either that or it was a drawn-out attempt to ward them off the scent.

Still the entourage followed, an atmosphere already sticky with tension becoming unbearable as the sun reached its peak. Chandler tried to focus his mind on the task but his body cried out for water and shade. Sweat gripped his uniform, dripping through his eyebrows and into his eyes, blurring his vision. As he passed under a branch, he tried to blink it away, and for a moment in the heat haze the slight figure of Gabriel morphed into the squat form of Arthur from all those years ago, the old man shuffling along, hunting in vain. Squeezing his eyes shut he shook the mirage from his head.

Just then Gabriel paused and looked around at the scenery.

'Do you need a break?' asked Mitch, his jacket slung neatly over his arm. His white shirt remained crisp and remarkably dry, as if he had no sweat glands at all. *A freak of nature*, thought Chandler.

'No,' said Gabriel sharply, as if angry at being distracted.

'What is it?' asked Chandler, stepping closer.

'The forest here looks familiar. That rock,' said Gabriel and set off, his pace quickening.

'What about it?' called out Chandler as he trailed behind.

'The bend in the horizon ...' Twisting towards them Gabriel stumbled, banging into an unyielding tree trunk, and fell to the ground.

'Are you okay?'

Gabriel winced and tried in vain to get up. Chandler grabbed him and helped him to his feet. 'I'm okay, but can I get rid of these? For now?' he said, presenting the cuffs that were bound behind his back. 'In case I fall again. It's hard to move.'

'I'm not going to be caught out like others, Mr Johnson,' stated Mitch.

'I'm not going to run.'

'I said no.'

Chandler approached his former colleague, voice lowered. 'What if he gets injured?'

'We make sure he doesn't. We look after him. *You* look after him,' said Mitch.

Chandler stared at him. It was like peering at a rock face, hard, chiselled and uncompromising.

'If he falls, he could sue us. And how will that look on your record?'

'No,' Mitch said.

Gabriel shrugged, turned and walked on. His pace slowed, possibly in protest, possibly in exhaustion from walking and talking, recalling details of his escape, a tree he vaguely remembered passing, a dried-out stream that conjured images from the day before. Closing his eyes in what he said was an effort to aid his memory, Gabriel persistently stumbled, causing Chandler, Mitch or whoever was nearest to lurch towards him and keep him upright.

It took half an hour of this sluggish progress to irritate Mitch.

'Take them off,' he finally ordered, to no one in particular.

Everyone stopped, including Gabriel. As Chandler stepped forward to remove the cuffs Mitch took charge. 'Mr Johnson, we're letting you out of these cuffs for now but I need to see more progress.'

Gabriel nodded.

Gabriel stuck to his promise and the pace immediately increased, the now freed man seeming to almost float over the ground. Chandler's senses heightened. In the cuffs Gabriel had been pretty helpless, but now they had a free-moving suspect with possible knowledge of his surroundings. Despite the increase in pace, the random zigzagging continued, dragging the group along behind.

The day swept on, the relentless sun fraying nerves and patience. As Chandler was beginning to think that it was a waste of time and that they should return and get Heath, Gabriel suddenly stopped, the group concertinaing behind him.

'What is it?' asked Chandler.

'I fell here,' said Gabriel, shivering, terror coursing through him. Chandler held back, as if contact would break the spell. 'He nearly got me.'

The tremor returned, even more intense. Chandler wondered what the hell they were going to do if their suspect had a nervous breakdown. Then suddenly, Gabriel set off at a sprint, the suddenness of the movement catching everyone out. He easily gained ten metres before the entourage had a chance to react.

'Stop!'

Mitch and Chandler yelled out simultaneously but this did nothing to slow Gabriel who moved with a sure-footed nimbleness.

Chandler led the chasing pack. Roper and others from Mitch's squad jogged up hard on the outside; Luka too, though it was increasingly hard to determine what team he ascribed to now.

Despite further calls to stop, Gabriel increased his lead. After a few hundred metres he disappeared behind a set of boulders. Unleashing his handgun Mitch ordered his officers to get their tasers out, find Gabriel and take him down.

Chandler charged onwards, panting for air. Rounding the set of boulders he expected to find that Gabriel had disappeared into thin air, but there he was, standing at the edge of a small clearing in the scrub, soil disturbed in rectangular patches, the edges too perfect to be natural. The gravesite.

'Freeze there, Mr Johnson!' shouted Mitch, his officers moving into position to let loose the electric barbs of their tasers if required. But Gabriel wasn't moving. He had his back to them, his shoulders jerking as he sobbed and continued to gaze at the clearing, even as Mitch forced him to his knees and reattached the cuffs.

Chandler stared at Gabriel. The horror was etched on his face, tears of relief staining his dusty cheeks. This is where he could have found himself. Underneath one of these six mounds of dirt, including the one nearest to them that looked recent. At the most, it was a few days old, the soil retaining an element of darkness, not entirely devoid of moisture, the sun-scorched clay crusted like freshly baked pastry on top.

28

The smell hung in the air, the drying soil offering little resistance to the unforgiving aroma of decomposition underneath. As Chandler turned his head to the side to stifle a retch, he spotted Mitch pacing around in the background, mumbling into his iPhone, calling in the forensic team and providing running commentary on what had been discovered.

The atmosphere was burdened by the stench and a searing hot mix of tension, anticipation and sweat. Turning his head from the grave, he risked another breath. He was determined to be there when they uncovered it. As he inhaled the searing air he found himself staring at Gabriel who watched on from the side, chewing his nails in a look of apprehension and shock.

Chandler turned back to the scene. A whiff of what lay under the earth invaded his nostrils. He could resist no longer. Making for the bushes he deposited his breakfast. And made the first discovery. A pickaxe lazily hidden under some rocks. Around the handle was a ripped section of shirt. Green checks. Chandler recognized the pattern.

'Over here!' he shouted.

Mitch scooted over, trying to maintain an air of authority through his palpable delight.

Chandler pointed at it. 'It matches Heath's shirt.'

'Good,' said Mitch, before addressing them all, loudly. 'This could be the breakthrough we need. Tape that area off for forensics to look at.'

As some of Mitch's team set about this, Chandler took a minute. Heath. Their killer. That would explain the state of his hands when he had arrived in the station: blistering caused by hacking through hard earth. The piece of shirt used as protection. Chandler's instinct had been wrong. Gabriel truly was the innocent party, merely trying to escape town and the clutches of a maniac.

Chandler had got it wrong. Completely wrong.

The forensic team funnelled out of the chopper as if dropped straight into a contagion zone, already bedecked in white smocks, equipment in unmarked cases. He didn't envy having to wear one of those full-body jumpsuits out here in summer. The team of eight stormed past him without greetings, professionals on a mission, stopping only to shake hands with Mitch.

Chandler got up to join in and watched on as they set to work, the entire team dropping to their knees around the graves, sweeping layers of crumbled soil away with their fine brushes. Chandler wondered what state they would find the body in and whether they would discover clothing or skin first.

'Let's keep going,' said Mitch to everyone. 'We have

evidence to tie one of the suspects to the scene. Let's see what we are tying him to.'

The deeper the forensic team probed the worse the smell became. Chandler watched them pass VapoRub around to smear under their noses to dampen the scent. Someone finally offered him the jar and he used it, but the sour, throat-clogging stench of death forced its way through the heavy stink of menthol all the same.

A sweep soon brought the first hint of body: a hand, bare and uncovered, the skin loose and grey like dripping candle wax, the nails cracked, rough and square cut, those of a man who worked with his hands, the withering of the skin giving the appearance that they had grown since death. Work paused and everyone absorbed the now visual confirmation that they had a body.

With delicate work the face was revealed, the eyelids thankfully closed. Chandler noted how well preserved the body was, the lack of moisture in the air assisting and making it hard to tell at first glance how long the body had been buried. His guess was at least a few weeks, given the decomposition. What he *could* tell was that the victim was male, early thirties, short brown hair with a broken nose – whether it'd been broken pre- or post-mortem, it was impossible to know at this stage.

'How did he die?' Mitch broke the silence to ask the question.

That was easy, even from Chandler's limited perspective. With the greying of the tissue-paper-like skin, the dark discolouration and frayed rope fibres around the throat, it was evident.

'Strangled,' he said, glancing at Gabriel to see how the proposed victim took the news. Gabriel was staring at the murdered body with a look of shock.

'With?' interrupted Mitch.

'Looks like rope,' said the lead forensic officer.

'Photograph it. Take some fibres and bag them,' said Mitch. He turned to the lead officer. 'I want to find out *who* the deceased is straight away. Check him for ID.'

Mitch turned from them and called over Yohan who held the satellite phone.

'We have one,' he bellowed down the handset. 'A body. Male, early thirties, no ID as yet.' A smile crept over his face, a smile Chandler knew well. Things were finally going Mitch's way.

With the first body discovered, the forensic team turned their attention to the other graves. Each patch of disturbed soil revealed another victim, soon numbering five in total, in more advanced states of decomposition than the first, the sex of each impossible to determine. But the manner of death seemed to be the same, strangulation, and an unspoken assumption that it had been a horrible demise.

As each grave was uncovered, Chandler studied Gabriel's demeanour. He remained at the fringes, eagle-eyed, giving little away. Chandler wondered if he were thinking about just how close he had come to having his own plot here in this unforgiving ground.

29

With the professionals in place, Mitch dismissed the majority of the others, posting a couple of his team as site security and another couple in the car park to monitor the reporters who would no doubt be desperate to find out what was going on now that the chopper had appeared.

Chandler approached Mitch. He nodded towards the still-handcuffed Gabriel.

'What do we do with him?'

'Has he asked to be released?'

Chandler shook his head. He had expected some sort of rant about being kept captive then dragged out here to relive his experience, but Gabriel had merely watched on as if shocked to the core as they had uncovered the bodies. 'No, but his lawyer will surely press for it, given that we know it's Heath.'

In response, Mitch bit on his oddly blue lower lip. Mitch's theory of the two being in partnership seemed to be in ruins but Chandler recognized the reluctance to acknowledge that he was wrong. Not that he was in any position to gloat.

The next question caught Chandler off guard.

'What do you think?'

Chandler paused. He waited for some ruse but there seemed to be none.

'I think that there is no harm keeping him around on the pretext of tying up loose ends. If we let him go he could disappear. He has no address and no reason to hang around after what has happened to him. He escaped once and was hard to find. If we give him a day's head start we might never find him.'

The nod from Mitch suggested that he agreed. It felt odd to work in true partnership once again, rousing a warmth in Chandler that was only partly due to the weather.

'There is a chance that he'll thank us for saving him,' said Mitch.

'A remote chance,' noted Chandler.

'If he starts making noises or threatening to sue, then release him,' said Mitch. 'But get some form of forwarding address.'

This was the answer Chandler wanted. Heath might be their killer, but a few questions still clawed at the back of his skull.

Chandler got ready to guide Gabriel back through the woods.

'Thank you for your help, Mr Johnson,' said Mitch, removing the cuffs from Gabriel's wrists.

'I was glad to help, but I'm also glad it's over. Out here it all came back to me.' He looked at Mitch, then Chandler. 'Now hopefully you can make it stick. Now you found his shirt.'

'We'll do our best, Mr Johnson,' said Mitch, before striding away to resume command.

Chandler could see that Gabriel was relieved, all nervousness and fear gone now that he was, in his mind, a free man, now that they had discovered the evidence incriminating Heath. But as yet the scrap of material was the only connection they had, important but circumstantial.

They set off back towards the car park. Soon he and Gabriel were alone with nothing but the trees, scrub and small talk to keep them company.

'It's a huge place,' said Gabriel as they crested a small rise.

'Very,' replied Chandler. 'What do you plan to do now?'

Chandler waited for an answer, but got another question in return.

'Do you come out here much?' asked Gabriel. Before Chandler had a chance to answer Gabriel continued, 'Probably not, I suppose. Too easy to get lost out here. Say I got lost how long would you – as in the police – spend searching for me?'

Chandler knew the answer all too well but didn't say. Gabriel hadn't been lost, he'd found his way out. One of the lucky ones. 'Until we found you.'

'Really? You lost anyone out here in the past?' After asking the question he stopped so abruptly that Chandler almost bumped into him. 'This place ... I dunno, it gives me the creeps. Like there are ghosts haunting this hill. Could have easily been mine if I hadn't escaped. But I suppose you have ghosts too, Sergeant.'

'What do you mean?'

'Haunted by people that you put in jail wrongly or failed to help?'

Chandler wondered what Gabriel was getting at. Was he aiming for the false imprisonment angle? Whatever it was, the conversation had turned very morbid for a now free man.

'I try. That's the best I can do,' said Chandler.

'That's not an answer, Sergeant.'

'Things happen and we try to rectify them.'

'And if you fail . . . ?'

'I try not to fail.'

'Very noble,' said Gabriel, sarcasm dripping behind the smile.

Chandler decided to search for his own answers. 'Why do you think Heath chose you?'

Gabriel shrugged. 'Could have been anyone. Anyone hitching that road.'

'But it wasn't. It was you.'

'It was,' sighed Gabriel.

'You mentioned God earlier. Do you think he helped you escape? Why do you think he chose you to get captured in the first place?'

'I suppose he has a plan for me.'

'And what is that plan?'

'I'm not sure. Something I have to do, have to continue. Or something that I must stop.'

'You've stopped Heath.'

Gabriel paused as if considering this. 'Not yet.'

'What do you mean?'

Gabriel looked back towards the now out-of-sight

graveyard. 'I suppose I need to testify, don't I? Get him behind bars for good.'

'Not if we get lost out here ourselves,' said Chandler directing him towards the burned-out shack and then the car park.

A quick call to Jim allowed Chandler to meet the car further down the forest road, out of sight.

Chandler escorted Gabriel back to the station and fed him and his lawyer a story that they had to process his release and that with so few officers available it might take a while. Though Gabriel seemed somewhat mistrustful, he didn't rail against it. He was confident in his innocence.

Mitch stormed in fifteen minutes later with a new vigour, ready to confront Heath with the evidence of his guilt.

'Get Mr Barwell strapped into the interview chair,' he said, striding into the office. 'And have that lawyer of his there too.'

Chandler nodded for Tanya and Jim to do it before turning to Gabriel.

'We'll get you out of here, before we bring him in,' said Chandler.

'It's okay, I can face him,' said Gabriel. 'I'll have to in court.'

'That may be,' said Chandler, 'but, as you say, he's already tried to murder you once, so why put yourself through any more stress?'

'I go back to the cells?'

'It's all we've got, I'm afraid.'

'Is there no other alternative, Sergeant?' asked his lawyer.

'He's disappeared once already. We don't want it happening again,' said Chandler, addressing the lawyer but staring at Gabriel.

'I'm not happy about this,' said the lawyer. 'My client stays here … for now. But only until I find him suitable accommodation elsewhere.'

Good luck with that, thought Chandler.

Chandler waited for Gabriel to resist, but there was only a reluctant nod. Then he walked towards the cells, as obedient as an innocent man as he was as a prisoner.

'We'll be as quick as we can,' Chandler called after him, but got the distinct impression that his captive was in no rush, exhausted after everything that he had been through.

He was still thinking about this as he entered the recording room. At Mitch's insistence Luka was at the control desk this time and on the other side of the glass the man himself had already begun the cross-examination, an evidence bag waved in front of Heath's face containing the missing piece of his shirt.

'Where did you find that?' Heath asked. Chandler noted the guilt in his voice.

'At one of the graves, Mr Barwell.'

'Okay,' said Heath. 'I lost it somewhere. Maybe when I fell.'

'I don't think you understand, Mr Barwell. It was wrapped around the handle of a pickaxe.'

Heath looked confused, a little flustered. 'A pickaxe? How did it get there?'

'You tell us.'

'I don't know,' said Heath, panic seeping from him, perhaps realizing where this line of questioning was headed. He glanced at his lawyer, a jowly man in his mid-forties, perched on the seat beside him. 'I didn't put it there. I didn't have a pickaxe.'

'It does explain your hands, doesn't it?' said Mitch, maintaining his calm.

'What do you mean?' said Heath, staring at his hands.

'The blistering. It's hard work digging a grave, no doubt.'

Heath held his hands up. 'This is from trying to escape. To get away from him,' he said, pointing towards the door and the cells beyond.

To press home the point, Mitch held the piece of cloth up against the larger evidence bag containing Heath's shirt. The ripped pocket matched exactly.

'How would he get your shirt, Mr Barwell?'

'He could have torn it off when I was unconscious. I don't remember when I lost it.'

'And why would he do that?'

'To pin the blame on me.'

'Really, Mr Barwell? It seems like a lot of effort to go to for someone he was intending to kill anyway, don't you think?'

Heath was lost for an answer, so Mitch continued, 'And now that the ball is rolling you can be sure we'll gather more evidence. Someone will have seen you pick up the other people on the list.'

Heath's voice turned adamant. 'I hadn't seen that list

until you showed me. I dunno anything about the graves other than I saw them. And I dunno anything about the killings other than I was going to be one.'

Mitch pounced. 'How do you know there was more than one killing?'

He was taking a risk with this line of questioning but Chandler could see that Heath was on the ropes. 'My client doesn't—' Heath's lawyer broke in.

Heath interrupted. 'Gabriel said I was going to be number fifty-five.'

'How did you kill them?'

Heath shook his head. 'I didn't!'

'Come on, Mr Barwell.'

The lawyer tried to intervene again. 'My client says that he didn't. You're trying to pressure him into—'

'I'm the victim here,' Heath yelled. 'I don't know how they died. And if you're so smart, get Gabriel to tell you!'

There was a sneering quality to the last comment that seemed to knock Mitch off stride. He went quiet for a moment, pacing the room before turning to face Heath, his hands on the table glaring down at his main suspect. 'We need the truth, Mr Barwell.'

Heath remained obstinate. 'I'm giving you the truth. You can't pin it on me.'

Heath's lawyer finally managed to interrupt his client. 'I think that's enough for today,' he said crisply.

'Just one last question,' said Mitch, standing up from the table. 'How did it *feel* to strangle them to death?'

Mitch didn't wait for an answer, but stormed out of the room, leaving Flo to officially end the interview.

242

Chandler met him outside. His ex-colleague tried to maintain the aura of calm but he looked flustered with the heat, the burden of finding proof.

'I'll grind it out of him,' Mitch scowled, loosening the tie from his neck.

He looked at Chandler. 'Has Mr Johnson been released yet?'

'No. His lawyer asked but didn't press. I think he thinks he's in the clear and he's trying to play nice.'

'As long as we've got him here, we might as well try and force something out we can use on Mr Barwell. A part of me still thinks that they're hiding something. A friendship, a past, something.' There was a calm fury in Mitch's eyes that Chandler was wary of. A look that suggested that he was capable of anything.

Gabriel agreed to the interview, again without his lawyer, seeming to think that he was now assisting the police. It was only when Mitch asked him how the victims died that his attitude changed.

'What is this?' asked Gabriel, staring at the one-way mirror.

'Just some questions, Mr Johnson.'

'They sound more like accusations. I thought you had your man.'

'We need to gather as much information as possible,' interrupted Mitch.

Gabriel fell silent.

'So?' asked Mitch.

'So ...'

'How did they die?'

'I don't know. Ask the other guy. You found *his* shirt there, what more do you want? If I hadn't escaped he'd still be out there. And I'd be in one of those graves. You, the police, would be none the wiser.' Like Heath, the attempted accusation had summoned a blast of defiance in Gabriel. Though with Gabriel, this defiance had a spirited cockiness to it. 'You want him to sign a confession? Break down and spill his guts? He's a killer, Inspector, a cold-blooded killer. Someone with a similar make-up should be able to see that he won't give up easily.'

Gabriel glared at Mitch. It was a jagged response, intended to hurt.

It worked. Mitch rose to the bait and shot Gabriel an arrogant grin. 'I've done this before, Mr Johnson.'

'And so has he. If you can't make it stick, bring in someone who can.'

Mitch's grin dropped and he narrowed his eyes. Chandler could see his old colleague getting wound up.

Gabriel laid his uncuffed hands flat on the table. 'If you're going to continue to detain me and ask me these types of questions then you probably better call my lawyer. You've held me without charge for a long time now and let's face it, I've done all I can to help you, and if I really wanted to, I think I could bring a false imprisonment lawsuit against you, against this station.'

Chandler knew that any threat to Mitch's status and career would aggravate him. The veins bulged from his temple, his lips so blue they shone dark grey in the light. His blood was boiling but Gabriel wasn't finished.

'It seems like the police want to stretch my goodwill to the extreme. And if I can't sue you, I can at least sell this whole sorry mess to the papers.' Gabriel leaned forward and glared at Mitch. 'With your name at the top, Inspector.'

Mitch returned the glare before walking away from the table and out of the room.

Chandler met him outside.

'Can you believe that fuck?' growled Mitch. 'Making us look like idiots.'

Making you look like an idiot, thought Chandler but went with, 'We'll have to bring the lawyers in.'

Mitch shook his head. 'I'm giving it one more try. To reason with him.'

'You're pushing your luck.'

Mitch just mumbled in return as Nick called from across the room. 'Zero-zero-one, Sarge!'

Zero-zero-one – a call from home. Chandler paced to the phone to tell his mum that whatever it was he would deal with it later. As he put the receiver to his ear his mum was talking, as if she had carried on, oblivious to whether someone was listening at the other end or not.

'– he's insisting on trying to paint the house on his own.'

Chandler jumped in. 'I'll sort it later, Mum.'

She wasn't to be appeased that easily. 'I don't like seeing him up the ladder.'

'I can't leave now, Mum.'

'The important thing is still happening?'

'Yes, Mum. Just tell Dad not to go up the ladder. I'll paint it this week. Bye.'

Chandler hung up the phone. He cursed silently, annoyed that his personal life was getting in the way of work again. Then he closed his eyes. He was doing it again. Putting work before family. He promised to rectify it soon.

He returned to the recording room. Luka was still in there but the monitors were blank, the recording equipment silent.

'He's finished the interview already?' asked Chandler, happy that Mitch hadn't pushed his luck.

Luka's response was to look anywhere but at Chandler, pretending to fiddle with the controls.

'Luka?'

'The inspector's having a private chat with Mr Johnson.'

Chandler looked at the blank screens. A conversation he didn't want recorded. Something on the wrong side of legal.

Bursting out of the recording room he made for the interview room. Yohan and Roper formed a formidable barrier in front of the door.

'Let me in.'

'We can't do that,' said Roper, teeth gritted, legs spread for balance. Expecting trouble.

'What are you going to do?' asked Chandler.

'Whatever we need to,' said Yohan.

Chandler prepared for a confrontation. Jim appeared beside him.

'What's happening?' asked Jim.

'I intend to find out.'

With the battle announced and lines drawn Nick joined

the fray. Three on two now. This was going to be unseemly but Chandler needed to get inside. The three local officers charged. Bodies collided in the narrow corridor. There were embittered cries as the pushing and shoving continued, Chandler catching a short-armed fist to the side of his skull, the corridor too tight to allow for a meaningful blow. In response Chandler thrust his hand up and found a sweaty face, forcing the head backwards, securing a gap to wriggle through and into the interview room.

There he was presented with the sight of Mitch kneeling across Gabriel's upper arms, pinning him to the floor. Gabriel was crying out in pain.

'Get off him, Mitch,' ordered Chandler, pulling at his superior officer, his fingers struggling for purchase on the silk suit.

'He attacked me,' said Mitch, attempting to retain his position on top of Gabriel.

'I didn't,' cried Gabriel, trying to free himself.

Chandler knew that Gabriel hadn't attacked Mitch, his instinct telling him that it was an effort by Mitch to see if roughing the suspect up produced greater results. Or simply revenge for threatening to bring a lawsuit against him.

'Get him off me!' cried Gabriel again.

Chandler got hold of Mitch's collar and dragged him to his feet. They faced off against each other as Gabriel scooted to the side of the room.

'What the hell are you trying to do, Mitch?'

'Get some answers,' replied Mitch through clenched teeth.

'By doing that shit?'

'It's my job to get results.'

'And what did you get?'

The flushed look on Mitch's face told him that he had got nothing but sweaty.

Chandler shoved him to the back of the room before helping Gabriel back into the seat.

'Are you okay?'

'Course he is, I didn't touch him,' said Mitch, pacing along the back wall like a caged animal.

'Is this one of those good cop, bad cop routines?' asked Gabriel. 'If it is, it's pretty fucking see-through.'

Chandler shook his head. 'No, it isn't, and I apologize for the inspector's actions.'

'Don't apologize for me,' snarled Mitch.

Gabriel took a few deep breaths. He looked to have recovered some of his cool. 'Go get my lawyer. I've got plenty to say.'

30

To Chandler's surprise, Gabriel didn't ask to be released, just for access to his lawyer. If he had there was little he could have done to prevent it, given what Mitch had done. Maybe a charge of harassment levelled against Mitch or the force in general was in the works. Adding another anchor to the investigation. After securing Gabriel in a cell he caught up with Mitch in his office.

'You going to explain to me what that shit was?' he demanded. 'Attempted beating of a suspect? Threats? Harassment?'

Mitch was unrepentant. 'I'm here to get results. Sometimes you have to apply force to get what you need.'

'Not in my station.'

'Remember who you're talking to, Sergeant.'

'I know full well who I'm talking to.'

The friend who shared his teenage dream of becoming a motocross champion. The friend who had dragged him out of Sully's Gorge after he'd taken a spill and torn most of the skin from his leg. The friend who had dated

Kelly Freeman's half-mutant sister just so he could go out with Kelly.

'My friend with the melted chocolate in his pocket who looked like he'd shit his pants,' said Chandler.

Mitch paused. His eyes narrowed. It wasn't a story he wanted rehashed. A story forever to hang over his head. Mitch spat back.

'Yeah, well I'm not that boy now, Chandler. I happen to be the *man* who's seeing your ex-wife.'

Ex-wife . . . what was he? The words made sense individually but as a collective Chandler was convinced he must have missed something.

'What are you talking about?'

'I'm seeing Teri.'

'What do you mean?' said Chandler, the implications of the words still unclear.

'What more clarification do you need, Chandler? Teri. And I. Are a couple.'

Teri and Mitch? A couple?

'Since when?'

'Since we got the call about an attempted car-jacking up in PH. From a Teri Pagonis. I tagged along to see if it was the same Teri Pagonis I used to know.' The familiar beaming grin had returned to Mitch's face. He was delighted at having sprung this on Chandler. He had probably been itching to tell him since he had arrived.

'How many Teri Pagonises do you think there are?' spat Chandler.

Mitch's shrug suggested he didn't care. 'She said that the two of you weren't together any longer. She still looks pretty hot. We've been seeing each other since last August. Just over a year now. She's cleaned up her act a lot since I knew her. Moved into her own place. Decent job in admin, decent prospects. But you know all this.' It was delivered with a snideness that suggested he knew Chandler didn't know, and he was correct in that assumption.

Mitch continued, 'Well, we decided to meet up for a drink, got to talking and found that we had more in common than we thought; we both like our own space, she enjoys order and I like things to be in order. We talked about this place a lot.' He looked at Chandler. 'Mostly about missing her kids.'

'She was the one who left us.'

'Let me finish,' said Mitch in typical reproachful fashion. 'She misses the kids but doesn't miss the place. Neither do I.' He leaned in to whisper, 'It's a bit of a shithole, frankly.'

Chandler let the disparagement of their home town pass.

'So I said to her; you've got a stable environment, why don't you apply for custody of the kids?'

Chandler clenched his fists tight, speechless.

'It's not like it's your exclusive right to have them, is it?' added Mitch. 'Now, to be fair, she's not sure she's earned the right to have them, but then again have you? From what I've seen, your folks do most of the parenting.'

'What the hell do you know about it?'

'This town has ears.'

'Who talked to you?'

Mitch sniffed. 'Remember I have family here,

Chandler. They told me those kids are never away from your parents' place.'

'They know fuck all,' said Chandler, seething.

Mitch laughed.

It made Chandler further enraged.

'You're probably right, Chandler, but *we* are,' said Mitch, emphasizing the '*we*', 'looking into gaining custody of the kids.'

'You've only been together, you said, a year?'

'It's serious, Chandler. A serious relationship. We're living together. I want to be a father, and I think it's better if the kids are ready made. Cuts out the messy early stage.'

'Fuck you—' spluttered Chandler. 'You, a father?'

'You might not believe me, Chandler, but fortunately it's not up to you. It's up to the presiding judge. And I know a *lot* of them.'

Every fibre of Chandler's entire being screamed out to punch Mitch. Mitch even kept his face and jutting chin right in front of him as if tempting him to do it. To do it and earn himself a reprimand and probably get thrown off the force. Do it and provide fuel for Teri's case. Give the judge another reason to rule in her favour. If Chandler stayed where he was then the chances were that he would plant one, or both, of his fists into that face.

There was only one solution. Chandler turned and left the station.

31

The day was blazing hot but Chandler barely noticed. Blanking the questions posed by the reporters hanging outside the back gate he continued down Harper's, darting between the scorching sun and the cool of the awnings. As he paced along one thought dominated his brain.

She was the one who left.

He did, however, understand why. There was a regularity to life in Wilbrook here that for someone as restless as Teri was dull. Mr Peacock sitting outside his hardware store letting customers roam around inside before coming to serve them in his own sweet time. Ansell Parker swatting away flies in his grocery store like Sisyphus. Mrs Cotterall watering her window boxes despite being warned over the egregious use of water, and maliciously soaking those walking below. These thoughts, which ordinarily were enough to distract him, were unable to prevent his mind from focusing on what Mitch had said; about what they threatened to take from him. Whether a judge had lack of insight enough to rip Sarah and Jasper away from him after everything Teri had done, or more appropriately, hadn't done. But if she had indeed cleaned up her act as Mitch had said then it was possible it could happen. That Teri – and Mitch – could gain custody of his kids. *Mitch and Teri*. Two people who had openly despised each other. Now, they were a couple – a *thing*. If she got the kids, he'd be forced to resume his weekly commute to the coast, this time to see his children with the loving couple. It made his skin crawl.

A car pulled up alongside him, the electronic motor of the window whirring as it rolled down. Mitch leaned over from the driver's seat.

'Chandler, we were going to tell you – honestly. *I* wasn't supposed to, Teri was, but ... well it happened. We wanted to see if we were going to stay together first before doing it. And now that we are, we both want the kids to grow up in the city. At least experience it before they decide where they would rather be. Surely you can see that would be good for them. No one can survive in isolation for ever these days.'

Chandler stopped and turned towards the voice. He spoke with a restraint he didn't imagine possible. 'You can take Teri, Mitch. Take her and keep her for all I care, but no way are you getting your hands on my kids.'

'We'll let the courts decide that, Chandler. In the future. We have a case to solve. Get in the car and I'll take us back to the station.'

'I'll walk,' said Chandler, not trusting himself to be alone with Mitch.

Chandler made his way back through town, noticing, as if for the first time, how barren and dusty a place it was, like a ghost town from some old cowboy movie, the tarmac scorching the soles of his feet and draining his remaining strength. Wilbrook was stuck in a different era, the ornate street lights, the delicate awnings, all built for footfall rather than vehicles. Maybe Mitch was right, maybe they were out of touch. Maybe Sarah and Jasper should be given the opportunity to decide where they wanted to live. Maybe he was restricting their development by forcing them to live here. But – as Mitch had said – that was for the future. There was something more pressing happening at the moment. A case of life and death.

Chandler walked straight back into discussions over what to do with the suspects. Mitch had settled upon Heath as the sole culprit given the new evidence. After making his case he asked for opinions. Not that he wanted them. As was expected, his team nodded their assent. Only Tanya offered a differing opinion, noting that neither suspect had backed down from their story despite the psychological – and physical – pressure.

'We have the shirt and the axe,' said Mitch. 'And the fact that Mr Barwell was brought in trying to steal a car. Probably to flee the area.'

'Gabriel fled too,' Chandler noted.

'He also gave himself up,' noted Mitch. 'Twice.'

'To a degree. But do you want to take that chance—' He broke off before he could call him 'Mitch'. If provoked, Mitch might have turned stubborn. What he wanted was to play into Mitch's fears of getting something disastrously wrong. ' – Inspector?' he concluded.

As it was, Mitch narrowed his eyes, clearly having heard Chandler's slight hesitation before using his title.

'We have both, we can charge both,' continued Chandler.

'Falsely accusing one man,' said Mitch.

'Until we are sure which one is innocent that is something we – and you – have to live with.' Chandler felt sick. Saying this, even thinking this went against everything that he stood for, depriving an innocent man of his freedom, but he could see no other alternative.

'So where are we?' asked Tanya.

'We charge them both. With murder,' said Chandler. 'There's no way around it. We've easily exceeded our window to hold them in custody, even applying generous time-outs for transfers, evidence collection, medical treatment and escape attempts. If we take the piss any further there's a danger of the whole thing collapsing, or our suspects claiming rights violations.'

There was a pause. All eyes were on Mitch.

Mitch gave a reluctant nod. 'The lawyers will make things murky,' he said, not disguising his dissatisfaction. 'I'd hoped to have this all ironed out before that happened. But we are where we are,' he continued. 'We'll charge them both. Now get to it.'

With that the meeting broke up.

*

With the suspects again cloistered with their lawyers, Chandler's thoughts returned to the earlier revelation. But ringing Teri to discuss it would do no good and he wasn't about to rehash it with Mitch.

Seeking a distraction he left to visit the forensic team who had taken over the town hall a few hundred metres down the street. The cracked, red-brick building looked like a warehouse with decorative windows. It hadn't seen this much action since the recruitment drives at the end of the Second World War when there had been a heated discussion on whether the town should be sending people off to fight another world away. That time it had ended up in a small riot, with the part-time mayor, part-time publican 'Rolling' Harry Winter, using the ceremonial chains as a makeshift lasso to drag the worst of the rioters away. This one act had made all the papers and secured Harry another ten years in the job.

As Chandler stepped inside, suspicious eyes trailed him everywhere. It was only after he flashed his credentials that he was pointed towards the officer in command, Rebecca Patel, her demeanour painfully formal and ultra-clinical. Perfect for the job.

'What do you have?' asked Chandler.

'Have? You'll need to be more specific, Sergeant.' Dr Patel wasn't one for time-wasting.

'Anything further on the bodies – on identifying who they were?'

She shook her head at him as if he were a small child who had asked her to summarize the meaning of life in five words or less. 'It's too early to tell anything as specific as that, Sergeant. We've only got preliminary results so far.'

'Preliminary's good enough for me.'

She raised her eyebrows. Dr Patel was a woman of little humour, as colourless as her smock, but Chandler supposed that she had to be in her line of work; meticulous in dress, meticulous in approach.

'We've identified the victims as four males and two females, all aged between twenty and forty, but that initial prognosis might alter for at least two of them. All were clothed but no ID was present. Currently we are working on recovering dental imprints in case that gives us something straight off. Initial tests reveal no signs of sexual interference. Importantly, and as I'm sure you are eager to know, all the victims look to have been strangled with rope. Ligature marks are visible on all the bodies, nothing subtle or unique about the application, just pure force.'

'That was preliminary?' Chandler smiled, searching for an ounce of humour.

Rebecca gave a simple nod. 'There's nothing more I can or want to divulge right now. We'll prepare the report in good time. And can I ask that you don't leak anything to the press that might have to be rescinded at a later date when we have sight of the full results.'

She raised her eyebrows hinting that she was open to any further questions he had, but that there shouldn't be any.

32

Chandler was back at the station when Mitch informed each suspect, in the presence of their lawyers, that they were to be charged with six counts of murder. Both were stunned. Both insisted that the police were making a huge mistake. Both were told to keep quiet by their lawyers who then reiterated their clients' complaints to Mitch in the strongest possible terms, claiming that their clients had pleaded not guilty and should be treated as such, angry that it had taken the police so long to call them in. It was like watching a verbal ballet, their complaints as in sync as their clients' testimonies.

Despite having the suspects held and charges laid, Mitch was angry.

'Heath's insisting on making a complaint. About our treatment of him.' Mitch shook his head, the tendons in his jaw pronounced. 'I've got him, and yet he, this serial killer, the one who'll make my name throughout all of Australia, maybe even the world, has the gall to complain about how we've handled it.'

'And Gabriel?'

Mitch seemed angry at the focus being drawn from Heath. 'Not a peep.'

'He might be saving it for later.'

Mitch frowned. 'What do you mean?'

'I mean – your assault on him. Gabriel might be saving it to use as a bargaining chip for later on.'

Mitch fell silent, the tendons at work again.

Flo appeared at the door. 'Press conference, Inspector.'

Slamming his hands on the desk Mitch stood up and stormed into the press conference to announce the charges. Chandler listened in astonishment as Mitch's usually pin-sharp delivery was missing, his air of confidence gone. His irritation with the reporters for badgering him overwhelmed him. He had lost the sheen of control and had reverted back to the stumbling teenager of old, as if some disease from his youth had risen from the soil he'd grown up on and infected him. The belligerence of the suspects was ruining his plans to storm in, round up the culprits and swan off back to the coast. With Teri. And Chandler's kids.

The announcement of the charges sent a buzz not only around the station but around town, locals joining reporters in gathering outside the station, eager to witness the evil that had ridden into town. Murder was not something that came often to Wilbrook. Mass murder was unthinkable.

But any discomfort was not kept solely for Mitch. With locals turning up en masse, Chandler was forced to explain to panicked members of his town that all was calm and that they had the suspects locked up. Sparra Talbot even made him swear to it.

Two official summonses were drawn up and issued, for one Gabriel Johnson and one Heath David Barwell to appear before the magistrate tomorrow morning.

Chandler had half-expected Mitch to insist that he stayed at the station, keeping him from the kids to help further his and Teri's case for custody, but Mitch was preoccupied with completing the prosecution notices, so Chandler went home.

With Sarah glued to her phone, Jasper dragged him to the garage and insisted on him retrieving the go-kart from it. Laying it on the driveway, Chandler could see that the back axle had worked loose over the winter and was in need of some work, but Jasper was in no mood to fix what was immediately serviceable. Plumping himself down on the plastic seat they had cannibalized from an old buggy he demanded that his dad push him around the yard. This carefree attitude to safety reminded Chandler of his own youth darting around on motorbikes. It was also the reason Jasper tended to get into scrapes, his grandparents too slow to keep up with him, usually arriving on the scene in the aftermath of an incident. Indeed the knobbly knees which protruded from Jasper's khaki shorts were presently crisscrossed with a series of cuts and scabs as if he had been dragged back and forth through a nest of brambles. The type of injuries that would cause whoever was ruling on custody to think twice. But Chandler was sure they would have to accept that kids could not be watched over one hundred per cent of the time. Tears were part of growing up and with Jasper they never lasted long anyway, his life a constant stream of adventure: fortresses and stunts, cops and robbers. And now, murderers.

After a pleasant family dinner, Chandler put Jasper to bed with a bedtime story, a fantastical tale of robots and spaceships on a distant planet where the water was sparkling soda and the scenery was edible, a rip-off of a nursery rhyme from his childhood he couldn't quite recall. Before he had turned the second page, Jasper was asleep, the evening's exertions taking their toll.

Next stop was Sarah. She was curled up in bed, the phone inches from her face. Chandler felt tentative as he entered, expecting questions that he didn't want to answer. He played it safe at first.

'How was your day, honey?'

All he got in reply was a mumble. A good or bad sign, he couldn't tell.

'Nothing exciting?'

'No First Confession yet.'

'Yeah, sorry about that. But there's—'

'Sophie says there's been a murder and that you have the murderer. Two of them.'

So much for caution. He cleared his throat. 'There's an investigation in progress.'

'Dad, I'm not a kid. You can tell me.'

'Even if that were true I couldn't tell you.'

'Is it true?'

'There's nothing to worry about. We have it under control.'

'Then why did you – they – stop the First Confession going ahead?'

'It takes time to clear these things up. It'll happen soon I suspect. Maybe in a few days.'

'Oh.' She sounded neither happy nor sad.

He settled on a change of subject.

'Do you want to go through it with me?'

She shook her head. 'I know it.'

'You know your words?'

'Yes.'

'And you know the sin you're going to confess?'

She nodded.

'And what is it?'

'I'm not telling,' she said, wide-eyed.

Chandler feigned shock. 'Is it that bad? Do I need to call Jim and Tanya in to take a statement?'

'Noooo,' she said, yelping with laughter.

'So why can't you tell?'

'It should be a secret,' she said, before looking up at him with big brown eyes. 'Unless you tell me what you confessed. Your first time.'

Chandler was stumped. He couldn't remember what his big sin had been. Probably something trivial that seemed like a big deal when he was eleven. If he were asked to come up with one now he knew what he would confess. Forgiveness for all those he had let down over the years. Teri ... Sarah ... Jasper ... Martin.

He left her with a gentle kiss on her forehead. She told him to go away and let her sleep.

As he went back into the living room, he saw that

his parents were engrossed in some TV game show, all flashing lights and overexcited contestants, whatever his mum's latest fad was. Everyone was home and everything was normal. Until the knock on the door.

'I'll get it,' said Chandler before his mum could wrestle herself from the sofa. He was glad he did.

Answering the door he was presented with a bedraggled-looking Mitch crowding the doorstep, today's suit tilted off his shoulders like the scales of justice gone askew, the shirt creased, as he leaned on the buttress of the porch.

'What are you doing here, Mitch?'

'Yes, *Mitch*,' said Mitch, holding up a half-empty bottle of brown liquid, probably bourbon. From the wide bottom and thick glass it looked like an expensive bottle. 'Not "Inspector" tonight, eh?'

'What do you want?' asked Chandler.

'A drink. A truce.'

Mitch's voice was loud. He was bordering on drunk and barely managing to disguise it.

'A truce?' What should have felt like old times – him and Mitch hanging around on the porch – felt more sinister. A souring of a memory.

'We got off on the wrong foot I think.'

Chandler sighed. 'Look, Mitch, I appreciate it, but it's late and I'm trying to spend time with my kids. You, drunk, on my porch is the last thing I need.'

'I'm not drunk,' said Mitch, raising his voice.

Chandler went to shut the door. 'Look, you have to go. We – I – have to get things back to normal tomorrow. The kids have school, Sarah has First Confession in a few days. I have to prepare for my ex-wife trying to steal my kids.' Not a subtle blow but it felt good.

Mitch threw his hands in the air. 'Ah, come on. It's nothing personal.'

'Nothing personal?' spluttered Chandler, glancing over his shoulder in case his mum was prowling. 'How ... when ... did you two decide to drag the kids – *my kids*— into this?'

Mitch shook his head, his upper torso following suit a second later in a long, inebriated swing. 'She had the idea a long time before we got together.'

'Just leave, Mitch. You're drunk.'

Mitch fought back. 'You want to know why? 'Cause there's nothing else to do 'round here. Those kids'll do the same – have nothing to do but become a *bogan* like you.'

Chandler glared at Mitch. 'Call me what you want. At least I'm not just out for the publicity like some media whore.'

'Christ, Chandler, join this century. Publicity's everywhere. PR is *king*. Quotas and press releases. Charts for charges and charges for column inches. I have to fight for a budget and to get it, things have to either work well, or have gone to complete shit. I prefer the former.' He narrowed his eyes, clinging to the buttress for support. 'Are you jealous?'

'Jealous?'

'Yeah, that I'm with Teri. Maybe you haven't moved on. Pickings might be slim around here but surely there's someone desperate enough.'

Mitch chuckled at his joke but Chandler had had enough and stepped out the door to confront him.

'Get out of here Mitch, before—'

'Before what?' said Mitch, pushing himself away from the pillar and finding the world a little rocky without the support.

'Before something happens we both regret,' said Chandler.

Deciding he'd had enough, Mitch stepped off the porch on to the dry, scorched garden.

'I regret coming down to deal with this shit,' he said, 'but I *will* deal with it.' Turning quickly, he stumbled on down the lawn and into the darkness.

Yet another dangerous character loose in town.

33

2002

Eighteen days in the search was shut down, forced upon them with the forecast worsening for the next few weeks, the temperature gauge cranking into the mid-to-high forties. Weather that made it unsafe to be out there with a limited supply of fresh water. So Bill and the heads from Perth took the decision from Chandler's hands.

On hearing the news, Sylvia's shoulders slumped, her body language suggesting that all remaining hope had been lost. Arthur's resolve, however, held firm. Fronting a hastily arranged press conference he stated his intention to continue the search, informing the reporters that the police might have abandoned Martin but that he and God wouldn't and that he was going out again, with his own plan of attack this time.

This revelation worried everyone involved, but there was little the police or anyone could do to stop him, thwarted as they were by a combination of public land

and free will. So Bill dragged Chandler and Mitch aside and asked them to stay on, to ensure nothing else went wrong and to try and persuade Arthur to stop. To prevent the family from jumping down the mineshaft to save Martin, only to succumb themselves.

But Arthur wouldn't be entirely alone in his search, the stipend of a hundred and fifty dollars persuading some of the remaining 'volunteers' to carry on. Those that were fit, able and had the guts to continue. This brought out the weird and the wonderful, some there for the adventure, some there for the money, but all definitely some form of crazy. So Chandler and Mitch, the two rookie cops, were left with this burden, babysitting a gang of unstable mercenaries and a slowly imploding family in the midst of forty-five degree heat.

Huddled in the shade of some eucalyptus trees, Mitch ran through the instructions to the group. There were only nine in total now, five being paid for the privilege, seven if he and Chandler were included. Seven mercenaries, an old man and a child to search for one lost boy. The orders, relayed by Mitch, were to stick close together, and included the warning that he would call back the chopper and airlift everyone out by force if he was disobeyed.

The threat was immediately ignored by the more experienced bushmen who believed they knew better than some rookie cops. This was their land and they would lead Arthur to his son by their own means, no matter how disparate or vague. Privately, Chandler warned them against that kind of over-optimistic dialogue but up here he understood he really had little authority over anyone. Up here, nothing was respected more than the ability to survive, the rule of law an unwelcome obstacle this deep in the outback. They had the uniform but no clout. They were bodyguards with shiny badges, nannying the family and the others, their own search taking a back seat to maintaining a watchful eye on their charges.

Straight away the group scattered across the land, frayed strands of a single piece of fabric, exploring by instinct rather than design, a strategy encouraged by their spiritual leader, Arthur. The old man believed that the way to find his eldest son was not by order, like they had been doing for the last eighteen days, but by a form of chaos. But this chaos meant that overall progress slowed and instead of ten kilometres a day they barely managed half that, the direction of travel random, guided by one cop who didn't want to be there and another who cared little for the emotional well-being of the group but more for making a name for himself.

Chandler did what he could, sticking close to Arthur and his son but regularly losing them, the boy scampering off on his own and slipping behind some rocks, or disappearing over the edge of a ridge causing Chandler to frantically scramble after him – only to find him engrossed by a shiny black insect in the dirt or tearing at the bark of a tree as if in his own backyard.

But the child was merely impetuous. It was Arthur

who worried Chandler more. The old man's mind was disintegrating. Chandler was left with trying to distract him from the search, discussing everything from the vastness of space to the latest football scores, doing his best to keep the awful truth from entering and consuming the old man's brain.

34

The day began with the publication of the preliminary forensic report. It confirmed what Chandler already knew: all six victims had been strangled with rope. Not the same rope, which was unfortunate for the investigators. There wasn't much else to note in it other than his delicate retrieval of the manacles had proved a bust, any DNA or fingerprint evidence destroyed in the blaze. He had been hoping it would at least confirm which one of them had been chained up. The report included confirmation that the perp was right-handed. Both Gabriel and Heath were right-handed so it didn't add anything. Traces of blood found on some of the less-damaged tools matched DNA with a couple of the buried victims, but again nothing regarding the suspects, the plastic handles melted into unrecognizable shapes like the death masks of the victims forensics were currently trying to piece together to aid identification.

What could be determined given the deterioration of the corpses was that the most recent victim – a male in his early thirties of slight build – had been dead three to four weeks. Bones in both legs had been broken but had since healed, childhood injuries rather than ones inflicted by his killer. Other than that, there were no signs of torture or mutilation, offering Chandler some relief that their killer might not have been quite as sadistic as believed. Deranged enough, however, to send at least six people to their maker.

John Doe was recent, the others weren't. The oldest victims were judged to be between two or three years old, nothing but bone and fragments of clothing left. There was hope that they could be matched to the list of missing persons via dental records, but that would be a lengthier, administrative process. The final line of the report confirmed what Chandler already knew: that the shirt found around the axe handle did indeed match Heath's.

Why would Heath be stupid enough to leave such a crucial piece of evidence there to be found? Of course he couldn't have known that the graves would be discovered but how could it happen? Had Heath been rushed into burying the John Doe while another victim – Gabriel – waited in the shed, like a conveyor belt of murder? But the body in the grave had been dead a few weeks. Why keep John Doe that long without burying him? His corpse would have stunk the cabin out in no time in this heat. And why keep it and then rush to bury him? There were no signs of interference post-mortem, sexual or otherwise. There was a chance that he was giving Heath too much credit for intelligence but there seemed only one feasible solution.

Against his better judgement Chandler sought out Mitch. As ever, he was stowed away in his sequestered office, the blinds shut tight, staring at a map of the town and the Hill projected on the wall, pretending not to be dealing with a hangover.

Chandler abandoned any attempted greeting and came right out with it, loud enough to make Mitch cringe.

'I have a theory.'

Mitch closed his eyes but didn't respond.

'About the piece of shirt we found—'

'Before you go on – about last night,' interrupted Mitch.

Chandler didn't want to discuss it. There was nothing to discuss. 'This isn't about last night.'

The hot, still air deadened the room. Mitch spoke first. 'Okay, go ahead.'

'I think Heath's being set up. By Gabriel.'

Mitch didn't react so Chandler continued.

'To make it look like Heath was responsible for the murders. We found the piece of Heath's shirt around the pickaxe, placing him at the scene. But by now you've seen the prelim report from forensics stating that the most recent victim had been dead three to four weeks.'

Mitch nodded slowly. 'Yes, and—?'

'Well, the soil around the body had been disturbed a lot more recently than that. There was still some moisture in it, so, either the victim was buried a few weeks after death – and you know in this heat the stink of a dead body would have made the cabin unbearable, so it doesn't seem likely the killer would have kept it around – or the soil was disturbed more recently. And there would be only one reason to do that. To plant evidence.'

Chandler expected at least a moment of quiet deliberation of his theory but Mitch shot back immediately. 'But Gabriel was caught first wasn't he? In fact, he handed himself in. Twice.'

'True, but as Heath has stated, he had no way to get here quicker. That's why he tried to steal the car.'

'But we have no guarantee that after stealing the car he was going to come to the station, only his word that he was, and that means nothing to me. The evidence we have, Sergeant, points to Heath. But while we put together something concrete, we'll keep them both here.'

'You're reading it wrong,' said Chandler. 'It's not Heath.'

'And you're clutching at straws, Sergeant.'

'But them working together makes no sense.'

Mitch interrupted, not raising his voice but insistence creeping through each word.

'Sergeant, we're charging both Mr Barwell and Mr Johnson.'

Ironically, given that under normal circumstances his daughter's First Confession would have been under way right now, Chandler headed to the church where the magistrate's court had been hastily convened in its hall. People with graver sins than his daughter would be offering their confessions.

To preside over the hearing, Eleanor White had been flown in. Eleanor had been the local magistrate for twenty-five years but even the tight bun that strangled her silver hair couldn't contain her excitement. Nothing in her long years of serving came close to this. Indeed, the case had brought the town to life for the first time in years, drawing to the surface a morbid fascination with death amongst its population that no amount of funfairs or amusement rides could hope to match.

Chandler's involvement was purely as a spectator, Mitch ordering his team to prep and move the suspects under close watch from their lawyers, the alert level raised to extreme, guiding them with excessive caution from the cells to the cars, one suspect in the back seat of each, flanked by a pair of Mitch's officers. Until the last second. Spying his chance, Chandler jumped in the back seat of Gabriel's transport ahead of Yohan. The squat officer shot daggers at Chandler but was outranked and minus the support of his boss who had left in the lead car with Heath, who had to be physically forced into it when told where he was going. As Chandler squashed up alongside Gabriel he gauged his reaction but got nothing that indicated that Gabriel was excessively worried, the suspect merely shifting around as if discomforted by the slick leather seats. Otherwise, he was placid.

The journey was unremarkable and at the hall, Chandler escorted his suspect from the car to the cramped lobby without issue. With the assortment of cops and officials there was little space to breathe and tensions were high. The suspects were watched over like hawks, and they, in turn, stared at each other from opposite sides of the lobby waiting for their name to be called. Chandler was confident that this was merely a formality. Both had indicated they would plead not guilty and neither would make, nor could afford, bail given the flight risk.

Heath was up first. Chandler accompanied him and his tired-looking lawyer inside.

The hall had been laid out in the manner of one of Sarah's terrible school plays, rows of seats thrown into casual alignment by the caretaker, to cater for the increased police and press presence. Even so, there were nowhere near enough places, the press muttering as they filed along the back and sides of the hall, notebooks and pencils at the ready to record the events. To lend the proceedings an air of authority the reverend's solid mahogany writing desk had been dragged from next door to the front of the stage where the Honourable Justice White sat looking very stately but very lonely, only the neatly stacked sheaves of evidence to keep her company. Convening the court, all her nervous excitement seemed to have disappeared. She was clear and deliberate in her speech as she read to Heath the charge of murder – a count of six. Heath whined that it wasn't him, loud enough for most to hear, the press eagerly noting the witness's intransigence and jittery body language. When the time came to enter his plea he did: Not Guilty. Delivered firmly, if emotionally. Chandler stared at the man he believed was innocent, unable to do anything to halt the process. He would just have to work on proving Heath's innocence.

After some more formalities, bail applied for by his

lawyer and refused, Heath was led out and directed to the worn pews that lined the lobby, his chest rising and falling in long breaths.

Gabriel was up next. He was perched not on the pews but curled up in a ball on the thick stone windowsill, rocking back and forth, looking almost foetal, the stained-glass window bathing him in a gentle blue light. His calm veneer had cracked. Mitch approached Gabriel's shoulder, and rested his hand on it, a cue to stand. Gabriel didn't move. Chandler got to his feet to help just as Gabriel finally unfurled himself and stood, head raised, focused not on Mitch, not on the wide double-door to the temporary court beyond, but on Heath.

The party began to move. As Mitch ushered onlookers out of the way Gabriel's attitude reminded Chandler of a dead man walking, taking his last steps before meeting his executioner, the grave silence broken only by the shuffled steps of the condemned. Chandler took up position as the suspects passed each other, barely six feet between them, closer than they had been since falling off the ridge together.

In a flash, Gabriel was free. With a dip of his shoulder he evaded Mitch's grasp, the cuffs that had been attached to his wrists sliding to the floor as he moved towards Heath who was propped rigidly on the pew.

The speed of the move took everyone by surprise. Chandler stood stunned as if he'd witnessed a magic trick unfold in front of his eyes, Gabriel's hands free of the chains, the escape artist wowing his audience into momentary inertia. Gabriel threw himself at the other man and wrestled Heath to the floor, trying to jam the serrated edge of a set of keys into his throat. Heath's screams wrenched Chandler from his stupor. Shoving Gabriel's lawyer out of the way, he launched himself at her client.

The tackle was good, forcing Gabriel off his prey and knocking both Gabriel and Chandler into an out-of-control roll, sweeping bystanders off their feet and causing him to lose hold of Gabriel, who slipped from his grasp.

As Chandler picked himself up off the faux marble floor, Gabriel was already up and sprinting for the door. Roper blocked the exit, reaching for his gun. Gabriel flew at him, hitting Roper in the midriff, knocking him over and relieving him of his firearm in one move, disappearing out of the church hall and into town.

Reaching the door, Chandler drew his gun. Lining the steps and car park, a mass of scared and eager reporters, cameramen and locals confronted him. Gabriel scampered across the tarmac parting the crowd by waving his stolen weapon in the air. Raising his own, Chandler aimed for Gabriel's legs, confident of hitting his target from this range. But as soon as Gabriel passed, the crowd closed in, the reporters turning to pursue the suspect, cameramen lugging their equipment, trying to keep up with their lead reporters.

'Out of the way,' yelled Chandler, bumping into one of the cameramen, his recording equipment swinging back and forth like a wrecking ball. Breaking through the main group, suddenly a line of sight opened up. Chandler got ready to shoot, but Gabriel disappeared around the corner of the station.

Chandler set off after him, Tanya, Jim and a motley crew of Mitch and his team close behind, the rabid press and a few determined locals also. Mitch's high-pitched and less than commanding cry of 'Get him!' rose above the sound of footsteps and excited squeals.

Before he even made the corner, Chandler had been overtaken by the younger and fitter pair of Flo and Sun, their firearms at the ready.

As the pursuit continued along King Edward Avenue, locals nosed their heads out of their doors and windows to observe the commotion.

'Back inside!' ordered Chandler, his legs already heavy.

His order was ignored. Until the first shot rang out. The residents scuttled back indoors as quickly as they had appeared.

'Don't fucking shoot,' shouted Chandler, trying to identify who had taken the shot, as the reporters swarmed him.

But desperation was helping ease Gabriel into the distance, already a couple of hundred metres ahead, Flo and Sun struggling to keep up.

Suddenly Gabriel darted on to the road, straight into the path of a chunky yellow Holden. It screeched to a halt. Miss Atherton, a local primary school teacher, threw herself out of the car as a gun was waved in her face. Getting in, Gabriel swung the hatchback around and zoomed off down Scott, pursued by another unidentified pot shot, a wild miss that screeched off into the distance.

And like that Gabriel was gone. For the second time.

Flo and Sun kept chasing in vain, following the car on to Logan's Way, tailed by the press looking for that final camera shot, but there would be no catching their suspect on foot.

Mitch stood by Chandler. He was fighting for breath. 'Why the fuck did you let him get loose?' Mitch cried.

'I didn't. He must have got the keys.'

'And how did he do that?' he spat. 'Your incompetent fucking officers, I bet.'

Mitch didn't wait for Chandler's defence, jumping straight on to the radio, putting the entire region on standby for the second time in two days.

35

Within ten minutes of Gabriel's escape, Mitch had corralled his forces and issued instructions. All vehicles were to be mobilized with the precaution that Gabriel was to be considered armed and extremely dangerous.

'What about Heath?' asked Chandler as Mitch finished his speech. 'We need to keep him under watch.'

Reporters gathered and yelled questions at them from close by, questioning what the police were doing about the murderer now loose in town. How did he get free? How were they going to keep the townspeople safe? The questions kept coming, spat like automatic gunfire.

Mitch paused, eyes rolling as if he had only just remembered his other suspect.

'We need to focus on the one not in custody, Sergeant.'

'I agree, but Gabriel's determined to kill him. For whatever reason. Has he got information on him? Something we haven't thought about?'

Yohan interrupted them. A yellow Holden had been seen near Lockridge. Going fast. Mitch ordered Yohan to get the word out to those already on the street. Almost instantly another report came in, verifying the first sighting, the police fanning out, Mitch in constant contact with his team, shrieking at the officers on the other end to catch Gabriel, then screaming at those nearby to keep the damn reporters back.

'I've got him in my sights.' A determined voice fought through the radio chatter. Tanya.

'Where are you?' butted in Chandler. He didn't care if Mitch didn't like it, Tanya was one of his officers.

'On Butcher's. He's trying to steal—'

The radio signal broke up. Chandler pictured Butcher's – a dirt road heading south, out towards the iron mines and unfarmable desert.

'Don't get too close,' ordered Mitch. 'Follow him.'

The signal returned; hard breathing and frantic motion filled their ears. A microphone rubbing on fabric. The voice cut in again.

'I can—'

The call dropped.

'Shit!' Chandler looked to Mitch who was already on the radio, ordering all available bodies to Butcher's.

'I'm going,' said Chandler.

Mitch nodded, then shouted at Luka. 'Luka, get us a car!'

A minute later a siren parted the reluctant horde, drowning out the questions from the press.

As they were barrelling into the car, a voice spluttered over the radio. It was Steve Kirriboo, a miner and father of six who farmed a few cattle further along Butcher's. His voice sang with worry. 'Chand? Sergeant?'

'Yes, Steve,' said Chandler.

'One of your guys – girls – is down out here.'

Chandler held his breath. *Down* ... had she confronted him?

'Chand?'

Chandler found some air. 'Yes, Steve ... she okay?'

There was no answer, Steve's drawl lost in the clamour of radio communication.

'Luka, step on it,' said Chandler.

Luka obeyed, the souped-up police car searing through streets that were otherwise eerily quiet, everyone either indoors watching the TV reports or crowded around the station and church hall.

'She better be okay.'

'As long as she blocked his escape,' said Mitch.

Chandler glared at him, the tarmac under the tyres changing into dirt, the rear end fishtailing with the sudden lack of grip.

A couple of kilometres up Butcher's they found the Holden outside Chucker Nelson's farm, angled towards the ditch as if forced to stop suddenly. The rear lights were on, the engine still running. As Luka pulled up behind it, Chandler was out of the vehicle before it stopped, other squad cars queuing up behind.

Just past the empty Holden, Tanya was propped against the foot of a fence post. She was alive, much to his relief, looking up at him in embarrassment, a narrow trail of blood appearing from her tight hairline.

'Sorry,' she said.

'Never mind that, are you okay?'

'Fine. A few bruises, a sore head,' she said, resting against the post for support.

'Why did you approach him?' he asked, more forcefully than he had intended.

'To try and stop him,' she said, suddenly angry.

He nodded in silent apology. 'What happened?'

'He was parked by the gate, trying to get Chucker's quad started. With the noise of the old thing I thought I'd managed to sneak up on him but I guess he saw me in the mirror. Hit me before I had the chance to take him down. I thought he was going to kill me but instead he just asked my name. When I told him, he pistol-whipped me.'

'Your name? He didn't say anything else? Anything about where he was heading?' interjected Mitch, impatient.

Tanya shook her head. 'Nothing.'

'Not even a hint?'

'No,' said Tanya, glancing at Chandler as if pleading for him to get Mitch away from her. 'In fact, he seemed almost, disinterested in me.'

'You're not the one he's after,' said Chandler.

'Or possibly because he has half the police force after him,' countered Mitch. He turned to Tanya. 'What direction did he go in?'

Tanya shook her head. 'I didn't see, but I'd guess further in. Somewhere we can't get to by car.'

'We need to get going,' grunted Mitch, directing this at Chandler.

'I'm not leaving Tanya.'

284

'She's fine, a bump and a bruise. We can't waste more time. My team will call an ambulance.'

Chandler looked to his senior constable. Her fury was barely confined. Her response was given through clenched teeth. 'Go. I'll be fine.'

Chandler put a hand on her shoulder. 'Not until—'

'Go,' she said again. 'Don't let the bastard disappear.'

Chandler ran back to the car to find Mitch behind the wheel. Circumnavigating the Holden, Mitch fought with the steering wheel on the gravel road as he increased the pace of the pursuit, his foot heavy on the accelerator.

'Why do you think he let her go?' asked Chandler, thinking out loud.

'I don't know,' said Mitch, sawing at the wheel. 'Maybe he doesn't want to kill a woman or a police officer?'

'There were two women amongst the bodies we found.'

'Maybe he isn't as crazy as we thought. Maybe there's a plan behind all this.'

'Maybe,' said Chandler. He hoped it was the truth. A plan was good news. Plans, by their very nature, could be discovered and foiled; random acts of violence were harder to determine and prevent. But to stop Gabriel, first they had to capture him.

Ten minutes up Butcher's and the road spluttered into a track that was barely navigable by car. Another five and it disappeared altogether, the brush accessible by quad or scrambler only. In desperation, Mitch ordered them to follow on foot but after half an hour of laboured progress and no sign of their suspect, the foot search was called off. Mitch radioed in a chopper and roused the state police to the exits at the far end in case Gabriel appeared there.

The ride back to town was dominated by questions over the escape, the ramifications of what Gabriel had done and what he might do next. The only good news that filtered through on the way was confirmation that Tanya was okay, the cut on her scalp minor, concussion protocol passed. She'd refused to stay in hospital, insisting on returning to work. Chandler was glad. He needed all the good officers he could muster. The town was on lockdown, the streets empty aside from a few nosy locals and the ever-present mass of reporters surrounding the station. As they made their way through the crowd the same questions Chandler had himself were fired at him, questions he had no answers for; how had Gabriel managed to get free and what were they were doing to find him? How many had Gabriel killed? How many would he kill? Chandler kept his head down and offered no comment.

As they entered the station, Chandler started the inquest.

'How *did* he manage to get free from those cuffs?'

The other officers looked at each other for answers. They drew a blank.

As he reached the door of the office, Mitch swung around. 'That doesn't matter now. We just need to get him.'

'Of course it matters,' frowned Chandler. 'The

procedure failed somewhere. And you're all about procedure.'

'I'm *all* about getting Gabriel back,' replied Mitch. 'So kill this convo and get back to work.'

The order was belted out to his team – plus Luka – and they returned to their desks. Chandler and his small crew remained in discussion.

'He didn't break the cuffs,' noted Jim, 'I checked 'em. They were unlocked, no scratches either.'

'So he had the keys,' said Nick from the front desk.

'It looks like it, but *how* did he get the keys?' asked Chandler.

'Pickpocket?' suggested Jim.

Chandler shook his head. 'His hands were bound at all times. And no one ever got that close to him. Only ...'

He turned to the office. Chandler suddenly knew. Yesterday, when Mitch had assaulted Gabriel in the interview room. Gabriel must have swiped them in the melee, then concealed them, waiting for the right moment to ambush Heath.

He followed Mitch into the stale air of his former office.

'So it was *you*,' said Chandler. 'He got the keys off you.'

Mitch paced to the far end of the room, head lowered, reeking of guilt. If only Gabriel had looked as guilty earlier, all this shit could have been prevented, thought Chandler.

'He must have taken them off me,' said Mitch, speaking quietly, refusing to go into details. 'But we need to keep it quiet.'

'Why?'

Mitch rubbed his ever-darkening stubble. 'If this leaks, we'll have a million more questions. From above and below. What matters now is that we catch Gabriel before he has the chance to kill again.'

Mitch looked desperate. It was the first time since the search for Martin that Chandler had seen his former friend like this. If only he was capable of looking vulnerable a little more often, then people might have considered him human. Despite this unexpected glimpse of humanity, a significant part of Chandler considered handing the information over to the press, a simple loose word or two that would spread like a virus and infect every news station with the tale of the bumbling inspector. Worse – the negligent inspector. But even though it was tempting, Chandler recognized the underlying truth to what Mitch had said: how Gabriel had got free was secondary to apprehending him again. If the distraction over the lost keys resulted in someone else getting killed, Chandler would never be able to forgive himself. So he made the decision – he would keep the information for now, save it as a bargaining chip.

Another realization forced its way out of his mouth. 'After taking them off you Gabriel had the keys all day. He could have escaped at any time but he waited until Heath was exposed.'

'So . . . ?' said Mitch.

'So, instead of me catching him outside the station, I think he purposefully turned himself in to stay close to Heath.'

'So there must be some sort of connection.'

Chandler nodded. 'Some reason to risk his freedom for that one chance to kill Heath.'

Heath was brought back into the interview room, his lawyer in tow. He was furious. This time Mitch made a point to invite Chandler to accompany him.

'There's no connection,' said Heath, his voice insistent. 'I swear it. I'm a victim.'

Chandler spoke up. 'And you're sure you didn't run into him earlier? On a farm, or on a job? Months, even years ago?'

'Yes, I'm sure.'

'Might you have done something to someone he knows – or loves? You didn't sleep with his wife, ex-wife, sister?'

'What? Are you asking if I brought this on myself?' asked Heath, tilting his head to the side in confusion.

'Yes,' said Mitch. 'You have quite an abrasive person-ality, Mr Barwell.'

'*I* have an abrasive personality? What about this fucking joke of a police force? I've told you that I'm the victim. Four fucking times now.'

'We're only trying to determine if there's a reason he's so intent on killing you. You didn't steal something, punch somebody, beat up someone?'

'Punch? Beat?' spat Heath. His voice was incredulous and his face livid.

'You did say that you committed an assault,' said Chandler.

'That guy was a friend of a friend,' spluttered Heath.

'Look – all I know is that I'm in here accused of a crime, accused of *murders* I didn't commit. I came close to being murdered twice by the same person, the *actual* murderer and yet I'm still being treated like I'm guilty. I want out of here now. I want outta this station and far away from this fucking place. Find him and then *maybe* I'll come back and testify. Or better yet I'll do it over video link and keep the fuck away from this shithole.'

Heath looked to his lawyer for help.

'Is there anywhere secure my client can be kept overnight?' asked the blonde lawyer.

'He's staying in it,' said Chandler.

'For your own safety, I think you are better off remaining here, Mr Barwell, where we can protect you,' said Mitch.

Heath glared at his lawyer and then at Mitch. 'You nearly got me killed.'

'That was an accident.'

'Yeah, there seem to be a *lot* of accidents happening around here. And just so you know, I'm going to sue you after this. All of you. False imprisonment, endangering my life, holding me without charge. I'll make a fortune,' he said, his anger morphing into a smirk.

36

With darkness having closed in, the hunt through the outback for Gabriel was put on hold. Mitch ordered some of his officers on to the streets to lend the appearance that things were under control.

Something was bugging Chandler. A conversation he'd had with Gabriel that first morning. He told Mitch that he was going home to check on his family. Mitch wanted all hands to the pump but they both knew Mitch was in no position to refuse considering how their suspect had got loose. And though he didn't have to, Chandler felt the need to tell Mitch, to tell someone what was bothering him – just in case.

'Gabriel knows where I live.'

Mitch frowned. 'How does he know that?'

'We were chatting when I took him to the hotel after questioning him the first time and I mentioned my family.'

'That was stupid.'

'I had no idea he would turn out to be *masquerading* as a victim. I was just trying to put a witness at ease.'

Mitch paused. 'Okay, what's done is done. I'll have a patrol car come by every half hour.'

Chandler nodded. 'Thanks.'

'Be back in a couple of hours, okay? We need everyone.'

'What are you going to do?' asked Chandler.

Mitch nodded towards the door. 'Go out on patrol myself. Lead the hunt. Check out some of the abandoned joints in town in case he's hiding out. It'll be a journey into the past.'

'You really want to go back there?' asked Chandler.

Mitch didn't answer.

Chandler fought his way through the forest of microphones without comment. The numbers of vans and reporters had multiplied like bacteria.

The darkness pervaded everything and as he drove home Chandler found himself peering into the murk of every house, garden and alley, wondering if Gabriel lay in wait and was unnerved to find himself frightened by the prospect, frightened by what lurked in the shadows of his own town. His small, laid-back town was now a pulsing mass, terror soaked into its very fabric.

The fear lingered even as he arrived home to find the kids settling in for a rare evening in their own house, Nanna watching over them. He quashed those plans immediately.

'Okay, everyone, pack some things. We're going to go stay with Nanna and Grandad tonight.'

'Again? Why?' asked Sarah, frustrated.

'I might have to leave in a hurry,' said Chandler.

It was hard to tell who glared at him hardest. Sarah or her nanna.

'Go pack,' he ordered and walked to the front window. He scanned the front garden, the mighty paper-bark tree in the yard casting long shadows in the washed-out porch light, shedding its orange-brown skin, moulting ... like the town was moulting, from peaceful existence to insidious terror. Chandler shook his head, trying to clear his mind.

Leaning forward he checked his neighbours, the Rizzos. Lights dotted their two-storey home, the garden swing twitching slightly in the breeze. There was nothing abnormal in the scene but all he could envision was Gabriel commandeering the Rizzos' house, lying in wait for him.

'What was that about?' asked his mum.

Chandler almost banged his head on the glass. He checked that the kids couldn't hear. 'It's best they stay with you.'

'I can stay here with them if you get called away. But they were looking forward to spending an evening with you.'

'Me too,' said Chandler. It was true, nothing would have been more enjoyable. An evening with both his kids, the world back to normal.

'It doesn't much seem like it.'

'I'll make it up to them.'

'You can't keep taking from the bank. You have to deposit some too.'

'I know.'

He returned to the window. Still Gabriel lurked in every shadow. Chandler had no doubt he was going to return like some nightmarish monster. He was resourceful, and smart, and moved with what seemed like unworldly stealth. Chandler cursed himself once again for not pressing Mitch to realize that their quiet, pensive prisoner was infinitely more dangerous than the constant whinger. A serial killer doesn't whine. *Or introduce themselves*, as Gabriel had noted.

His mum was helping the kids pack when the shrill ring of the landline interrupted his stakeout. A call on the landline signalled trouble. An unknown caller.

Leaving his post at the window he answered. His instinct was right. It was trouble, the voice causing his stomach to try and escape his body.

Teri.

'Are the kids there?' she asked, a little frantic.

'Yeah,' he answered. If she wanted to speak to them he would refuse. He'd claim that they had already gone to bed.

'I'm comin' to get them,' she blurted out.

'No you aren't,' said Chandler, louder than he wanted.

As ever, Teri took this as a challenge and raised her voice in return. 'I'm coming and taking them to the city where they'll be safe.'

Safe. He realized what must have happened. She had been talking to Mitch who had pumped her full of fear, possibly out of genuine concern but more likely as leverage in the coming custody battle. The perfect opportunity to prove that she was ready and able to look after the kids in a time of crisis. To assume the role of their protector. Chandler wasn't prepared to let that happen.

'No, Teri, it's too dangerous.'

'I know. I know what's happening there.'

Chandler stabbed his sword at the chink in her armour. 'And how's that?'

'How's what?'

'How do you know what's going on here?'

'I—'

There was silence from the other end. Chandler decided to swing the sword again.

'Teri, I know about you and Mitch,' he said, before lowering his voice so as not to be overheard. 'About you wanting to take *my* kids.'

'That's—' stumbled Teri before going on the offensive. '*This* is the stubbornness I wanna get the kids away from.'

Chandler let the slight pass. 'I'm going to fight you, Teri. All the way.'

'Go right ahead,' she replied. 'Mitch knows people.'

'And they know Mitch,' said Chandler.

From the background his mum announced that the kids were ready to leave.

'I'm going now,' said Chandler.

'Let me—'

He cut her off, and hung up. He left the phone off the hook in case she decided to call back.

Chandler hustled the kids and his parents out of the house to the car. Ignoring the kids' suggestions of who should sit where, he shoved them inside. Putting Jasper in last, he looked behind the car. Something or someone was skulking in the distance. Chandler was sure of it. And sure of who it was. Gabriel. He looked back at his family. His muscles twitched to leave them and go after Gabriel but he would have to leave them exposed.

Deciding against it, Chandler jumped in and pulled away. As he peered in the rear-view mirror, a set of headlights appeared from nowhere, tracking a hundred metres behind as he turned on to Harper's, keeping a consistent speed and distance from him. A tail. Not a subtle one. He wouldn't have time to lose it if he went the direct route to his parents' house so instead of shooting down Tunney's, he pulled sharply on to Mercado, the tyres screeching, his mum shrieking at him to slow down.

As he turned the corner, the headlights disappeared only to reappear moments later. Then they began to close in rapidly. Chandler's sense of danger heightened. He wanted to speed up but any faster and they were liable to plough into something solid. So he decided to slow down, force the car to go past and identify who was behind the wheel.

It pulled up alongside him in seconds. Chandler glanced over expecting to see Gabriel and wondering what he would do.

But it wasn't Gabriel. The driver was a man in his early fifties, brown hair washed back from his forehead, focusing solely on the road in front as he drove down the wrong side of it. Leaning over from the passenger's side was someone he did recognize, Jill SanLuiso, Channel

Nine reporter for the Pilbara, her jet black hair stylishly streaked with grey, distinguished and pretty for her advancing years.

'Can you tell me what the latest situation is, Sergeant?' she shouted across the face of her driver.

Chandler couldn't believe it. They had followed him home, hunting for a scoop. Rage made him grip the steering wheel tight. 'The latest situation, Miss SanLuiso,' he said, his words curt, 'is that you're driving down the wrong side of a residential street, breaking the speed limit while hassling a policeman and his family.'

'You know what I mean, Sergeant. What's the latest with the serial killer out there?'

Chandler almost swerved into them in anger, glancing in the rear-view mirror to witness the look of concern on his kids' faces.

'No comment,' he said, his eyes fixed on hers. 'And I ask you not to mention anything more in front of my family.'

'Just a few words.'

'I have a few but you won't be able to broadcast them.'

Turning sharply on to Prince's he drove off. Miss SanLuiso didn't follow.

A minute later they were safely ensconced in his parents' house. Chandler's interrogation had only just begun.

'What did she mean by serial killer, Daddy?' asked Jasper.

'What it means is—' started Sarah.

Chandler interrupted her. 'What it means, Jasper, is that someone has done something bad and now the police are looking for him.'

'And you dunno where he is, Daddy?'

'Not yet, but Daddy's friends have it under control. We'll find him and put him in custody.'

'Can I help?' asked Jasper, his voice eager.

The honesty in the offer helped ease Chandler's tension. 'You can help by going to bed on time and without a tantrum.'

'I will.'

'Good boy,' said Chandler, ruffling his hair.

Chandler glanced around and then looked at his mum. She was frowning.

'Are you leaving? Now?' she asked. It was a question – and a thinly disguised order not to even think about it.

'No,' said Chandler. Given the scare they'd had on the way here, Chandler wasn't about to go.

'Daddy?' asked Jasper, his sister having scampered into the living room to lay claim to the majority of the sofa.

'Yes, Jasp.'

'Why are you putting the bad man in custody, like us?'

Chandler frowned. 'What do you mean?'

'You are putting us in custody too. I heard you on the phone. Would *we* have to go to prison?'

Chandler paused. Jasper must have overheard him on the phone to Teri and got the wrong idea. Again the shame of neglecting his family – his kids – rose to the surface. There was only one thing to do. Taking the young boy into the living room he sat him on the sofa beside his sister to explain it to both of them. His mum followed, both witness and judge.

'It's a different type of custody. It means that your mum wants you to go live with her.'

'Just me?' asked Jasper.

'No, you and your sister,' said Chandler, looking at Sarah. She was sitting up on the sofa, staring at him. Her semi-permanent look of boredom had been blown away.

'And you?' asked Jasper. 'Us living together again with Mum?'

'No, you and her and Uncle ... Mitchell.' The words were like poison on his tongue.

'When did this happen?' asked Sarah.

'It hasn't happened yet. It's something your mum wants.'

'Since when?'

'A few months, a year, I'm not sure,' admitted Chandler.

'All because she suddenly became an adult,' added his mum. Chandler agreed with her on this but glared at her to keep quiet.

'Daddy?'

'Yes, Jasper,' said Chandler, focusing on his son.

'If we go there, how will we get to school? It's lots and lots and lots of miles away.'

Though the shame had left him feeling empty inside Chandler couldn't hold back the smile. 'It's not definite yet, by no means, but I need to know how you feel about it. They'll ask you—'

'I don't want to leave here,' interrupted Sarah.

'I don't want to leave unless you're coming, Daddy,' said Jasper, throwing himself at Chandler, clasping his arms around Chandler's neck like he would never let go.

The sheer insistence of their responses made Chandler feel a little better and he settled into playing a few games of Jenga with his kids. For a while he even forgot about the looming spectres of Gabriel, Mitch and Teri.

It was almost bedtime when the phone rang. His mum answered before Chandler could get to it. It wasn't Teri this time, but the station. The call to return.

'Tell them I'm having a shower or something,' said Chandler as she covered the mouthpiece. He was in no mood to leave his family, not while it was dark and Gabriel was still out there.

As he put the kids to bed, the phone rang again. Tanya this time. Chandler nodded that the same excuse should be used. Still in the bathroom.

He had finished Jasper's bedtime story when the next call came. This time the order came from the very top. Mitch wasn't accepting Chandler's well-worn excuse.

'He won't get off the phone,' said his mum. The frown she now wore changed her welcoming and open face into a haggard one. 'Go in,' she said. 'The kids won't get any sleep with the phone ringing every minute. Plus, eventually he'll come out here and drag you back.'

'I can't go in,' said Chandler, forcing the gulp down.

'Why, son?' Even his dad's concentration had been torn from the TV over his son's reluctance to leave.

'He knows where I live.'

'Who does?' asked his mum.

'The one we're looking for. The killer.'

'How does he know that?' asked his mum, her expression one of shock.

Chandler took a deep breath and explained his mistake. Both were silent for a second before his mum spoke up. 'There's nothing to say he's coming back, son. Why would he?'

'He did before. We think he will again.'

There was a moment's pause before his dad rose from his armchair with intent. Taking a key from a chain around his neck, he entered the kitchen and unlocked the cabinet affixed horizontally on top of the cupboards. From it he pulled out the old shotgun, the wood chipped and worn but, as far as Chandler knew, still in perfect working order.

'I'll keep watch,' he announced, clicking the barrel open and slipping two red shells inside.

'Dad, you don't need that thing,' said Chandler, even if he did feel a little more secure in its presence.

'Can you even use that still, Peter?' warned his mum.

'Of course I can, Caroline. My fists might be brittle and my wits might be gone, but I can still pull a bloody trigger.'

He gripped the gun, hunched as he had been the last few years. His stubby fingers eased over the butt, the fingernails as cracked and chipped as the paint on the old Ford Mustang that lay in the back of the garage.

'I only want you to point it, not use it,' said Chandler.

'What's the use in that?'

'Take out the shells, Dad,' said Chandler, his hand out.

'What do you mean, take out the shells? If I'd wanted a club, I'd have bought a club.'

'No shells,' said Chandler. His dad mumbled under his breath but popped the barrel and removed the cartridges. Chandler took them and passed them to his mum. He trusted her not to let him have them.

His last action was to go and kiss the kids goodnight. Sarah let him kiss her on the forehead but waved him out of the room as she stared into the glowing screen of her phone. Jasper was asleep and he was about to creep out and leave him be when the young boy awoke.

'Why are you going, Daddy?' he asked, his voice drowsy.

'I have to help the town.'

'Because of that serial killer?'

'Yes,' said Chandler, hoping that Jasper wouldn't ask any difficult questions.

'Why does he hurt people, Daddy?'

'I don't know, Jasp. Some people are just bad people but Grandpa and Nanna will keep you safe while Daddy catches him. Now it's time to get some sleep. We'll go out on the go-kart again tomorrow.'

Chandler left his son smiling at the thought. In the living room his dad was perched by the front door, staring out the front window.

'Chances are—' started Chandler then stopped. He didn't know what the chances were of Gabriel coming here so he settled upon, 'Just keep calm, okay?'

'I am calm,' said his dad, adjusting the empty shotgun across his knees.

37

Back at the station Nick brought Chandler up to speed on the hunt. The initial search in town had been fruitless; garages, gardens, sheds, shacks, houses and stores on the main street had been searched and in some cases, ransacked. That had taken a while. There'd been plenty of them to clear; the once numerous small, independent stores abandoned, as dried up as the desert beyond. The latest reckoning was that Gabriel was still in the outback, bedding down up there, possibly in an emergency hideout of some kind.

Chandler joined the rest of the team in Mitch's office.

'Kids all right?' said Mitch with a cheerless smirk.

Chandler nodded. 'Find our *escaped* suspect yet?'

Mitch dropped the smirk.

Mitch carried on. 'Come daylight we'll send the plane and chopper up. Exmouth are lending us theirs too. Hopefully we'll spot some movement or sign of a camp.'

'What about sending a group in tonight? Catch him cold,' said Roper, his head bandaged after being taken down by Gabriel earlier.

'We'd see nothing,' said Chandler, 'and the last thing we need on top of this is a case of friendly fire.'

Mitch weighed in. 'Besides, he'll be too smart to light anything.'

'Unless he tries to destroy evidence like last time,' added Tanya, sending a murmur of possibility around the room.

'Can we be sure he's still out there?' asked Chandler. 'There's a chance he double-backed and bedded down in some barn on the outskirts.'

'We've searched as extensively as we can,' said Mitch. 'And even if he has, we're left with the same needle in a haystack problem.'

'Well, do we need to be *seen* to do something? Rather than sitting around waiting for him to make the next move?' asked Luka. It was a solution designed to plaster over the cracks, saving face. The positive projection to the public. He *was* slowly turning into Mitch.

'Sitting still may be our best bet, Luka,' said Chandler. 'He attacked the guy we have in our cells when he had the chance. Maybe he'll come back to finish the job.'

'Whatever the decision, the press need to be updated,' said Mitch. 'This time I think it's best that one of you local guys do it.' Though he didn't look at him, Chandler understood that the buck was being passed.

'Why local?' asked Chandler, wanting some reasoning behind it.

'To show that both local and state are working in harmony to protect the town.'

As Chandler expected: a bullshit reason. 'So what you

want is for me to go out there and tell them that we've got nothing, putting my face on the incompetence of the police force.'

Mitch shook his head but the thin smile was telling. 'No, Sergeant, I want you to go out there and do your job.'

'You're the ranking officer here,' said Chandler.

'That's right. And I'm ordering you to take the conference.'

'And tell them what? That we don't have any leads; just to strap themselves in, hunker down and wait for the Devil to appear?'

'Not in those words.' Mitch paused. 'You need to learn to deal with disappointment and setbacks, Sergeant.'

'I've learned,' said Chandler. He couldn't hold it back any longer. It was time to play his joker. If Mitch was going to try and put him in the shit then they were both going to be covered. 'The whole reason we're in this mess is because Gabriel stole the keys from you, when you attacked him in the interview room.'

To Chandler's surprise, the revelation did not shake Mitch's cool. It was almost as if he expected this. Contrary to intention, the chill ran down Chandler's back. He had walked right into the trap

Mitch stepped back from the table and straightened to full height. 'Now is not the time to go around throwing blame, Sergeant. The press will do enough of that. We have to close ranks. Remain as one,' he said, appealing to the entire table.

'And don't you think that should come from the boss?' said Chandler.

'It's about keeping a united front.'

'Behind a leader we can trust.'

Chandler looked around the table. Where once he might have been able to judge loyalties, the exertions of the last few days had blinded him. He found it hard to tell if Tanya, Jim and Nick retained enough faith in him as a leader to believe his accusations. Luka was a lost cause.

'We made a false step. It's time to recover,' said Mitch, teeth gritted slightly.

'And it's up to you to lead that recovery,' said Chandler.

Mitch paused then ushered Chandler to the side, keeping his voice low. 'I didn't want to have to remind you, Sergeant, but remember, I write the report on this. You already let Gabriel go once, it's easy to believe you let it happen a second time.'

Chandler took a deep breath. 'When did you become such a bastard?' As he said it Chandler realized that Mitch had always been a bastard. The selfishness had always been there, even in his teens. The badge had only released the maniac within. He reworded his question, 'When did you start throwing everyone under the bus?'

Mitch wasn't riled. The thin smile suggested that he might have even taken it as a compliment. 'Your career's going nowhere, Chandler, not after this, not after details are leaked of how you – *and* your team – had the killer and let him go twice. So I suggest that if you – and they – still want to have a job after this is over, get out there and feed the dogs the story. How would it look to a judge if Sarah and Jasper had a single dad with no income?'

The urge to punch that smug, sanctimonious face was overwhelming. Chandler glanced across the office to the rest of his team. He didn't want them going down with his ship. Jim had his elderly parents to support, Tanya her three kids. Nick was only starting out and Luka ... well, he would be just fine. Any clone of Mitch would survive like a cockroach in an apocalypse. Plus, Mitch was right; losing his job would hand Teri the advantage.

Biting the bullet, he stepped out of the front doors. Camera flashes blinded him as the reporters' questions tried to pierce his armour, the floodlights framing him. Trying to compose himself he raised a hand. The questions died down.

He relayed the current situation to the gathered horde. He repeated their standard description of Gabriel and pleaded that people call the police rather than approach him if seen, before finishing with an appeal for the public to remain indoors.

As his statement finished the questions were fired at him again. *How dangerous was Gabriel? Was it true that they originally had Gabriel locked up and let him go? Could he confirm the identity of the six victims? Was there a chance he'd kill again? Was the second suspect still in custody? Why was the second suspect still in custody?* Chandler answered them all, dazzled by the light. He even explained exactly how Gabriel got free, the official version, a procedural fault, the system to blame rather than a specific individual.

As he spoke he peered into the crowd. Despite the pleas to disperse it seemed to have swollen and he searched the faces, looking for Gabriel hidden amongst them. It would be exceptionally brave or stupid of Gabriel to return, but he had proved himself both capable and daring. He scanned for beards and hats, simple disguises that Gabriel might use. He looked for tanned faces and men of a certain height. There was no one fitting Gabriel's description so he asked the reporters to disperse until morning to let the police do their job.

He slunk back inside the station feeling like a criminal himself. He was now part of the cover-up. Lying to the press.

But Chandler couldn't contemplate his dishonesty right now. He focused on catching Gabriel and answering the one question charging around his skull. Why was Gabriel so fascinated with killing Heath that he voluntarily had himself arrested and waited for the – almost – perfect moment to attack?

Maybe there was something he hadn't thought to ask Heath. Chandler moved through the office and into the holding area. Heath came right up to the door of the cell.

'I'm not talking to anyone without my lawyer.'

'Look, Mr Barwell ... Heath. I don't think that you have anything to do with this,' said Chandler.

There was a pause before the angry response. 'A bit late for that. And if I've nothing to do with this, can I leave now?'

'We need to keep you safe until we find Gabriel. I

believe he's still after you. I think he got himself arrested just to get close to you.'

The prisoner shook his head. 'But why? I don't even know him.'

'I'm trying to figure that out.'

'If you let me out of here I'll stick around. Or you can escort me out of town. Bulletproof car or whatever.'

'That I can't do, sorry. You're safe in there.'

'Like hell I am! At least out of this cell I have a chance to run. Given that you're so convinced he's after me, you did a great job making sure he was close enough to try and kill me. And then you let him escape. So forgive me for not being overwhelmed with confidence in your abilities.'

'I know you're angry, Mr Barwell, but we have the right to keep you here if we believe that your personal well-being is in danger.'

'What kinda fucked-up system is this?'

'One that might keep you alive.'

Through the slat in the door, Chandler saw a frown ripple the suspect's forehead.

'*Might*. That's comforting.'

Chandler spotted Heath's defences relaxing, his attempt at procuring release having failed. He tried a sneaky question. 'Do you think Gabriel chose you deliberately?'

Heath sighed and shrugged. 'It could have been anyone hitching that road. It was wrong time, *very* wrong place.'

'And there were no indications? None at all?'

'Of what?'

'That he had something else planned for you.'

'No, as I've told you numerous times, it was all fine. Nothing but general conversation ...' Heath paused, staring at the side wall before turning towards Chandler. Once again the frown rippled his skin. 'He did seem intrigued by my name, I suppose. More than most. My mum loved *Wuthering Heights*, but thought calling me Heathcliff would have been cruel ... but the way he repeated my name was as if it was personal to him. I remember asking him if he knew someone else called Heath but he shook his head. Why? Do you think I remind him of someone?'

'We'll try and find out,' said Chandler.

38

2002

The days stretched out, long and unforgiving, the search petering out. Martin's ultimate fate remained officially undetermined but inevitable. It had been over three weeks now, and Christmas was approaching fast.

Chandler had a front seat view of the show, witnessing the mercenaries – even the Murray River teenager – pocket the cash each morning before feigning effort throughout the day. Arthur had been wooed by their fantastical ideas and by charts and diagrams drawn by a laundry list of psychics and mediums stating that they knew where Martin was – and could tell him if only Arthur would pay them, allowing their spiritual talents to be nurtured by physical cash. Only that morning, one of the mercenaries, a shamanic figure from Darwin called Blazz, put forward the latest theory about what Martin had been searching for in the forest: a hidden cave of gold, buried by some turn of the 19th century outlaw.

Chandler's vexation was such that he was forced to seek out Mitch as the voice of calm.

'Did you hear that?'

'I heard it,' said Mitch. He didn't seem annoyed by it at all, which wound Chandler up further.

'We can't let that go.'

'We're meant to keep the peace, not verify what these weirdos claim. That's not our job.'

'I don't really know what my job is anymore,' admitted Chandler.

'It's keep your eyes down and ride it out,' said Mitch.

'That's the kind of police work you want to do? Sit back and let the family destroy themselves?'

Mitch didn't answer, spitting his chewing gum into the dirt.

'Chunks the size of footballs,' announced Blazz at the top of his lungs; bombastic and insistent.

'There's no cave in here stocked with gold,' said Chandler, unable to let it pass.

'The wind told me,' said Blazz, his voice carrying the belief of his convictions.

'The wind? Bullshit.'

'Just because you don't understand, Officer, doesn't mean it's wrong,' said Blazz, the ringlets in his hair dancing, despite the sweat that rolled down his temples.

Chandler stepped closer. 'I understand that you don't mind stealing an old man's money, but don't feed him bullshit as well.'

'It isn't bullshit. I was told by the wind. I can sense these things.'

312

'*Your senses haven't located Martin yet, have they?*'

'*We're close,*' *said Blazz in a whisper.*

Close to joining Martin if you keep up with this, *thought Chandler.* 'Just focus on searching. Enough with the spiritual crap.'

Blazz started uttering gasps and croaks, conversing in an odd language that sounded like he was having a fit, spitting and retching. Chandler wanted nothing more than to have to call in the chopper to take Blazz away. But Blazz suddenly stopped and announced: 'You are cursed now, Officer. And remember these hills are my friends not yours.'

Chandler stepped forward. 'Was that a threat?'

'That was a curse.'

'That does . . . ?'

Blazz smiled. Chandler took another step forward willing to forcefully extract the truth from Blazz when his shoulder was grabbed. It was Arthur.

'What are you doing, Chandler?'

The simple question dazed him; what was *he doing?*

Arthur continued, 'These people are only trying to help.'

Chandler stared at him. The old man was clearly deluded. What his exact role was out here might have been lost in the dust and trees but he remembered one of the main tenets: protect the public.

'They aren't trying to help, Arthur.' *It was time for the old man to learn the hard truth.* 'They're only here to take your money. All these utterings of divine intervention and omens. They're just trying to swindle you.'

He had said it. Immediately Chandler felt lighter, the earth no longer sapping the energy from his limbs.

The response he got was a simple nod. The pressure slowly increased once again, anchoring him to the earth.

'I know that. I believe in God but I'm not stupid, Chandler.'

Chandler frowned. 'Then why?'

'If one set of eyes, paid or not, can find my son, then I would give everything. My money, my house, my eternal soul. It doesn't matter.'

Chandler didn't know what to say. He was wrong about the old man. He had voluntarily hopped on the ride in the faint hope that someone on the carousel would find Martin, his son. Chandler thought of Teri and his newborn child. What if it were him? He didn't want to think about it.

It was a turning point for Chandler. From wanting to leave the outback and abandon the search, he found himself drawn closer to father and son, living through the pain with them, the weight continuing to fall off Arthur every day as if he were giving part of himself to the outback as a ritual sacrifice to get his missing son back. Day by day his barrel chest and booming voice became cowed, hardly heard over the chattering of the insects in the brush, searching for kindness in people, searching for hope in others. He talked about back home, the family accountancy firm that he'd intended to pass on to Martin, but Martin had shown neither aptitude nor desire to follow his father into the business. He talked of his wife, Sylvia, afraid that she would never recover sufficiently to be a good mother for their remaining son, essentially giving up on him because she had failed the first. She spent her days locked in the hotel surrounded by photos of her lost boy. Donated by friends and colleagues, it had become a bittersweet treasure trove of pictures they had never seen of him; Martin with friends and girlfriends, passed out drunk or dancing at a random house party. These were flashes of their son at play, happy and content, out walking, rambling and climbing in the great outdoors. It was these pictures of their son outdoors that hit home the hardest. They had spent many nights crying themselves to sleep, lost in their spiralling grief.

As such, Chandler found himself grasping on to anything to keep the old man distracted. Today the topic was exercise, Arthur stating that he had never done as much walking in his life and wishing that he had kept in some sort of shape, so he could cover the ground quicker.

'It's not about covering the ground quickly, it's about covering it well,' said Chandler, walking behind him, within the footstep of the old man's shadow and the old man in the footstep of his son's. 'You said that he loved the outdoors.'

'He did – he does. It's something I never understood. Maybe I can't appreciate it. Just how massive it is. How it would feel to live here.'

'It wouldn't be very pleasant,' Chandler told him. 'Your only neighbours are a thousand snakes and a million spiders.'

To *this* the boy turned, *eyes wide with intrigue.* 'Really? Coooool,' he said, *dragging out the 'O' for a good five seconds before his dad warned him to keep his eyes in front when walking.*

Arthur reached out to keep him on the straight and narrow. He had spoken to Chandler already of his worry that his other boy shouldn't have to do this, not at his age ... not at any age. He had looked up to Martin since he was born and was struggling to understand why his brother had come out here alone. And stayed out here. And refused to be found. Arthur had admitted to Chandler that he didn't have anything to tell him. What could he tell him that wasn't a lie or as hard-edged as the truth? Chandler was ashamed that he had nothing to give the old man, nothing but choked words and a horrible, guilty relief that it wasn't his own family.

39

Dividing the town into sections, Mitch sent crews out to hunt for Gabriel, not out of expectation of finding him, but more to provide a reassuring presence on the streets.

Orders were to stop and search with caution – 'Free rein to detain' – as Mitch put it. People were paired: Luka with Yohan; Tanya with Jim. Nick was again left stuck on the front desk, alongside a base crew of Roper, Flo, MacKenzie and Sun.

Minus a partner once again, Chandler left the station on the back of a promise to get Nick into the action before long. The look of disillusionment he received made him realize that he would have to make good on his promise soon.

First stop was to check in on his parents. As he strode up the baked but neat garden, his phone buzzed. A message from Teri stating that she was on her way, disregarding Chandler's warning. He pressed the button to call her back even before he fully realized what he was doing. She answered immediately.

'Teri, you can't come here,' he said though he knew she wouldn't listen. She never had.

'You don't control me.'

'No one's *ever* controlled you. I'm just asking—'

'I'm already on my way.'

'The state police won't let you past.'

'You get me past them.'

'I don't *want* you past them. In fact, I'll order them to detain you.'

'I'll get through.'

'Talk to Mitch. He'll tell you the same thing.'

'Maybe,' she said, her stubbornness shining through. 'But you forget that I know my way around there. I'll take a back road. You can't cover them all.'

'Teri—'

She gave a short, defiant chuckle. Giving up, he said, 'Stay safe. And watch out.' She had already hung up.

With the prospect of Teri bursting on to the scene, Chandler entered the house. Everyone was up, including the children.

'Who were you arguing with?' asked Sarah, eyes cast to the floor in a semi-stupor, awake and not happy about it. Jasper couldn't speak, his incessant yawning blocking any attempt to communicate with words.

'No one. Nothing important,' he replied.

'It sounded important,' said his dad, positioned by the front window, the shotgun tucked down behind the seat, out of sight from the kids.

Chandler convinced himself that there was a valid reason for not telling them. He'd lost count of how many times over the years Teri had promised to come and not shown up – or worse, appeared out of the blue, throwing everyone on to high alert. Five years ago, on Sarah's fifth birthday, she'd made one of her unannounced visits. The kids had been thrilled, believing she was moving back home. When he explained she needed to give him some warning, she told him she could do what she liked; *they're my kids too*. But back then Chandler knew she didn't really want them. Not permanently, anyway. So the party had continued, Teri on the receiving end of a mass of cold shoulders from the gathered adults, before she made her excuses and left Chandler to soothe his bawling kids.

The night was getting late and the children were ordered back to bed. After being tucked in Jasper fell asleep straight away but Sarah wanted to discuss her upcoming First Confession again. Chandler was more than happy to, as much to distract his mind from the case as to ease her fears.

As he sat on the edge of the bed she skimmed through the stories chosen by the priest for study: Cain and Abel; the sellers in the temple; the Prodigal Son. Typical First Confession fare.

'I want to get rid of my sins,' she said abruptly.

'Honey, you don't have any sins.'

'I *do*,' she said matter-of-factly. 'For a start I steal food from Jasper at dinner or sneak a cookie from the tray when Nanna bakes them. Also, sometimes I get angry that you're not here and curse.'

'You do?'

Tilting her head to the side as if he were slow, she said, 'I know curse words, Dad.'

Chandler shook his head. He'd assumed she knew curse words. 'No, not that. You get angry that I'm not here?'

Sarah nodded. 'But I get angry that Mum isn't here too,' she said, sweeping the curtain of jet black from her face.

He nodded and tried to force the next question out. It stuck in his throat. He needed to ask it though he wasn't sure he wanted the answer.

'Now you've thought about it, would you want to live with Mum?'

'In Port Hedland?'

'I guess.' The alternative he hadn't considered until now chilled him to the bone. Mitch and Teri living in Wilbrook and having to see them every day as parents to his kids. The idea made him sick to the stomach.

'And you're coming too?' she asked.

'No, without me.'

'Maybe if I get rid of all my sins and pray you could live with us too—'

Chandler gave her a wan smile. 'The fact that your mum and me aren't together isn't yours or Jasper's fault. Plus, it would take more than a few Hail Marys to get us back together.'

'I'll pray for it.'

'You do that,' said Chandler, kissing her on the forehead.

*

320

After a final check that his dad hadn't slipped a couple of shells into the gun, Chandler left. Even now, late at night, an insistent residual heat from the baking-hot day rose from the tarmac, making being outside and exposed even more sticky and uncomfortable.

He navigated the quiet streets, passing nobody but Mitch's officers in their unmarked cars. Lights beamed from windows of houses, but no one was framed by them. It was as if everyone in town had vanished.

His unhurried cruise was filled with thoughts about his daughter's stories. Stories of sins committed and paid for. Of forgiveness and rough justice. Cain attacking his brother Abel, killing him. It got him thinking: were Gabriel and Heath brothers? He shook his head. Surely it couldn't be. They looked nothing alike, in voice or appearance. There was something else going on . . .

Cain and Abel . . .

The names returned. He recalled seeing them recently, written down. The newspaper? Perp sheets? A list of something?

It came to him as he turned on to Harvey Street and he almost lost control of the car. He had seen them on a list . . . the one retrieved from the shack. He struggled to picture it, picture the names. He recalled some. There had been an Adam, a Seth, a Jared, a Sheila. All familiar and all relatively common, but he could have sworn he had seen them grouped together before. It might have been the lack of sleep scrambling his memory but maybe there was a nugget of truth in there.

He turned on to Prince's. The names continued to nag him. The list in his head was added to: Adam, Seth, Jared, Sheila. Noah too. Cain and Abel. His memory thrust another vivid recollection to the front of his brain. He *had* seen the names before. In a book. He was sure of it. A book with a red cover and gold . . .

He slammed on the brakes at the junction leading on to Harper's. There were no cars around to honk at him.

Chandler remembered.

40

His tyres scraped the kerb as he pulled up outside his house and jumped out. Gabriel had stated that religion was part of his upbringing. He had even noted that the one thing everyone had in common when born was needing their parents and being comforted with some form of religion. And that he had been failed by both.

Skirting around the back of the house, Chandler walked through his never-locked back door and aimed for the bookcase in the corner between the kitchen and living room. The red cover should have stood out amongst the second-hand bestsellers that he'd bought and never read but it didn't seem to be there.

Next he tried Sarah's room. He spotted it on the bedside table surrounded by a litany of mobile phone paraphernalia: covers, screen protectors, and spaghetti-string headphone cables. Red cover. Hardback. For some the ultimate read.

Not knowing where to start he flicked to page 55. The number had come up in both Gabriel and Heath's

statements. The page spoke of the parting of the Red
Sea. The followers hungry in the desert. Bread falling
from heaven.

Did that mean anything? Being able to make the sea
part on command? Did that suggest wanting ultimate
control? Killing that many people could create that kind
of delusion. What about bread falling from heaven?
Going hungry in the desert? Had Gabriel been leading
followers up there? Trying to convert them to a religion
or a cult that he had invented? Did he kill them when
they resisted? Or had going hungry up there made him
mad? There had been no sign of cannibalism on the victims, even the latest one where the flesh was more intact,
but it was a possibility. Still it was nothing but more
speculation – nothing to bring him closer to the truth.

Noting the paragraph numbers set in superscript
at the side of the page he searched page to page for
paragraph 55s.

He found only two. The first was a psalm. A lament
about being surrounded by betrayers and enemies. The
enemies weren't named specifically, but it could be proof
of a rampant paranoia. But Gabriel hadn't come across
as paranoid at any stage. He seemed much too calculating for that.

The other was Isaiah 55: an invitation to the thirsty.
It talked of the grace and power of God and ended
with the transformation of life. There was one basic
transformation that Chandler could think of: the transformation from life to death. Was this what Gabriel
meant? Transforming these people from their hell on

earth to God's side? It was possible but it was a big jump and still vague. The paragraph ended with a powerful collection of words: *an everlasting sign that will endure for ever.* Was it a statement? That Gabriel would endure for ever. The notoriety of a serial killer? Destined to be discussed and studied for years to come? The chance to live for ever.

Stalking into the kitchen Chandler skimmed through the case notes on the table looking for some inspiration. Though there was nothing that would stand up in court he remained convinced that the Bible had something to do with all this. One of those paragraphs held the key, both were too portentous to be coincidence. Thinking that it might come to him if he immersed himself in the details, Chandler reviewed the causes of death; the names of the suspects; the summary of their lives; an inventory of items found in the cabin and what was retrieved: blood, hair, clothing and significant markings. He went through the statements of Gabriel and Heath again, the list of names, the note that declared 'named at the Beginning'. Still any sense of clarity or link eluded him.

If he had been getting somewhere, all that disappeared as a shadow flashed past the front window. The handle of the front door turned cautiously, stopping after a few centimetres, the door locked. Someone was trying to get into his house.

Gabriel had returned.

Sliding into the kitchen, Chandler raced to the back door.

Easing outside, he closed it gently behind him. Around the side of the house, he heard Gabriel coming. With no time to do anything else he ducked to the other side of the path and pressed up against the high brick wall of the shed, affording him the perfect place to stalk ... and, if needed, attack.

He listened to the steps shuffle quickly across the uneven path. Gabriel would find the back door open but Chandler wouldn't let him get inside. As soon as the moment was right he would jump him and force him to the ground.

He slid his gun from the holster. He didn't want to use it but had to assume Gabriel was armed. As a last resort only, he reminded himself.

A shadow edged towards the back door. Chandler curled up, ready to pounce.

The dark shape stepped into the glare of the porch light. 'Teri?'

The shock in his voice startled her and she leapt forward, bouncing off the screen door almost back into his arms. Regaining her balance she turned to him. It had been nearly three years but she still had the beauty to force him to pause, her Greek skin tinted a beautiful caramel, the two dark, round beauty spots on her cheeks only accentuating her overall attractiveness. Her face was as he remembered, like a cherry blossom tree in spring. A face that was spectacular in full bloom but which remained susceptible to any sudden change in the weather. From the look on her face it was early spring, an overcast day that could swing in either direction.

'What are you doing in the fucking bushes?' she spat. Age hadn't tempered her language.

'What are you *fucking* doing here?' he yelled back at her. 'I almost shot you.'

Though she only stood five-foot-four in heels her voice filled the backyard, insistent.

'The Camry ran out of gas. I had to hike a couple of kilometres. I tried to phone ...' She paused. Chandler assumed that she had tried to contact Mitch and had failed. 'Cops stopped me a couple of times on the way. As if I look like a serial killer?' she said, offering a thin smile.

She went to enter the back door. 'I want to see the kids.'

'They're not here. They're at my parents.'

'*What?*' said Teri. 'You're telling me there's a serial killer on the loose and you aren't even looking after them. This, *Chandler*, is the kinda shit I left you for. Trying to save others and sacrificing your own kin.'

'I don't need this right now. The kids are safe.'

'They *will* be.'

'Leave them alone, Teri.'

'No. I've taken a back seat too long on this. I'm taking you to court for Sarah and Jasper if you don't hand them over.'

'They're not hostages, Teri. And this isn't a negotiation. You can't force them.'

'No, this isn't a negotiation. This is their decision. But all this – ' she said, waving her hand in the air, 'this is the type of shit I want to get them away from.'

'This type of shit doesn't happen regularly.'

'Leaving them with your folks?' smirked Teri.

'No,' said Chandler, shaking his head, 'having a serial . . . a murder suspect loose around town.'

'But yet I hear they're always with Pete and Crazy Caroline.'

Chandler let the insult pass. 'Something better not happen to them 'cause you distracted me here.'

'If something happens it'll be because *you* let the killer go.'

Chandler glared at her. False information she could only have garnered from her boyfriend. Trust Mitch to sell him out, even now.

'The advantage of an inside contact,' she continued, flashing the thin smile again and tapping a nose that had always been a little too large for her face, prominent and sharp.

'He's welcome to you,' said Chandler pushing past her and into the house. All he wanted was to pack up his notes and leave.

As he shoved the notebook and other scribbled pages into a backpack, she poked around the house. 'Bit messy in here. The kids will be better suited having two parents, don't you think? Me and Mitch.'

Chandler didn't respond. He had larger fish to fry. Bundling his notes into the car, she went to get in the passenger's side. Chandler kept the door locked.

'What are you doing?' he asked.

'Going with you.'

'This is police business. You can walk. It's not far.'

Chandler felt a puerile but pleasing inner glow at his response.

'I thought you said there was a killer out here?' she said, standing back from the door, looking vulnerable and alone.

Chandler felt the warm glow turn into anger. She had him again. He couldn't let the mother of his kids walk around with Gabriel out there somewhere. Unlocking the door, he pushed it open.

'Get in. But don't talk.'

Teri offered no promises and slid inside.

As he drove to his folks' place, she talked about how much the piece-of-shit town hadn't changed, throwing up her hands in anger and frustration that she had to be here at all, a primeval, instinctual mannerism to make herself look bigger than she was, her green eyes flashing, teeth bared for action.

He dumped her off with his parents, both sides affronted at this turn of events. As ever, Teri couldn't modulate the volume of her voice, waking the kids who sprinted into her arms for a hug. Chandler listened as Teri promised that she would protect them. When Jasper asked from what, she said from the tickle monster and chased him around the kitchen. Chandler's mum and dad looked at him for an explanation, his dad not making an effort to hide the gun. Chandler merely told them that he had to go.

41

Despite the numerous orders to disperse, the reporters remained outside the station, trying to work their way inside like semi-sentient zombies. Mitch had returned, conducting the symphony, running through leads phoned in by his team and by locals, more in charge than Chandler ever had been. He even had Nick and Luka working efficiently.

Chandler entered Mitch's office.

'Mitch?'

Mitch flinched at the informal addressing but didn't retaliate.

'I need to talk to you,' continued Chandler.

Grabbing another set of papers from the cluttered desk Mitch pretended to read them.

'I have a theory about the victims,' Chandler said, undeterred. Mitch turned another page, disinterested. 'The names of his victims: they're all linked to the Bible, somehow. Some religious angle he's following,' said Chandler. 'Something he mentioned earlier about being let down as a child – by his parents and religion.'

For a moment Mitch continued to pretend to read before he finally acknowledged Chandler's presence – by waving the bunch of reports in his face.

'Forget your theories, Sergeant, and check these out first.'

'You've got a team for that,' said Chandler.

'Which you're part of.'

Chandler stifled a laugh. 'I'm on the bench, at best. Where you put me. And by the way Teri's made it to town in case you were wondering. The Camry ran out of juice and she hiked to mine. She said she was trying to get in touch with her boyfriend.'

Leaving Mitch with his unchecked reports Chandler went to the cells and sat outside Heath's, hoping to confirm something with the victim.

'Mr Barwell?'

There was no answer. No one wanted to talk to him it seemed.

'Did Gabriel seem like a religious man to you?'

Still no response.

'Think back to when you were captured. Was anything said that seemed out of the ordinary? Completely out of the ordinary. Did he pray at any time? Say a prayer? Cross himself? Did he mention God, or anything like that?'

A weary voice replied, 'What more can I tell you?'

'That's what I want to know.'

There was a long pause. Heath let loose a dry cough. The voice croaked in again. 'He mentioned something about God. I can't remember exactly.'

'Please, Mr Barwell ... Heath. It would be helpful.'

A frustrated sigh blew through the slat in the door. 'I recall him saying something about the land out here being so dry God must have forsaken it, as if he was angry with it in some way. But he also said that it was beautiful. Like it was in the beginning, like everything was.'

'In the beginning?'

'Yeah.'

There was that phrase again – *in the beginning.* What beginning? The beginning of his murder spree? Was it something that he felt he had to do? Or – did he like the beginning of the process only? Capturing and getting to know his victim. The killing was merely something that had to be done and which he didn't even enjoy.

'Did he mention anything else about the beginning?'

Heath sighed again. 'Like his childhood, you mean? Given what he's done I'd say it wasn't good, don't you think?'

Heath stopped there. Chandler had hit another dead end.

'But he did mention a place, said it was *the beginning.*'

The alertness in Heath's voice made Chandler jump.

'What place?' asked Chandler, now equally alert.

'I don't know.' Heath's voice faded away, the moment of clarity quickly lost.

'Please try,' said Chandler.

'I am,' said Heath, sounding flustered and angry.

Chandler backed off. Silence descended over the cells. He felt tense, wondering if he had just hit upon another dirt road to nowhere.

'Singleton,' said Heath.

'Singleton?'

'Yes.' The voice was shaky, unclear. 'He mentioned it a couple of times in the car. I thought he was just pointing out somewhere he'd been or a farm that might have some solid work available, but I suppose it did seem a little out of place. He always said the word with passion. It was about the only thing that stirred him.'

'And he said it was the beginning?'

'Yeah, I think so.'

'And what did he say this Singleton was?'

'Again, I don't know. A place, a farm, a person ... And before you ask, I don't know what it was the beginning of.'

Chandler didn't know either. But it was something.

Using Tanya's computer he looked up Singleton. The search brought back a bevy of results: a software pattern, a whiskey, a few famous people with the surname Singleton and other links inviting him to social media and dating sites to meet up with singletons. Removing all references to dating sites and famous people he was left with a town in New South Wales, a few others in England and the United States, plus a vast number of Australian suburbs, buildings and institutes.

Even though it was across the far side of the country, the town north of Sydney on the banks of the Hunter River in New South Wales would need looking into, but it was the suburb at the southern reaches of Perth that grabbed Chandler's attention. Gabriel originated from Perth, or at least his accent indicated as much. From the picture onscreen the suburb looked like nothing more than a small outpost dotted with rundown bungalows, houses and a few essential stores, the last reaches of civilization, a greener version of Wilbrook. The only building with a website was an orphanage. He clicked on the link.

The website was professional, the photos of the building proving it to be nothing like Chandler had imagined. It was small, and almost quaint, a building that looked like something from one of Sarah's Harry Potter novels. He got the impression that the layout of the website and the angle of the pictures were designed to mask the flaws.

Putting a late-night call into the IT section of Central HQ in Perth, he was directed to the female operator on duty. He asked her to send over the admittance records at the orphanage from the last thirty years.

Ten minutes later a massive folder crashed into his inbox, the computer refusing to open it as if the contents held a secret it was under pain of death to keep. A second attempt was more successful and he forced the machine to search for Gabriel Johnson amongst the names. It brought back no results. Chandler tried Heath Barwell. Again it brought up a blank. A search for Seth brought up a couple of results that were busts. Out of ideas, Chandler was left with thousands of records accompanied by photos. He settled in for a long night.

The first half hour brought nothing, no photos that even resembled the image of Gabriel implanted in his brain; none that might even have resembled Gabriel in his youth. After an hour staring at the screen, his eyes began to hurt. His search became more cursory, continuing to flick through the records as he considered the next angle to pursue. There had to be some connection to *the beginning*, to religion, to what had made Gabriel this way. Chandler knew it in his gut.

It was an hour later, as he worked through alternative possibilities, that Gabriel's photo appeared on the screen. In fact it took Chandler so much by surprise that he sped through another couple of images of orphaned children before scrolling back. The image that confronted him was definitely Gabriel, a younger version, his hair cropped close to his skull, accentuating the gaunt quality of his face. He looked like a concentration camp survivor rather than an orphan, but it was unmistakably him. David Gabriel Taylor.

Chandler's heart raced as he studied the attached file and notes. The occasional bout of bed-wetting and emotional – bordering on violent – outbursts, but nothing more than the struggles of a scared young boy. Unfortunately the record ended as abruptly as it had started. Gabriel had been allocated a foster home after only six months, the name and address of his foster parents scribbled in a column at the side. Dina and Geoffrey Wilson from Glendon, situated on the outskirts of Perth.

Chandler made the call. It was answered after a few rings.

'Is this Mr Geoffrey Wilson?' he asked.

'It is indeed.'

Expecting to have to mollify an irate householder woken from sleep, he was surprised to encounter a pleasant, deep, gravelly voice.

'I'm Sergeant Chandler Jenkins from Wilbrook Police Station. I'd like to—'

'Sergeant Jenkins from where?' interrupted Mr Wilson.

'Wilbrook, up north in the Pilbara.'

'What are you doing up there?' asked Mr Wilson, before rephrasing. 'I mean, why are you phoning me? At this hour?'

'I have a couple of questions regarding a David Gabriel—'

The gravelly voice interrupted, the politeness gone.

'I know Gabriel.'

'Well, I have a couple—'

'I – we don't want anything to do with him, Sergeant.'

Chandler's interest was piqued. He heard a rustle from the other end, the sound of a receiver about to be hung up. He jumped in. 'Please, Mr Wilson, just a couple of questions. Don't you even want to know why I'm phoning?' Chandler hoped that curiosity would keep his caller on the line.

'No,' said Geoffrey, firmly. 'We – me and my wife – tried to teach him right from wrong and he threw it back in our face.'

'Right from wrong? Like in a religious sense?'

'Yes – in a religious sense, Sergeant.' The voice remained calm but insistent.

'So you're religious then?'

'We are. And proud of it,' said Mr Wilson sternly, as if

there were some insinuation in Chandler's question. 'We tried to bring him up in a good way, a righteous way, especially after what happened to his family.'

'What hap—?'

'A car crash, Sergeant. A horrible experience for a boy at that tender age no doubt, but one *we* believed he could recover from. We wanted to teach him that despite what God had thrown at him, the Lord was good and would guide him. *If* he repented for his sins and obeyed His word.'

The direction the conversation had taken caused the hairs to stand on the back of Chandler's neck. 'And how did you make him do that?'

From being open and talkative Mr Wilson suddenly clammed up. It left Chandler to guess how: lessons, chores, lectures or worse. Something disturbing enough to turn an orphan into a killer. He decided to tread carefully. 'When did David – Gabriel – leave?'

'At eighteen.' A brusqueness had developed in the voice. A need to finish this call. 'And he hasn't been back since. We don't want him back. He turned our house into a den of sin, Sergeant, a *den* of *sin*. Like something from Sodom and Gomorrah, harlots invading my house, parading around as naked as Eve in the Garden of Eden. Me and my wife had to scrub the floors and furniture clean.'

There was a rustle from the handset on the other side and Chandler thought he could hear sobbing. The gravelly tone was replaced by a woman's voice. Dina.

'You've upset my husband, Sergeant. We just want to

forget all about that boy. That Devil child!' She spat this out. And hung up.

Chandler leaned back in the chair, letting it all soak in. From lacking any credible leads, he was struggling to identify the most lucrative avenue to follow. What he did know was that something had happened in that house. A set of foster parents trying to instil their zealous beliefs into a vulnerable teenager, leading to an event, or series of events that sent young Gabriel over the edge.

42

With a theory and the foundations of some evidence Chandler went to corner Mitch again.

And nearly made it. But for the phone call. It was one of hundreds that had come into the station, offering information on the man they were busy hunting. But this time the caller was different – it was Gabriel himself.

From the front desk Nick waved his hands frantically, catching Chandler's attention. Covering the microphone on the headset, he whispered, 'It's him.'

The station immediately went quiet. Everyone knew who the young constable meant. None more so than Mitch, who charged out of his office to demand that the call be put straight through to him.

The officers gathered around the meeting table in what had once been Chandler's office. Perched by the speakerphone Mitch glared at each one of them. 'Everyone stay quiet. I'm doing the talking,' he said, jabbing a finger at his chest to hammer home the point.

The light on the phone started to blink. This was it. Mitch switched the phone on to speaker and pressed the button.

'Mr Wils—'

Gabriel interrupted immediately.

'I'm calling to let you know that I've changed my target for the moment.'

Mitch quickly recovered his stride. 'Changed from?' he asked.

'Instead of fifty-five I'm taking ninety.'

There was a brief pause as they waited for more information on who, what, when, or why, but nothing further arrived, the information as vague as the faces around the table.

Mitch broke the silence. 'Mr Johnson, I have to ask you to turn yourself in. It's not too late.'

'I already have, Inspector. Twice,' he reminded them. 'Now I have work to do. If you are going to prevent me from taking Heath then there are plenty of others who are worthy.' There was a clarity in his voice that suggested he believed what he was saying.

'Does this game of yours have something to do with the Bible?' asked Mitch.

Chandler was surprised by how tentative Mitch's question was. Rather than stating it as known fact, he presented his query in the insecure manner of a school kid, as though afraid of being mocked.

'The Bible? That's a pretty hazy theory, Inspector.'

Witnessing Mitch losing the chance to maintain the upper hand, Chandler jumped in. 'How about something to do with your parents? Or your *foster* parents, Dina and Geoffrey?'

Mitch glared at him but didn't speak. Neither did the killer on the other end of the phone.

'Mr Johnson?' asked Mitch, his glare still aimed squarely at Chandler.

A dead tone sounded. Gabriel was gone.

Flo broke the silence. 'What did he mean by taking ninety rather than fifty-five?'

This question was directed at her boss. Mitch's mouth moved up and down as if he hoped some words would ride to his rescue but nothing came out.

'Does it mean that he's slaughtered – or he's *going* to slaughter a load of people somewhere?' asked Tanya.

'Thirty-five more people,' confirmed Luka.

Spoken out loud it seemed a colossal number. In the absence of direction from Mitch, Chandler sprang into action.

'Nick, have we had any reports of gunshots, or disturbances of any kind coming over the radio?'

'Nothing,' confirmed his constable.

'Okay. That leaves a possibility that he's holed up at one of the remoter farms, close to where we last saw him,' Chandler explained to his audience.

'Maybe,' said Tanya. 'But nowhere has as many as thirty-five people – I doubt there's even thirty-five people living that close to each other.'

His senior constable was right. To murder thirty-five people would mean Gabriel would have to travel to multiple locations – quickly.

'Is it a bluff?' Chandler asked the room.

'To what end?' said Mitch, finding his voice.

'To get us running around like headless chooks.'

'He's killed six people, Sergeant. That was no bluff. So we have to consider that he isn't bluffing now, either.'

Again a pall of silence descended over the office.

'Any ideas?' asked Chandler.

'The Boltons and Easts live close to each other,' shouted Nick from the front desk. 'That's about ten.'

Tanya stepped in. 'Add in the Cartys and you have sixteen, if you include the dogs.'

'What about local bars? The medical centre?' offered Flo.

'What medical centre?' spluttered Mitch.

Tanya answered regardless. 'Anne Tuttle told me the reverend was considering having a bunch of his congregation meet in the church hall for a midnight prayer.'

'How many?' asked Chandler.

Tanya shrugged her shoulders. 'I don't know. Thirty or forty wouldn't be extraordinary if they've been scared by what's happening.'

'Is it worth taking a look?' asked Flo.

'Everything's worth taking a look,' said Mitch. 'We cannot not respond to this threat.'

'What if it's a diversion to get rid of us so that he can make another attempt at killing Heath?' said Chandler, thinking of the crowd outside, imagining Gabriel amongst them waiting for the station to empty.

'We have to follow up this threat, Sergeant.'

'And we have to protect our own prisoner.'

342

'And we will. There's not a chance in hell that Gabriel's going to get in here.'

A plan was drawn up. First stop was the church hall, then the local bars, then the Carty, East and Bolton farms. After that other farms with an abundance of people in close proximity were identified: Toady Cook's, Izzy Cheelie's, Old Ma Reisling's, Mincey Amaranga and their families.

Chandler phoned Reverend Upton, waking him. It was long past the reverend's 9pm bedtime. Though annoyed, he confirmed that the idea of a midnight prayer had been broached but that the public opinion was to stay safely indoors. Nothing was happening in his church hall and nothing would without his stamp of approval.

Three crews were sent to the local bars, and Mitch phoned the farms. Roxanne Carty answered on the second ring, angered that she had been disturbed from her TV show. Izzy Cheelie growled down the phone that there was no one at his farm who he hadn't invited. There was no answer at the others. Though service could best be described as sporadic out there the silences were worrying.

Mitch dispatched cars to check out the people who hadn't answered the phone – via the church hall to make doubly sure. The teams fled for the cars, a game of musical chairs no one wanted to lose. Chandler pulled Tanya and Luka to the side.

'I need you two to stay here. In case he comes back for Heath.'

'I don't want to,' said Luka.

'We need to keep—' started Chandler.

'Constable, why have you not left?' interrupted Mitch, prowling around the office, rubbing his thumb and fingertips together in anxiety.

'I want Luka to stay here,' said Chandler. 'As protection.'

'And I want him out *there*,' said Mitch. 'As enforcement.'

'I want to be out there,' pleaded Luka, inching towards the door.

Chandler stared at his eager young colleague, begging not to be kept inside like a grounded child.

'Go,' he said, sighing.

Luka didn't need to be told twice and sprinted off to join up with Flo. Chandler turned to Tanya.

'I'll stay,' she said, with a solid nod.

'Don't worry, you'll have company, Tanya,' announced Mitch. 'I'll leave Roper with you,' he said pointing to the large man awkwardly wedged behind a desk.

Though he felt awful at leaving Tanya – and Nick, again – behind, and sick at the possibility of this being a wild goose chase constructed by Gabriel to leave the station open for attack, Chandler knew he had to be out there, leading the search of the farms to put some of the jumpier residents at ease and to make sure that his townsfolk were safe. No one in town had been killed and he was desperate for it to remain that way.

43

Chandler led Sun and MacKenzie up to Brian East's farm, the unpaved, untended lane extra treacherous in the dark. Reaching the front gate he switched off his headlights and coasted to a gentle stop. A single light beamed from the one-storey farmhouse; the kitchen or living room. It was ominously dark for a six-bedroom house with four kids below the age of twelve.

Climbing out of the car he flexed his hands to ward off his nervous anticipation. He was joined by his two colleagues, appearing out of the darkness dressed all in black. Meant to inspire confidence, out here amongst the dirt and rusted barns it looked conspicuous.

'Stick close to me,' whispered Chandler. 'And keep your guns in your belts. There are kids in there.'

They stalked up to the farm, wary of the ditches and fences hidden in the gloom, Chandler almost tasting hard earth a few times before they made it to the chicken shed and were greeted by the mumbled clucks of hens disturbed from slumber.

He murmured instructions to his two colleagues.

'You two go around the sides. Check the windows but don't put your face right up to them in case you scare the kids. If anything seems unusual meet back here. Okay?'

Sun's expression remained as emotionless as ever, MacKenzie agreeing on his behalf with a solitary nod before they set off, splitting up as they skirted past the oil tank and moved out of sight.

With the others gone, Chandler focused on the kitchen window. Approaching it, the residual light from the living room illuminated it sufficiently for him to see that it was empty, and typically messy, plates in the sink, crumbs littering the table. Nothing out of the ordinary.

Sliding along the side of the dilapidated wooden structure he made it to the living room window. For a moment he dared not look but steeling himself he peeked inside, hoping to find a family at ease in front of the telly. He wasn't disappointed. Brian East was there, sprawled in his armchair, fighting for foot space on the chaise longue with his wife and the eldest two kids, bare feet battling bare feet, the telly bathing them in a stupefying blue glow. Chandler breathed out hard in relief. The Easts were okay. Finding them alive and in one piece tied another ribbon on his theory that Gabriel was sending them on a wild goose chase. Chandler decided not to disturb them.

Suddenly Diane East looked across to her husband who sat up quickly, knocking his can of beer to the carpet. They'd heard something. Chandler knew what. He made it around the back just as Brian was taking a wild swing at a mysterious figure in black, looming on the porch.

'Brian, Brian, it's me!' shouted Chandler.

Brian drew his fist back and squinted into the darkness. 'Me who?' he growled, his voice slurred.

'Sergeant Jenkins,' said Chandler, staying out of range of any fist the former amateur boxer might unleash. Now up close he could see Sun and MacKenzie had trained their firearms on Brian.

'Fuck you doin' up here?' asked Brian.

Though he was on edge, Chandler felt a little relieved. From Brian East this was a polite, almost reserved response. He waved his hand to get Mitch's officers to lower their weapons. Neither responded.

'Put those away,' insisted Chandler, waiting until both reluctantly re-holstered their weapons.

By now Brian's wife, Diane, was poking her head out the door, holding back her entire brood of four.

'Who is it?' she said.

'Back inside,' ordered Brian. His family didn't move.

Brian turned back to face Chandler, a bushy eyebrow raised, wordlessly questioning why Chandler was here.

'We're just checking on something,' said Chandler, answering Brian's raised eyebrow.

'Checkin' on what?'

'Someone we thought was up here.'

'And?' said Brian peering into the darkness around them.

'Nothing. You can go back inside and enjoy your evening.'

There was a frown on Brian's face that indicated he

wasn't satisfied. His eyes narrowed as if he suspected the police of being up to something.

'Don't go around poking in my things,' he said.

'What would we find?' Sun had finally spoken, his voice lyrical and unexpected.

'Nothing,' said Brian, bluntly.

'We're not going to poke around,' said Chandler. There was little to poke at, now it had been determined that Gabriel wasn't in the house.

'Brian, come inside,' ordered Diane.

But Brian was curious himself now. 'Who are these two?' he asked, nodding his head towards Sun and MacKenzie.

'They're helping us,' said Chandler, leaving it at that.

'Well they're lucky they didn't get their heads kicked in,' growled Brian as he backed off towards the door.

Chandler watched him go inside before turning to Mitch's officers.

'I warned you about drawing your weapons.'

'He threw a punch,' said Sun, unmoved by the rebuke.

'You were sneaking around his backyard in the dead of night. You're lucky he doesn't have a gun.'

'If that's the case, then he's lucky too,' said Sun, chillingly.

It was a lot easier at Mincey's, the man himself out on the porch to greet them, enjoying a late-night rollie. He invited them all in for a beer despite being strictly teetotal since his first wife had left him. He answered Chandler's questions in good humour. He'd seen nothing out of the ordinary that night other than his youngest son, Wayne, trying to climb out the kitchen window because he'd been dared to. There had been no cars, no bikes, in fact no movement at all until Chandler and company had arrived.

Calling it in, Chandler received an update from Nick about the other searches. It was the same everywhere, the farms, the bars, the church hall, and even the church itself, all quiet. Gabriel was nowhere to be found.

All crews regrouped at the station en masse.

Mitch was pacing the floor, nervous. 'I want all the other farms checked in case someone's being held hostage or putting him up for the night.'

'That'll take until morning at least,' warned Chandler.

'I know.'

'How do you want it done, Inspector?' asked Luka.

Chandler was annoyed by how keen to please he sounded. Within a couple of days Mitch had brought the wild horse to heel.

'As with everything,' said Mitch. 'Start at the beginning.'

Start at the beginning. There it was again. Another reminder of the note in the cabin: 'They have been named at the beginning'.

As Mitch launched into a motivational speech about redoubling their efforts, Chandler reviewed what Gabriel had said on the phone: the declaration that he was going to kill ninety. It was a shocking boast, possibly one designed to make them panic and abandon the station to leave Heath exposed, but there had been a poise about the way he had said it that made Chandler think that he had an exact plan of how to go about it. But killing thirty-five people could not be an exact science so maybe in stating the number ninety he meant just that. He was intending to kill *ninety*; not total kills, but the number.

'Gabriel said he was going to kill ninety.'

Chandler said this out loud, interrupting Mitch as he accelerated into full flow.

'We know that, Sergeant. We're trying to prevent it,' said Mitch, more exasperated than angry.

'No. He said he was going to kill – ninety. As in the number. Heath mentioned it in his statement, that the killer said he was going to be number fifty-five. We've been looking at it like Heath was going to be the fifty-fifth victim, but what if he was *number fifty-five*?'

Mitch was getting visibly frustrated. 'What do you mean?'

'Well, if he has killed fifty-four people why are there only six graves and eight names on the list that we can make out? What if it's the name he's going for, as if Heath's name was on a list?'

'What list?' said Mitch, impatient. 'The one in the cabin?'

'Yes,' said Chandler. 'Or a list somewhere else.'

'That's not very helpful, Sergeant. Come back when you have—'

Chandler continued nonetheless. 'He mentioned that Gabriel said, "They have been named at the beginning." But the beginning of what?'

'I know what you are getting closer to the end of, Sergeant,' spat Mitch. 'Your career.'

Chandler ignored it and looked at his audience.

'It would have to be the beginning of a book,' offered Tanya.

'What book?'

There were more bemused looks. Some of the assembled officers chatted amongst themselves, doubting Chandler's theory or simply his sanity.

Then the answer came to Chandler.

'Genesis. The start of the Bible. A list of names.'

He turned to Tanya but she had already dug out the black hardback Bible from her desk drawer, a copy that had been well thumbed but remained in one piece. She opened it at the start, at Genesis. The first few pages revealed a list of names.

'What's fifty-five?' he asked.

She counted up. The officers began to mill around, their attention now with Chandler rather than Mitch, who was trying to get them to focus on the command he had issued.

'What is it?' asked Chandler, impatient.

'Give me a . . .' said Tanya. She nodded her head as she counted the last few. She stared up at him. 'It's Heth.'

Chandler looked at Mitch. Upon the uttering of the name he could see the realization wash over the inspector's face, his lips shading to a royal blue once again. He called out the other names from the list found in the cabin. 'Adam, Seth, Eve.'

Tanya scanned the pages. Another excruciating wait.

'All there. In some form.'

'Jared, Sheila, Noah.'

She nodded again.

'And number ninety?' asked Chandler.

'Wait,' said Tanya as she counted out loud. Finally she had the answer. 'It's Sarai,' she said, pronouncing the hard 'i'.

'We got any of those in town?' cried out Mitch, aiming this at Chandler and his team. He was met with the shaken heads of Tanya and Luka. 'No babies with weird names?' he added hopefully.

Chandler didn't answer, grabbing the Bible from Tanya. 'There's—' he said, remembering something he was taught in Bible study many years ago. Flipping over the pages he found it. It sent a chill down his spine and he struggled to get the words out. 'Sar-*ai* was renamed Sar-*ah* at the annunciation of the birth of Isaac.'

44

Without a word Chandler bolted out of the office, barely hearing Mitch bark out the orders for a list of all the Sar-ai, Sar-a and Sar-ahs in town and the surrounding area.

Rushing out the front door, Chandler pushed his way past the reporters, jumped in his squad car and sped off. Turning the corner on to Beaumont he called his mum's mobile. There was probably no need to worry, he told himself. Another wild goose chase. The sick bastard sending them in circles with Chandler on the blunt end of his knife this time. The phone continued to ring, each unanswered blast heightening his sense of panic.

It was still ringing as he swung on to Prince's, the front axle trying to bury itself into the hot tarmac. Where the hell was she?

On the tenth ring it was picked up.

'Mum?' he asked, relieved. 'Are you—?'

'Try again,' said Gabriel, his soft voice infused with glee.

Chandler almost ditched the car into a lamp post, fighting to regain control.

'Gabriel?'

'Correct.'

'What have you done?'

'Nothing,' he said, innocently.

'You better not have hurt them,' warned Chandler, his foot to the floor now, gaining speed, the trees, the cars – his life – flashing by.

'They're safe.'

'Don't do anything,' warned Chandler.

'You either,' said Gabriel. 'And don't think of informing Mitchell or any of the others.'

'Don't hurt them,' pleaded Chandler, throwing the car on to Mellon's. The road was now a blur in front of him. All he could picture was his parents' house and what might be happening there. He blinked hard to try and block it out.

'You might be too late,' said Gabriel.

The threat of violence filled the car to bursting point.

'Let me speak to them,' said Chandler, his parents' house not appearing fast enough but the roads too dark and too angular to go faster.

'You *will* speak to them again – *if* you do as I say.'

'Don't you—' started Chandler, barely containing his anger. The tyres screeched as he turned on to Greensand. 'What do you want?'

'A swap.'

'What do you mean – a swap?'

'An exchange, Sergeant,' said Gabriel. 'Heath for your daughter. For Sarah.'

Chandler tried to let the demand sink into his over-loaded brain. What did he mean, Heath for Sarah? The man in the jail cell in exchange for his daughter? That couldn't be.

Gabriel continued, 'As a rule I'm not a huge fan of killing kids unless absolutely necessary. Of course, it's also true that being Catholic she was born a sinner, but I can't hold that against her before she has had a chance to redeem herself.'

To this Chandler couldn't find words, shocked into silence. His fugue was such that he was only stirred from it after swiping the pavement and knocking over a 'For Sale' sign, the wood shattering as he tore it apart.

'Are you still there, Sergeant?' said Gabriel, revelling in the power.

'I—'

'Surely it's a simple decision. Isn't it?' said Gabriel. 'It's not like the people buried on the Hill, or some loudmouth stranger like Heath, mean anything to you. I mean, you're a family man; a *policeman*, not a grief counsellor, aren't you?'

Through his confusion Chandler understood he had to keep Gabriel on the phone. Another couple of minutes would be enough.

'Hurry up, Sergeant. Make your decision.'

'I need time.'

'Time for what?' The soft, mocking voice grew an edge. 'This is an *easy* choice. Your kids – your own flesh and blood – in return for a man you don't know. A man who you don't even like, I'm sure.'

Gabriel had got that right. Even though he had been proved to be the innocent victim, there was nothing in Heath's demeanour that Chandler had warmed to, nothing that marked him as a good person, a person worth saving. But, then again, who was he to judge? Chandler stalled some more.

'I'll need time.'

'To decide something as simple as this? No wonder you can't catch me.'

'No. I'll need time to get him out.'

Chandler was on Howe Street. Sixty seconds and he'd have Gabriel surrounded. Blow his head off if necessary.

'You have one hour.'

'No, wait—' said Chandler.

Gabriel continued, 'And if I meet any police, state, army, or that ex-partner of yours, I'll just as easily kill them all. You see, Chandler, God, the police, or even the innocent cannot be allowed to thwart the Devil's work.'

'I want to see that she's okay.'

'And you can. Once you bring me what I asked for. And remember: you come by yourself. I'll tell you where. I know you know your way around the woods.'

Chandler was on Crowe Street now, gunning towards the porch light, which guided him like a beacon.

'What do you mean?' asked Chandler.

But Gabriel was gone.

45

He bounced on to the pavement with a jolt that threatened to throw him through the front window. As he got out of the car and drew his weapon what Gabriel had said spun around and around his head. The threat and the comments, words and phrases delivered as inside jokes that Gabriel seemed to assume Chandler would get. As if he should know Gabriel, or Gabriel know him. Sly remarks about Chandler not caring about the victims and moving on after the cases were over.

You're a family man, policeman – not a grief counsellor, aren't you?

Plus he knew that Mitch used to be Chandler's partner. How? Had he overheard something in the station? Or was it that obvious? Or did he just *know*? He couldn't be someone they had arrested. Chandler knew this from the date of birth on the orphanage records. Gabriel was too young to have been one of theirs, back when he and Mitch had worked together. Perhaps Gabriel had lied about his age to match Heath's – to help his story fit Heath's. There also existed the possibility that Gabriel was someone that Mitch had wronged down in Perth – but then why bring that up here and involve Chandler and his family, if his grudge was solely against Mitch?

Reaching the front window, he peeked inside. The light was on but his dad wasn't on guard. The room was empty, the TV off, the piano in the corner unused. Everything looked normal. His hopes grew that Gabriel hadn't been here after all and the phone call, all of it, had been nothing more than a sick joke played by a sick bastard, leading them – especially him – around for kicks. Hope, however, was an emotion easily extinguished and fear rose to encompass the whole of Chandler's being as he opened the front door and slipped inside.

The living room was indeed empty, his heavy footsteps echoing on the wooden floor. The desperation to see his kids, to see them alive, swelled in his heart but he resisted calling out and giving Gabriel forewarning that he was here.

With his gun drawn, Chandler crept to the edge of the kitchen. Thoughts of the worst possible kind began to fill his imagination, visions of blood and agony, of savage terror. Still he could see no sign of a struggle, no signs of blood or splattered bloodstains, no awful groan of the mortally wounded. Another thought forced its way in. What if no one was here? Could he take that as a good sign or not?

Sucking in a deep breath, he swung around the corner. The barrel of his gun caught sight of a shape in the middle of the floor, bound to the handles of the kitchen cupboards and struggling to get free. It was Teri, her mouth gagged, her legs flailing on the slippery tiles and failing to find purchase. Her eyes were full of fear and he tried to read if what he saw in them was a warning of danger. She cast her eyes desperately to the right. Chandler followed them. In the far corner of the kitchen, two more figures were slumped on the floor, his parents, bound together, his dad bleeding from a head wound. He ran to them.

'Are you okay?' he asked both.

His mum nodded. His dad moaned in pain.

Taking a quick glance over his shoulder, he asked, 'Is he still here?'

His mum shook her head. Chandler untied them. She pulled off the gag herself.

'He took them,' she said, gasping.

Being prepared for this didn't soften the blow. Suddenly his extremities felt numb as if all the blood had drained from them.

'Both of them? Where?'

'I don't know,' his mum sobbed.

'How long ago?'

'Half an hour. He took my phone with him. Your father tried to stop them—'

Chandler pulled the gag from his father's mouth.

'Sorry, son,' he said, his eyes narrowed in pain.

'Did he hurt—'

He couldn't finish the sentence.

'No, he just took them with him. Warned us – warned you – not to tell the police.'

From behind came a distraught mumble.

Chandler returned to Teri and untied her. Her face was a mirror image of his: the same bottomless pit of worry. Expecting a torrent of abuse she instead wrapped her arms around him and hugged him tight, the first time that they had been close for years, united in fear.

He moved them all to the house of one of their closest friends a few streets over, his dad reluctantly leaving the shotgun behind so as not to arouse suspicion, and his mum and Teri having to be persuaded not to roam the streets looking for Sarah and Jasper. This time, the reporters backed off as he stormed into the station.

Expecting the station to be abuzz, it was largely empty. Chained to the front desk and ignoring the buzzing phone, Nick's face lit up.

'Sarge!'

Chandler nodded once and put his finger to his lips. 'Where is everyone?'

Nick clicked the mouse. 'At Pete Stenzl's place. Tom DeVrai rang in about lights being on in Old Pete's shed and the sound of screaming. They think he's hiding something.'

'He probably is,' said Chandler, 'but it's not Gabriel.'

Nick looked confused. 'How do you know that?'

Chandler paused. There was no need to reveal what he knew. 'Just a guess. Pete's probably got a stolen vehicle or two stowed there. The screaming could be the grinder at work.'

Nick nodded eagerly. 'He was asking where you'd gone.'

'Mitch?'

'Yeah.'

'What did you tell him?'

'That you went to check on your family.'

Chandler tapped the desk affirming that this had been the correct response.

'He was going to send a car out to check on you and Sarah if you didn't come back,' continued Nick.

The breath caught in Chandler's lungs. He didn't need any officers poking around and wondering why the house was empty.

'They're all okay. No need to disturb the kids. They're asleep.'

Chandler hoped that he had sold the lie. He changed the subject.

'Who've we got looking after our prisoner?'

'This is it,' said Nick, pointing to Roper and Flo hammering at their respective keyboards.

Two was manageable, thought Chandler.

'And is the prisoner all right?' asked Chandler, raising his voice so that he could be heard.

Roper answered but didn't take his eyes from the screen. 'Complaining as usual.'

'Thinks we should have more officers guarding him,' said Flo, concentrating on the screen.

'He's calling himself the VIP,' said Nick. 'Says that we have to protect him at all costs.'

'That's why we have to move him,' said Chandler.

Flo raised her eyes from the screen, suspicion written across the dark lines of her forehead. 'We weren't informed about that order, Sergeant,' she said. There was no hiding the distrust in her expression and tone.

JAMES DELARGY

'Your boss ordered it,' replied Chandler, locking his gaze on both of them, trying to ooze authority.

'Move him to where?' asked Roper, standing up from the desk. His sheer size remained impressive but the slight twitch in his stance suggested he hadn't fully recovered from Gabriel's assault. If it came down to a fistfight, Chandler would stand a chance, a fifty/fifty chance at least.

'Is he not safe here, Sarge?' added Nick, his tone steeped in wariness. If anyone was going to recognize Chandler wasn't acting normal then it would be his young constable.

'We *believe* Heath isn't a target anymore,' said Chandler, moving to the wall cabinet to retrieve the cell keys, 'but we're not happy that Gabriel knows where he is. He could change his mind. Heath's name is still on that list.'

Flo nodded slowly. 'I just need to call the inspector to confirm this.'

Chandler paused looking for an excuse to prevent this. Nothing came to mind.

'Go ahead,' said Chandler. There was nothing he could do but gamble on Mitch being out of radio contact up at Stenzl's farm.

With what he hoped was a crushing confidence he continued with the plan. Grabbing the keys from the cabinet he strode towards the cells. So far the balance of power lay with him. It was still his station. At least until he did what he was planning to do.

*

Heath paced his cell, his puffy red face somehow even sweatier, coated in a thick, impenetrable layer of grease.

Trying to balance his nerves and anticipate the questions his prisoner might ask, Chandler opened the cell.

'You got him?' asked Heath, hopeful.

Chandler shook his head. Heath cursed and looked around, perhaps in a futile search for something soft to kick inside the cell.

'But it's fine,' said Chandler.

'How's it fine?' spat Heath, long past the feeble assurances of the police. 'You won't let me out 'til you've caught him. Or he catches me.'

Chandler ground his teeth. To get this done he needed Heath calm and pliable. 'He's moved on to another target,' he said, his tone as flat as Flo's had been.

Heath abruptly stopped pacing, suddenly interested. 'Yeah?'

'Yeah.'

'You're telling me the truth?'

Chandler nodded.

'Well. Thank. Fuck. For. That!' he said, beaming, a smile that Chandler didn't return. If Chandler hadn't fully committed to what he was planning to do with Heath, the man's next comment shoved him off the fence.

'Let some other poor bastard suffer.'

Chandler took a few seconds to let his anger pass.

'So I can go?' said Heath.

'No.'

'What do you mean, *no*?' exploded Heath.

'We don't want to take the chance that he's bluffing us like before. We can hide you somewhere more comfortable. A hotel. All expenses paid.' This was his bargaining chip – comfort and food after two nights in a barren cell.

The offer seemed to leave Heath uncertain. Chandler's offer wasn't absolute freedom but ... He came to a conclusion. 'Anywhere's better than this shithole.'

Ushering Heath from the cell, Chandler led him towards the office. Both Roper and Flo were on the phone. Trying to contact their boss.

'Did you get through to him?' asked Chandler, fighting his nerves.

'No, but—' said Flo.

'I'm coming with you,' said Roper, walking towards them, a slight hitch in his step.

Chandler shook his head. 'No. No one but me and your boss are to know where he'll be.' He shot Heath a nod of reassurance but all Chandler wanted was to get out of here. Every second they stayed increased the chance that Flo would get through to Mitch.

'Added security,' said Roper.

'I don't think Mitch would want to lose a valued member of his team to babysitting duty.'

'Hey!' said Heath.

'You know what I mean,' said Chandler.

'You shouldn't transport him alone,' said Roper. 'We go in twos.'

'Normally I'd agree,' said Chandler, 'but, as I said, this needs to be kept secret. That's the whole point.' He looked to Flo. Her headset was on as she tapped at the keyboard, dialling her boss's number again.

'This guy's right,' said Heath, pointing at Roper. 'I don't want to go out there alone.'

Chandler weighed up his options. The situation was getting out of control.

'Okay,' he said, pointing at Roper. 'You come with me to the place.'

Roper glanced at Flo and paced across the room towards Chandler. Chandler set his feet firm and prayed that the big guy's resolve had been weakened by the earlier attack. Waiting until Roper was just past him Chandler dragged his handcuffs from his belt and slid them over Roper's wrist. In the split second it took for Mitch's goon to react, Chandler had shackled the other half to Heath's wrist. Heath and Roper were now conjoined.

'What the hell?' said Heath. His confusion was matched by Roper's, though this ended abruptly as Chandler pulled out his gun and cold-cocked the policeman on the side of the head, pounding his already damaged skull. Roper went down in a heap, taking the shackled Heath with him.

Chandler turned towards Flo. She stared at him and her colleague spreadeagled on the floor and pressed her hand to her headphones. *Had Mitch answered?* As Chandler closed the distance she drew her gun. Swinging his hand, he knocked it from her grasp and across the floor. Grabbing her, he pulled her athletic frame into a headlock before dragging her towards the cells like a disruptive prisoner. Within seconds, and despite her vigorous resistance, he had tossed her into Heath's old cell. The door slammed closed behind her as she slid across the floor, cursing him.

Returning to the main office, Nick had left his desk and was standing over a terrified Heath and the prone Roper.

'Sarge? What are you doing?' asked his young constable, staring at him, hands by his sides. His voice was confused, weak. No training had prepared him for this.

'He's gone mental, for fuck's sake!' answered Heath, trying to move but unable to get far with Roper's dead weight attached to his wrist. 'Stop him! Shoot him! He's caught whatever disease the other fucker had.'

'Sarge,' pleaded Nick. 'Just let this go.'

Chandler stepped forward. 'Nick, I can't explain. I have to.' He balled his fists. He didn't want to hurt his young colleague. He didn't want to hurt anyone.

'You *can* explain,' pleaded Nick. 'Whatever it is.'

'Yeah, *fucking* well explain,' added Heath, still struggling to pull his wrist from the loop of the cuff.

Chandler sat down in the nearest chair and took a deep breath. From the corner of his eye he watched Nick close in.

'Whatever it is we can fix it,' said Nick, sounding as scared as Chandler felt. 'We'll get the inspector and the others and find this guy. It's not your fault he escaped. We all did our best.'

By now Nick was standing over him. Chandler

waited for it; the supportive hand gently rested on his shoulder.

Springing to his feet Chandler grabbed the hand and twisted it behind the young man's back, forcing Nick's face down on to the hard plastic table as he cried out in pain.

'I'm sorry, Nick.'

Bending him over and using his arm like a rudder, he steered his young colleague towards the cells, depositing him into the middle one. Two cells occupied, one to go.

'Sarge ... Chandler ... don't do this,' pleaded Nick.

'They're going to fire you if you don't let us out. Throw you in a prison like this one,' echoed Flo from the far cell.

Chandler ignored their pleas, returning to the office and Heath who was screeching for help as he crawled towards the front door, dragging the unconscious Roper with him.

As Chandler caught up he stopped crawling and assumed a defensive stance. 'What is it you want?' he begged. 'Are you working with him?'

The accusation caused Chandler's temper to flare. Frustration at being unable to explain that he hadn't gone crazy. That there was a plan.

'No, I'm not working with him.'

'Then what the fuck is this?'

Chandler unlocked the cuff from Roper's limp wrist and attached it to the pipes on the wall, securing Heath inside the office.

'You wanted to leave the cell, didn't you?'

'Not like this. I wanted to be released, not taken hostage by a different psycho.'

Grabbing Roper by the arms, Chandler dragged the unconscious officer across the floor before dumping him into the final cell. He left to another chorus of pleas from Nick not to do anything stupid.

Too late.

As Chandler left the cells and approached the frightened man rattling the cuffs in vain, something occurred to him. Gabriel had known of him and Mitch – *and* from what he had hinted at over the phone, of their search on the Hill all those years ago. But how could he have known those details? Who the hell could have told him? One of his colleagues who was in the force back then? One of the crazy mercenaries they'd pissed off? The family?

The family. The collective noun, impersonal.

Chandler tried to recall their names. They didn't come back immediately which filled him with shame.

But come back they did, into focus slowly and filtered through everything else charging around his head. There they were: Arthur, the old, portly accountant forcing himself to trek through the outback for weeks. The mother – Sylvia. The proud, well-heeled woman who had eventually crumbled under the pressure. And their youngest son with the long, straggly hair and the name that was as lost in Chandler's mind as their eldest child had been in the bush. The *boy* as Chandler had always thought of him. They were all there, images implanted deep in his memory despite having tried to blank them out. The entire episode in there waiting for the memories to crawl once again to the surface.

Chandler might misremember what had happened, but he would never forget it.

46

2002

The morning radio communication from base urged Chandler and Mitch to ramp up their efforts to persuade the family to stop the search. Twenty-five days had gone by with nothing to show for it. The opinion from up top was that Martin had disappeared into thin air and in all likelihood was dead – though under no circumstances were they to put it to the family that way.

Mitch was in full agreement with this decision, his face and arms scorched from the sun, his feet blistered, and ankles bruised from numerous collisions with exposed tree stumps and rocks. He took the opportunity to complain for the umpteenth time that he was out here walking himself into a fucking crisp in search of a person he didn't know and no longer cared about. If he ever had in the first place.

After that came the morning ritual: a group prayer, which Chandler had now become drawn into for the old man's sake, then payment, the unkempt mercenaries huddled around Arthur, their withered old paymaster, almost slobbering as the cash emerged from his inside pocket.

Mitch nudged Chandler while easing the boots over his prominent blisters. 'You gonna let him keep getting fleeced with no hope of finding the guy?'

Mitch was probing for a response. Chandler knew it – but gave in anyway. 'You don't get it, Mitch; they have hope. They'll always have hope.'

His colleague's reply was sharp. 'Hope – but no chance.'

'You wouldn't give up if it was one of your family.'

'None of my family are stupid or suicidal enough to get themselves lost out here.'

'It might have been an accident,' said Chandler, though he didn't believe it himself.

Mitch raised an eyebrow. 'You know this isn't an accident. No one could wander this far by accident.' He pointed to either side of the vague path they were cutting through the rough terrain, each searcher forging their own slice of Australia. 'He could be anywhere. Lying not two metres from us and we'd never know. And even if by some miracle he is still alive, the longer we go without finding anything, the more likely it is that we never find him at all. Maybe he's already headed home and is waiting for us.'

To this Chandler had a comeback.

'But if he did surely he would get in touch with someone?'

'Or maybe he's enjoying the attention, even deriving

some sort of sick pleasure from it. His fifteen minutes of fame. For all we know he can't stand his family. Maybe this is his revenge, hurting them like they hurt him.'

'Your theories are growing as crazy as theirs,' said Chandler, nodding to the Murray River teenager who was tucking his cash into his socks for security.

'The mercenaries will know to quit though when the well has run dry. Maybe it's time you tell the family the same.'

Breaking off from the conversation, Mitch barked out the order for everyone to get moving, leaving Chandler to stew over the options. Chandler knew that Arthur would listen to him if he made it clear that his son was gone from this earth. But could he do it? Could he extinguish their last vestiges of hope? And what would they do once the search was called off? How would the family piece their life back together?

In the end Linda Keeler and a lack of money did it. On the twenty-seventh day of Martin's disappearance, Linda made the headlines, a young housewife who walked out her front door and into the Blue Mountains in nothing more than her wedding dress and a pair of trainers. Her husband had left her for a co-worker, and Linda's mind decided it was time to depart as well. The hunt for the pretty housewife immediately went into full swing and with her distraught family owning the second largest trucking business in New South Wales, the remaining mercenaries left the search for Martin to venture to greener pastures. No apology, no goodbye, just gone. All apart from the Murray River teenager, who ducked out with almost a sheepish goodbye to Chandler. But Chandler wasn't that sorry to see him go either. Over the course of the search the teenager had become more swindler than bushman.

So despite temperatures that topped forty every day and their shattered minds and bodies, the group went out again, now reduced to four: Chandler, Mitch, Arthur and his son.

Understanding time was running short, Arthur barrelled through the scenery like a rock tumbling down a ravine. Chandler had at times resorted to physically grabbing the soaked collar of the older man's shirt, ringed yellow with sweat stains, salt granules icing a neck that was now slim if not entirely healthy.

'Arthur.'

'What?' said the old man, seeking to free himself from the embarrassing restraint like a punished child.

'Don't get separated from the rest of us.'

Arthur flung off Chandler's hands, charging onwards. Chandler watched him for a few seconds, the bright red wrecking ball of his sunburned face crashing through the thin undergrowth before realizing that the boy hadn't set off after his father but was studying him alongside Chandler. Their eyes met, the boy seemingly in two minds over what to do, worried wrinkles around his eyes that no kid that age should have. Chandler wondered if at that moment they were thinking the same thing: whether his dad had become a danger to himself and everyone around him.

From his other side, Mitch said, 'Why are you bothering? If he has an accident it might get him to stop this shit.'

Mitch had already voiced his thoughts on the matter. There was no glory in finding a set of bones. There would be no individual acclamation for such a discovery, merely a statement in the paper proclaiming that after nearly four weeks of searching the police – in generic terms – had discovered the remains. True to form, Mitch was thinking purely of himself.

As the boy ran after his father, Mitch continued, 'You have to explain to them that it's pointless. The time, the effort, the money they're wasting.'

'They need to come to that conclusion themselves,' said Chandler. He wasn't sure he had the capacity to ask them to stop, no matter how much he wanted to get back to Teri.

'What if they never do?'

Chandler believed they had to. At some point.

'They're fucked,' said Mitch. 'Their heads are fucked. We need to bring this to a stop. You need to. If anything happens it'll be on your head. If anything happens to the other kid ...'

'Then you tell them,' said Chandler. If Mitch was so keen to stop then he could deliver the news.

'I've tried,' said Mitch, 'but you're closer to them.'

The tone seemed to insinuate Chandler had done something improper by developing a bond with the family.

'Why would they listen to us?' said Chandler. He rephrased it, 'They aren't listening to us.'

'Make them,' growled Mitch. 'Every fucking step out here is grinding my nerves.'

Mitch slowed down and let Chandler forge ahead pursuing Arthur.

Chandler called for a break. They needed some time to breathe, to take on some water and any food they could force down.

Arthur kept walking. And walking. Chandler considered going after him. Suddenly the old man turned. He looked exhausted, his limbs barely preventing him from crashing to the ground.

Chandler brought him some water.

'Are you okay?'

Arthur nodded but didn't speak, swigging the water. His son took a seat beside him and did the same.

'I think I saw something down there,' spluttered Arthur between swigs, staring at his feet, but pointing into the distance.

Chandler followed the finger. He couldn't see anything out there but trees and dirt. 'Something?'

'A piece of cloth it looks like. It might indicate—' He turned to his son. 'Go, check it out.'

The boy scrambled to his feet and was about to set off in the direction his dad had pointed in.

'No. Stay here,' ordered Chandler.

Arthur looked up at Chandler with hurt and tired eyes. 'It was there ... blowing in the wind.'

'We're all blowin' in the wind by now,' said Mitch, out loud and full of contempt.

'Show some respect,' said Chandler.

'You show some decency and tell him the truth.'

'What truth—?' started Arthur but Chandler had turned on his partner.

'The truth? The truth is that you're a self-centred bastard, Mitch, and you better pray this never happens to you.'

'It won't. I'm not going to be stuck in this backwards shithole for ever. I'm heading to Perth to deal with some real crime, not arseholes too stupid to find their way back after a hike. If they even wanted to be found in the first place. Like you said yourself: we're policemen, not grief counsellors.'

Chandler looked at Arthur. His head hung low, too tired or cowed to raise it, his fists clenched as he stared at the red earth. Chandler felt like stepping up and doing the job for him by punching Mitch in the face. But that wouldn't negate the fact that what Mitch had said was true; he had uttered those words. But that was before. He wanted to explain himself to Arthur but words failed him.

Mitch turned and stormed off back towards camp alone, against all rules and common sense.

'I'm clearing up and heading back,' said Mitch without turning. 'You can continue babysitting the fucking Taylors if you want to.'

47

Taylor. Arthur Taylor. A surname that should have been hard to forget given the circumstances but Chandler had lost it amongst the unusual names out there. Mercenaries called Chaz, Blazz, Bagboy and Yippy, deliberately obtuse. But Taylor ... it rang a bell.

Suddenly Chandler remembered why. He had seen it recently.

He paused by the desks, filtering out Heath's bleating cries. Even the chorus from the cells drifted into nothing but a background hiss as he struggled to comprehend what this information meant. He was still struggling even as he loaded up the foster records Perth HQ had sent. It now suddenly made sense. Why Gabriel knew so much about the search for Martin, why he knew so much about his and Mitch's past. And the Hill.

He had been there.

Gabriel Wilson had been previously known as David Gabriel Taylor, the younger brother of Martin Taylor, his new name burying the past to clear the way for the future.

The memories flooded back. The kid – Davie, as Chandler now recalled Arthur calling him – had been eleven or twelve at the time of Martin's disappearance. And eleven years later he had returned, only twenty-two or twenty-three, though he looked older, his skin ragged, his body scarred and beaten, nothing like the innocent floppy-haired kid he had been back then.

With the truth laid in front of him Chandler wondered how he hadn't recognized him before. Gabriel had certainly recognized Chandler, though he supposed he hadn't changed much over the years. Still a cop in Wilbrook, only a few kilos and a couple of kids heavier. But Gabriel – Davie – looked like a completely different person.

Why had Gabriel come back? Revenge? And if so, revenge for what? And why had he killed six people before presenting himself? The sweat dripped down Chandler's forehead and splashed on to the desk. His body felt like a pressure cooker with no vent, building and building, about to explode at any second. His entire life about to explode. He tried to focus. The reason for Gabriel's return was important but wasn't the most urgent issue – his kids were in danger. Other possible motives forced their way into Chandler's mind. Did Gabriel – David – feel they gave up the search for Martin too early? Or that they hadn't done enough to help? But if Gabriel truly was after revenge for his brother, why did he not take it earlier, as soon as he knew Chandler still lived here? And if he was after revenge and just wanted to kill Chandler's family, why was he offering a swap?

To kill them all? To take his kids and the witness? To finish them all off?

All he wanted to do was speak to Gabriel. Now. Speak to him and speak to his kids.

A cry from the cells interrupted him; Nick pleading for Chandler to give himself up. To not do whatever he was planning to do.

'I know who he is – who Gabriel is,' said Chandler, replying to thin air. 'I know how he knows this town and why he knows me. Why he knows Mitch. *Everything*. I'm going to meet him.'

'Not with me you're not,' said Heath, rattling his cuffs in vain, his voice desperate.

'Let us out, Sergeant Jenkins,' Flo shouted from the other cell. 'You're just making this worse for yourself.'

'I'm not sure it can get any worse,' said Chandler.

'If you're going to meet him, you'll need backup,' shouted Nick. 'I can help, Sarge.'

With Nick's offer to help, a plan formed in Chandler's mind. A plan that he couldn't carry out on his own. He needed a third person. Nick could be controlled. He hoped.

'Have you ever shot someone, Nick?' asked Chandler. The lack of a reply told Chandler all he needed to know.

'I don't know who's the biggest fuckin' nutjob.'

Having given up on trying to break free, Heath had listened with growing incredulity as Chandler explained what was happening.

'I have to get them back,' said Chandler, trying to invite support from his hostage.

It failed.

'By trading me in? Like a fucking casino token.'

'It's a trap. I've got it worked out.' Chandler didn't reveal that though he had figured out the basics, his supposition was still less than comprehensive. 'I need your help.'

Heath shook his head vigorously. 'You're not gettin' it.'

'Nick will be covering us.'

Nick stood at the far wall, hands out in front of him wearing the cuffs Chandler had insisted putting on him before he let his young constable out of the cell. Chandler was still trying to ascertain if Nick was going to assist or resist.

'Well that fills me *full* of hope,' said Heath, his voice dripping with sarcasm. Suddenly his face lit up. 'Ha! Well you'll never get me out of here without me blabbing to the press out there. I'll tell them what's going on, that you've flipped and—'

The ringing phone interrupted him. They all stared at it. If it was Mitch or one of the others ringing in and it went unanswered they would grow suspicious.

'Sarge, you can't take him,' said Nick. 'You're a police officer. And he's a member of the public you've sworn to protect.'

Chandler squeezed his eyes shut. He didn't need Nick to remind him of his oath but the images of Sarah and Jasper imprinted behind his eyeballs superseded all other considerations.

'I have two other members of the public to protect, Nick.'

'And what makes them better than me?' spat Heath.

A million things. Every fucking thing. Chandler closed his eyes and took a deep breath before speaking.

'Sometimes it's necessary to take a risk,' he said.

'Not with my life.'

'I have no choice,' said Chandler.

'There's always a choice, Sarge,' offered Nick.

Chandler shook his head. 'Not this time.'

As eager as Chandler was to exchange Heath and get his kids back, a major sticking point remained: how to get a non-compliant hostage and possibly non-compliant Nick out of the station without being seen. The phone continued to ring in the background, halting for a few seconds, before returning with vigour.

An idea formed. A shot in the dark but with a central tenet he knew would hold firm: the curiosity of the press.

Leaving Nick and Heath, Chandler exited the front door to address the assembled crowd. Shouting over the questions fired at him, he swiftly informed them that Gabriel had been found and surrounded. He tried to keep his demeanour calm and assured as he 'accidentally' let it slip where the ongoing siege was taking place, naming the abandoned Potter farm south of town, far from Wilbrook, far from any phone coverage.

A few follow-up questions were aimed in his direction but they were choked short as equipment and vans were hurriedly loaded, directions googled and relayed, each crew desperate to be first on the scene, first to report on the story of the summer.

Chandler watched them leave; the press running off,

the locals drifting home to follow the updates as best they could on television.

Before long the car park was empty. He scanned the surroundings for the demonic figure of Gabriel but there was nothing.

Ducking back into the station, he looked at Heath and Nick as he dug something from the charity clothing box. 'Time to leave.'

'What did you do?' asked Nick.

'I gave them a better story,' said Chandler. He leaned down towards Heath who cowered against the wall. 'Now, Mr Barwell – Heath – I'm going to uncuff you from the pipe. Are you going to remain calm?' Chandler glared at him, trying to intimidate him into compliance.

There was no response. Heath's eyes were glassy.

Chandler turned the key, pulling the opened metal loop from the pipe. 'Your other hand please,' he said, then continued, 'You won't be hurt.'

'You don't have to do this,' stuttered Heath.

'I do,' said Chandler. 'This is the only way to stop him. You'll be a hero.'

'I don't want to be a hero. Heroes die,' said Heath.

'Not this time.'

'Can I at least get a gun?'

'You don't need one. I'll have one. And so will Nick.'

Slipping the cuff over Heath's other wrist, Chandler closed it and helped his reluctant prisoner to his feet. He led them both outside.

On taking his first step into the night air, Heath yelled for help, his voice carrying across the empty tarmac and buffered between the concrete buildings. It was a disappointing but expected response. Chandler leaped forward and stuffed the old T-shirt he had taken from the charity box in the office for this purpose into Heath's gaping mouth, stifling the yells.

While Heath continued to scream into the gag, Nick remained pliant. 'Where is everyone?' he asked.

'Gone to witness Gabriel's arrest,' said Chandler, pushing Heath into the back of the police car. Before he could do the same to Nick his young colleague held his hands out.

'You said you needed me, Sarge. For the plan. So you can take these off.'

'Not yet,' said Chandler.

He didn't need any more surprises. He needed time.

48

Chandler drove back towards the dirt car park where they had gathered earlier to follow Gabriel back out to his burned-out lair. This was the designated meeting point and it now made perfect sense. This place was as much a cruel memory to Gabriel as it was to him.

At the beginning.

As he snaked the car up the dirt road, Chandler explained the full situation to his passengers, that Gabriel had taken Sarah and Jasper hostage and wanted Heath in exchange for them. He then explained the plan as Heath, through the gag, made his feelings quite clear on what he thought about being the bait, his stubborn kicks against the back of the driver's seat as expressive as words. But Heath's role was merely to be present at the exchange. It was Nick's help that Chandler required. He hoped that now Nick had a complete understanding of the situation, the young man would do his job. If everything went to plan, Nick would be the real hero.

If everything went to plan. The lack of assurance made Chandler almost throw up.

Not wanting to come to a complete halt in case Gabriel was tracking the movement of the headlights as they approached, he slowed to a crawl before the car park came into view, stretching over to unlock Nick's cuffs. There was a tense second as Chandler waited for his reaction. If he decided to resist ...

But his young constable didn't make any move to attack, opening the door of the car and diving out of the slow-moving vehicle, disappearing swiftly into the darkness, his heels only briefly flashing red in the glow of the brake lights.

Chandler continued his slow crawl to allow Nick time to get into position. He was terrified. This was the first time that he had allowed Nick out of the station, to participate in an operation, and his life, Heath's life and the lives of his children were all on the line.

He hit the brakes at the entrance of the car park and scanned it for any sign of activity. Nothing moved apart from the gradual spread of condensation on the inside of the windows. Reaching back he pulled the old shirt from Heath's mouth. His prisoner gasped for air.

'Where are we?' he demanded.

'Close to where this all started,' said Chandler.

'How are you going to ensure I'm safe? They might be your kids, and I'm *very* fucking sorry for that, but I don't want to give my life for them.'

'Do you trust me?' asked Chandler. This was the part he needed to go smoothly, the part out of his control.

'Trust you? You've kidnapped me!'

Ignoring Heath's outburst, Chandler continued,

'What's going to happen is that I'll bring you over and ask for the exchange to happen at the same time. You – for my kids. When you and they pass in the middle Nick will take the shot.'

Spoken out loud, the plan sounded reckless and exceptionally risky, each word rotten and diseased, poisoning his guts.

'And how good is he?' said Heath, understandably searching for some hope to cling on to.

'He passed weapons training and simulation.'

'*Simulation?* You mean he's shot at some fucking cardboard cutouts! Give *me* a gun,' pleaded Heath. 'I've at least shot some kangaroos. Distance shots too. I can get close and take him out.'

'Or shoot me,' said Chandler.

'You have to trust me,' said Heath with a sneer.

Chandler stared at Heath. Though there seemed little virtuous about him, he was a human being. And he was innocent. Chandler couldn't force him to put his life on the line.

Chandler climbed out of the car.

'Where are you going?' shouted Heath, his screech dulled by the reinforced windows.

Chandler leaned back inside. 'To the meeting.'

'Without me?'

'Without you.'

'And you're just leaving me here? What if he kills you and then comes get me?'

'If he kills me, Nick will shoot him.'

With that Chandler left the squad car behind and

walked up the lane towards the car park. He hoped he was doing the right thing. He hoped that he had given Nick enough time to get into position. And that the kid was able to shoot.

The gravel shifted under him with each heavy step. Chandler felt like he was getting nowhere, as if hiking through the forest again searching for Gabriel's brother.

49

2002

With Mitch gone Chandler joined father and son underneath the trunk of a well-foliaged tree. The worries of the father were now mirrored on the boy's face, ageing him prematurely.

'Maybe he's right,' said Arthur, speaking as he exhaled, the words falling to the dry earth. He looked at his son and then to Chandler.

'He's only right if you feel he's right,' said Chandler.

'I can't make judgements on how I feel,' said Arthur. 'I don't know how I feel. I don't know if I ever will.'

The old man was looking for Chandler to make the decision to leave. And though Chandler wasn't sure where they came from, words started to tumble out. And once they started he couldn't stop them.

'Call it off, Arthur. Martin's lost and there's no need to lose you and Davie as well. He wouldn't have wanted that.' Pausing to suck in some hot, dry air, he continued, 'Not everything out here, maybe anywhere, can come to *a closure. There will always be an element of mystery but it's up to you – up to us – to keep Martin alive in our hearts. He's part of the earth now, part of this forest. And always will be.'*

Chandler looked at them. With the truth out in the open he felt relieved. It was more than could be said for father and son. Arthur's head had sunk between his legs but Davie stared at Chandler, his face filled with shock as if trying to come to terms with what the voice of authority was telling him. With the limber ease of a child, he picked himself up and wandered away. Chandler searched for words to stop him but found none.

Arthur's voice floated into the silence between them. 'I don't want Martin's spirit to wander here.'

'You have your wife and Davie to look after. You've done your best,' said Chandler. The old man began to sob, reality becoming apparent to him in all of its nause-ating glory. But Chandler couldn't dwell on the old man's misery. There was what to do next to be considered. First up – a call to base to get the chopper in the air and out to them. Then press statements confirming the conclusion of the search and thanking everyone who took part in it.

It was a sobering and tiring thought. What came next? The page would be turned in time, the contents of the last chapter steadily forgotten.

Chandler looked up. Davie was gone. The younger brother had disappeared like the older one.

'Davie?' shouted Chandler into the patch of outback where the boy had last been.

Helping Arthur to his feet he prepared to chase the boy. The tears had gone from the old man's eyes, replaced by dread. Abandoning all precaution that had become instinct, they set off after him, stumbling through bushes and shrubs, crying out for an answer and getting none. Chandler's panic grew. Mitch had been right. He should have called this off earlier. When the surviving family were still safe.

He crashed through the low canopy of the trees, a rotten branch snapping his stupidity back at him. Arthur quickly fell behind, only his warbled yells overtaking Chandler as they scoured the landscape for the clash of the bright blue jumper against the dull red earth. Chandler's feet scuffed the earth, ripping seedlings from the harsh soil. His hair tangled in branches that dragged him back as if it didn't want him to see something. Surely the boy couldn't have got far? Unless he had started running.

The flash of synthetic blue up ahead burned his eyes, unnatural, but beautiful all the same.

'Davie!'

The boy didn't turn, frozen to the spot and staring at something in the bushes ahead. After all this time, all the kilometres trekked and as they were about to finally give up, they had found Martin. In the absolute depths of desperation they had found success.

As sure of this as of anything in his life, Chandler tore through the landscape with abandon. What he hoped to see – Martin alive – clashed with what he expected to see.

Closing in he found out it was neither what he hoped or believed – but also why the boy was so transfixed.

The hoof stuck out from the bushes, attached to the recently deceased body of a camel; a hulking mess of fur and flesh, its guts ripped out and partially eaten, maggots swarming through the putrid, pink mess. The stench that rose into the air was both natural and disgusting, off-putting and alluring, remnants of a life that was once there and was now gone.

50

Chandler visualized the animal rotting in the bushes and the boy transfixed by it. Davie then, Gabriel now.

He could picture the young boy clearly in his mind now. Forced to face the cold brutality of life and death at such a young age, the discovery of the animal carcass serving as confirmation that nothing could survive out there and nothing would be found of his brother.

'*Stop there!*'

The voice rumbled from the darkness, nothing soft in its intonation. Chandler tried to make out a figure flanked by two smaller shapes but his eyes located nothing in the darkness.

A torch flickered into being, blinding Chandler but hopefully providing a target for Nick to aim at. He tried to shield his eyes from the beam, but his retinas were flooded with light they couldn't expunge.

'You're alone,' said the voice, a little softer now but lined with disappointment.

'Yes. But—'

'But what? You're not fulfilling your end of the bargain, Sergeant.'

'I want to talk to you first,' said Chandler. 'I have a few confessions to make.'

There was a slight pause, the torchlight wavering.

'It seems to be in the blood,' said Gabriel coldly. 'Your oldest – Sarah –' he almost spat the name out, 'she's been talking about confession too. Trying to calm her brother. It's been making me very angry.'

Chandler released the breath that he had been holding in. *Been making me*. It suggested they were still alive.

Gabriel continued, 'Tell me, Chandler, *why* does she want to join a religion that ultimately wants to control her? And *why* are you allowing her to? Maybe I'd be doing her a favour – ending her life before you ruin it.'

The threat tore through Chandler's skin, puncturing his lungs. He now wished that he had brought Heath and had handed him over. He could have dealt with the guilt later, gone to confession alongside his daughter and purged his soul.

'Please, don't,' said Chandler. 'Just tell me where they are.'

'They're safe. For now.'

For now. Chandler could feel his hand itching to go for his gun. Gabriel could obviously see it too.

'You don't want to do that, Chandler. Then you won't be able to save your children. God only saves souls – not the bodies they belong to.'

'Please, I'll—'

'You'll what? Go back and get what I asked for?'

Chandler considered the request. What did Heath's life matter? As opposed to his two kids? Surely two for one was a fair trade? His eyes adjusted to the faint light at the edge of the beam, allowing him to identify the dark, almost silhouetted figure in front of him, a solitary shape. The urge to shoot Gabriel there and then fought to the surface.

Again Gabriel seemed to read his intentions. 'Sergeant, your kids will be in big trouble if I don't return.'

'Where have you put them?'

'Ah. That I can't tell you. Not yet. Now, take out your gun – slowly – and leave it on the ground.'

'I know who you are,' said Chandler.

Gabriel didn't respond.

'David Taylor. Davie Taylor.'

The silhouette smiled, the teeth catching the faint light, a true smile, maybe the first genuine emotion that he had witnessed from Gabriel.

'That took a while, didn't it?' There was an element of relief in Gabriel's voice. 'I honestly thought that you would have recognized me earlier. It was really my only worry ... but after seeing you in the station, talking to you and riding in the car with you to the hotel, I realized you didn't have a clue. You'd forgotten about me just like you forgot about my family.'

'What do you mean?' asked Chandler.

'What do I mean? Nearly eleven years ago we left here and that was it. The book closed, no one there for us after. Job done. Job failed. On to the next one. Abandoned, another failure by the police swept under the carpet. The others, like your partner Mitchell, I expected it from. But you, Chandler, I remember you being close to my dad. On us like glue, comforting us, guiding us, praying with us. Leading us nowhere.'

'I ... I tried to be a friend,' said Chandler. He didn't know what else to say.

'If you were such a friend, why weren't you in contact with us after? Not even a phone call. A simple call to ask how we were coping. That might have been enough to stop it.'

Chandler searched for an excuse. And found none. He could have got a phone number, he *should* have got a phone number. He had no excuse but tried anyway.

'My girlfriend back then ... my wife. My *ex*-wife—'

'The one I met at your parents?' interrupted Gabriel.

Chandler clenched his teeth, remembering his injured father.

'Yes. She was nine months pregnant at the time. About to give birth. Well, after the search she did. She gave birth to Sarah and other things took over. Trying to live took over.'

Gabriel growled. 'Trying to live took over my family as well. Only they couldn't do it.'

'What do you mean?'

'What I mean, Chandler, sorry, *Sergeant*, is that they died in a car crash three months after we came home.'

'I'm sorry.' Chandler meant it.

'I'm sure you are now.'

'Was it an accident?' asked Chandler.

'They found nothing wrong with the car,' said Gabriel, matter-of-factly.

'Were you—?'

The shadow nodded. 'Yes, but I was wearing a seat belt. They weren't. They died instantly,' said Gabriel, a little tremor in his voice.

'So Geoffrey and Dina took you in?'

'Tell me, Chandler, those kids of yours ... have you ever punished them?' Again the soft voice turned sinister, the torchlight shaking. Gabriel's emotions were taking over. Chandler wasn't sure if that was a good thing or not. Did he want a calm, rational man who might see sense, or an irate Gabriel who might make a mistake? A fatal mistake?

'Of course,' said Chandler, hesitantly.

'No, I mean, *really* punished them.'

'A smack across the backside if they did something really awful when they were younger, but that wasn't often.'

'Would you punish them even if they were good?'

'No.'

'For instance,' continued Gabriel, 'would you punish Sarah for not getting her lines right at her First Confession?'

With the conversation drifting back to his children, Chandler sought to keep Gabriel talking, to heighten the chances of him divulging where Sarah and Jasper were being kept. But he knew he needed to tread carefully, given the subject and noticeable quiver in the beam aimed at him.

'Of course not. Nobody's perfect,' he replied.

'Exactly,' said Gabriel, some softness returning, obviously pleased at the response. 'Nothing and nobody's perfect. People aren't perfect. Would you want your child to be taught at the end of a stick? Beaten and abused for failing?'

'Is that what happened to you?'

There was a pause as the torchlight readjusted.

Chandler continued, 'Because when I asked them—'

Gabriel exploded with anger. 'You talked to them?'

'I was trying—'

'*Why* did you talk to them?'

'To find out what might be going on inside—' He had said too much.

'Inside my head?' spat Gabriel. 'My head is clear. My actions are clear. I am of solid mind and body. Those zealot bastards however . . .' Gabriel trailed off.

Chandler jumped in, attempting to get on Gabriel's good side again.

'They refused to speak to me. About you.'

'Out of guilt,' spat Gabriel. 'I've heard all I want to from them; leaned against the wall and whipped as they read out the start of that book to me.'

'Genesis.'

Gabriel paused. 'Yes. Genesis. Whipped and told how we were all sinners. All sinners but it was only me that was punished, as if I was their conduit to salvation: spare the rod, beat the child. They gave me this.' He shone the flashlight up to his ear, revealing a four-inch scar normally covered by his shaggy hair.

By focusing the light on his ear, Gabriel revealed his head as a target. But Nick wouldn't shoot, not until the exchange. At least Chandler prayed that he wouldn't.

'One time they struck me right here,' he said, caressing his scar, 'splitting the flesh. It wouldn't stop bleeding so they took me to the doctor. The doctor was from the church too. He didn't ask questions. He stitched it back together and told me that God would only heal it with silence.'

'Their evil doesn't mean you have to hurt others.'

Gabriel snorted. 'They took away the last link I had to my parents. God's love. They taught me that I am evil, and evil does as it pleases. If I am the Devil as they claim, then I must carry out the Devil's work, the Angel Gabriel sent back to punish those that have been named. I am the Devil's hands.'

'What about all the names you've missed?' asked Chandler.

The beam danced as Gabriel shrugged. 'I take them as I come upon them. I do not choose which order but carry out what is written down. Imagine, Chandler, imagine reciting those names over and over again, the beatings lasting as long as it took me to read them out. And if I made a mistake? After a stray lash struck bone? Then I'd have to repeat the list. Right up until Chapter Thirteen.'

'Why Chapter Thirteen? Because it's unlucky?'

'No, because it first mentions Sodom and Gomorrah. Words that our beloved Geoff and Dina didn't want spoken in their home. As if depravity had not already seeped into the walls. There are times I even forget the names of my brother and my parents – if only for a split second – but those names are ingrained into my skull.'

'But everyone you took is innocent.'

'How do you know that?' said Gabriel. 'No one named in that book is truly innocent. They are all cursed with the sin of association.'

Though his voice remained steady, Chandler could see that Gabriel was beginning to fray. Chandler needed to buy time, so he continued to probe him.

'Why kill them out here?' asked Chandler. 'Surely this place only brings back bad memories. It does for me.'

'And there I was thinking that you'd forgotten.'

'Never,' said Chandler, abruptly – maybe too abruptly. It sounded like an admission of guilt.

'When I freed myself from the zealots and their idea of paradise I tried to go as far away as possible. I got access to the money from a trust fund my dad had set up years ago and travelled around for a couple of years. New Zealand, Thailand, Malaysia. Then somehow I found myself back in West Australia. Something possessed me to seek out this place again. I found nothing had changed – the landscape, the smell, the feel were all the same. As if time had stood still. As if the deaths of my mum, my dad and my brother had meant nothing in the grand scheme of things. Like they had been forgotten. I started walking. Maybe I wanted to do what Martin did. After a couple of days trekking and sleeping in my car I found the shack and began to treat it as home. I moved in and lived up there. It's amazing what you find out about yourself out here all alone at night.'

Gabriel paused for breath. Chandler considered making another heartfelt plea for his kids' well-being but instinct told him that Gabriel was not in the mood to be distracted.

'There's a lot of pain in this forest, Chandler, pain that was heaped upon me. *People* have brought me nothing but pain, *religion* has brought me nothing but pain, so it's right that I take revenge on these things, out here where it started, offer something to the soul of my brother, the souls of my parents. They didn't die out here but this is where they were lost. They deserve some company out here.'

All of a sudden Gabriel let out a humourless chuckle. 'The first victim was called Adam,' he continued, glancing at Chandler. 'Ironic I suppose – but unplanned.'

'When?' asked Chandler, the policeman in him taking over.

'Nearly three years ago. January the fourteenth 2010. He was hitching to find work like Heath. Those are the easy ones, the desperate ones. He was a talkative lad, a bit older than me, eager to make some money for a holiday. He was obsessed with himself; Adam did this, Adam did that, repeating his name over and over and over. Hearing it repeated like that – well the urge to kill him suddenly came over me. I *needed* to kill him. But I had no idea how to do it. So in the middle of nowhere I pulled off the highway on to a dirt road. Told him I needed to have a piss, grabbed the rope from the boot, climbed into the back seat and strangled him.'

Gabriel stared at him. 'It was hard to do, harder than I'd imagined it would be but I felt charged, like I had gained some measure of revenge.'

Chandler wondered whether Gabriel's intention was to kill him too. He had, after all, been lured out here in the middle of the night. He didn't think his name was in Genesis but anything was possible, his name could be twisted into something from the Bible; even Canaan might have been close enough for Gabriel to believe Chandler should be punished.

But Chandler realized something further. There was nowhere else he would rather be. He would go to the depths of hell to get his kids back.

Gabriel continued, 'The next couple I abducted in the hope that they could help look for Martin's remains but keeping a hostage for longer than a day proved difficult. They were always whining.' There was incredulity in his tone. He was apparently amazed that people might not like being held prisoner. 'It's not that easy getting supplies up here either and I ended up spending more time looking after them than I did searching. I tried to explain to them – Seth and Eva – why they had been taken. They called me crazy and worse, but I'm not crazy.'

Chandler bit his tongue.

Chandler could see that Gabriel had truly convinced himself that by murdering others his brother would be somehow returned.

'But I can let Sarah go. In return for Heath. I might be what you and everyone else considers evil but I'm not a monster. You did try to comfort my dad, even though you told him to give up.'

'It was best for your family.'

'How can you say that when they're all dead?'

'I couldn't have known—'

'And you didn't.'

There was a brief silence, the stolen gun glinting as it flashed in Gabriel's hand.

Gabriel continued, 'Bring me Heath and I'll happily hand them over.'

'No one else needs to die. Your dad wouldn't—' said Chandler.

Gabriel interrupted. 'People die, Chandler, that's what they do.'

'Heath, Sarah, Jasper – they don't deserve to die. They haven't done anything wrong.'

'Neither had my brother, my mum, my dad. But God saw fit to take them.'

'You're angry and you're right to be, but you can't do this ... Davie.'

'This *is* what I have to do. I don't have a choice but you do, Chandler, a simple one: him or them.'

'Tell me where they are.'

'Now, Chandler ...' Gabriel's grin peeked out from the gloom.

Chandler battled for an advantage. 'If you had this so under control, how did Heath get away?'

In the faint light Chandler could see Gabriel's brow knit together.

'Is this a ploy to waste time until backup comes?'

Chandler shook his head, blocking the beam with his hand. 'There's no backup. Do you think that they'd just let me kidnap Heath and hand him over?'

Gabriel's grin wormed its way through the darkness. 'That's the kind of dedication I respect.'

'So how did he escape?'

'As we said: he managed to hack through the manacles,' said Gabriel, stunting a laugh. 'In a way I admire him; it must have taken a hell of a lot of willpower. He got out of the shack and ran, I caught him and we fell over that ridge. When I woke up all I had was a piece of his shirt. I knew he'd head downhill towards the road but I also knew that it was a long way on foot so I went back and got my car. I intended to run, get out of the state and hide. In those brief moments I forgot what I was tasked to do, as if I was being tested. So I decided to head him off and made for town. Maybe I was a little curious too. About whether God would allow me to get away with pinning the blame on an innocent person. Surely the supreme overlord wouldn't allow them to be punished? It was like being God: having control of someone's life – but in a different way to killing them. It was intriguing. *New.* If I was truly evil and God truly had the ultimate power then I wouldn't get away with it. So I left it down to fate. If God deemed it, He would allow Heath to escape my justice. Otherwise I would act as the hand of fate.'

'Fate doesn't need an executioner. Fate happens. It's unavoidable,' said Chandler.

'In *your* opinion. I used to be a passenger of fate too,

JAMES DELARGY

until I realized that both my hand and its are equally as unsteady at the wheel. Why should it steer me, when I can steer it myself? It had already allowed me to escape the car crash.' Gabriel stared at Chandler. 'Martin always believed in fate.'

Chandler had no answer to this.

Gabriel continued, 'And think about it, happiness is never celebrated for as long as sadness is endured, is it? Is that because we anticipate sadness lurking around the corner? Well, I tested it out—'

'Tested what?' asked Chandler. He was growing sick of Gabriel's half-arsed philosophy, the supposed justification for his actions. He wanted his children back and as the gun wavered in Gabriel's hand and he offered his validations, Chandler began to worry that Nick was going to get impatient or nervous and take the shot before Chandler got the information he needed.

'Suffering fate. One day I was on top of a rock overlooking a valley searching for Martin when I slipped and fell down an embankment. A long way down. I got to the bottom still conscious but with an ankle twisted badly enough that I couldn't climb out of there. So I lay at the bottom, the sky and the trees around me unmoved by my suffering. I got to wondering if this was what happened to my brother all those years ago, waiting to die, lost and alone. I thought I should feel at peace, but I still felt unfulfilled, as if there was something I had to achieve before the end. So after an hour or so I found a sturdy branch and hobbled up the incline back to the cabin. I spent the next long, cold month stuck in there, out of supplies within two weeks, shivering to sleep at night and starving to death during the day. I wondered if my fate was to die up there but again, the peace that I thought should have been forthcoming didn't arrive. So I picked a day to live or die. I managed to hobble back to the car and drove to Port Hedland. To hospital.'

'So you survived,' said Chandler. 'Fate didn't take you. Shouldn't you be glad? Shouldn't you want to help people, not hurt them?'

'Why? No one helped me. I tested my fate, others can test theirs.'

'Not two kids.'

'And they won't have to. *You* will take the test for them.'

'But then *I* am deciding Heath's fate.'

'No,' said Gabriel. 'You are only handing him over. His fate is decided after.'

Chandler shook his head slowly. 'Why did you come back after you escaped from the hotel?'

Gabriel smiled. 'To see if you would recognize me now. Or maybe, somewhere deep down, I was looking to be caught. I also prefer to finish what I start. It's cleansing. But what do you know about finishing what you start?'

Chandler had nothing in response. The overwhelming silence hung for a few seconds before Gabriel continued. 'But I'm prepared to give you one last chance. Bring Heath to me or else I'm afraid I'll have no choice.'

To make his point Gabriel raised the gun and pointed

it at Chandler's head. 'I've already killed one Sarah. A nice girl, quite flirty as I recall. Let's see if fate's still on Heath's side or your daughter's.'

'Don't,' said Chandler, his voice choked and quiet. By now he had a full picture of who Gabriel was and what he had endured. Losing his family in what might have been a suicide pact, orphaned, then shacked up with the foster parents from hell. He had endured so much pain, but Chandler couldn't allow his children to go through the same. He had to give Heath over. He was about to become the hands of the Devil.

A shot rang out, the echoes held by the trees and spat out again and again.

In front of him the torchlight fell.

Chandler rushed forward as the beam hit the ground and span around, illuminating the prone form of Gabriel. The soft yellow light highlighted the dark patch spreading rapidly across his chest. The narrow, soft-spoken lips were open but nothing uttered from them, no gasps for help, no pained cries. Silenced for good.

'Where are they?' said Chandler kneeling beside the lifeless body. 'Where are my kids?'

He grabbed Gabriel by the collar and pulled him up. Gabriel's head lolled back. 'Where are they?' he shouted, loud enough to wake the dead.

But Gabriel didn't wake.

Why the fuck did Nick shoot? That was not the plan. But Chandler recognized that the plan had been flawed from the start. He should have ... should have what? Called backup? He had needed a willing accomplice and

Nick had been the only one he could trust. Gabriel had pointed a gun at him so Nick had decided—

'Is he dead?'

The voice wasn't Nick's. Nor Heath's. As Chandler swung around, the lanky figure stalked towards them, weapon drawn. Mitch.

'Is he dead?' repeated Mitch.

'What the fuck were you doing?' yelled Chandler.

Mitch was beside him now, staring at Gabriel's body. He seemed pleased with himself.

'I needed him alive,' said Chandler.

'He was pointing a gun at you.'

'He wasn't going to shoot me, he wanted Heath.'

'Yeah, the innocent man you took to trade.'

'He has Sarah and Jasper.'

'I know, Chandler, but that doesn't give you the right to choose one person's life over another.'

'I wasn't going to trade him,' said Chandler, convincing himself it was the truth. 'I needed to buy time. Get him to reveal where they were.'

'And?'

'You shot him.'

Mitch's face was unmoved.

Chandler pointed at the body. 'Do you understand who he was?'

Mitch shrugged his shoulders and slipped his gun back into his holster, safe in the knowledge that the killer wasn't getting up.

'It's David Taylor. Davie.'

Mitch's face twitched. Recognition flared in his eyes.

'Davie? No ... The kid whose brother we couldn't find? Him?'

'Yes.'

'I wouldn't have ... I didn't recognize him. So was this— All this shit was about revenge?'

'Not exactly,' said Chandler, 'but I don't have time to explain.'

'You do and you *will* explain. At the station. About exactly why you used a suspect as bait.'

Mitch was attempting to be forceful but Chandler was in no mood to obey.

'I need to know where my children are, Mitch. He said they would be in trouble if he didn't return.'

'Probably a lie.'

'He abducted them from my parents' house. From Teri. Roughed my dad up. That was no lie,' said Chandler. 'We need to get planes in the air. Search for someplace out here that he could have been hiding them.'

'I give the orders, Chandler.'

'Well give the fucking *order*, then.'

51

Back at Chandler's car, Heath had been uncuffed. He responded to the news of Gabriel's death with a rant that included threats to press charges against Chandler, the state and the police.

Chandler tried to ignore him as he and Mitch, each on a radio, tried to organize a ground search immediately and an air search at first light.

As Chandler diverted manpower from the roadblocks on the highways to the new search, Heath continued to rant that he was going to sue them all. Chandler shoved a finger in his ear to listen for the response from the Staties, running close to the edge of his patience.

Just then, Mitch dropped his radio and turned to Heath. 'Why don't you make your way out of town, Mr Barwell?'

'Oh, *now* you want me to go,' laughed Heath, entirely without humour.

'Go, then come back with a lawyer and we'll talk,' said Mitch, calm and assured. 'Until then, leave us to our business. We have two kids to search for.'

'I'm not going to forget this.'

'I'm not asking you to forget,' said Mitch, 'I'm asking you to fuck off.'

Within the hour twenty-four people were recruited to the search team: Mitch's crew, including the still aggrieved Roper and Flo, Nick, Tanya, Jim and Luka, breaking into pairs and setting off into the outback in a desperate scramble to find Chandler's kids.

Chandler went too, quickly pulling away from Nick who had been assigned as his partner, crashing through the undergrowth, crying out every few steps for his kids. He shone his torch over the ground but in this terrain it was useless, the long shadows creating a false impression of the layout of the earth, full of darkness and little light, the bushes creating shadows that in his mind were Sarah and Jasper.

His voice soon grew hoarse as he fought with the realization that they could be anywhere out here or in town where a smaller team, bolstered with the help of eager locals, was scouring every dive and dump for any sign of his children.

On he drove through the undergrowth, pursuing the echo of his cries but never catching up. He pushed on harder because he was panicked and he pushed on harder because of the tears streaking down his face. He didn't want anyone to see his hurt, immersing himself in the trees, dirt and despair, Nick just a few steps behind, his protector. In the short time Gabriel had he couldn't have taken the kids far. That was the hope he clung to. That they had to be somewhere nearby. With enough effort, with enough people, they should be able to find them.

His thoughts turned to consider Gabriel as he was and Davie as he had been back then. The boy that had turned into a serial killer, driven by revenge, driven by hatred of what had happened to him. All of which traced back to the search on this hill all those years ago. He wondered whether this was indeed his plan, his final revenge: to have Chandler crawl through the woods in a desperate attempt to find his children; Chandler turned into Arthur. Nobody, not even the Devil, could be that cruel. To put him, nearly eleven years later, on the other side of the search.

But this time he would not give up. Not if it took him the rest of his life.

Chandler stayed out all night, burrowing through the trees, heading in the general direction of the burned-out cabin, not because he thought his children would be there, only that it was as good a direction to go in as any. It was only Nick reminding him that they should check in to see if anyone else had news that made him turn, storming back towards the car park via an alternative route that proved equally as fruitless as the original.

Nothing was found that first night, the search now focused solely on the Hill, the extensive search of the town proving a bust.

During the next two days the search increased in scale, quickly outgrowing that held for Martin, which seemed bitter irony to Chandler as he traipsed through the brush leading off from where Gabriel had been gunned down.

Overhead, drones whirred just above the level of the trees, sent up at first light and remotely controlled from the base in the car park. So far, all they had beamed back was a carpet of pale green, dotted with vivid red, no Sarah, no Jasper.

It took sixty hours for Chandler's body to shut down, forced into two hours of restless sleep before continuing, against all advice, into the night. People sought to give him sympathy, which he merely deflected. He couldn't have cared less for fucking sympathy. He didn't need or want the negativity. He didn't need or want anything, the hugs, the words, the attempts at providing comfort, food, air – he needed to walk until he found them.

His bubble of fear only had room for one. Even watching Mitch comfort Teri meant nothing to him. The whole world could swallow him up as long as he found them.

As the days wound on they started to blend into one, the fleeting, often impromptu fits of slumber nothing more than restless dozes that made him feel ill with shame, before commencing another arduous shift. Days were characterized by long shifts and false hopes, sightings that turned out to be nothing but a fallen log or campfire long since dormant. And with each of these discoveries he understood. For the first time he *truly* understood what the Taylors had gone through, the fluttering highs and crashing lows, his entire existence distilled into nothing other than walking, searching and trying to maintain hope. Calling out their names in the faint hope of hearing something in return. The volunteers shouted their names too. He wanted to tell them all to shut up and to let his children breathe.

He slammed his fist into a tree. It shook but stood firm. The pain carried through his knuckles and up his arm but failed to shake the terrifying thoughts from his head.

52

As the search wound down on its fourth day Chandler was angry. He, more than anyone else, recognized the telltale signs of people beginning to lose belief. It had only been *four* days. It would be another ten before the kids would be in serious trouble of starvation. Dehydration was, of course, a different beast. He had snapped at Luka yesterday for staring at his phone as he trekked through the woods. Today he had torn a strip from some poor constable dragged in from Newman who had dared wonder if the kids were dead already. Nick and Mitch practically had to drag Chandler away, pointing him in a direction he had never been before and letting him loose to walk off the anger like a wind-up toy.

The past played on his mind. How they had given up on Martin. How the teenager could have been out there and alive, if only they had chanced upon him. But nature buried everything eventually, including the sins of the past.

But his children weren't dead. Chandler knew it. He pursued those thoughts through the deepest, darkest parts of his brain, beat and mauled them until they never existed. Sarah and Jasper were alive. There was nothing else. They were alive. But were they together? Had one of them managed to escape and gone off to get help? Without a compass or some form of orientation it would have been difficult. Without water the same. An unseen hand twisted his stomach into knots. Why had he never taught them to navigate by the sun, or given them tips to survive in the wild? But who needed those in this day and age? Maybe if Sarah had her phone and it had some type of compass feature on it then she could navigate her way towards town. It was a possibility. Once again he had fought away the dark thoughts only for hope to rear its, by now, ugly head.

No, his kids weren't free. If they were they would have headed towards the foot of the Hill. They knew that much at least. They had to be confined somewhere. The terrors quickly returned, his imagination let loose. They were both locked up – chained up – in a shed somewhere out here. He refused to believe that they were out in the open where they would freeze to death long before they would die of thirst. The list of killers in the wilderness was long and brutal. Mitch had only shot one of them.

He glanced behind. The past continued to haunt him, this time in the form of Mitch. Today he had appointed himself Chandler's guardian, genuine concern written across his haggard face. The same bastard that had killed Gabriel. If his kids did die – and they wouldn't, he reminded himself – it would be his fault. And Chandler couldn't quite say what he would do.

53

A week passed in a blink of an eye. Like one of his fitful dozes.

The all-party search continued, the police not about to give up on one of their own easily, all resources falling under Mitch's command, experts from West Australia and further afield dialling in via satellite phone to offer advice and tactics.

Chandler continued his torturous regime of walking twenty hours a day with a couple of short breaks for refreshment that did anything but; water that only reminded him that his children were thirsty, sandwiches that scraped his throat as if Sarah and Jasper's fingernails were scratching at it.

Camp was moved close to the site of the burned-out shack to maximize time in the field. From his bivvy bag Chandler looked up at the stars, sleep as far away from him as they were from the earth, wondering if his children were watching the same sky, wishing once again that he had taught them some of the constellations for navigation purposes. As a good father rather than an absent one. The shame pushed sleep even further from his mind, the faces of his children now dotted amongst the same constellations.

He climbed out of the bag, the night air attacking his sweat-soaked clothes. The shaking began, quickly taking over his entire body. He couldn't control the muscle spasms and involuntary twitches. He couldn't control them and he didn't want to. He glanced around at the rest of the team. They were asleep, the soundness of their slumber irritating him further. He could understand their exhaustion but not how they could sleep when his kids were still out here somewhere. He tried to remember what day of the week it was. He failed. All he knew was that it was day nine – AD 9. Nine days after his world collapsed.

54

2002

He watched Arthur sink to the earth, his legs surrendering, staring at the decomposing camel as Chandler eased Davie away from it. The image and odour of the rotting corpse proclaimed the truth more succinctly than Chandler ever could; nothing survives out here for long.

'It's over,' he said to Arthur, so softly he was initially unsure he had even uttered it. He eased the boy away further.

'It's over,' repeated Arthur, all hope gone.

The utter relief that burned Chandler's guts felt shameful, nauseous at having forced them to give up.

Chandler looked at the boy. He too was lost, staring at Chandler with an expression that cried out for meaning. Chandler had none to impart. He must have understood it was over, but whether he understood that he would never see his brother again, Chandler didn't know. Given the finality of Arthur's last two words, nothing needed to be said, the day continuing forth, life continuing on evermore, the wind easing through the trees like a silent assassin, the sun crossing the sky in the same brooding silence.

Chandler cast his eye around for the last time. Martin was out here somewhere, enjoying the same silence, dead now, his eyes eaten out, his tongue too, the soft fleshy parts the first to go. Eventually, after all the flesh was picked clean, he would turn into a cluster of bones, slowly bleaching yellow in the unforgiving sun.

55

The picture formed as he stood shaking. Sarah and Jasper, their bodies slowly rotting away, abandoned to the earth.

Taking the knife from his belt Chandler drew it across his forearm, deep enough to remove everything from his mind other than pain. Angry, bitter pain. He re-sheathed the knife as the blood trickled off his fingers to the soil. It was early but he was going to head out. No point waiting around.

Packing what he needed with as little noise as possible, he prepared to leave.

A whisper floated across the camp. Mitch.

'Where are you going?'

'I can't ... I have to go.' Chandler turned to see his former friend peering up from his own bag, his hair cast this way and that. He looked like a timid teenager again, on one of their outdoor camp-overs.

'You'll get lost if you go alone.'

Chandler continued to pack. Mitch might have been right but Chandler didn't care.

'What happened to your arm?'

Chandler glanced at the blood dripping from the cut and threw the backpack over his shoulders. 'Focus,' he said and got ready to leave.

'I'm coming with you,' said Mitch, sliding with ease out of his bag. *Like a snake*, thought Chandler.

'This isn't about getting your name in the papers, Mitch.'

He recognized that his pain was finding voice and trying to hurt those seeking to help. Like the family had done to them all those years ago.

'I know that. I want to find them too,' said Mitch.

Chandler stared hard at him.

'I'm leaving,' he said.

'Two minutes.'

Chandler didn't wait but started off slowly. He wanted to see if Mitch would let him go. If he was still full of bullshit.

With nearly an hour before dawn was scheduled to break it was hard to navigate in the darkness but the early hours' silence let Chandler hear the footsteps approach from behind, the long, even strides coming up directly behind him, then beside him. Chandler looked over at Mitch. Against all his instincts, he was comforted by his presence.

Traversing a slight incline, their headlamps piercing the indigo of the night soil. Mitch spoke up.

'I'm sorry.'

'What for?'

'For shooting Gabriel – Davie – whoever he thought he was now. For coming here and taking over. For not telling you about Teri. For losing contact. For Teri wanting the—'

Chandler interrupted the apology, Mitch's contrite tone sounding alien. 'I don't care about any of that, Mitch. That's the past.'

They continued in silence, walking until daylight reared up slowly between the trees. Then an unusual sight interrupted the characteristic landscape of trees, rock and dirt, a colour unnatural to the outback. The rusted grey of a group of old shacks gradually emerged from the rising light. They were ... they could be ...

Chandler increased his pace. As he stalked closer, struggling to keep his balance, he could see that they were forestry shacks, maybe even military shacks left over from manoeuvres undertaken out here many years ago in preparation for a war that was real or imagined. Four shacks in total. The explosion of hope cramped his stomach. He could see the same hope spread over Mitch's face.

'I'll take the two on the left,' spluttered Chandler, fighting a mouth that was suddenly as dry as the air he breathed. He started running.

'Okay, but watch out,' said Mitch. 'These have been here a while. Who knows what's in them.'

Chandler ran over to the first of the sheds, the corrugated iron worn and curled from the summer heat. He touched the door expecting to be burned by it but found an icy coldness. Undoing the bolt lock Chandler held his breath. The door opened with a prescient crack, the hinges rusted and dry, unused in a long while. Pulling harder he wrenched it open, the beam of his head torch filling the small space. He was met by a litter of electronic equipment and machinery from the seventies that had decayed to dust, a bevy of tiny insects scurrying across the floor and table tops to flee the predator invading their home.

No Sarah and Jasper. Hope rushed from his heart and flowed out the soles of his feet to the dirt floor.

But there were three other buildings.

'Chandler . . .'

Mitch's voice was unsure, brushed with an urgency that seemed to border on disturbed.

As Chandler exited and sprinted across to him, Mitch stood by the door of a shed, the tin similarly worn and rusted, abandoned for years. His old colleague was shaking and sobbing, his mouth opening but no words issuing forth. Something beyond the reach of words had occurred.

The torchlight that had been directed inside the shed swung around to shine into Chandler's face, blinding him.

Chandler moved towards the light.